P9-DHQ-263

GO EAST, YOUNG MAN

GO EAST,
YOUNG MAN

Harrison Lebowitz

Copyright © 2008 by Sleeping Dog Press

All rights reserved. No part of this book may be reproduced or transmitted in any form or by any means, electronic or mechanical, including photocopying, recording, or by any information storage and retrieval system, without the written permission of except where permitted by law.

Designed by: SilverCloud Designs, LLC
silvercloudsolutions.com

Printed in the United States of America

Dedicated foremost to my inspiration,
Molly, Tess and Jared

This is also dedicated to the entrepreneurial spirit. When the major publishing houses rejected this novel, my agent received the same reason from each. They all enjoyed the writing very much (and all wanted to see my next novel), but because this book did not fit into a particular genre, they had no idea how they could market it. Well, I would like to show them how, and, in doing so, I would like to show that, perhaps, something different is a good thing. So, how can you help the little guy take on the big boys and make this an independent best-seller? I'll tell you. If you like this book, tell ten people about it, or only tell one if that one happens to be Oprah. You can also be the first on your block to throw a "Go East, Young Man" party, where you can sign up a great number of book buyers at the one time while dressing up as your favorite character; we'll talk commission later.

1

"Times are gettin' a hard." We all nodded in agreement with Pa's statement, although I never understood why Pa stuck an "a" in front of "hard".

It was September 23rd, 1987 and the sun had just about bid farewell to Grangerland, Texas for the evening. In truth, me, my brothers and Pa lived smack dab in the middle of a triangle formed by the towns of Cut and Shoot, Security and Grangerland. But I had learned that it was easier when I said, "We live near Grangerland" than "We live smack dab in the middle of a triangle formed by the towns of Cut and Shoot, Security and Grangerland." See, too many words put people to sleep, as Pa always said, but in not so many words. Anyhow, with a town as important as Grangerland nearby, and you know it's important when Grangerland's Broncobuster Motel just received a recommendation in the AAA road guide, I assumed that just the mention of Grangerland anywhere in the world would have us pinpointed immediately. 'Course, I've never been out of the triangle too much, so this is all conjecture on my part.

"Yep," Little Ben said as Big Bill tossed another log into the campfire. A few ashes flew from the blaze which Big Bill proceeded to stamp out.

At this point, the conversation lulled. 'Course had you been privy to sitting around the evening fires, you'd have a pretty good argument that the fireside conversations lulled sometime last year when we started running low on topics besides the weather. But especially tonight, after Little Ben's mouthful of reaffirmance, there really wasn't much else to say.

Big Bill sat down next to Little Ben and rubbed his feet. I was proud of my oldest brother. Almost thirty, he had the reputation of having the toughest feet in Montgomery County, beating out challengers half his age. For as far back as I could remember, I don't think I had ever seen Big Bill in anything but his barefeet. He just felt it wasn't natural to wear boots. He never had aversions to shirts, pants, scarfs, holsters and hats, just boots. And even though, sometimes, sitting downwind from Big Bill in front of the campfire after a long day of working the ranch was a might unpleasant, I was still proud of him.

I looked away from the fire and could still make out the ranch house in the distance. Of course, no one was there right now. All the hands were here with me, my brothers and Pa. When we all determined that the ranch, being situated as it was, couldn't pick up any television or radio stations, sitting around the fire became the nightly activity. We all enjoyed this until around mid-July when it seemed a little silly to be sitting around a hot fire. 'Course, no one would dare say anything to Pa. So when summers came, we just sorta quietly sat back a couple more inches than usual from the fire.

Pa, Tex "Eugene" Henry as he is known to others, was born and raised here on the Old Miss Ranch. His pa, who started the ranch, chose this location due its proximity to the west fork of the San Jacinto River, which he mistook for the Mississippi, which explains the name. Ma, a city girl from Grangerland, met Pa during one of his trips into the nearby town. Ma's pa was a hidetrader who often purchased cattle from Pa's pa.

Ma said it was love from the moment she saw Pa driving twenty of his pa's Red Branguses down Grangerland's Main Street. She said she had always related to a "Big Red Muley", but to this day, I don't know if she meant Pa, who used to have red hair before Tiny Bob came along and turned his hair gray, or the cows. Anyhow, early on in their courting days, she'd often wake up to find a prize heifer tied to her front porch. Ma thought this a nice gesture on Pa's part, but felt that a sprawling metropolis like Grangerland just wasn't conducive to livestock grazing in one's frontyard. She discussed this with Pa, but getting him to see reason was no easy matter once he got a notion stuck in his head. Eventually, they reached a compromise: roses would be substituted for cows. From that day on, which is still referred to in these parts as "Eugene Henry's Great Compromise", until the day they were married, Ma would often wake up to find roses tied to her front porch.

I seem to remember that Ma often recounted tales of their courting days. 'Course, towards the end, when Ma's memory was fading, I vaguely recall hearing the same story over and over, but I believe that I enjoyed it just the same.

"Scorpion," Tiny Bob yelled. "Over by the fire." The shout brought my attention back to the campfire. If there was one thing I hated, it was a scorpion. The only thing I hated more was two scorpions. And the thing I hated more than that was three scorpions. I could continue, but I think you get the progression.

By the flickering light, I saw a small darting object over near Tiny Bob's seat by the fire. I could tell by its poised tail that Tiny Bob was unfortunately correct in his identification. Luckily, though, I felt a safe distance from the critter, and Tiny Bob was not afraid of scorpions. As a matter of fact, Tiny Bob had a collection of scorpion belt buckles, which, unbeknownest to him, was an ingenious way of keeping me from using his belts. Tiny Bob's fear was of rattlers. He hated rattlers, and the only thing he hated more was two rattlers and so on.

The scorpion turned, and for a moment I lost it in the shadows of the fire. A cold sweat broke out on my forehead. "What if this scorpion has faced this challenge before?" I thought. "Even now it could be lulling us into a false sense of security, making us believe that it is retreating, only to resurface later. Maybe even next to me!". A cold sweat broke out over my entire body.

My head felt a little light, making my thoughts a little fuzzy, but the crunch brought me back to my senses. I looked over to see Big Bill pulling pieces of scorpion out of his foot.

"Ya okay, Even Tinier Bert?" Big Bill asked. All eyes turned towards me.

To say I was embarrassed by everyone recognizing my fear is an understatement. Here was a man who had just single footedly tackled a scorpion, without shoes no less. But the seven pairs of eyes were focused on me.

"Yeah, I'm fine," I answered, trying to think of something to add to save face. "You know, maybe next Christmas, I'm going to buy myself a scorpion farm." The ensuing laughter took a full five minutes to settle down.

Big Bill, holding the remains of the now deceased scorpion in his hand, turned to Tiny Bob. "Ya want these?" he asked.

Tiny Bob inspected the offering. "Nah. Ya stomped a little too hard," he said. "Smushed scorpions don't make for good buckles." And the general consensus was that it was true.

"Bill Boy," Pa said. "Git yer feet on over to the fire."

"Yes, Pa," Big Bill said, moving his massive six foot six frame closer to the fire and bringing his feet to within inches of the flames. It was Pa's concern that with Big Bill's feet being so tough and all that if he was ever to get stung by a scorpion, he'd never know it. So whenever Big Bill stepped on something Pa felt was a potential source of trouble, Pa would make sure that Big Bill properly sterilized his feet.

The sky was now full of millions of twinkling stars with the only sound being Big Bill's feet sizzling in the fire. As I looked around the campfire, I could see each member of the Old Miss Ranch. It was a shame that on such a peaceful night, each man looked so sorrowful. Pa's gray, rugged face showed his fear of the almost certain collapse of the cattle ranch that he had worked so hard to keep going. The face of my twenty seven-year old brother, Little Ben, showed the same concern.

While I was the only family member who had had any formal schooling, Little Ben's brain was to brains what Big Bill's feet were to feet. I don't mean dense. I mean that his brains were something special. He was so smart that he could get his entire point across using less words than anybody else around. Little Ben of little words. So, more than anyone else, he understood what had happened that morning.

In his usual cryptic manner, Little Ben had explained the situation to all of the Old Miss Ranch personnel, and the faces of the two hired hands, Willie McCoy and Clint Johnson, now reflected the resulting inevitable unemployment.

B.B., the cook, on the other hand, wore his typical "What will I ever do with the leftovers?" expression. Tiny Bob's sorrowful expression probably had something to do with the loss of a potentially new scorpion belt buckle, while Big Bill's was probably related to the fact that his feet were on fire. It was a shame his reputation stopped him from saying anything about it. He did, however, remove his black cowboy hat, exposing a full head of brown, matted hair and wiped the sweat from his brow. All of us Henry boys have brown hair, except not quite as matted down as Big Bill's was now.

"Mr. Henry," Willie said, a sympathetic frown peeking out from beneath his pepper colored mustache. "The whole thing's a shame. A dern shame."

I expected to hear from Clint at any time, and I wasn't disappointed.

"That's right, Mr. Henry," Clint said. "The whole thing's a shame. A dern shame."

Willie had been with the ranch since the time I was born, and he was practically family. An ex-rodeo champion, he had left the circuit at the fairly young age of twenty. It seems that one day the bucking bronc Willie was riding did what its name implied. Poor Willie landed on his head. When he finally came to, Willie was a conglomeration of broken bones with a head attached. Old Doc Buford told Willie that if he stayed with the rodeo, his days were numbered. Although Willie was confused by this statement (seemed he believed every day had a number anyway, or at least every time he had looked at a calendar it appeared that way) he decided to hang up his rodeo spurs. Willie, who was big like Big Bill and strong like Little Ben, is still one of the best steer ropers around, and I'm just sorry that I didn't get to see him in his prime.

Clint, on the other hand, was the other hand. And as far as ranching went, he was a pretty good hand at that. He was squat, but muscular. Problem was that he wanted so much to fit in that he often got under your skin. It had become so bad that Pa was afraid to use pesticide around the ranch for fear that Clint might keel over.

The thing that bothered me most about Clint, though, was his habit of repeating whatever somebody else had just said. Behind his back, we had started calling him "Mynah Bird" Johnson. Now, this was in no way meant to be disrespectful to our great Lady Bird Johnson, but you can now see the humor if you didn't before. In Clint's defense though, I guess he figured why tax his brain with original thoughts when repeating something just said was an equally good way of joining in a conversation? Now I know I mentioned that I was the only one with formal schooling, and I don't want you to get the idea that that makes me a know-it-all smarty pants, but I figured out a way to turn the tables on Clint. After much study, I found that when me and Clint were alone, if I didn't say anything, Clint had nothing to repeat. One day I think I'll let the others in on my secret.

"A dern shame," Clint harped. "That's what it is. A dern shame."

"We heard ya the first time, Clint," B.B. shouted, probably more perturbed at the leftover situation than at Clint. Usually, it took four or five "Clintisms" before anyone would erupt.

"And there ain't much to do about it now," B.B. continued. "'Course, I knew somethin' was gonna happen. Couldn't tell when. But I said so to Eugene a couple a days ago."

"One of your inklin's?" Little Ben asked.

B.B. nodded affirmatively.

B.B., you see, suffered from a condition we called "inklings." He got funny feelings when something was going to happen. It wasn't exactly like being able to see the future, but it was the closest thing to it that we had ever seen. The source of these inklings, B.B. figured, was this lump growing out of the middle of his forehead. He never had any kind of powers before the lump, but now as either the lump grew larger or his receding hairline made it look like the lump was larger, B.B. was getting more and more inklings. For this reason, B.B. was mighty proud of his lump. Personally, if it was my lump, I'd have gone cross-eyed long ago from trying to stare at it. 'Course, pretty soon, it will make a nice place to hang a hat. "Then this morning, I had just finished figurin' out what to do with the breakfast leftovers, when the inklin's got real strong like," B.B. continued. "Strongest they've ever been. Strong and powerful. To me it said that today was gonna be a day of reckonin' on the Old Miss."

And he was right.

2

MORNINGS JUST DON'T GET much better than the morning of September 23rd. As I got up, the sun was already shining without a cloud in the sky. For me, though, the day hadn't really begun until I had climbed safely down from my bunk and avoided all contact with Tiny Bob sleeping somewhere below. You see, my fifteen year old brother didn't exactly appreciate a foot being the first thing to greet him hello. 'Course, the way he slept, all scrunched up under the blanket, I could never quite tell what was Tiny Bob and what was not. So, every morning, I played what I called "Bob Mine". If I miscalculated and stepped on a fatal area, the Bob Mine exploded. The one draw back of the Bob Mine compared to a real mine was that a wrong step on a Bob Mine had day-long repercussions. At least with a real mine, it would all be over. Several times I had tried to point out to the Bob Mine that he was lucky that it was me and not Big Bill sleeping over top of him. But there was just no defusing a Bob Mine.

I took a few deep breaths and mustered up my six a.m. courage. I kicked my legs over the bed frame and gingerly slid down. I paused, waiting for a sign, any sign. Luckily, an unexpected snore from the Bob Mine gave me a bearing, and I was able to safely plant a foot on the bed below me. As I reached the hardwood floor I thought, "I shall live to see another day."

I quickly and quietly got dressed. Too much noise could also set off a Bob Mine. I hadn't heard anyone else in the house stirring, but I could tell by the smell of frying bacon that B.B. was already up preparing breakfast. I knew I had to hurry if I hoped to get back in time to eat. B.B. had set feeding times. They began the minute he rang his metal triangle and ended the minute he said, "stop."

Nothing aggravated him more than to find one of us sneaking around his kitchen after hours. We never made any bones about it because as Pa said, "A man's entitled to set the rules of his domain." 'Course, this only seemed fair if you happened to have a domain to rule. Now, I guess you could consider my top bunk a domain, but I don't think people would much care about any rules I set up about it.

I hurried out the front door to find the can of white paint and paint brush that I had left out on the porch the previous night. The air was still and warm. The familiar odor of dirt and cattle hit my nostrils almost immediately. You might not appreciate the smell, but to me, it meant home. I proceeded to survey the scenery. The ranch house, being situated as it was on top of a ridge, afforded a panoramic view of the entire Old Miss.

The Old Miss spread in every direction for as far as the eye could see. And on a beautiful morning like this, if you looked to the south and squinted, you could even see the San Jacinto. Pa's pa must have had some eye troubles because even at this distance, the San Jacinto did not look large enough to handle a riverboat.

Now, the Old Miss didn't come close in size to the King Ranch or even the L.B.J., but to me, it was the best ranch in the world. It had everything on it that a person could ever want — corrals, pig pens, silos, chicken coops, feeding troughs, a barn. It even had a private swimming hole that everybody except Clint knew about and was a good place to escape to. All of this swell stuff was, at the most, a horse ride away, which seems to me to be just about the right size for a ranch to be. Any bigger, Pa would have to hire more hands to work it. Any smaller and Pa would have to let someone go. That someone would probably be Clint, but I'd suggest Tiny Bob's name anyway.

So as it stood, there was just the right amount of good, hard work for everybody with the ranch the size that it was. This was mainly because there were five thousand head of cattle haphazardly roaming wherever they pleased. Because the Old Miss offered such good eating, with only a few spots covered by weeds and bluebonnets, cattle spread themselves far and wide. Contrary to popular belief, cattle are not stupid. I knew that they probably congregated and mingled once darkness hit and only parted company in every which way upon my imminent return. "Anything To Make

Life Difficult" was the cow's true motto, and I was almost certain that an ornery stray was welcomed back to the herd as a hero.

But we didn't care. Hard work was in our blood. Pa would say that the smell of sweat was our cologne. 'Course, he did use fancier stuff when he was courting Ma. My own feeling was the harder the work, the better the feeling after the work was done.

With these enterprising thoughts lingering in my head and the paint and brush lingering in my hand, I hopped off the porch and walked over to the corral. Raw Speed was already waiting by the fence for my arrival. The old brown mare had belonged to Tiny Bob, but she was mine now. Tiny Bob had named her "Pokey", but I renamed her "Raw Speed" in the hopes that she would take the hint and live up to her new name. Unfortunately, she still was quite content to be a "Pokey", and some days, I would swear that she thought her name was "No Visible Sign Of Movement". Of course, the exception was at feeding time. Then she was Raw Speed.

"Good, Raw Speed," I said, patting her on the head. I pulled out a sugar cube from my Levi's, which was the real reason for Raw Speed's feigned excitement over my arrival. I placed the cube in her mouth. "Ya ready to go, girl?" I continued.

Raw Speed neighed. Had I been able to understand horse, I'm sure the response was "No". But as I am not one to let nonhumans dictate, I saddled her up and mounted. A well-placed kick got her from "No Visible Sign Of Movement" to "Pokey", and soon we were out of the corral.

We slowly made our way down the main road heading toward the front entrance. We passed semi-eaten green fields on either side dotted with cattle plotting their strategy. A big dillo scurried past us. Actually, it more like "moseyed on by", but I had to be careful with my choice of words for fear that Raw Speed might develop a complex, being passed by a fat armadillo and all. Ten minutes later we came upon the same dillo dead by the side of the road. Passed by a fat armadillo who was on its last legs no less. Raw Speed, however, appeared unconcerned as she plodded by the defunct dillo.

Eventually, we arrived at the front entrance to the Old Miss. Approaching from the rear, as we had, you saw a large wrought iron gate overtop of which were the words HCNAR SSIM DLO. Of course, from the front, it said OLD MISS RANCH. But from my vantage point, I felt that this was probably the way the Hebrews would have spelled the ranch's name. If one ever wandered onto the property, I made a mental note to ask.

I dismounted and tied Raw Speed to the back of the gate. Raw Speed immediately lay down in the grass. Usually a down horse was cause for grave concern, but not in Raw Speed's case. Raw Speed was just a true horse of leisure.

I stepped back onto the road with the paint and brush in hand and walked under the wrought iron arch, kicking up a little dust with every step. Once through the entrance way, I put down the paint and brush, turned around and gazed back to where I had just passed.

You could not help but admire the work that went into the wrought iron gateway, with its large letters that spelled OLD MISS RANCH from the front and HCNAR SSIM DLO from the back. On either side of the gate were small red brick walls which ran a mile in both directions. 'Course, these walls might have been good for stopping an occasional dillo, but anything bigger could step right over, and anything smaller could always walk through the ever open front gate. And even an extremely stupid critter would only have to stumble a mile in either direction before it was on the Old Miss. I, therefore, assumed that these walls were built strictly for their aesthetic quality, and that is why I admired them.

I gathered the paint can and brush and walked over to the brick wall left of the entrance way. A white wooden sign hung there which read," Member — Texas and Southwest Cattle Raiser's Association". Scrawled underneath stood Willie's handiwork from two nights before, "Vegatarians Are Us".

You could always depend on Willie for his practical jokes. Another thing you could depend on was that the scope of Willie's practical jokes was directly proportional to the magnitude of his liquor intake. Obviously, one too many Shiner's at Prairie Dog By The Sea in Grangerland had resulted in this, the latest of Willie's triumphs.

When Pa discovered Willie's joke, he was furious. It wasn't that Pa didn't have a good sense of humor. He enjoyed sticking manure down an empty boot along with the next guy. But with the way business had been going, I guessed that he was afraid that someone might just believe the sign and take what little business was left to someone who knew something about beef.

The only other explanation I had for Pa's anger was that Willie had misspelled "Vegetarian", which could make the whole ranch out to be a bunch of illiterate imbiciles. Now, I might be the only one with any formal education, but the Old Miss hands are far from buffoons, especially, as I've told you, Little Ben. As a matter of fact, Little Ben, with no education, was the first to point out to the Grangerland School Superintendent that two of the three R's taught in the school system don't begin with R's at all. Thanks to his keen observation and the Old Miss hands' insistence, students in the district now learn the three M's: Math, Material Comprehension and Material Inscription.

In any event, Pa was irritated, and as our saying goes, "When Pa gets irkin', we really get workin'". So, being the youngest, it was my job to fix the trivial things around the ranch, and I guessed that Pa categorized this misspelled word as trivial. 'Course, it could have meant that Willie had a learning disability, which is far from trivial in my mind, but I didn't want to raise this point with Pa.

I opened the paint can with the knife that I always kept attached to my belt. My belt was a fancy hand-tooled leather belt complete with a silver buckle displaying an enameled Appaloosa. Thought you'd just like to know. I paused for a moment, contemplating which course of action to take. I figured that I could either delete the entire phrase or just fix the spelling. Not knowing the source of Pa's anger, I decided it would be best to paint over the whole phrase.

Very carefully, I painted two perfectly parallel white lines. Stepping back, I saw that not only had I completely covered the writing, but I had retained the aesthetic quality of the entire wall as well. I felt a swell of pride and knew in my heart why Pa always depended on me for trivial matters.

My self congratulations were almost complete when I heard B.B.'s meal bell off in the distance. I quickly wrapped the brush in the bandana, grabbed the can of paint and ran to Raw Speed. Raw Speed was already up, sensing food was on the horizon.

Once untied, Raw Speed immediately broke into an all out gallop home. She obviously couldn't be bothered with those in between stages like walking, trotting and cantering when food was involved. Unfortunately, she hadn't given me proper notice of her intentions, and about the only thing correct about my riding form was accidently getting my right foot somehow into my right stirrup. How this happened riding at a ninety degree angle to a horse running at full tilt, I don't know. I did know, however, that stuck in such a predicament, holding onto the paint and brush for dear life seemed kinda pointless.

I was desperately clinging to the saddle horn and shouting, "Where's that Pokey we all knew and loved?" when we arrived back at the ranch house. Raw Speed came to an abrupt halt at the kitchen door. Actually, she came to an abrupt halt upon reaching some scraps of scrambled eggs B.B. had left out by the kitchen door. The kitchen door itself was inconsequential. I, however, came to an abrupt halt after flying head first into the kitchen door. For me, the kitchen door had real meaning.

I picked myself up and straightened myself out. I examined the hole my head had made in the door. It was an impressive hole. You could look right into the kitchen through the four inch circle of emptiness and scalp where oak once was. It really hadn't hurt too much when I made it either. Maybe with some practice, I could get my head as hard as Big Bill's feet. Then I'd bet that people would pay a pretty penny to watch two such talented brothers crush things in unusual manners.

As a token gesture, I tied Raw Speed to the porch railing, the dead dillo had a greater chance of moving than did Raw Speed. I then entered the kitchen.

"Yer late," B.B. said, looking up from the sink. "'Course, I knew you'd be late." He smugly tapped his lump and winked.

"Sorry," I said, grabbing a plate from the counter. "Had to fix the sign down by the entrance."

"Yeah, I heard that Willie misspelled "vegetarian"," B.B. said, shaking his head in disgust. "Lucky nobody done saw it or they would have thought us fools." He returned to washing pans."Now Even Tinier Bert, you'd best hurry 'cause I'm a yellin' stop in about seven minutes."

I took a glass from the pantry, which I filled with milk, and headed towards the dining room.

"By the way," B.B. added. "Nice hole." He looked my direction and smiled, adding to the many wrinkles on his face.

With a grin on my face, I opened the door leading into the dining room. As I did, I heard the voices of the Old Miss hands who were all gathered around the table. They were just finishing a discussion on what would have happened had Big Bill and Little Ben been reversed. There was a general agreement that Grangerland would have become a tourist haven, with crowds of people looking for a famous clock in the vicinity. The thought of my oldest brother's picture on the post cards that they hawked over at the Broncobuster Motel amused me as I entered to the smiles and nods of the others.

"Bert Boy," Pa said. "Ya'll done?"

"Yeah, Pa," I said. "I was even able to keep the aesthetic quality of the wall." A general sigh of relief followed.

I placed my plate and glass down at an open space on the table between Willie and Tiny Bob. As I squeezed down onto the bench, Willie gave me a sheepish grin.

"Heard some noise" Little Ben said.

"Raw Speed threw me," I said.

Even though a cowboy is usually embarrassed by being thrown by a horse the likes of Raw Speed, I knew that no one at the table would rib me, except maybe Tiny Bob. They felt sorry for me because no matter how hard I tried, I just didn't have the coordination to be a decent cowhand. My falling off a horse was as predictable as a coyote howling at the moon. But even a good cowboy might have been thrown by a food-crazed Raw Speed.

"I landed on my head and knocked a nice hole in the door," I added. "Can you pass the bacon and eggs, Clint?"

"Pass the bacon and eggs?" Clint said passing the scrambled eggs and bacon. "Sure I can pass the bacon and eggs."

I was almost sorry I had asked. First, I had given Clint a chance to talk and second, the bacon and eggs were one step short of petrified. I took a biscuit from the plate of biscuits in front of me. At least this was still warm.

"Hole in the door, huh," Pa said, tactfully precluding Clint's continued discussion on the fascinating subject of eggs and bacon. "Sounds like a trivial repair. Bert Boy, why don't ya fix that thar hole after ya eat."

"Sure, Pa," I said grinning.

B.B. entered from the kitchen. I wolfed down my eggs, bacon and biscuit figuring that B.B. had come in to yell "stop". Instead, B.B. walked over to Pa.

"Trouble's a comin', Eugene," B.B. said.

"Felt a strong inklin', did ya B.B.?" Pa asked.

"No, saw it comin' through the kitchen window," B.B. said. "E. Lester Shapes just pulled up."

A collective look of concern suddenly appeared on the faces of the Old Miss personnel. E. Lester Shapes was the local banker, President of Fertilizer Bank, formerly known as Chemical Bank until it turned out that some other bank, somewhere, had already used that name. A diploma from the National Correspondence School certifying him as a Bank President hung prominently in his office. For deposits of a hundred dollars or more, he'd let you look at his Dallas Cowboys Cheerleaders' poster. That's the kind of person E. Lester was.

'Course, no one was quite sure what the "E" in E. Lester stood for, although, with the exception of Big Bill, everyone had their ideas. Little Ben figured it stood for "Enormous", which was appropriate for the three hundred pound E. Lester Shapes. He was so big that he had to special order clothes. He said they were from a fancy store called Neiman-Marcus, but I once saw him removing a "Besty Ann's Maternity For Men" label and sewing on one that said "Neiman-Marcus."

Clint believed that the "E" stood for "Enormously Fat", but we told him that if that was the case, it would have been "E.F." and not plain "E". Willie thought it stood for "Ecky", but I didn't have the heart to tell him it was spelled "Icky". Tiny Bob invented the word "Eeoogie", which did describe E. Lester to a tee. I just said it stood for "Eyesore".

Pa was not too concerned with what the "E" stood for. What was more important to Pa was what "E. Lester Shapes" stood for. According to Pa, E. Lester stood for legalized, state approved robbery. On money Pa gave E. Lester to use, Pa received 5¼% interest. On money E. Lester gave Pa to use, Pa had to pay 8½% interest. To Pa, it just didn't make sense. Through investments, E. Lester was already making money on the money Pa had given him. So, it only seemed right that E. Lester should return the favor and charge Pa no more than 5¼% or E. Lester's money.

Now, E. Lester had once tried to explain the difference, saying that one was a savings account rate, while the other was a loan rate. But since E. Lester could not deny the fact that he used Pa's money rather than let it sit around the bank, we saw no reason why Pa's account was not called a loan account and Pa paid accordingly. E. Lester became so flustered that he truly resembled an Eeoogie, and could only spit out from his big, fat face that the whole thing was legal. We hated bankers.

There was a knock at the front door. Everybody turned to Pa.

"Oh, let him in," Pa said. "Maybe he's a come to tell me he's changed his mind 'bout my interest rate."

Big Bill got up from the table and went over to the front door. When he opened it, just like jello being poured into a mold, the entire door frame filled with E. Lester. And somewhere between the chins, I thought I detected a smile.

"Big Bill," E. Lester said slapping Big Bill on the back. "Yer lookin' good, boy." E. Lester took off his Stetson, which was probably a Grangerland Discount and Surplus Store copy, and handed it to Big Bill.

Big Bill took the hat and had started to cross in front of E. Lester on the way to the hat rack. It was then that I heard the crunch.

"Sorry," Big Bill said. He knew without even looking that he had stepped on one of E. Lester's feet, and it really didn't matter which one. A boot is just no protection from Big Bill.

E. Lester tried to keep his smile on his chins as we helped him over to the table. I looked back to see Big Bill hanging E. Lester's hat on the rack. He saw me and gave me an 8½% grin.

E. Lester slowly sat down on the bench. His face showed more colors and gyrations than the Broncobuster's pinball machine. With a couple of broken toes, he was obviously in some pain. Still, through his pain, he was able to see that there were some biscuits left on the table. With a slight grimace, he reached for a biscuit. And with a trembling hand, he brought the biscuit towards his mouth.

"Stop," B.B. yelled. "Time's up." He grabbed the biscuit right out of E. Lester's hand.

E. Lester turned to Pa. "Tex, I'm in some great pain here," E. Lester moaned. "I might even blank out if…if I don't get some food into my system."

"Now, E. Lester, ya know B.B.'s rules," Pa replied.

"But, Tex," E. Lester pleaded. "Ask B.B. to bend the rules. I might just be dyin'."

"If I asked B.B. to bend the rules, they wouldn't be rules, now would they?" Pa asked. "Ain't ya the one who's always a tellin' me that? 'Sides, nobody's done died from a few broken toes. Worse comes to worse, Old Doc Buford cuts 'em off."

E. Lester just sat there, turning more into an Eeoogie with every word he was hearing.

"So, B.B.," Pa continued. "What do ya want us to do?"

"Leave," B.B. replied. "Else I can't clear the damn table and start gettin' ready fer lunch. Did ya think I was kiddin' when I said "stop"? And I don't want no fat-assed banker in here tryin' to disrupt the law of my kitchen. Now, everybody git."

We swiftly rose from the table and made our way into the den. Big Bill had one of E. Lester's arms around his shoulder and was dragging him along behind. A bang and a deep sustained wail suddenly filled the air.

"Sorry," Big Bill said to the now purple and dizzy E. Lester Shapes.

Seems in his haste to drag E. Lester out of B.B.'s domain, Big Bill had caused E. Lester to stub his already injured foot on the door leading into the den. Tiny Bob later said that he really didn't know that E. Lester was hurt further because it sounded more like an Eeoogie mating call than a cry of pain. All I know is that when I turned back, I saw B.B. in the dining room, putting away the remaining biscuits and smiling an 8½% smile.

Now, the den at the Old Miss ranch house was a sight to see. Cactuses, barrels, shotguns and branding irons abounded. In the middle was a big old stone fireplace complete with a couple of decorative cow skulls on the mantle. Over the top of the fireplace hung the Lone Star. Across the way stood a couch covered with burlap. Pa said that there was no sense using real material when it was just us sitting on it. Over top of this was a painting of Sam Bass, an outlaw who made his living robbing banks. It was under there that Big Bill placed E. Lester.

E. Lester just laid there on that couch, and actually, he was mighty lucky that he was injured. Pa frowned on anyone caught laying on the couch with their shoes on. He was afraid that someone might dirty up the burlap. And because once you were through admiring the cowskulls, the couch became the center of attraction, his concern was well justified. But, under the circumstances, I guess Pa was letting E. Lester slide. So, as E. Lester just laid there with his shoes all over the good couch, we pulled up barrels and formed a sorta circle around him.

"Think this time he's dead?" Willie asked after about ten minutes of staring at the still Eeoogie.

"Nah," Pa said placing some chaw into his mouth. "Bankers don't die. They go away to law school."

Pa revved up and spit some tobacco juice in the general direction of his spittoon, a brass container molded into the shape of the Alamo. Unfortunately, because the spittoon was nearer the couch than it was to Pa, most of the brown sludge landed on E. Lester's leg instead. Pa, seeing what had happened, simply shrugged his shoulders, figuring that there wasn't much sense apologizing to an unconscious banker.

"Think wavin' a biscuit under his nose would bring 'im to?" asked Willie, turning to Little Ben.

"Yep," Little Ben answered before pondering a few more moments. "If ya find it."

Little Ben had made an astute observation. With the way E. Lester was positioned, his nose was lost somewhere in one of his chins.

"That's also assuming you can sneak into the kitchen and grab a biscuit without B.B. seeing you," I added.

A cold chill went up and down the spines of the Old Miss hands. No man had ever been caught in the kitchen after hours and lived to tell about it. I think it had more to do with B.B.'s belief in three square meals a day than with the protection of his kitchen. But, for whatever reason, B.B. was fully prepared to lay down his life in a kitchen shootout, whether with an intruder or merely a potential in-between meal snacker. Needless to say, we at the Old Miss were a pretty trim, healthy lot. But, because we were only human, B.B. did allow us an occasional s'more at the campfire.

"Well if he ain't dead, I'm sure sick of starin' at him," Willie said.

Willie rose from his barrel and approached the rolls of fat christened E. Lester Shapes draped on the sagging burlap. I could clearly hear the couch pull and creak under the tremendous strain. Willie was just about to bend down next to E. Lester's head when B.B. entered armed with a shotgun.

"What are ya plannin' on doin'?" B.B. asked, pointing the gun in Willie's general direction.

"Well, I'll tell ya one thing I ain't doin'," Willie said quickly standing up. "I ain't figurin' on comin' into the kitchen. So ya can just point that gun somewheres else."

"It ain't pointed at ya," B.B. said. "But I ain't a crack shot neither. So, I'd be backin' off if I was in yer shoes."

Now Willie knew that B.B. was a terrible shot. What Willie was unsure of was just how terrible. Still, it was kinda hard to picture anyone being that short a distance from a target like E. Lester and missing. 'Course, that's the stuff of which legends are born, and Willie, recognizing the unpredictable "legend" factor, backed off.

Pa spit another wad of tobacco juice on E. Lester.

"Now, B.B.," Pa said. "What's this all 'bout? Ya done got yer biscuit out of his hand."

"I had some real strong inklin's, Eugene," B.B. said, closing the wrong eye and taking some sorta aim. "E. Lester's bringin' nothin' but trouble."

"We don't know that," Pa said, even though he knew that B.B.'s inklings were never wrong. "The man ain't done much more than moan since he got here. 'Sides, we can't go 'round shootin' people just 'cause they might have somethin' to say that we don't wanna hear."

"Not even a banker?" B.B. asked.

Pa was silent for a couple of minutes. "No," Pa replied solemnly. "Not even a banker."

Disappointed, B.B. slowly lowered the shotgun. We all felt an immediate sense of relief, that is, until the ringing sound of a shotgun blast filled the air. It seems that in lowering the gun, B.B. had forgotten to take his finger off of the trigger. Fortunately, the blast hit above the wagonwheel chandelier hanging down over the couch, and the only result of any consequence was that large chunks of plaster fell onto E. Lester below — the kinda chunks you get when the ceiling's made of Plaster of Peoria rather than Plaster of Paris. 'Course, having no idea of what was going on, everyone else, including B.B., dove for cover. Everyone else, I should say, except Pa, who was too busy staring at the new hole in the ceiling.

"Bert Boy," Pa said, still staring at the ceiling. "When ya finish with the door, ya can fix this hole too."

Since B.B.'s shotgun only held one shell, everybody figured that it was safe to stand and inspect the damage.

"Nice shot, B.B.," Tiny Bob said examining the hole. "Ya huntin' ceilin's?"

"It was a warning shot," B.B. said. Pointing his finger at E. Lester, he continued, "So ya'd best take the hint. Take yer bad news and git 'cause I ain't a plannin' on warnin' ya twice."

"And I reckon, he'd surely appreciate the warnin' if he were awake," Pa said sincerely. 'Course it sounded so funny that the rest of us laughed.

"Well, thar ain't no doubt that ya kilt it," Willie said, lifting one particularly large chunk of ceiling off of E. Lester's face. "Does this mean we're havin' fresh plaster for dinner?"

Again, everybody except Pa and B.B. laughed. B.B. turned and headed back to the kitchen.

"I think I've made my point," he said while exiting. "But unlike you Yahoos, I got better things to do."

"Like shootin' the ceilin' in the kitchen," Clint yelled after him. 'Course, no one except Clint laughed. Even with a good cause for ribbing, there came a point when enough was enough.

Willie bent down next to E. Lester's ear. After a few clears of the throat and a quick look to make sure that B.B. had no thoughts of reloading and returning, Willie began his impression of bacon frying on a hot griddle.

It was pretty much a given that a person could not put in a claim to be the area's best practical jokester if they could not do impressions. At least, that was the current popular theory in Grangerland. Willie was probably somewhere in the top three. He could do impressions of just about anything, and fortunately, there were no deductions for spelling. He once hid behind Pa and did this great impression of an attractive available heifer. Well, this big old bull named George heard the call, took one look at the origin of the noise and fell in love with Pa. And had that bull been able to get down on one knee and talk, it would have proposed to Pa on the spot. 'Course, even though Ma was dead, Pa wasn't interested. We all thought this was mighty funny except that George never recovered and went on to be a lonely, heartbroken bull.

Anyway, I could almost feel grease drops splattering on my arm as Willie continued with his impression. And sure enough, I soon started to detect some movement under the plaster and the unmistakable sound of licking chops. Willie, his job accomplished, moved away.

"What, what happened?" E. Lester asked from beneath the pile of rubble. He moaned slightly as he sat up and brushed off the pieces of plaster.

"Yep," Little Ben said looking skyward. "Strong twister."

"Mighty strong twister," Pa repeated.

Slowly, E. Lester inspected the room. He seemed puzzled by the fact that the only evident damage of the tornado was on him.

Pa continued, "We coulda all been kilt. Lucky fer us, that thar wind just swept off a small part of ceilin'."

E. Lester sniffed the air.

"I thought I smelt bacon," he said.

"And the bacon," Pa said, slapping himself in the forehead. "I clean forgot that the wind swept that off too."

E. Lester still appeared confused.

"So the only thins the twister got were some ceilin' and some bacon?" E. Lester asked as Pa nodded affirmatively. "Well, what was a twister doin' inside?"

Pa seemed stumped. He looked to Little Ben, but I don't think either of them had expected such a tricky question from someone with broken toes who had just been conked by plaster.

"It was an internal twister," I said, jumping in. "The ones that have been the talk of all of those scientific conferences. You know, the ones that have been in the news almost every day."

All of the Old Miss hands looked at me in a sorta shock. I think they thought that I had really come across something called an internal twister through my schooling. And even as I'm telling you this, I still haven't told them otherwise, figuring that I might be able to use it as an excuse for something in the future. But not to disappoint you since you now know better, I was just playing a hunch that E. Lester's only reading consisted of the menu over at Claudia's Beauty School and Diner.

"Oh yeah, I've read about 'em," E. Lester said not wanting to appear uninformed.

"Yeah, them dern internal twisters," Clint said.

Now, we knew that Clint said what he said because, as usual, he had nothing else to say. But E. Lester took it to be a confirmation of the existence of internal twisters. E. Lester and Clint then spent the next ten minutes discussing the subject of internal twisters. Finally, when we all had more than enough of the discussion over a subject that even if it had existed would have become boring after five minutes, Pa interrupted.

"E. Lester, it was certainly nice of ya to stop over," Pa said. "But the boys gotta git started cleanin' up this here twister damage."

"Not really," E. Lester said. "That's what I came to talk to ya about."

E. Lester fumbled with his string tie and took a few deep breaths, which made his chins look like an accordian held straight up and down, before he continued.

"Now, Tex Henry, we've known each other a long time," he said. "Hell, my daddy and yer daddy used to play together. So ya gotta believe that I wouldn't be sayin' what I'm a gonna say unless there was no other choice. But a man's gotta feed his family, don't ya think? That's why, well, that's why I'm callin' in my loan."

We all sat there silent. I tried to picture Pa's pa playing with E. Lester's pa. From what I remembered about E. Lester's pa, he was even more of an Eeoogie than his son. So, unless Pa's pa played mountain climber with E. Lester's pa playing mountain, I doubted that they ever played together. I didn't buy the feeding of the family line either. One look at E. Lester's family showed that most food never made it past the head of the table.

"Just what's that mean, yer callin' in my loan?" Pa asked.

"It means that I need back all of the money that I lent ya or I'm a gonna have to take the ranch," E. Lester said.

"But I've been payin' ya, E. Lester," Pa stated.

"First of all, don't think I don't know that ya only been payin' a 5¼% interest rate," E. Lester said.

"It was a matter of principle," Pa stated.

"It was a matter of interest, Tex," E. Lester replied. "But forgettin' about that, ya ain't paid me nothin' in over two months."

Now knowing Pa, he had to have had a good reason not to pay his debts. He once walked clear over to Athens to return a dime that Old Man Grubbs had lent him. When he got there, he found out that Old Man Grubbs had just died. Well, damn if Pa didn't track down Grubbs' grave and bury the dime next to him. I thought this little story told alot about what kind of man Pa was, although some low lifes claimed that the only reason Pa went to Athens was for the Miss Black-Eyed Pea Pageant.

"Business has been a bit off," Pa said. "Some kind of rumor goin' 'round that beef ain't healthy. People are bein' told to eat more vegetables and less meat. The Cattle Raisers are promisin' me that they've got some sorta reverse campaign startin' soon. It's some-thin' like, Meat is healthier than vegetables. Just look around you. There are a lot more rabbits dead by the side of highways, than there are cows. So, I expect business to be a pickin' up real soon."

"But, Tex, in the meantime, I'm goin' bust," E. Lester said. "If it ain't you, than it's the oil fielders who can't pay their loans or the guys who went off to work in Houston. Hell, people are leavin' Houston faster than customers in a Nun-runned whorehouse."

Not ever having gone to a Nun-runned whorehouse, and not really even knowing what one is, I had no idea of how fast we were talking. All I knew about whorehouses was that Willie told me that if I ever had a chance to frequent one, never tell them my name was Even Tinier Bert.

I looked around to see what Willie thought about the whore-house analogy, but I guess he had left the room while I was busy contemplating. Maybe he went to teach B.B. how to shoot.

"So, ya see, Tex," E. Lester continued. "I ain't got no choice. I wouldn't be askin' for the loan money if I didn't need it. And it's only because ya defaulted on payments that I gotta ask fer the whole thing. I never woulda otherwise."

E. Lester slowly stood while emitting piglike grunts. Then, with all the grace of a boulder in a landslide, he made his way out of the den and back to the front door. We all followed behind, like the little pebbles that trail a boulder in a landslide. He removed his phony Stetson from the hat rack.

"I'm gonna need a little time, E. Lester," Pa said watching E. Lester position his undersized hat on his oversized head. Plaster of Peoria flakes fell from his hair.

E. Lester turned back to face Pa.

"Tex, I'll tell ya what I can do," E. Lester said. "Bein' how you did save me from an internal twister, I can give ya two days to come up with the money 'fore I take the ranch, cattle and any other collateral."

E. Lester proceeded to wobble out the front door and head

towards his car. Pa remained silent. We watched E. Lester painfully stuff his body into his Rolls Royce, a 1968 Ford Falcon painted silver to which he had attached a Rolls Royce hood ornament. The car kicked up a cloud of dirt as he drove off. Willie appeared through the settling dust.

"Willie," I said running up to him. "E. Lester gave Pa two days to pay the loan or he's going to take everything."

"Good," Willie said.

"Good?" I replied, confused by the response.

"Yeah, good," Willie reiterated, opening his jacket and displaying part of a 1968 Ford Falcon water pump. "I wouldn'ta wanted to feel guilty 'bout a guy with broken toes havin' his car break down miles from anywhere."

3

I APOLOGIZE, BUT IT seems that one flashback chapter just wasn't enough to bring you up to the campfire. So, I'll tell you what happened next, and that should about do it.

Right after E. Lester left, Pa got on the horn — our telephone's shaped like a cattle horn. We remained quiet, seeing as how Pa seemed all riled up, although with Pa, it's hard to tell. He never yells and never curses. He does, however, start grumbling when he's really angry, and, right then, I felt like I was in the middle of an active volcano field. Finally, the lava subsided as Pa hung up and told everybody to get into the truck.

Me, Tiny Bob and Big Bill were crammed in the flatbed while Pa and Little Ben sat in the cab. Big Bill's legs were hanging over the tail, and because the rear bumper fell off sometime in 1971, rocks of all sizes were bouncing up and hitting him in the feet as we drove along. Needless to say, Big Bill was in ecstacy. Tiny Bob was having a good old time examining bugs and bug pieces on the cab's rear window. Next to Big Bill's feet, the truck's front and rear windows were the best places to find belt buckle ornaments. And it was only because the truck would sometimes only work in reverse that Tiny Bob presently had such a fine selection to choose from. As for me, I was just crammed.

We had passed a broken down 1968 Ford Falcon some twenty miles back on Route 105. E. Lester was over by the side of the road waving. So as not to appear inhospitable, we all waved back as we drove on by. We crossed under Highway 45 and were now approaching the outskirts of Plantersville. Had we turned south on Highway 45 and driven about thirty miles we would have hit Houston. As I saw it, that wasn't all that far away, but Pa had never made that turn. I knew it was the biggest city in Texas, but without ever having been there, I couldn't compare it to Grangerland. Still, Houston made its presence known daily. You see, the Houston Intercontinental Airport had a flight path that ran directly over the Old Miss. Through the noise created by the plane followed by the stampede of frightened cattle, I often looked up and wondered where those people were coming from and where they were going, and whether I would ever be joining them.

Right before we hit Plantersville, Pa pulled off Route 105 and into the driveway of an ugly white stucco house. The mailbox in front of the driveway read, "Cyrus H. Squirrel, Esq." Pa shut off the engine, but that didn't stop the old Dodge from running. Pa said that it was better to have a truck that always ran rather than one that never ran. Truthfully, I think I'd prefer one that ran when it was supposed to. 'Course, I don't drive, so no one really asks too much about my preference.

The engine was still running when we got to the front door. Partway down the door was a wrought iron knocker.

"Look, he has a door knock in the shape of a gavel," I said.

"No, it ain't," Tiny Bob said. "That just shows what ya know. It's a crab mallet."

"Now why would a lawyer want a door knock in the shape of a crab mallet?" I asked.

"To show that he enjoys eatin' crabs," Tiny Bob replied.

"That's stupid," I said. "A gavel is a symbol of our great justice system. And because Mr. Squirrel is part of the system, it'd only make sense that this thing is a gavel." I hated showing off my education, but I thought that Tiny Bob deserved it.

"Boys," Pa said. "I know that tempers are runnin' a might hot right now. But it's real important that we all stick together, okay?"

Both me and Tiny Bob looked at our feet in shame. Not that we were embarrassed by them, but because Pa was right. When Pa really needed us to act like men, we were acting like little immature kids, especially Tiny Bob.

Pa lifted the door knock and banged. "Now, Bob Boy," Pa continued. "Did ya leave yer bugs and bug pieces in the truck?"

"No, Pa," Tiny Bob replied.

"I ain't too sure Cyrus would want 'em in his house, are ya? Pa asked rhetorically. "Why don't ya put 'em in the glove compartment."

I could tell by the look on Tiny Bob's face that he could not believe that a person existed who would not want prime bugs and bug pieces in their house. Still, he obeyed Pa and ran back to the truck just as the door opened.

"Tex," Cyrus said, nodding slightly and twitching his cheeks.

"Cyrus," Pa said, returning the nod.

"Come on in," Cyrus said, his eyes sweeping in all directions. He took a step back, allowing room to pass.

Pa, Big Bill and Little Ben walked into the house. I stayed back at the door. Cyrus watched me for a moment, then approached.

"I was just admiring the door knock," I said.

"Oh," Cyrus said, squinting his darting, jet black eyes. "It's a crab mallet. It's to show that I enjoy eatin' crabs."

I quickly looked around and saw that Tiny Bob was just on his way back from the truck. As I entered, I hoped that the subject of the door knock would not be brought up in conversation.

"Cyrus," Pa said, as Tiny Bob entered and Cyrus closed the door. "Ya remember my boys? Big Bill, Little Ben, Tiny Bob and Even Tinier Bert?"

We each took turns shaking Cyrus's very small, hairy hand. As I shook his hand, I discreetly searched it for nuts.

"Lookin' for nuts?" Cyrus asked.

Startled, I looked up. I was relieved to see that Cyrus was talking to Big Bill, who was staring at a big tin marked "Pecans".

"Got some in the kitchen," Cyrus continued, puffing his cheeks. "You can have a few. Just don't throw the shells away."

Big Bill exited. Pa walked over to Cyrus while the rest of us found places to sit, which wasn't as easy as it sounds. From the looks of his living room, I was pretty sure that Cyrus had never thrown away a thing in his life. The place was cluttered with just about everything known to man. Because we were afraid to move anything, I sat on top of a pile of books while Little Ben and Tiny Bob sat in what looked to me like two piles of trash.

"These are them loan papers I was tellin' ya 'bout," Pa said handing some documents over to Cyrus. "Can E. Lester take every-thin'?"

Cyrus cleared off the top of what appeared to be an uprooted tree stump and sat down. With his cheeks twitching, he hunched over and began reading the papers. His head moved back and forth like a windshield wiper. There were no other sounds but the turning of pages, that is, until Big Bill dropped what sounded like some pecans in the kitchen. The noise caused Cyrus to immediately stop reading, sit up straight, lift his head and listen. His brownish-gray neckhair stood on end. I half expected him to jump up on the stump, although I'm glad he didn't because, by now, I was biting my lip to keep from laughing as it was. I think that it was because Cyrus was so amusing that Pa tolerated him. As you probably figured, lawyers ranked right up there with bankers in Pa's book.

After a minute of staying absolutely still, Cyrus relaxed and returned to his hunched over postion and his reading. His neckhair receded.

Big Bill came back in from the kitchen and found an old potty to sit on. The room was quiet again for a couple more minutes.

"Well," Cyrus said, lowering the documents and jerking his head up. "Seems that a clause here calls for an acceleration upon default, meanin' that if you miss a payment, the whole thing becomes due."

"So yer sayin' E. Lester's got a right to the ranch if I don't come up with the money," Pa said.

"The ranch, the cattle, the horses," Cyrus said.

"The burlap sofa?" Big Bill asked.

"Yep," Little Ben replied.

"You're right, Son," Cyrus said, shifting his eyes to Little Ben. "He gets everythin'. But there might be somethin'…"

Crack. Cyrus lifted his head and froze. I looked over to see Big Bill picking shells and nuts from his toes. Well-mannered as always, Big Bill offered the pecans to everyone. Cyrus was relaxed by the time Big Bill got around to him and took a few. He immediately stuffed them into one of his cheeks, after which he began chewing rapidly. Again I bit my lip to stop from laughing.

"Anyway," Cyrus continued as if no time had passed. "There might be somethin' we can do to keep you in possession of…"

Crack. Cyrus sat up, lifted his head and froze. Pa looked over to Big Bill.

"Bill Boy," Pa said. "Can ya hold off eatin' them thins 'til we're finished? Or else we ain't a never gonna get outta here."

As Big Bill put the nuts away, Cyrus relaxed his state of alert and continued.

"I think there's somethin' we just might be able to do," he said standing up and quickly walking in my direction. "Boy, I'm gonna need one of them books you're sittin' on."

"Yes Sir," I said jumping down from my pile.

Cyrus bent down to read the titles of the books which were written on the bindings. I swear I saw him sniff each book, wiggling his nose as he went along. He proceeded to pull out the second book from the bottom. It was a large green volume entitled, "Bankruptcy Deskbook". Standing back up, he flipped through a couple of chapters before he stopped and read.

It seemed like hours before he lowered the book. "I think your best bet is to file for voluntary bankruptcy under Chapter Eleven," Cyrus finally declared. "The court'll have to appoint a trustee and all the credtors'll have to get together before anyone can do anythin'. In the meantime, it'll give ya'll a chance to reorganize and most important, it'll put an automatic stay on actions against you or the ranch."

I looked over to Pa to see what he made of the gibberish.

"Can't do," Pa said. "E. Lester would head the creditor's committee, and fer all I know, he mighta snuck into court already and filed a lien givin' him a priority claim."

"But," Cyrus said a bit flabbergasted.

"Then thar's the figurin' of prepetition set off," Pa said.

"But, but," Cyrus stuttered.

"And worryin' 'bout the trustee's power to avoid anythin' resemblin' a preference," Pa said, his voice lowering an octave.

"B-b-but," Cyrus spit out.

"And then determinin' which property is exempt," Pa grumbled. "No, I just won't do it. Boys, let's go home."

Tiny Bob, excited by the thought of returning to his bugs, sprung from his trash mound while Big Bill rose from his potty. I helped Little Ben up from his heap, and we all met Pa at the door.

Cyrus, looking like he was trying to muster up some courage, held the door open for us. The truck was still running. And it looked like Cyrus was about to say something besides "But" to Pa when the truck backfired. Now, we were used to occasional backfires, which began about the time Tiny Bob started playing torpedo tube with the tailpipe. But Cyrus, hearing the bang, scurried back into the house, perked up his ears and remained still only after he was a safe distance away. Pa closed the door behind him and we left without Cyrus getting a chance to say what he was going to say. 'Course, for all we knew, this might have amounted to just chirps, and no one felt like hanging around for those.

Little Ben later told us that Pa grumbled the whole way home. I reckon that Pa believed that he had been given bad advice, and now, worse than that, Cyrus was probably going to bill him for it. That's why Pa had the natural inclination to hate lawyers just as much as bankers. However, as a source of entertainment, me and my brothers felt that Cyrus was worth every penny. But not even Cyrus's amusement value could save him now. Little Ben heard Pa specifically grumble about the fact that lawyers weren't put here to entertain. 'Course, now everybody's stumped because if they weren't put here to entertain, we had no idea of what their purpose is.

4

"C'MON, EVEN TINIER BERT," B.B. said. "Yer S'more's been in the fire way too long."

I removed my stick from the fire. B.B. was right. My marshmallow was engulfed in flames. By the time I had the fire under control, my marshmallow was nothing more than a pitch black blistery blob.

"Ya ain't gonna stick that on yer gram, are ya?" Tiny Bob asked. "I bet ya can use it to trap some bugs if ya whack 'em with it while it's still hot and gooey."

I stared at the marshmallow, a glimmer of its former self and handed the stick to Tiny Bob.

"Thanks," Tiny Bob replied. He immediately took aim against an ant hill unfortunate enough to be in his line of attack. Whop. Whop. Whop. He brought the stick up to the light of the fire, which revealed a burnt marshmallow covered with dirt and many fairly unhappy ants.

"Look at them ants go," he squealed with delight. 'Course I took this to refer to the ants' legs kicking wildly in the air because it was obvious that these particular ants weren't going anywhere.

In a way, it sorta looked like our situation, except that E. Lester hadn't hit us with a hot charred marshmallow. But like these ants, here we were, a group who had spent a lot of time and effort building a home, only to have an unconcerned individual wipe everything out. And now everybody was stuck, held at the mercy of, well, Eeoogies. Yes, it was sorta ironic that the word Tiny Bob invented to describe E. Lester was probably being used by these ants to describe Tiny Bob. You've got to forgive my triteness, but, "What goes around, comes around".

"Even Tinier Bert," Big Bill said. "You've been mighty quiet."

"I've been thinking about B.B.'s inklings, and you know, if today doesn't qualify as a day of reckoning, I don't know what would," I said, not wanting to get into the ant analogy.

"Chapter Eleven," Little Ben said with disdain.

"Yeah," B.B. replied. "Just what the hell was that goddamn lawyer thinkin' of? What if we couldn't explain the loss of certain assets? I'll tell ya. We'd be denied a discharge. And ya know what that means, don't ya? Eugene's non-exempt assets would be liqidated and any future earnings, exempt assets and property acquired after the bankruptcy filin' could be reached by E. Lester."

"Yeah, what the hell was that lawyer thinkin' of?" Clint reiterated.

"Does this here lawyer have a car?" Willie asked.

I looked over to Willie, who had practical joke written all over his face. Seems he had picked up a piece of burnt wood when no one was looking and used it as a charcoal pencil. I started laughing so hard that I fell off my log. Willie saw those old low spirits hanging around and, as usual, came through with a joke like a champion. That's because nothing good ever came from low spirits. I mean, a person just can't do their best thinking when their brain's stuck on one track and the train's coming in.

"Willie, go and wash them words off yer face," Pa said, chuckling.

With a smile, Willie rose and walked over to the water basin. We could tell by Pa's tone of voice that he was mighty glad that Willie had succeeded in improving everybody's outlook and in spelling "practical joke" correctly.

"Anybody want 'nother s'more?" B.B. asked. I took this as another sort of optimistic sign. B.B. offering seconds on dessert happened about as often as Raw Speed turning down food.

Big Bill jumped at the opportunity and immediately helped himself to seconds. Clint then followed suit. 'Course, this had nothing to do with manners. Even when it came to food, Clint couldn't act on his own accord. Willie returned and made both himself and me some s'mores. Only a slight trace of the practical joke was left on his face.

"Mr. Henry, if it'd help any, ya don't gotta pay me 'til yer able," Willie said. "Money turns into beer and beer turns into trouble."

Willie took a bite of his s'more. Some chocolate and marsh-mallow got caught in his moustache. Big Bill was watching him. He was either amused by the stuck food or, knowing Big Bill, curi-ous as to what kind of trick it took to turn money into beer.

"You don't gotta pay me neither, Mr. Henry," Clint said out of reflex. But almost immediately you could tell that he was sorry for not having paid attention to what he was going to say before it slipped out of his mouth.

"No, ya men are always the first to git paid," Pa said. "I'd rather give ya my money than E. Lester any day." Clint breathed a sigh of relief.

"Eugene," B.B. said, "I got me a few shares a stock tucked away. Thar all yers."

"I appreciate it, but they might not be worth a whole lot," Pa said. "I heard they're predictin' some sorta market collapse."

"Then Pa," Big Bill said. "Shouldn't we git to Grangerland 'fore it's too late and help build up the walls at the Piggly Wiggly?"

"I'm sure they'd appreciate it, Bill Boy," Pa said. "But we just can't spare the manpower right now."

Pa looked my way and winked. He knew that I knew what he and B.B. were talking about since I was the only one who read the monthly edition of The Grangerland Daily. Now, as I saw it, you had three factors that were going to cause the market to crash. You had your takeovers, your deficit and your insiders. And when you put all three together, you had misvalued companies bought with misvalued currency by people who missed values. Needless to say, rather than explain, it was easier for Pa to just let Big Bill think the Piggly Wiggly was falling down.

"What if ya sell off some of the herd?" Willie asked.

"Thar just ain't no market 'round here so long as people ain't a eatin' beef," Pa said.

"Drive 'em," Little Ben suggested.

"That'd be fine 'cept thar's no place that I know of where we could drive the cattle to, sell 'em and be back in two days," Pa said.

"Then why don't we drive them to a place where we'd get a good price and start all over?" I said.

My statement stopped the conversation dead in its tracks. Everybody turned to Pa. Pa looked my way with the most pensive face I had ever seen, then closed his eyes.

Starting over meant leaving the Old Miss. True, I was the youngest and last to arrive here, but you know how I felt about this place. I didn't make my suggestion because I wanted to leave. However, given the choice of losing everything in two days time or getting out now with a little something, well, there just didn't seem to be much choice, was there? And here was Pa, having to balance this one single fact against the many, many memories.

Pa remained quiet for a long, long time before he spoke.

"Where to?" Pa asked, his eyes still closed.

We joined Pa in thought. I had been so pleased with myself for coming up with the idea of the cattle drive that I had forgotten that a drive sorta needed a destination. Otherwise, it's not a drive at all, and, I guess, we'd have to call it an aimless wander. Now, while I do recall reading books about cattle drives, I can't ever recall reading anything on aimless wanders. And since Pa would only do things by the book, I assumed Pa would not lead an aimless wander of cattle. That's how important a destination was. Unfortunately, I had no idea of where beef was fetching a good price.

"How 'bout Oklahomee?" B.B. suggested.

I was not sure if B.B. really knew whether this was a particularly good place to go, or whether he just wanted the opportunity to say "Oklahomee". You've got to understand that B.B. enjoyed saying certain words that ended in "a" as if they ended in "ee". And "Oklahoma" was one such word.

"Yep, Olkahomee ain't all that far," B.B. continued, being sure to emphasis the "e"s.

"That's the problem, B.B.," Pa said. "Thar ain't that much call fer beef thar neither. We need to go farther."

"Then how 'bout Montanee?" B.B. suggested. "South Dakotee? North Dakotee? Minnesotee? Nebraskee?"

B.B. was on a roll.

"Iowee?" B.B. continued, then quickly apologized. Not because it was necessarily a bad idea, but because Iowa was not one of the "a" words that he normally changed.

"Well, thar all farther away, that's fer sure," Pa said. "And I reckon we do need a place to go 'cause I ain't leadin' no aimless wander. But do ya know how meat's a sellin' in them thar parts?"

B.B. tapped his lump. After a couple of seconds, he shrugged his shoulders. He didn't have a clue and his inklings weren't helping. It was then that Little Ben, who had been extraordinarily quiet since the topic of destinations began, spoke up.

"New York City?" Little Ben said.

Believe me, this got all of our attentions. We kinda looked at Little Ben, not altogether sure that we had heard right.

"New York City?" Pa said opening his eyes and lifting his head.

"Yep," Little Ben said, pausing a moment. "Heard New York's nothin' but a big meat market."

Everyone looked at each other with a "That would be great if it's true" expression. Pa turned to me.

"That true, Bert Boy?" Pa asked.

Now, I had heard the same thing about New York City. I had also heard that the city was full of animals. And once, while in Grangerland, I saw a bull running down Wall Street on a television advertisement. So, maybe it was true.

The problem was my gut reaction told me otherwise. Not that I knew any more about the place then what I had read in my text books, but I couldn't figure New York being a meat market, at least not in the sense we were all talking about. I mean, I had seen pictures of the place — the Statue of Liberty, the Empire State Building, Carnegie Hall, men sitting behind sewing machines and wearing beanies in the Textile District. All those buildings, all those people. Where was there to put the cattle?

I looked over to Pa, who, for the first time all day, had a look of hope showing on his old lined face. He thought that he finally had his destination. The last thing I wanted to do now was disappoint Pa. It was enough that he was losing everything that he and his pa had worked for. Besides, I would be questioning Little Ben's intelligence if I revealed my doubts. This was akin to insulting Big Bill's feet. I got to thinking how much easier life was this morning when all I had to worry about was trivial repairs.

I took a deep breath. "I heard the same things about New York," I said. "It's just one big old meat market."

I crossed my fingers behind my back, praying that this was so. Right now, I didn't even want to consider the consequences of my gut reaction turning out to be true. Besides, it would be months before we would know the real truth, and anything could happen enroute. Still, the sick feeling stayed in my stomach. I think it was because I may have deceived Pa for the first time in my life.

I looked over to Willie. Willie had a grin on his face a mile wide. It would have been a mile long except the marshmallow on his moustache changed the direction of his mouth. In any event, that cock-eyed grin told me that my gut reaction was right — either New York wasn't a meat market or at least wasn't the right kind.

Still, Willie kept silent. A quick nod in my direction pretty much told me what I had figured, knowing Willie and all. Willie had reached the same conclusion. Whatever the truth might turn out to be, what mattered most was here and now and Pa.

"Well, then," Pa said, his voice full of excitement. "Everbody, we have ourselves a cattle drive. Tomorrow we leave fer New York City."

An airplane flew overhead on its way out of Houston Intercontinental Airport. I looked up and saw its lights blinking in the dark Texas night.

5

I WISH I COULD SAY that the sound of B.B.'s breakfast bell woke me up. However, I spent the whole night tossing and turning in nervous anticipation. And now, tomorrow was today, the day of contradictions, the day deemed to be both the happiest and saddest day in my life.

Still, excitedly I hopped out of bed.

"Ouch!"

Bob Mine.

In my haste, I had detonated the Bob Mine. I immediately tried to apologize, but to no avail. The Bob Mine seemed more interested in ranting and raving. That is, until I pointed out that we were on the verge of missing breafast. Still in his underwear, Tiny Bob ran out.

Breakfast. The last breakfast. The last breakfast at the Old Miss. Everytime I added another word or two, I grew a little sadder.

A little more solemnly now, I put on a long sleeve flannel shirt and my thickest pair of dungarees, which I fastened with my hand-tooled leather belt complete with silver buckle displaying an enameled Appaloosa. I stepped into my riding boots, immediately getting a spur stuck in the wood floor. After a brief struggle, I dislodged the spur and strapped on my leather chaps. Finally, I put on my suede jacket, slipped on my riding gloves and set my tan cowboy hat on my head.

All hands were already in the dining room by the time I strutted in, clinging and clanging.

"Bert Boy," Pa said, suppressing a smile. "We ain't quite ready to go yet." Looking around, I saw that everyone was still in their underwear.

Sheepishly, I sat down at the table. The table was covered with food and maps, looking like something that would fit right in with the decor at Cyrus H. Squirrel's. It turned out that only Tiny Bob had been able to sleep, the others had been up for sometime wondering about a route to New York. It seemed that the only thing they knew about New York was that it wasn't in Texas.

Mistakenly, I had thought that we had ourselves a cattle drive because we had our destination picked. But upon reflection, Pa felt that it wasn't a real cattle drive until he had found a route to get there. He said he was sorry for saying that we had ourselves a cattle drive when in fact we still had ourselves an aimless wander, but he, too, was swept up in the excitement. To put our minds at ease, he added that choosing a route wouldn't be too hard.

I should explain that Pa had a firm belief in itineraries. Even when I went to play with friends in Grangerland, I had to leave Pa a note detailing who I was playing with, where I was playing, how I was getting there, the anticipated time of play at each location and phone numbers in case of emergency. I, therefore, assumed that Pa wanted to choose a route to New York so that he could leave an itinerary with Uncle Ray and Aunt Tammy Faye. 'Course, this itinerary would probably just be for Uncle Ray since Aunt Tammy Faye won't read anything that doesn't include pictures. She wouldn't even read her pa's obituary in the Grangerland Daily until they stuck in a photograph next to the copy. 'Course, it probably would have been better had we known the person whose photo the paper used.

I reached across the table, careful not to let the tassles from my riding gloves fall into the blueberry jam, and took a piece of bacon, my last piece of bacon, my last piece of bacon at the Old Miss. By the time this sad moment passed, the others had determined that New York was somewhere north and east.

"We'll head north through the Sam Houston National Forest, cross the Trinity, then up through the Davy Crockett Forest," Pa said pointing at the deluxe AAA map. "That'll put us here."

"Twenty miles outta Lufkin," Little Ben said.

Pa saw me nibbling on my bacon. "Bert Boy, when ya finish, start writin' all this down," Pa said. "We're a gonna need an itinerary."

"I ain't never been further north than Lufkin," Big Bill said.

He had indeed gone to Lufkin once for the Southern Hush Puppy Olympics. Maybe with the exception of Willie, none of the rest of us had been that far north and were kind of jealous. Not because we necessarily wanted to travel north, but because we had the Olympics practically in our own backyard and missed them.

"Best fritters I ever did eat," he continued, then quickly looked over to B.B. "Next to B.B.'s, I mean."

Pa put his finger in the map and continued, tracing the route as a visual aid to anyone who was interested. "Then we'll follow the Neches, go 'round Lake Palestine and that'll put us in Tyler," Pa said.

Using a pencil and a Patsy Kline album, which I'm sure we would have enjoyed had we had a record player, I began to write all this down.

"Good thinkin', Bert Boy," Pa said. "Maybe with Patsy's picture on the cover, Tammy Faye'll read our itinerary." I smiled as I looked at the deluxe map to check the correct spellings. Uncle Ray was from Pa's side of the family which meant that he was also a stickler when it came to spelling.

I saw from the map that Tyler was the first town that we would hit on our drive. And according to the map, Grangerland was an itty bitty black dot, while Tyler was a great big orange wagonwheel. Chills ran up and down my back.

"Tiny Bob, git that spider off yer brother while he's a workin'," Pa said.

Tiny Bob removed the daddy longlegs from my back which he had placed there. Like I told you before, setting off a Bob Mine had its day long repercussions. But I decided that I wouldn't let it interfere with the excitement of seeing another metropolis besides Grangerland.

"We'll restock in Tyler," Pa continued. "I'm sure they got some kind of store thar, being the size of a wagonwheel and all. Then we'll hit Interstate 20 and start headin' east."

"Pa?" Big Bill asked.

"What is it, Bill Boy?" Pa replied.

"Can ya keep usin' yer finger to point out the route?" Big Bill said. "I find that to be a perticularly good visual aid." The rest of us agreed.

"Whenever it comes to somethin' that stimulates education,

ya know I'm a glad to oblige," Pa said, returning his finger to the map. "From here, we'll follow Interstate 20 outta Texas and into Shrevesport."

"Louisianee?" B.B. asked.

"Yep," Pa replied. "And we'll keep a goin' east on 20 until here, Atlanta, where we'll pick up Interstate 85."

"Why not 59?" Little Ben asked, pointing at a highway outside of Birmingham.

"By the time we get 'round thar, it'll be startin' into winter up north," Pa explained. "So I'd rather travel down south as long as we can." As usual, Pa was thinking ahead. 'Course that's why Pa was Pa.

"I agree with Eugene," B.B. said. "I'd much prefer a goin' through Georgee." By now, you've figured for yourselves that B.B.'s reason probably had little to do with warm weather.

"And we'll stay on 85 north through South Carolina and North Carolina, and all the way into Virginia," Pa said. B.B. squealed with delight as he heard each of the states' names.

"Pa, what 'bout crossin' this here mountain in South Carolina?" Big Bill asked pointing at the map.

From my vantage point, Big Bill was indeed pointing to a large object looming in the northwest corner of South Carolina.Pa studied the situation closely for a moment or two, then removed the mountain from the map.

"Boys, ya gotta be more careful where ya drop yer scrambled eggs," Pa said, tossing the ex-mountain to the wayside. Looking at it laying on the table, I saw that had it been a mountain instead of a scrambled egg, it would have been a formidable opponent. Still, it made you think.

"Here at Petersburg, 85 hits 95," Pa continued.

"Yep," Little Ben said. "95 into D.C."

Washington, the nation's capital. Not that I was a skeptic or anything, but it took a long time for my teachers to convince me that Austin was not the nation's capital. This had to do with the fact that since politicians said the nation's capital was Washington, and because I had learned that politicians do not tell the truth, I assumed that they were lying again.

This had everything to do with Mayor Pete Crudins of Grangerland. He had been born Peeper Crud, but had decided early on in his political career that he needed to change his name to something that did not evoke an ugly visual image. Not that it mattered, mind you. People loved to refer to him as Mayor Crud and Old Crusty Eye. People figured that it served him right, seeing as how his pa and ma probably spent many hours coming up with such an orginal name only to have their son go off and change it. But the silly thing was, who cared? No one else wanted to be mayor of Grangerland.

Anyway, whenever there was some kind of event that called for the services of a mayor, Old Crusty Eye would be there telling everybody how great a job he was doing. Problem was, around here, things are easy to check up on. For instance, I remember not too long ago when Mayor Crud gave a speech at Old Lady Cooder's funeral, although I think it was supposed to be a eulogy. Partway through his fond memories of Old Lady Cooder, he began talking about the new tennis court that had just been completed down by Grangerland High School, thanks to his administration.

I think Mayor Crud felt confident boasting about the court, figuring that none of us would make the trek over to Grangerland High in our time of grief. What he didn't realize was that no one had seen Old Lady Cooder in three years, and we all figured she had secretly kicked the bucket some time ago. So, while it was true that we were all shocked to find that Old Lady Cooder hadn't really been dead at all, until now that was, the only grief we were feeling was in having to sit through Mayor Crud's long-winded speech. And since none of the funeral attendees had ever seen a tennis court before and most had no idea what one was, we thought that it'd be an interesting thing to see after viewing the body.

When Mayor Crud got wind of our intentions and realized his grave misjudgment, he tried everything he could to stop us from wandering over to Grangerland High. He even offered to dismiss all parking tickets. When we pointed out to him that Grangerland did not issue parking tickets, he offered to start issuing them.

'Course there was no new tennis court. Mayor Crud, being sly and all, did try to convince a group of early arrivals at the school, who were a bit dim-witted to start with, that the trash dumpster was the tennis court. Well, the Old Miss hands saw through this and confronted Mayor Crud. After apologizing for his misinformation, Old Crusty Eye directed our attention to a large mound of dirt where construction of the court had just begun. 'Course, being familiar with my future high school, I knew that that mound of dirt had nothing to do with the construction of a tennis court. That mound was affectionately known as "Critter Hill" and Biology classes had been burying their projects there for years.

Needless to say, you can see why I don't believe a thing politicians say. This was especially true of the Mayor's patented line, "I'll get to the bottom of this", which, incidentally, was the way he ended the tennis court episode. Translated, this line meant, "I'll forget about whatever `this' refers to, knowing that after a while, everyone who heard me will either have forgotten or dropped dead." But I'll let you in on my little way of fighting back. Every month, I send Mayor Crud an anonymous note asking him how the tennis court was coming. By now, I bet he's weeing in his Wranglers.

And now we were planning on going through Washington, D.C. The place where the Mayor Cruds of the country congregate. The place where people who don't know us pass laws about us. I actually hoped that Pa let us stay there a spell. I needed the time to determine scientifically who produced more manure, our cattle drive or the Mayor Cruds.

I returned my attention to Pa whose finger was already somewhere in New Jersey. I saw that he had followed North 95 out of Washington and up through Maryland and Delaware. Now, I'm not too sure, but I think Maryland's another one of those states where they use crab mallets for door knockers. I don't know a thing about Delaware, except that it looks so itty bitty from the map that I can't figure out how they can stuff all those corporations into it. I quickly scribbled these points to keep in mind on Patsy's face, as well as all of the itinerary from Washington up to and including Pa's finger.

"See, we got ourselves a number of ways we can go once we hit here," Pa said. His finger was on the outskirts of New York City. It appeared that the city was surrounded by water.

Pa studied the situation for a couple of minutes. "And I reckon the best bets are this here Lincoln Tunnel or the Holland Tunnel," Pa continued.

"Don't want to go to Holland though, Pa," Big Bill chimed in. "Thought we wanna go to New York City."

Nobody thought it necessary to correct Big Bill. To explain to Big Bill that the Holland Tunnel did not take you to Holland seemed even harder than explaining the Piggly Wiggly situation.

"What about goin' up here?" B.B. said pointing at a spot a little farther north. "Looks like this crosses into New York City."

"The George Washington Bridge," Pa read off the map. "It's a possibility."

"No it ain't," Willie said. "I ain't goin' over that thar bridge. Look at that warnin' they all give ya."

Willie pointed at a word in parentheses directly underneath the words "George Washington Bridge" on the map.

"See, see the warnin'," he continued. "Trolls. They got trolls! And I betcha they wouldn't give ya no warnin' unless they were some big old trolls lurkin' under that bridge too." Although he had never seen one, Willie's only fear in the world was of trolls.

Pa squinted at the fine print Willie was referring to.

"Willie, damn if one day yer bad readin' and spellin' don't put an end to ya," Pa said. "It says `Tolls'."

I could see by Willie's face that he would have been embarrassed by his faux pas had he not been so confused. To him, it made perfectly good sense to warn someone about trolls. But it seemed awful silly to warn someone coming into New York about the ringing of bells.

"Then what 'bout usin' this here bridge?" B.B. questioned. "The Verrazano Narrows."

"Sounds too small," Little Ben said. We all agreed.

"So, boys, looks like our choices into New York are the George Washington Bridge, the Lincoln Tunnel or the Holland Tunnel," Pa said.

"But Pa," Big Bill interrupted.

"Right," Pa replied. "For Bill Boy's sake, we'll just forgit 'bout usin' the Holland."

"How 'bout swimmin' 'cross that old river?" Willie said pointing at the Hudson, which according to the map was the name of the river that separated New York from New Jersey. "Looks kinda puny to me."

I think that Willie, being a true cowhand and all, was a little bothered by the fact that we were diverging from the original cattle drive form. For instance, in a true cattle drive, when you got to a

Go East, Young Man> 43

river, you didn't use any of those new fangled tunnels or bridges. You did things the old fashioned way. You drove the herd down to the river bank and swam them across. I'm just about sure this was what Willie was thinking about. 'Course, that's unless he was considering the fact that when you did things the old fashioned way, you didn't have to worry about trolls.

Pa pulled out a deluxe AAA map entitled New York City and Vicinity. He unfolded it and spread it out on top of the other maps. He took a few moments to locate the Hudson.

"It looks kinda big here, Willie," Pa said. "And after this long haul, I don't right know if them cattle'll want to swim."

You see, cows have a natural aversion to water to begin with. That's why they all lay down when it rains. If they stood, you might get the impression that they were taking showers and were enjoying it. 'Course, laying down, you might get the impression that they're taking baths and enjoying it, so go figure

"Sides, by the time we're thar, the river'll be too cold to swim," Pa continued. "So, figure on takin' the bridge or tunnel. Any thoughts?"

"George Washington," Little Ben said. "Honor our country's father."

"Then I say the Lincoln," Willie said. "'Cause of his honesty." And because of the trolls.

"B.B.?" Pa asked.

B.B. tapped his lump. "George Washington," B.B. said. "Cause he lived for a long time in Virginee."

"Lincoln, Pa," Big Bill said. "'Cause he made the logs that I used to play with when I was little."

"Lincoln 'cause he made logs," Clint said, confused.

"Bob Boy?" Pa asked, but Tiny Bob too was preoccupied with making daddy longlegs into daddy shortlegs. "How 'bout ya, Bert Boy?"

I thought for a moment and then a bell went off.

"Time's up on chow," B.B. said, striking his triangle with his clanging stick. "Chicken fried-steak for lunch." He took a few plates out from under the maps and went into the kitchen.

"Anyway, Bert Boy," Pa said. "Ya got yerself a preference 'tween Lincoln and Washington?"

Again, I thought. Truthfully, I didn't have a perennial favorite.

It wasn't as if I knew either of the two gentlemen. And both had strong arguments in their support, although I believe that Lincoln was more of a politician than was Washington.

Finally, with nothing better to say, I spoke. "How about taking the one that's closer to where we want to end up?" I said.

"Why, Bert Boy, that's a mighty fine idear," Pa said. "That way we wouldn't have to insult either of these great two Americans and the fine structures that represent 'em."

Everyone applauded my idea, except for Tiny Bob, who just stuck out his tongue.

"Where we endin'?" Little Ben questioned.

Pa leaned down and hovered over New York City and Vicinity. After a short spell, he pointed to a large green shaded area symbolizing grass. In the middle of this were a couple of blue shaded splotches which represented either lakes or smudged blueberry jam.

"Right here," Pa said. "We're a goin' to Central Park."

"Looks big enough," Little Ben said, studying the situation.

"And much closer to the Lincoln Tunnel," Willie said, looking relieved.

"Then that's it," Pa said. "We come in through the Lincoln, take this here 40th Street, turn on Eighth Avenue and head on up to our new homestead, Central Park."

"Hey, B.B.," Little Ben called out as I wrote these final directions down. "Come here."

B.B. entered, holding a pot he was cleaning.

"What is it?" B.B. asked.

"We've got ourselves a location for the ranch," Pa said jubilantly. "Central Park in New York City, the biggest meat market around." I crossed my fingers behind my back.

"I had an inklin' it would be Central Park," B.B. said with tears forming in his eyes. "Home of the New Miss."

"Yep," Little Ben cheered.

"We got ourselves a final destination!"Willie said.

"And we have ourselves an itinerary!" I said.

"That means we got ourselves a cattle drive!" Pa said, reinstating the official title.

Pa gave us a chance to finish our whooping and hollering before he continued.

"Now there'll be a plenty of time fer celebratin'," he said. "Bert Boy, take some of them duds off 'til later. The rest of ya, git dressed. Thar's thins that got to be done 'fore we leave tonight. I got a list fer each of ya. Now, let's get started."

Pa handed us our lists as we all got up from the table, still whooping and hollering. Walking back to my room to remove some of my layers, I thought to myself that, yes, this time we really had ourselves a cattle drive.

6

I KNOW I SHOULD HAVE been hurrying to the barn to start on the first chore on my list, but I couldn't help but take my time. Everywhere, eveything brought back some kind of memories. Some were good, some weren't, but it still took some time for my brain to bring the memory into focus so I could tell whether it was worth getting teary-eyed over.

I walked past the corral on the way to the barn. The corral had been around longer than I had. And every nick, every scratch on every inch of the corral's fence had a story all its own. Willie had a post where he kept a notch for every bronco he busted. Clint had a post where he kept a notch for every bronco Willie busted. B.B.'s post had a notch for every time he had told Clint to stop keeping track of Willie's notches. Little Ben's post had a great number of markings on it which I correctly identified as the Dewey decimal system. Seemed Little Ben was secretly working on a system of cow classification. There were still a few problems with the system, like in getting the cows to remember their group numbers, but that's a cow for you.

Now, Big Bill had his special rail where he would sit and carve off slivers of wood and use them as tooth picks. Pa also had a rail on top of which he would sit and whittle away. 'Course, I think Pa's whittling was his way of venting anger over Big Bill using the corral fence for tooth picks. Tiny Bob had a rail where he whittled just to see how many splinters he could create. And the rest of the nicks and scratches on the posts and rails were signs of where my head had made contact with the wood after being thrown by some animal or another.

Raw Speed, who was in the corner of the corral nearest the

barn, had seen me coming and had laid down. She had also closed both her eyes, pretending to be asleep, but not even Tiny Bob could fall asleep that fast. As I walked by, I thought I detected a slight crack in Raw Speed's right eye and could feel her big old horse eye following me beneath the slighty parted lid. Once past the corral, I swore I heard her neigh a sigh of relief.

I continued on toward the barn. Ah, the barn. I had helped Big Bill paint it when I was much younger. I seem to recall that I got more paint on me than on the barn, and that the paint tasted pretty good too. When Big Bill saw me, the living canvas, he just shook his head and laughed. 'Course, this was what Big Bill always did when he was speechless. This was true even if the underlying cause of the speechlessness wasn't particularly funny. And even though he's speechless quite often, I couldn't fault him on this occasion.

I remembered Ma coming out of the house to see the reason for Big Bill's speechless reaction. She took one look at me and called me Michelangelo. 'Course, not knowing whether this was one of Ma's clear moments, I reminded her that my name was Bert. Pa came over from the corral and said that he'd bet that I'd grow up to be a darn good painter once I found out where the paint was supposed to go. He reckoned that even though I was covered with paint from head to toe, I was still, somehow, able to retain the aesthetic quality of my shirt and pants. Pa had foresight, which was why Pa was Pa.

I stopped and took a long look at the big old two story barn. It could have used a new coat of paint. Just red, nothing fancy. Nothing that would ruin the aesthetic quality. But then, again, why should E. Lester get a freshly painted, aesthetically pleasing barn? If only I had the time now, and a little more Willie in me, I would have painted the whole thing chartreuse and in big brown letters on its side written, "Eeoogie Go Home".

I entered the barn. The sun came through the door and bounced off the golden hay, illuminating the dust floating freely in the air, and brought with it fond memories, long forgotten. Memories of childhood, playfulness, innocence, sneezing.

Me and Tiny Bob used to jump from the hay loft into the hay stacks below that Pa kept in the barn to feed the cattle. After a while, Tiny Bob decided that it was more fun not to land in the hay. At first, I thought that maybe he had just started to dislike hay. Finally, I realized that it was not his dislike of hay, but more his love of casts and splints. And I'm kind of embarrassed to tell you this, but he's still jumping from the loft.

One of my fondest memories returned as I looked around the rustic interior for what could be the last time. It was the time last year when I thought I had found myself here alone with Sue Sue Watkins. Alone with Sue Sue Watkins! It was a dream come true. She was a girl and I was a boy and, well, we were alone. Did I say that she was a girl? She still hadn't grown those woman type things yet. Still though, I did find myself getting urges. I guess they were akin to B.B.'s inklings except that they affected a different part of the body.

Anyway, the reason Sue Sue and me found ourselves alone on that particular day had to do with something that had happened in school. I was sitting in history class. We were discussing our neighbor and our friend, Mexico. And along with the rest of the class, I started to doze off, which was the best way to take in a lecture by Miss Putz. My eyelids felt like a ton of Mayan granite and slowly, steadily were approaching the out-for-the- duration position. Suddenly, I felt a sharp sting on my neck and heard the voice of Smuley Hogwrench snickering behind me.

"Yowl," I screamed as I jumped from my one piece desk and chair unit. I turned around and saw Smuley with a rubber band stretched between his thumb and index finger and a desktop full of paper projectiles. Then came the horrible realization that I was standing and that I had screamed and that my scream had probably startled an entire class from a dead sleep.

Slowly, I turned to face the front of the room. Miss Putz was looking at me and clapping her hands.

"Exactly," Miss Putz squealed. "All of those ancient artifacts from the Teotihuacan Ruins are now on display at Yale. Bert Henry, all I can say is A plus, A plus, gold stars all over your forehead."

Well, Sue Sue came up to me after class while I was rubbing my neck and everyone else was stretching their arms and yawning and told me that she didn't know I was that smart.

Now, up to that day, I didn't think Sue Sue knew that I was even alive. That's because all the rest of the boys made such a fuss over her that I could never get through the crowd. She was far and away the prettiest girl in the school. Bred for her beauty it was said. And I know for a fact that that had something to do with how she got her name. Rather than name her something like Sue Ellen or Sue Ann, her parents said that not only was she a Sue, but she was double the Sue any other Sue could possibly be.

So here I was talking with Sue Sue. Me, just plain, old non-repetitive Even Tinier Bert.

She asked me if I could help her with her history, being as how I was so smart and all. She told me that if she could be smart as well as beautiful, she'd be three times the Sue any other Sue could be and her Pa would change her name to Sue Sue Sue. I just couldn't turn her down.

That afternoon, with books in hand, we went back to the Old Miss. Actually, I carried the books, and Sue Sue carried her brush and mirror. When we arrived, we found all the hands taking a break and playing cards in the house.

"Willie," B.B. said. "Got any threes?"

"Nope," Willie said with a smirk. "Go fish." B.B. picked up a card from the pile.

"Willie," Clint said. "Got any threes?"

I interrupted the game and made my introductions. We probably would not be able to get any studying done with a raucous game of "Fish" going on in the background and decided to go to the barn to study. As we left, we heard Big Bill asking what the word was that he had to yell to win, but it didn't sound like anyone was going to tell him. Sometimes there was just too much competition at the Old Miss, and I was embarrassed that Sue Sue was there to see it rear its ugly head.

We entered the barn. Still amazed that Sue Sue was with me, I propped us up two tufts of hay, and we sat down. As she opened her book, I gazed at her and saw a goddess. Her hair was golden like the straw we sat in, except not as dirty. Her eyes were as green as the olives in an olive loaf. And I'm sure if she would have had those woman type things, they would have been beautiful too.

"Are you going to open your book?" Sue Sue asked.

"Oh, yes, my dear, yes," I said from my daze. 'Course, my idiotic and embarrassing response immediately brought me back to reality. I could not believe what I had just said, not to Sue Sue. I realized that I should have asked B.B. how he controlled his inklings.

With my hands trembling, certain that I had just ruined any chance I possibly had with Sue Sue, I lowered my head and opened my Texas history book to the chapter entitled "Our Friends To The North: The Rest Of The United States And Canada".

We sat quietly and read. Or I should say Sue Sue read. I still could not concentrate on any subject except Sue Sue. A chance blurt brought us together and now a stupid blurt would drive us apart. And what if Sue Sue went back to school and told everyone of my starry-eyed statement? But she wouldn't do that. No, not my Sue Sue. Not my angel, my fantasy, my religion. Yes, if there were a religion called Sue Sue, I would surely convert and be her devout follower.

My eyes were clouded. My head was spinning. My palms were sweating. I was in love and all else, including Our Friends To The North, seemed irrelevant.

Sue Sue looked up from her book. I smiled at her. She actually smiled back. I only prayed that she wasn't smiling because of something embarrassing, like drool running down my chin.

"You know," she said. "If you help me get an A in history, I might consider letting you kiss me."

Blood almost popped out of my ears. My heart had shot clear past trot into gallop. I cupped my ears, not to keep the blood in, but because I was afraid that they weren't working right. But they were! I pinched myself thinking that this was all a cruel joke. But it wasn't! I wasn't in one of my believable dreams, I was in the midst of an unbelievable reality.

"So what do you say?" she continued. "Would you like that?"

"Oh Yes, My Dear, Yes!" was the response. Unfortunately, I wasn't the one who blurted it, being as my mouth was too dry to say much of anything. It came from up above, from the loft.

Next, we heard "Geronimo" followed by a thud as Tiny Bob hit the floor not more than two feet from Sue Sue. Startled, Sue Sue screamed and tossed her Texas history book at least a hundred feet. You know, thinking back, we never did recover that book. So, in a way, we lost the Alamo for a second time.

Anyway, Tiny Bob twice tried to pick himself up from the floor, but fell back over each time. Finally, laying on his side with the back of his head facing the now standing, semi- hysterical Sue Sue, Tiny Bob removed his hat.

"How do," Tiny Bob said. "My name's Tiny Bob. I'm a better lookin' older brother."

I started to fume. Not only had he dropped in unexpected and scared the daylights out of Sue Sue, but now he was going to try to steal her from me.

"Ya ever seen a cracked rib 'fore?" he continued. "Cause if ya ain't, I think I got one. If we're real lucky, it might even be stickin' out."

Tiny Bob wriggled on the ground, trying to get in a better position to lift his shirt. Sue Sue screamed again.

"Wait," Tiny Bob called out as he momentarily stopped his wriggling. "Would ya rather see a scorpion? I got me a brand new one in my pocket…if I didn't land on him." He reached into his pocket.

Sue Sue screamed for the last time and made a dash for the barn door. I stood and watched her run. Rather than chase her, I turned back to face what I reluctantly called my brother laying on the floor. I took two steps towards him and lifted my boot, ready to test that old rib of his. That's when he started to lift the scorpion remains out of his pocket. The next thing I remember was almost knocking Sue Sue down as I passed her on the road leading to the front entrance.

She never did talk to me again, which was a shame since it was obvious we both shared a mutual fear of scorpions. And since that time, I have never again been alone, or what I thought was alone, with another girl.

Oh, as for Tiny Bob, Big Bill happened upon him a couple of hours later. Seeing him just laying there, well, Big Bill was kind of speechless, so he started to laugh. Pa came running and determined that Tiny Bob had only bruised a rib. And seeing as how Tiny Bob was enjoying watching red ants in action from eye level, Pa just left him there on the floor

"Bert Boy," Pa said, entering the barn. "The wagon in good order?"

"I'm sorry, Pa," I said returning to the here and now. "I haven't checked it out yet."

"Well, we're sorta pressed fer time," Pa said and then paused a moment. "This place sure holds alot of memories, don't it?" I'm sure that Pa had noticed the far away look in my eyes. And if Pa ever decided to leave the cattle business, he'd make a great psychiatrist or advice column writer.

"Are you going to miss this place?" I asked.

"Sure am," Pa said sitting down on the spot where Sue Sue had sat, while I sat down where Tiny Bob had landed. "I was born and raised here. And since I'm almost five times yer age, I've got almost five times the memories."

Pa spat some tobacco juice on the wall. I know it was meant to be left there for E. Lester to find.

"I'm excited about traveling," I said. "Going to all those places that I read about in school. Or at least I was. I was until I realized that this isn't a vacation. We aren't packing up our bags, we're packing up our home."

"Yep," Pa replied. He chewed his tobacco a little slower now. "Our new home's out thar miles and months away, and somewhere above that thar Mason-Dixon Line. But right now, it ain't much more than a hope and a dot on a deluxe map."

Pa fiddled around with the straw beneath him before he continued.

"Ya know, yer Ma always wanted to travel," he said, rising. "Said thar people and places worth seein' beyond Grangerland. Not that she didn't like Grangerland and the people in it, mind ya. She just had that pioneer spirit in her. She always wanted to know more. Ya got that quality from her, Bert Boy. She woulda focused on how excitin' it was to be leavin' the Old Miss, goin' to all them places we'd only heard about. This cattle drive is somethin' she woulda wanted."

Pa paused again.

"Pa?" I said softly.

"I'm real sorry she'll only be a travelin' in our hearts," he said. "She was a great woman, yer ma. It's a shame she passed on 'fore ya got to know her."

"I remember her reading bedtime stories to me," I said. "Then, she'd sing "Back In The Saddle Again" until I'd fall asleep."

"That used to be yer favorite song," Pa said. In a way, it still was.

Pa continued. "I didn't right know what to do when ya asked me when yer ma was a gonna come back to sing to ya again."

"Is that when you started singing to me?"

"I figured it was easier than havin' to explain dyin' to a five year old. Yep, fer awhile thar, I guess I had to do the thins yer Ma used to do to keep ya from askin' too many questions."

This sunk in just enough to cause a sudden realization. "Pa," I said. "Did you act like Ma for anyone else?"

Pa pondered this a moment. "No, yer brothers were all older and understood," he said as he began to smile. "So, I reckon ya were the only one unfortunate enough to have yer pa actin' like yer ma too."

"Lucky enough," I said softly.

I went over and hugged Pa. We both had tears in our eyes.

"Hey, how was my singin' voice compared to yer ma's?" Pa asked.

"The best," I answered, and we embraced again.

"I'm a turnin' into a softy in my old age," Pa said after a few minutes.

"No you aren't, Pa," I said. "We all have a right to feel our feelings." I realized that this didn't make much sense, but from the look on Pa's face, I couldn't have said anything more fitting.

"Well, Bert Boy," Pa said as he let go of his hold on me. "I guess we gotta move on."

"Yep," I said as I rose. "How's everybody else holding up?"

"'Bout the same as you and me," Pa replied. "I can't find Bob Boy, but I found Ben Boy out starin' at the cattle. Willie's sittin' and starin' at the corral. Clint's starin' at Willie. Bill Boy's a starin' at his feet. And B.B.'s starin' at the breakfast leftovers. If I see one more glazed look, I'll start thinkin' that everyone 'round here has turned into Old Mac."

Old Mac sold apples on a street corner in Grangerland. He had lost both his eyes in a mine explosion long before I entered the world. So, as replacements, he bought two glass eyes which he could remove at will. When they were in, they would just sit there and make it look like Old Mac was in some kinda trance. Often, though, especially when they were bothering him, he would take them out. And on these occasions, he would let us hold them.

Now, Old Mac, having a great sense of humor and knowing that very few people could duplicate this trick, would always have fun with strangers who didn't know any better. You see, for some reason, a guy selling apples on a street corner is the first person people come to for directions. So, on too many occasions to count, a car would pull up, loaded down with bags, a wife and kids, and some guy would hop out with a map in hand and head right for Old Mac. Too preoccupied to realize Old Mac's predicament, the

guy would thrust the map in front of Old Mac and ask for directions out of Grangerland. Very casually, Old Mac would say something like "I'll need to get a closer look at that thar map" and
proceed to pop out his right eye ball and hold it up to the map.
Then he would say something like "Nope, it ain't east, so it must be
west" and pop the other eye out, holding it up to the left side of the
map. By now, the guy with the map and his wife and kids would be
screaming, while everyone who was watching Old Mac's antics
would be rolling on the ground with laughter.

I chuckled as I pictured Old Mac and his glass eyes. "Well, I
think I'm about ready to work on the wagon," I said.

"Good, Bert Boy," Pa said. "Good."

I walked Pa over to the barn door.

"We might be losin' our home, but we ain't losin' our family,"
Pa continued. "We just gotta keep rememberin' that this is what Ma
woulda wanted. And 'cause of that, I'm dedicatin' this drive to
her."

Together we stepped into the bright morning sunlight. Pa continued on back to the corral as I stood in the doorway a moment
longer. The day had taken on a brand new meaning. My spirits
were now such that I barely heard the thud back in the barn behind
me. Oh well, I thought, even Tiny Bob was entitled to one last jump.

7

I FINALLY REALIZED WHY it was called a chuck wagon. The old thing should have been chucked long ago. It took me clear to lunch to put in some new floorboards. I guess it would have taken even longer had there been any floorboards to remove first. The old floorboards had rotted and fallen off about the time Texas declared independence from Mexico.

Now I once read an article about these boats where you could see all the stuff underneath you as you went along. Unfortunately, I had told Tiny Bob about this. So, about a week later, without anybody knowing, Tiny Bob hitched up the wagon to a couple of horses and rode into Grangerland to offer rides on what he billed as the "Critter Wagon". His pitch was that you could sit on the sideboards and watch the critters run under the wagon as you rode along.

Now, Tiny Bob attracted quite a few takers, and soon he had a full load of people sitting on the sideboards peering into the empty space where the floorboards once laid. With everything in place, he started up the horses on the Critter Wagon's maiden voyage.

Unfortunately, there were some big differences between the Wagon and those boats. The most important, of course, was the fact that the boats had bottoms, glass bottoms, to look through.

Well, needless to say, when the wagon hit its first big bump, Tiny Bob lost all of his passengers. With nothing to grab onto or balance themselves with, they just all sort of fell into the open floor space. Luckily, no one was run over, but had anyone been fortunate enough to weather that bump and stay onboard, the only "critters" they would have seen scurrying underneath the wagon would have been the other paying customers.

Lunch gave me a short reprieve from fixing up the ex-Critter Wagon. As promised, B.B. had gone out of his way to fix the Old Miss' favorite chow, chicken fried steak. In case you've never had this culinary delight, it consists of a poor cut of meat that is fried like chicken. And tradition dictates that this recipe must not vary. As a matter of fact, rumor has it that the gunfight at the O.K. Corral was actually begun when the cook tried to use filet mignon in this dish. That shows how time honored this recipe is.

Fried okra and fried jalapenos rounded out the lunchtime menu. It was just a shame that we had to almost inhale our lunches and get back to work because we hadn't experienced the pleasure of so much greasy food from B.B. in a long time.

After lunch, I went back to working on the wagon. I had to replace a cracked wheel, and I had promised B.B. that I'd have the wagon ready for him by the time he had finished boxing up the pots and pans. This meant two things. One, that I really had to hurry, and two, that we'd be having cold chicken fried steak, cold fried okra and cold fried jalapenos for dinner.

While I was busy with the wagon, Willie and Clint were busy rounding up the cattle and branding any non-branded ones they came across. Like everyone else, they, too, were behind schedule due to early morning sentimentalities and were now frantically try-ing to make up the lost time. But as Pa said, "Haste and branding go together like Northerners and string ties". And since Willie doesn't listen to Pa's sayings like I do, he'll now be wearing the OM label on his butt for all time.

Now, Little Ben was spending the afternoon at the corral pre-paring the horses that we were bringing along on the drive. At lunch, he told me that we'd probably have to tie Raw Speed to the back of the chuck wagon and dangle some food in front of her or she'd never keep up. Actually, unless food was stuck in front of her, I don't think Raw Speed'd stand up, never mind keep up. 'Course, being tied to the wagon and all, I guess if she didn't stand, she'd be dragged from here to New York. But, just to play it safe, we found a little bit of food that B.B. hadn't packed away to use for "Hanging-The-Apple-From-The-Stick-In-Front-Of- The-Horse". Or, perhaps I should say, in this case, "Hanging-The-Slab-Of-Old-Green-Moldy-Spam-From-The-Stick-In-Front- Of-The Horse".

Pa and Big Bill had spent the morning in the house packing up the necessities, like the cattle skull. After lunch, Pa went to Uncle Ray's and Aunt Tammy Faye's to drop off Patsy Kline and her face full of itinerary. He left Big Bill the chore of rounding up all the rest of the livestock, including Tiny Bob. Of course, Big Bill took this duty very seriously and spent the afternoon chasing and lassoing chickens. Luckily, Little Ben was keeping an eye on Big Bill to make sure things didn't get too out of hand, or mark my words, there would have been a yard full of hog-tied chickens. Instead, only a rope-bound Tiny Bob adorned the front of the ranch house.

It took me until three o'clock to mount a new wheel. In case you're wondering where the new wheel came from, well, I thought I was pretty clever. I used the wagon wheel light fixture from the den. 'Course, I couldn't cut off the attached electric cord, so we'll be subjected to the "thump, thump…thump, thump…thump, thump" of it flapping the whole way to New York. But, then again, we can still plug the wheel in if we happen to make a night stop and come across an electrical outlet. This would then give us a chance to see what B.B. was dishing out of the wagon.

I had just finished screwing on the last lug bolt when Big Bill came in to see what I was doing. I told him, and thought that I explained it pretty well. That is, until he questioned why we would take a chance on being in the middle of nowhere and not being able to find an electric outlet. He figured if we just brought one along with us, we wouldn't have to worry.

I tried to think of how Pa would have responded if he were around, but drew a blank. So, instead, I just told Big Bill that it sounded to me like Tiny Bob was getting loose from his ropes out front. 'Course, Big Bill took off immediately.

I stepped back and inspected the wagon. Somehow it looked different with a floor and four soundwheels…well, a floor, three wheels and a light fixture. Seeing all this new handiwork, I only wished I had the time to replace the sideboards, running boards, hitch, main frame and axles.

With everything looking pretty good, I ran out of the barn and back to the ranch house. I went around to the kitchen door and knocked- even though it was the last day, it was still not meal time.

"B.B.," I shouted. "It's me, Even Tinier Bert."

"Come in," B.B. replied from inside. So, I did.

"I'm all finished with the wagon," I said.

"And I'm 'bout finished with the boxes," B.B. said cutting himself a nice length of twine. "If ya give me a hand finishin' up here, I'll go help ya hitch up the wagon."

As I assisted B.B. in tying up the last box, I got a free lesson on the art of packing kitchen utensils.

"Ya gotta be careful packin' away utensils," B.B. said. "Ones we're a gonna need, ya gotta put on top. Ones that can break, ya gotta put on top...'cept if they're real ugly and ya got 'em as a present from somebody. Then ya can pack 'em on the bottom and hope they break. See, then ya can tell that person that while ya really loved them dishes, these thins happen when ya move. And see, while that person is bein' understandin' and sympathetic and all, what ya really got yerself is a good excuse fer dumpin' 'em with no one gettin' hurt feelins."

Well, this caused me to wonder whatever happened to the ten fancy brown and green dinner dishes I had given B.B. one Christmas. In the center of the plates was a sheep wearing an apron saying, "Lick yer chops, here come slops". I had purchased them from the Grangerland Gift and Feed Store and they were of such fine quality that they had come with a money back guarantee. It was strange, but after B.B. had opened the box, to the "Oohs" and "Ahhs" of the Old Miss hands, I don't recall ever seeing that fine china again. But, I wasn't about to say anything to B.B. about it now.

"Then each box has gotta be labeled proper-like or ya could be in a heap of trouble," B.B. continued. "Say fer instance, yer dyin' of thirst in the middle of the desert and, suddenly, ya come across some water. The last thin ya'd want to do with the little strength ya had left is to break open a box of forks and knives lookin' fer a glass. Right?"

"Well, I guess," I said. "But couldn't you just sorta stick your head in the water and take a drink without worrying about opening any boxes?"

B.B. thought a moment.

"It just ain't right not to label the boxes proper-like," he snorted. "It just ain't right."

With that, B.B. took the box we had just finished tying, marked "Glasses", and tossed them clear across the kitchen to an empty spot where they crash landed on the floor. They must have been extremely ugly presents.

"I'm sorry," B.B. said, closing his eyes. "Them glasses weren't all that ugly."

"I'm gonna miss the Miss," B.B. continued. "I spent all mornin' starin' at leftovers."

"Pa told me," I said softly.

"Even thinkin' 'bout all them "ee" states couldn't cheer me up," B.B. said, opening his eyes.

We started walking to the door. "If it helps any, Pa reminded me that we aren't losing our family," I said.

B.B. smiled. "Yep, that's why your pa is Pa," he said, and drew a deep breath. "The man sure knows what's important, don't he? But, damn, if he ain't right. Ya know, when I first got here, I had nothin' and nobody. But yer pa's pa made me feel like family right from the start. And when they needed a new company cook and I volunteered, even though I'd never set foot in a kitchen, well, like family, they suffered right along with me. Praisin' my good meals, like fried cat fish, and pretendin' to like my experiments, like B.B.Q. dillo."

B.B. opened the kitchen door, and we walked outside. We stood on the porch for a minute or two.

"Yeah, we're family alright and even a fat-assed banker can't do nothin' 'bout that," he continued. "Even Tinier Bert, I betcha didn't know that I'm the one who gave Tex his nickname."

We hopped off the porch and started towards the corral.

"You mean you gave Pa the nickname Eugene?" I said kinda shocked. You see, I had always thought that Pa's pa had nick-named Pa after a semi-booming metropolis on the Willamette River in Oregon. 'Course, I had no reason why I thought this or why Pa's pa would have been so enamoured of that city so as to give his son that particular nickname. I guess it was just an inkling on my part, but I could now see that it was perhaps best if I just left the inklings to B.B.

"Ya bet," B.B. said still smiling. "Nicknamed him after a semi-boomin' metropolis on the Puget Sound up thar in Washington."

"You mean on the Willamette River in Oregon," I said.

B.B. stopped dead in his tracks. A shadow passed over his face.

"Where's Eugene?" he asked.

"In Oregon," I said.

"Then what semi-boomin' metropolis is on the Pugent Sound?" he asked.

"Seattle," I answered.

B.B. slapped himself on his lump and laughed. "All these years and we never knew that he was walkin' 'round with the wrong nickname," B.B. said. "Well, that's what happens when ya nickname someone after a place ya ain't never seen before."

"How'd you get your nickname?" I asked.

B.B.'s smile dropped. "How'd ya know 'bout my nickname?" B.B. asked as another shadow crossed his face.

"B.B.?" I asked.

"B.B.?" B.B. said. "That ain't a nickname. That's my real name. My ma and pa, rest their souls, were charter members of the N.R.A. They loved guns so much that, damn, if they didn't name me after a pellet."

"Then I guess I didn't know you had a nickname," I said, as I thought to myself that, sometimes, certain things come to light in the strangest ways, at the strangest times.

B.B. shuffled his feet and stared at them for quite awhile. This was the first time that I had ever seen B.B. at a loss for words. Finally, he spoke, but it was not the same gruff, gravelly voice I grew up with.

"Used to," B.B. said softly. "Used to be called "Wee B". Kids thought it was funny, me bein' so scrawny and all when me and yer Pa were young."

Looking at B.B. now, tall and hefty, I could never picture him being scrawny when he was younger. 'Course, I couldn't picture him being younger either. To me, he had always been gray, wrinkled and balding.

"Yeah, kids used to pick on me," B.B. continued. "Used to call me Wee B. and throw rocks at me. Could be this here lump was caused by one of them rocks bouncin' off my noggen. But yer pa, he'd stand up for me, even when I'd run. I think he spent most of our childhood protectin' me." B.B. quickly wiped away the beginning of a tear.

"So it's a good thin I sprung up or he might never a had the time to run the Old Miss," B.B. said. "He's a good man, yer pa."

I had always felt a certain closeness to B.B. Despite his inflexible attitude to the rest, he'd often turn his head the other way where

I was concerned. I knew it and appreciated it and never took advantage of it. And like now, he'd trust me with his other side, his rarely seen emotional, sentimental side. But, sometimes, he was also sterner with me than with my brothers.

Yes, he'd treat me special. He always had, for as far back as I could...Then it dawned on me. Pa hadn't been alone in raising me! There was someone else, someone he trusted, his best friend who took over when he was unavailable. Someone who was equally responsible for what I was and, probably, what I'd become. Someone who could look at me in pride or shame, but see what he had helped to mold and shape just the same. He was more than the uncle I never had. He, too, had stepped into the shoes that Ma had left behind.

"You're a good man too, B.B.," I blurted as I grabbed him and hugged him.

"Now don't go gettin' sappy on me," B.B. said, looking around to make sure that no one was in sight. Awkwardly, he returned the embrace.

Releasing me, his voice once again became gruff and gravelly. "And don't ya go tellin' no one 'bout none of this, includin' this here discussion."

I promised, and we continued walking to the corral as if nothing had happened. But, I knew differently.

"Got even with them kids that used to tease me," B.B. whispered as a grin formed. "One day, after I was bigger than 'em all, well, I gathered 'em all together. I gave each one a pointy hat to wear and made 'em all sit on stools. Then I made 'em say, "Wee B. sorry" and I'd yell, "Bad Grammar!" I reckon this went on fer 'bout three hours 'fore I had to leave. I told 'em to keep on goin' without me, and, fer all I know, they're still at it."

I started giggling to myself. Unfortunately, real cowboys don't giggle. Girls giggle, cowboys chuckle. But I can't get my voice to chuckle yet. So, arriving at the corral, I tried to drop my voice down an octive, hoping that I would, at least, emit a manly giggle.

Little Ben was just finishing tying up the last of the fifteen horses. "Got four horses fer ya," he said to B.B. as he stepped over the rail right into a fresh mound of manure. "Damn dung!"

Little Ben looked down at his boots, then quickly in my

direction. "Nothin' funny 'bout dung," he continued. "Quit yer manly gigglin'."

I bit my lip and thought of scorpions. It worked, except I was truly sorry that Little Ben was now sore at me when I wasn't laughing at him at all.

After Little Ben cleaned his boots off on a nearby post, we all hopped into the corral. Me and B.B. followed Little Ben to four quarter horses tied to the railing closest to the gate. B.B. took a couple of minutes to inspect them. 'Course, we knew that B.B. knew nothing about horses, so this was strictly for show.

"Hmmm, good backside colorin'," B.B. finally mumbled to himself. "Yep, mighty fine backside colorin'."

It was nice that B.B. approved of the end that he'd be staring at the whole way to New York. But, it was even nicer that these fine colored rumps came attached to the four strongest horses we had - Odysseus, Sampson, Hercules and Shirley.

After a bit more inspection and the keen observation that horses don't have toes to wiggle, B.B. declared these horses fit for wagon duty.

"Let's hitch 'em then," Little Ben said.

Little Ben untied Odysseus and Sampson and led them out of the corral in the direction of the barn. I was in the process of untying Hercules when Big Bill's voice echoed from the front yard.

"Go see what he wants," B.B. said, untying Shirley. "I can handle this."

I was confident that B.B. could handle the equestrian task of walking two horses fifty feet to the barn, so I handed him my rope. I then ran across the corral and jumped the fence, landing in the same pile of manure that Little Ben had landed in. He was right. There was nothing funny about stepping in a pile of manure.

After wiping off my boot, I went around the house to the front yard. There I found Big Bill standing underneath a large oak tree.

"Git down, git down from thar," Big Bill shouted.

Big Bill's hat was tipped back, his hands were on his hips and he was looking straight up the tree. Suddenly, a hog-tied chicken dropped out of the tree and hit Big Bill square on the head, knocking his hat off.

"That does it," Big Bill said, picking up his hat and dusting it off. He reached down and found a nice sized rock. 'Course, "nice size" varies with the dimensions of the person throwing it. He wound up and was about to toss the rock skyward when four more hog-tied chickens pelted him from above.

Now, you don't have to be a genius to know who was lurking in the tree. While Little Ben was distracted, Big Bill had hog- tied the chickens and Tiny Bob was on the loose.

Big Bill drew his Colt 45 out of his holster.

"Big Bill," I said, thinking quickly. "There's alot more work around back." And even though he was simple, I still couldn't rightly boss him around because he was older. I also feared what his feet might do in a fit of anger. So, I added, "At least, according to what Pa wanted us to do."

"Yeah, well, then ya talk to Tiny Bob up thar," Big Bill said with a huff as he pointed up the oak.

"I will," I assured Big Bill.

Big Bill took a long, hard look into the upper limbs of the tree. He squinted, either searching for Tiny Bob among the leaves or because a gnat had flown into his eye. He then lowered his head and wiped his eye, so I guess it was a gnat.

"Then I'll be 'round back," Big Bill mumbled as he replaced his gun into his holster. "Thought I had 'im tied up real good, too."

Big Bill turned and walked away, pouting. I watched him kick dirt with every step until he reached the corner of the house. There, he paused to uproot a shrub with his feet. At one time, the ranch house was lined with shrubs. Now, it was lined mostly with holes. I guess Big Bill was what you might call an impulsive landscaper.

I looked up the tree.

"Tiny Bob," I shouted. "Tiny Bob, do you hear me?"

A hog-tied chicken passed within inches of my head, answering my question.

"Pa'll be home soon," I continued as I turned to my right and saw a cloud of dust coming up the road. "Matter of fact, here comes Pa now. Do you want me to tell him what you've been up to?"

There was a rustling of leaves followed by a moment of silence. Then, whoosh, crack, THUD.

Tiny Bob flew by and hit the ground behind me. From the angle of his plunge and the way both his feet were now sitting behind his right ear, I reckon that he must have been three quarters of the way up the tree.

I hovered over Tiny Bob and waited until his eyes started to open. "When you get up, you unhog-tie these chickens, you hear," I said.

"Ggggood jummmppp, huh?" he finally muttered. "Fffun jump."

True, it may have been a record jump for Tiny Bob. But, to me, there were probably things more fun than ending up with your feet wedged in behind your right ear. Luckily, now was not the time to debate. "Just make sure you take care of the chickens," I said. "I'm going to see if Pa needs any help."

I left a still dazed Tiny Bob who, upon closer inspection, resembled an isosceles triangle, and headed to meet Pa.

The old truck came chugging and sputtering up the drive. I had never noticed before, but with each chug and sputter, the land became blessed with a little piece of Dodge. Pa must have dropped five pounds of bolts, nuts and rust just traveling these last few hundred feet.

Pa pulled up and parked on the side of the ranch house. I went over to meet him.

"Hi, Pa," I said greeting him as he exited the truck.

"Hey, Bert Boy," Pa replied. "How go thins?"

"Fine," I answered over the chugging and the sputtering. "The wagon's fixed. Little Ben and B.B. are busy hitching it up right now. And B.B.'s got the kitchen all packed up and ready. How're Uncle Ray and Aunt Tammy Faye?"

"Fine," Pa said. "They told me to tell ya that that was one of the best darn itineraries they ever did lay their eyes on. Told 'em we'd call 'em when we hit Tyler…Ya think ya can help me with this here box?"

I saw there was a large box sitting in the flatbed. I bent over and lifted it out. It was a might heavy.

"What's in here?" I asked, trying to grunt and groan rather than whine. Real cowboys don't whine.

"Some stuff we forgot," Pa responded. It must not have been stuff that was too important or Pa would have thrown a "plumb" in front of "forgot".

I followed Pa around to the back of the ranch house as the truck imparted a twenty one backfire sendoff.

"Stopped by Mademoiselle Laurent's House Of Fine Camping

Equipment," Pa continued. "Picked us up some extra tents, sleeping bags, lanterns and skeeter repellant." Skeeters, like dillos, are another pest whose name Texans love to shorten. It's just a wonder we haven't done it with other crits.

"Lucky yer Aunt Tammy Faye reminded me that skeeters are still trouble this time a year, 'specially in the woods," Pa added.

And Aunt Tammy Faye would know. Seems she knew everything anyone would ever want to know about blood sucking insects. She was best on questions about leeches and ticks, but skeeters were right up there. At times, I think that Tiny Bob was probably meant to be her son. And one day, I might just ask her if she is interested.

Me and Pa reached the back of the ranch house and found Big Bill stacking boxes from the kitchen onto the porch.

"Hey, Pa," Big Bill said, dropping a big old box marked "fragile". For that matter, all of the boxes marked "fragile" were either thrown about or lying under other boxes.

"Hey, Bill Boy," Pa said, pulling out a wad of tobacco and beginning to chew. And the harder he stared at the boxes marked "fragile", the harder he chewed.

I added my box to the pile as Big Bill returned to the kitchen. Pa looked at me and simply shrugged his shoulders and spat. But let me tell you something, and I promise it's short because it seems that some people don't particulary like dwelling on the subject of spit, the velocity of Pa's spit here could have knocked over a good sized oil rig.

As Big Bill approached with a box labelled "paper products", which he gently set down, we heard the shrill sounds of old rusty wagon wheels and a light fixture approaching. We looked over in the direction of the barn and saw the chuck wagon being pulled by the team of four horses. Little Ben was leading the horses toward us as B.B. walked along side. The thump, thump...thump, thump... thump, thump of the electric cord could barely be heard over the creaks and screeches of the wagon.

"Hot damn!" I shouted, immediately sorry for cussing. But the wagon worked! True, it looked sorta wobbley from a distance, and as it got closer, the wobbleyness increased from sorta to somewhat to pretty to mighty, but it still held together.

"Good job, Bert Boy," Pa said, slapping me on my back and

wiping a potentially embarrassing dribble of spit from his chin. I was happy that I had pleased Pa and taken his mind off of Big Bill.

The wagon came along side us.

"Whoah," Little Ben said jerking the reins. The wagon stopped. Little Ben looked at me and winked.

"Might make it," he said.

"Still, it ain't no Critter Wagon," B.B. added with a smile.

"Speakin' of Critter Wagons, where's Bob Boy?" Pa asked as Big Bill again left for the kitchen.

My heart stopped. Well, not really 'cause then I'd be dead, and I can't right say that it "jumped" because hearts are pretty much imbedded in that space they sit in. So, let's just say that my heart did something when Pa asked about Tiny Bob. I didn't want to know where he was or what he was doing.

From the back of the chuck wagon, a voice cried out, "Here I is." Tiny Bob stuck his head out from beneath the wagon's flaps. "Now, c'mon, ya varmints."

With that, Tiny Bob jumped out of the wagon. He carried with him a rope which led under the flap and back into the wagon. He gave the rope a tug and forty chickens came tumbling out.

I looked down at the chickens and saw that each had one of its leg tied to another's leg, forming a sorta chicken chain-gang. Six of the gang members showed fine lumps on their noggens and exhibited extreme dizziness.

Before Pa could say anything, Big Bill returned with another box marked "fragile", which he threw to the ground. Pa bit down real hard on his chaw. B.B., who, from experience, knew to expect a missle of a spit, quickly went over to Pa.

"Don't worry, Eugene," B.B. whispered while tapping his lump. "I Bill-proofed the boxes. Ones labelled "fragile" ain't, and vica versy."

Pa surveyed the entire scene, including Warden Tiny Bob marching his prisoner chickens, and a grin spread across his face.

"Well… at least nuthin's broken," I heard him say to himself. He then took a moment to let his jaw and cheek muscles relax.

"Boys," he began at normal volume. "All in all, ya done real good and I'm awful proud of ya, 'specially with the short time we had. Now it looks to me like we're just 'bout set here."

"Just gotta load up the wagon and we're ready to move 'em out," B.B. confirmed.

"Good," Pa declared. "And I stopped by the herd on my way back from Ray and Tammy Faye's. Willie and Clint have got 'em all rounded up by the north gate. They're gonna wait fer us thar. So, Ben and Bill Boys, ya git the horses out of the corral and rounded up over here. B.B. and me'll load the boxes on the wagon. Bert Boy, ya gather up the thins that everone's a bringin' and that should just 'bout do it fer yer list." I glanced down to my list of chores. Indeed, last on the list was "Gather Up The Thins That Everone's A Bringin'."

Pa continued. "Willie told me to remind ya not to forgit his stuff. Clint told me to remind ya not to forgit Willie's stuff. Don't worry 'bout my thins. I've got 'em all in that campin' box ya carried over."

"Ya don't gotta worry 'bout me neither, Even Tinier Bert," B.B. said, moving a duffle bag over to the scatter of boxes. "If it ain't in here, it just ain't a goin'."

"And Bob Boy," Pa said.

"Yeah Pa?" Tiny Bob replied as he yanked his rope. At least one leg from each chicken was immediately pulled out from underneath it. 'Course, this led to tremendous squawking as most of the chickens lost their balance and fell over.

Pa silently studied the situation for a moment.

"Bob Boy, ya just keep good watch over them chickens," he finally said. I knew that it was something Pa had to do to keep Tiny Bob happy and out of trouble. But I could still tell from his tone that Pa felt mighty sorry for the chickens attached to Tiny Bob's imbecilical cord.

"Just watch 'em," Pa continued. "No more yanking, 'kay?"

"'Kay," Tiny Bob replied with a semi-smile. Had Pa allowed him to keep on yanking, it would have been a full smile.

I ran into the ranch house to get everybody's except B.B.'s and Pa's personal effects. We had all packed the previous night, after the campfire. So, all I really had to do was gather up the one bag we were each allowed to bring. Little Ben figured that one bag a piece would use up the rest of the room on the chuck wagon. However, Big Bill said that if we ran out of space on the wagon, then he'd unpack half his suitcase.

Now, let me tell you, if you've never tried it, it's awful tough trying to fit your whole life into one bag. I'm at the age where I could have easily filled up two or three bags, especially when you figured that clothing wasted a lot of space. That left only a little room for all the mementos and artifacts that I had gathered over my life. Although, you'd probably call this stuff junk, to me, it had meaning, and there was a lot of it to sift through. And what's more, each time I'd look at the stuff and then at the bag, I'd swear that the bag was shrinking.

But, knowing my own dilemma, I could only imagine what Pa and B.B. went through while they were packing. They had tons more mementos and artifacts. And they were at the age where you'd probably call their stuff "collector's items". This made it that much harder for them to pick which things to pack than if their stuff had been just plain old junk.

I entered my room first. My bag was right where I had left it, next to the bunkbed. I checked it closely and saw that the little piece of hair was still sticking out from the closed clasp, meaning that the Bob Mine had not tampered with its contents.

Tiny Bob's bag was lying on his bunk. 'Course, he hadn't bothered locking it. So, just to get a rough idea of how heavy it was going to be to carry, I looked inside.

MILLIONS of bugs and bug pieces! Absolutely no clothes, just disgusting dead insects and parts. Strictly out of reflex, I slammed the suitcase shut and jumped back, panting.

After a spell and one last deep breath, I went over to the window and removed the curtain rod. Then, holding it at arms length like a branding iron, I crept back over to the bed. I stopped when the tip of the rod touched the latch of Tiny Bob's suitcase, which was still way too close if I had had any real choice in the matter. I then poked at the latch with the rod until the latch finally snapped shut. If someone had happened by, they would have thought I was trying to wake a sleeping skunk.

Feeling better now that the dead bugs, their pieces and me were separated by a lock, I took both bags into the hall. I carried mine by the handle, while pushing and sliding Tiny Bob's with my feet. That done, I went into Willie's and Clint's room.

Most of Willie's pictures from his bronco busting days had been taken down from the wall. I guessed they were now packed away in his bag. 'Course, Clint, not having any mementos or arti-facts of his own, might have packed some away too. I took the matching suitcases, which were imitation leather but looked like genuine plastic, and put them in the hall with the others.

Finally, I went to Big Bill's and Little Ben's room. Both bags were sitting on Big Bill's bed. On his bedpost hung his second place ribbon for the Lufkin Southern Hush Puppy Olympics. He must have overlooked it while packing because, while it wasn't the type of thing you bragged about on a daily basis, a second place finish in the Olympics was an achievement not to be forgotten. So, I took the ribbon from the post and opened Big Bill's suitcase. Looking inside, it was amazing how many more mementos you could bring along when you didn't have to pack shoes. I folded up the ribbon and proudly tucked it away next to an autographed pic-ture of Dr. Scholl.

Pa and B.B. had just placed the last kitchen box onto the wagon as I arrived with the suitcases. Seated on his mount, a dark horse named Dukakis, Little Ben was leading the rest of the horses, with the exception of Raw Speed, towards us. Big Bill was already tying Raw Speed to the back of the wagon.

"How'd you get her over here so quick?" I asked Big Bill as I dropped the suitcases.

"One good stomp next to her ear," Big Bill replied.

While Pa and B.B. loaded the suitcases, I made one last quick sweep of the Old Miss from where I was standing - the house, the suitcases, Pa, B.B., the wagon, Big Bill, Raw Speed, a tree, some grass, strung chickens, Tiny Bob, a tree, open space, the corral, the road, approaching horses, open space, the barn, the road, an uprooted shrub, a new hole and back again to the house. I spun around just quick enough to take it all in without the scenery being blurry and without me getting dizzy.

"Quick look `round," Little Ben commented, looking down from Dukakis.

I smiled and was going to say something important, like "yeah", when B.B. interrupted.

"It ain't gonna fit," B.B. said. "Thar just ain't enough room." I looked over and saw that all of the suitcases excep for Big Bill's had been loaded onto the wagon. And the wagon looked mighty full.

"Then I told ya'll I'd take half my thins out," Big Bill said.

"It's the size of the suitcase that matters!" B.B. snorted. But, this fell on deaf ears as Big Bill opened his suitcase and began taking out clothes.

"Eugene," B.B. pleaded. "Do somethin'."

"Let 'im be," Pa said. "I guess the boy's just gotta learn the hard way."

With half of his clothes out, Big Bill shut his suitcase. We all watched as he stood and stared at it. After a couple of minutes, he started to scratch his forehead.

"Ya see, ya see," B.B. said to Big Bill. "Thar ain't no dif…"

A tremendous stomp interrupted B.B.'s statement mid-sentence. When the dust cleared, we saw that half of the suitcase had been completely crushed. Big Bill ripped off the smashed half and threw it aside. He then took the undamaged half and placed it in the wagon where it just fit.

"Well I'll be damned," B.B. said with his mouth hanging open. Sure enough, Big Bill had proved us all wrong. You could change the dimensions of a suitcase.

"I'm a proud of ya, son," Pa said as he patted Big Bill on the back. Big Bill's clever solution outweighed the fact that he had just pretty much ruined a good suitcase.

Smiling broadly, Pa shouted, "Let's head 'em up and move 'em out!"

Pa got on his horse, Ma, which had originally been named Petunia but had been renamed as a living memorial to Ma after her death. It was a beautiful gesture even though we often had to explain the name whenever Pa would declare in public that he was off to mount Ma.

Pa trotted Ma to the front of the troop while B.B. climbed on the wagon. Big Bill got on his horse, a Palomino he named No Olive Loaf. Without going into detail, Big Bill confused Palomino with Pimento and just wanted everyone to know that his horse was not going to be the main ingredient in his least favorite luncheon meat.

Tiny Bob hopped on his horse which he named Fido when Pa wouldn't let him have a dog. He walked his horse to the front as his train of chickens, now tethered to his saddle horn, unwillingly followed. Little Ben turned Dukakis around and took up the rear as I mounted You Romantic You, a wedding gift from Ma's pa to Pa.

You see, Ma's pa gave Pa the choice of a big wedding and a honeymoon anywhere within a ten mile radius of Grangerland or a horse. Pa spent two days wracking his brains with the decision. Actually, that's not altogether true. In Pa's mind, there was no choice. So, he really spent the two days contemplating whether or not to let Ma name the horse. And as if I even had to tell you, Pa decided to show his love to Ma by giving her the honors.

"Forward Ho!" Pa shouted, giving Ma a soft kick. Everyone else then shouted "Forward Ho!", except for B.B., who shook his reins and shouted, "Yah Mules!".

As we surged forward, I turned and looked at the ranch house for the last time. I shouldn't have. Yes, it was the adventure I had hoped for, and, yes, I was with my family, an even more important family than first realized. But I was leaving a place I could never return to. Never. And that's a long time, especially when you're still sorta just a kid, like me.

Thankfully, my melancholy was short-lived. As the Old Miss procession plodded on down the road, its horses and wagons kicking up great clouds of dust with every step, I had time to turn my head and look at the barn as we passed by. I rubbed my eyes twice to make sure I wasn't seeing things. But there it was. The entire side of the barn had been painted chartreuse and in big brown letters was written, "Eeoogie Go Home".

That's Willie! That's family!

8

It didn't take us long to get off the Old Miss once we finally reached the herd. Unfortunately, a small mishap slowed us down, so it took awhile to actually reach them.

As we were coming down hill and picking up speed, Big Bill broke his horse into a canter. All of the other horses then broke into canters. Now this was usually fine and dandy and what was to be expected. What we forgot was one of the first tenets of the range: chickens don't canter. So, as Tiny Bob's horse took off, well, it wasn't a particularly pretty sight. You had your basic string of bouncing chickens squawking their noncantering heads off with so many tailfeathers in the air that you'd have thought we were having a blizzard.

Now, unfortunately, that's just what B.B. thought. So, B.B. tried to pull the wagon over to the side while yelling, "Batten down the hatches, secure the fort, we've hit a snow squall." 'Course, his horses didn't pull over, probably because B.B. was tugging on his lasso instead of the reins. But he did succeed in scaring his horses, who panicked mainly because they heard the screaming and couldn't figure it out because they knew it wasn't snowing.

So, B.B.'s team broke into a gallop, which caused the other horses to break into a gallop, which caused the chickens, well, one of the second tenets of the range is that chickens don't gallop. More bouncing, more squawking, more feathers. Had I not been so preoccupied with trying to hang onto my saddle horn for dear life, I would have liked to have measured the amazing height that some of those chickens were hitting. Had they not been tied to a rope, some of them might have bounced right into orbit around the earth.

Pa and Little Ben finally got things under control, but not until all we had left were an awful lot of bald chickens. Fortunately, very few of them died which, I hate to say, was probably because of Tiny Bob's tree dropping, which sorta acted as a training program. It still took us some time get things back in order as many of the chickens needed splints, bandages and mouth-to-beak resuscitation.

But, we finally did arrive at the north gate and found all five thousand head of cattle grazing there. About half of the head were those Red Branguses, a combination of Brahmans and Red Anguses, and the other half were red Shorthorns. Basically, the breeds looked alike except that the Red Branguses don't have horns and the Shorthorns, being originally from England, have a slight accent when they moo.

As we arrived, Willie and Clint were sitting on the gate, watching the herd and singing "One Million Bottles of Beer on the Wall", which they hoped would cover them through to New York.

"Nine hundred ninety nine thousand nine hundred and twenty nine bottles of beer on the wall," Willie sang. "Nine hundred ninety nine thousand nine hundred and twenty nine bottles of beer. If one of those bottles happens to fall, nine hundred ninety nine thousand nine hundred and twenty eight bot...Howdy everbody. We've been a waitin' fer ya."

Willie hopped off of the fence and came over to meet us. Clint followed.

"Some nice lookin' bald chickens ya got there, Tiny Bob," Willie said surveying the situation.

"Had us a little trouble," Pa said.

"B.B. said it was one of them snow squalls," Big Bill said.

"Let's just forgit 'bout the whole thin, okay," B.B. snapped, now covered with so many feathers that chickens began to flock around him with a look of love in their eyes.

Willie looked from the chickens to B.B. "Don't ya know one of the first tenets of the range is that chickens don't canter?"

"Well, fer yer information, I've just done saved myself a lot of time pluckin' these critters later," B.B. snarled. "Just like I had planned. So, unless you know what yer talkin' 'bout, don't go lecturin' me on cookin' techniques."

Willie grinned that cockeyed grin of his, making it look like his mustache was starting to crawl up his face. He then turned west and studied the reddish orange sunset.

"Mr. Henry, we still got us a little light left," he said. "I've done scouted the old cattle trail and it's clear through to the Sam Houston. So, I reckon if ya wanta take off now, we'll still be able to hit that old forest 'fore dark…'course that's assumin' we don't hit no more snow squalls."

Willie's mustache crawled a little more as he looked in B.B.'s direction. Luckily, B.B. was too busy kicking love-struck chickens away to have heard Willie's rib or we might have had us a little altercation.

Speaking of love struck, Old George had seen Pa ride up and had quickly weaved his way through the herd and over to the fence closest to where we were mounted. He was now courting Pa with a rendition of "Moolight Serenade" as he gazed at Pa with those big old bull eyes of his. 'Course, this was the one time when you could probably say that the bull's eye was way off target because, as I said before, Pa just wasn't interested.

"That'd be real fine if we could reach the forest 'fore dark," Pa said.

"What?" Willie asked.

"Said that'd be real fine," Pa replied.

"What?" Willie again asked.

"George, shut up," Pa said, turning to face the old bull. "I told ya, I just ain't interested."

Old George ceased his crooning, lowered his head and once again walked away dejected. But knowing Old George, he'd be back. He wasn't about to quit until Pa was his.

"I said it'd be real fine if we could," Pa continued, turning back to face Willie. "Then we could set up camp right outside the forest and start in first thin tomorrow morn'."

"Good 'nough, Mr. Henry," Willie replied as he turned to Clint. "You heard 'im. Ya take the gate. I'll git 'em movin'."

Clint hustled over to the north gate as Willie walked over and mounted his steed, Clint's Pickle.

Willie had named his horse "Clint's Pickle" knowing exactly what would happen. Clint named his horse the same thing and, well, now pretty much everybody in Grangerland enjoys coming up to Clint and telling him that they are certainly impressed with the size of his Pickle and the fact that he can keep his Pickle stand-ing so long, and that his Pickle must get cold in the winter, being all exposed and all, and things like that. 'Course, the joke sorta back-fired too in that people also come up to Willie and ask him how it feels to sit on Clint's Pickle. But, that's a practical joke for you. Even the best of them sometimes aren't perfect.

Willie perched atop Clint's Pickle forged his way through the herd until he reached the rear. There he awaited Pa's signal from outside the fence.

"Ben Boy, ya take right point," Pa said. "I'll put Clint on left point. Bob Boy, ya'll back up both points. Bill Boy, ya got the horses. Willie said it's clear through to Sam Houston, so I'll lead today and let Willie bring up the rear. Bert Boy, yer in charge of the drags. And B.B., find some place in the wagon fer them chicken friends of yers."

"Need me to make ya some space?" Big Bill asked.

"Nah," B.B. replied. "Without all them bulky feathers, I'm a sure I can find some place to stuff 'em…Just like I had planned."

"Then head 'em up and move 'em out," Pa shouted.

At once, there was a pasture of activity. Pa gave Ma a soft little kick and trotted over to Clint to tell him his drive position. Little Ben cantered Dukakis to the far right of the herd and waited while Tiny Bob loped Fido to the far left of the herd. Big Bill took No Olive Loaf over to the few extra horses we were bringing along. Me and You Romantic You just stood our ground seeing as how there really weren't any strays to search for before a drive actually started.

I watched B.B. stuff the calvacade of chickens into the wagon. And would you believe it, without the feathers, they all did fit. 'Course, I can't quite say that chickens were suppose to bend the way B.B. bent these birds, but regardless of whether he ever had a plan, B.B. had lived up to his word. Pleased with himself, B.B. hopped on the wagon.

As I glanced around at all the pieces in place, it reminded me of the start of a game of checkers. I mean, except for the fact that there was no board and no one was wearing black or red, the Old Miss players were spread out, forming a big square boundary and waiting for the first move.

And the move came as Pa raised his arm high in the air for all to see and yelled "King me". Clint immediately opened the gate as

Pa turned Ma in the direction of the old cattle trail andspurred her into a gallop. Willie saw the signal but waited until Pa was nothing more than a dust raising speck before moving the herd.

"Yah! Yah!" Willie shouted as he put Clint's Pickle into a lope behind the herd. "Last one through the gate is ground beef!"

Not wanting to be tonight's hamburger, the cattle began a big surge through the open gate. People left Preacher Jim Earl's church after Sunday services in exactly the same fashion. 'Course, Preacher Jim Earl never had to threaten to turn anyone into ground beef or anything else for that matter to get them to leave. People would rush the church door and start pushing and shoving the minute they thought services were over. I'm not exaggerating, but once, Preacher Jim Earl made a mistake and paused between Psalms, and, well, the church was empty by the time the 35th Psalm began. So, the problem wasn't in getting the people to leave, but in getting them to stay. And Preacher Jim Earl solved this by threating those who didn't stay with eternal damnation. 'Course, he also had to promise not to pause anymore.

"Yah, Brisket, Yah, Round Roast!" Willie continued, causing the herd to quicken its pace through the gate. "Slow varmints end up pork chops!" Again, the cattle moved a little faster. By this time, they were just too involved in what they were doing to really consider Willie's last threat.

In the meantime, Clint, not wanting to resemble human salsa, had climbed over the gate the minute he had opened it. He had then run down to where he had tied his Pickle, and proceeded to quickly mount then whip his Pickle into a gait, heading for the left point. Even though some of the cattle had a head start, it didn't take long before I saw that Clint had them cut off on the left and, together with Little Ben, succeeded in channeling those cattle who weren't in danger of becoming ground beef towards the old cattle trail.

What a sight! Cattle shooting through the gate to join the thundering herd on the open plain. A picture perfect sunset illuminating a horizon filled with dirt, dust, cattle, horses and chicken butts sticking out from a chuck wagon. The ground trembling with the beat of horse and cow hoofs, the air resounding with moos, clucks, nays and shouts. Was I excited? Don't answer, that was rhetorical. Even though I had done no more than sit here straight and still on

You Romantic You, by God, for a moment, I felt just a little bit like a real cowboy.

"Yah," I shouted for no particular reason. I pinched myself to see if I was dreaming. True, I pinched myself on my thick leather chaps, so I wasn't able to feel it, but, still, I knew I was awake. I pulled up my bandana to keep the dust out of my mouth and eyes. By God, real cowboys did this! 'Course, I had to lower it just a little because I had completely covered my eyes and couldn't see, but a little mistake wasn't about to damper my first brief feeling of real cowboyness.

The last of the cattle came running through the gate, closely followed by Willie"…If one of those bottles happen to fall, nine hundred ninety nine thousand nine hundred and eighteen bottles of beer on the wall," he sang, his voice fading as he loped off to bring up the rear.

"Let's go, ya lazy nags!" B.B. shouted when Willie had passed. "Git this wagon movin', ya four legged plugs!"

The wagon jerked forward as his team of horses went into four hoof drive. So long as B.B. did absolutely nothing, his horses would instinctively follow the herd. The problem was he was shouting again. However, I also saw that he was still tugging on his lasso. And the featherless fowl, my nom deplumed for the chickens, were tightly packed away. So, while I can't quite say I breathed a sigh of relief, I did breath a sigh of no disaster yet. My reckoning was that if everything remained status quo, well, hopefully his horses would ignore him and things would be fine.

It was a minute or two before Hercules, Odysseus, Sampson and Shirley had the wagon going at full tilt across the plains. I soon lost the bouncing wagon in all the dust, but I heard squawking for sometime, B.B.'s that is — the chickens couldn't have been quieter.

Me and You Romantic You sat there waiting for the dust to clear. Even with the bandana off my eyes, I couldn't see more than fifty feet to the north. I thought it showed good sense to wait, figuring that if I tried to go through now looking for drags, I might end up one myself.

So, much akin to watching grass grow, we sat there watching dust settle. Pa called it desert snow, and it was true that particles did flutter down and glimmer in the sunlight as they fell. 'Course, from what I remembered, snow didn't make you cough when it ended up in your lungs, and I didn't know if every two dust flakes were different, although Tiny Bob once took a plate full of what he believed to be a representative sample to find out.

Now contrary to my suggestion of using a microscope, Tiny Bob, wanting to get a real, real close look, started sticking dust particles in his eyes. Well, eventually, Old Doc Buford had to come over to flush out Tiny Bob's peepers so he could see again. When his vision returned, Tiny Bob concluded that, based on what he saw before his eyes clouded up, no two dust particles were alike. But I pointed out to him that the experiment wasn't conclusive. He had only gone through half his sample before he was blinded. So, I tried to convince him to study the other half. But you know Tiny Bob. Already bored by the whole thing, he poured water into the rest of his sample, made a mud pie and ate it.

Now, I hope you're not disappointed in not knowing for sure whether all dust particles are different. However, recalling this little anecdote did give time for all the dust to clear. Everybody and everything was out of sight and it was very quiet.

"Well, this is really it," I said, my voice echoing in the emptiness. 'Course, it wasn't empty in any real sense. There was still the gate and fence and trees and shrubs and the ground covered with lots of cow and horse pucks. No, the place was empty in another sense. Gone were the people and livestock that gave the Old Miss its heart and soul. Without us, the ranch would be no more than deserted buildings and the ghosts of over ninety years of the Henry family.

A couple of generations had left their mark on the land. I found it strange to think that someone else would now be taking over. Would they build upon what we had left, or would they disregard all that we had worked for? Of course, I guess I couldn't blame them one way or the other. Nothing that they'd find would mean what it meant to us. They'd be the owners of our intangibles, strangers on their own property.

A gust of wind blew the trees on the hill leading back up to the ranch house. No, whoever lived in our stead could never take our place. Sure, they might sit in the living room in front of the fireplace on a cold winter night and listen to the wind howl, like we used to do, but they'd never know how it really felt; we built that fireplace.

Maybe it was symbolic that the only reminder of the lifeblood of the ranch left behind were the cow and horse droppings. Even I realized that sometimes in life, you're just going to get dumped on. And there's just not much you can do about it, except realize what it is before you step and try to avoid as much of it as possible.

Still, I felt a pang the moment I gave You Romantic You a little kick and we took a step off of the Old Miss. So, we stepped back on.

"Don't be such an emotional sap," I said to myself. "This isn't home anymore." And while home isn't exactly where the heart is, unless you're small enough to live in that chest cavity, home is where old memories are remembered and new memories are formed...where food has that special taste that makes it, well, homemade...where family abounds...where seldom is heard a discouraging word and the skies are not cloudy all day.

I then concentrated on a single thought which ran through my mind like a steam locomotive, "Real cowboy, real cowboy, real cowboy".

I grabbed the reins and gave them a mighty shake. Good bye Old Miss. Good bye.

9

BY THE TIME I ARRIVED at the campsite, there were already millions of stars out. The sky was beautiful, like a painter's black boot covered with tiny white paint specks, except without the shoelaces.

I had taken my time traveling up the old cattle trail from the Old Miss. I'm happy to report that on the first evening of travel, not a single drag was seen. I thought I had spotted one a little after dusk had set in, but it turned out to be just a log. Willie had stuck horns and a blown-up rubber glove on top of the log, so in the shadows from a distance it looked like a cow. 'Course, as I rode over to check it out, I did think it was a little strange that this cow had udders on top of her body. And even stranger was the fact that on her side was painted "Cow". But when you're concentrating in looking for strays, you just don't think too much about these things.

You may not believe this, but I didn't feel foolish when I discovered that this was just a practical joke. I actually felt kinda proud. After I had realized that the cow was really just a log in disguise, I looked around and saw that there weren't any other trees in sight. So, I figure that you can say that I did find myself a stray, even if it was just a log.

I rode up to where the other horses were tied, which was about a fifty yards from the campsite. I could barely make out the Old Miss figures sitting and talking around the campfire from this distance. The campfire was the only light for miles around and with the stars shining, it made for a very pretty sight. As I got off of You Romantic You, I saw in the moonlight that the rest of the horses were standing in a circle of dirt, while just out of reach in every direction was grass. It didn't take a genius to see what was going on. Raw Speed was bloated and all of the rest of the horses looked hungry.

I took You Romantic You by the reins and walked her over to a grassy area a little ways off where I tied her to a tree. I then started to move each of the other horses over to this spot. All I can say is, boy, were those horses ever happy to be away from Raw Speed. They began to eat almost immediately. But being more well-mannered than Raw Speed, they made sure that there was plenty left for their fellow horses.

I was just tying up the second of Clint's Pickles, the last of the horses to be brought over to the grassy spot, when I heard a voice behind me.

"Don't move and hands up, ya Rustler!"

"I'm not a Rustler," I said. "And it's impossible to not move and put up my hands at the same time."

I turned around and saw it was B.B., and he was pointing a rifle. However, in the darkness, I don't think he realized that he had the gun pointed at himself.

B.B. squinted as he drew nearer. "Even Tinier Bert, is that you?" he asked.

"Yes," I replied.

"I coulda shot ya just now," he said lowering the gun. I kept quiet, although knowing his aim, pointing the gun at himself may have been the only way he would have hit me.

"Where've ya been?" he asked.

"First day on the trail, I wanted to take my time. I wanted to do a good job."

"That'll make yer pa real proud. Now, ya better hurry over to camp and et 'cause I'm a gonna be yellin' stop real soon." Even though the Old Miss was behind us, I realized that some things just weren'tgoing to change.

We started walking towards camp. "How did you see me from way over by the fire?" I asked.

"Didn't," B.B. answered. "Had myself an inklin' that someone was over by the horses."

"You seem to be getting more inklings, don't you?"

"Yep. More and stronger."

"Oops!" I exclaimed. In the darkness, I had tripped over a small fallen tree.

"Hey!" The tree shouted back, which scared the living cow pucks out of me.

"Sorry, tree," I said still shaking.

"I ain't no tree, it's me."

I unfortunately recognized Tiny Bob's voice. B.B. leaned over the spot where Tiny Bob laid. "Ya want anythin' else to eat, Tiny Bob?" he asked.

"Nah thanks," Tiny Bob responded.

"Okay, then, we're headin' to camp," B.B. said as we resumed our walk towards the campsite.

"What's he doing lying on the ground?" I asked more out of curiosity than concern.

"Well, when we got close to where we were a figurin' on stoppin' fer the evenin', he tried jumpin' off Fido onto the back of a bull, 'cept he sorta missed."

"Sorta?"

"Well, he missed the back, but caught the tail. And ya know Tiny Bob. He was too dang stubborn to let go. So, that nostril flairin' critter done dragged Tiny Bob 'bout a mile and a half to the spot where he's lyin' now. And I'm a tellin ya, that crazy bull woulda kept on draggin' Tiny Bob forever had his tail not popped off from his behind. I swear, in all my days, I ain't never seen a tail just pop off a critter like that before... 'course, that's not includin' lizards."

I looked off to the left and, in the moonlight, I could now see the herd. They all seemed to be grazing peacefully after their first run. It was hard to believe that somewhere among those five thousand tired, hungry cattle was a bull whose tail had just popped off from his behind.

"Even Tinier Bert, ya done got an education," B.B. continued. "Ya know if bulls can grow new tails?"

We entered the campsite as I pondered the question.

"I don't think so," I finally said. "I think that only happens with animals that naturally lose their tails." I wanted to add "not when its yanked off by a moron", but I didn't.

"Oh!" B.B. exclaimed. "Regeneration! I thought as much."

B.B. looked at his watch. "You best git goin' on the grub," he added.

I quickly ran over to the chuck wagon, almost striking my

head on the slab-of-old-green-moldy-spam-on-the-stick. I grabbed myself a plate and dished out a big portion of grub, which I couldn't identify in the weak light, so it'd just have to be known as grub until I got closer to the campfire. With my plate full, I walked over to join the others.

"Bert Boy," Pa said as I entered the light of the fire. "We were a startin' to worry 'bout ya."

"Just making sure I didn't miss anything," I said sitting down between Big Bill and Willie.

"Any strays?" Little Ben asked.

"No," I said looking at my food. It was some sorta stew, but even by the light of the fire, I could't make out the exact kind.

"Not even a cow with utters on its back?" Willie asked with a smile on his face.

"Yeah," I said returning the smile. "I did find a stray log."

"Good fer ya, Bert Boy," Pa said. "Good fer ya."

I took a bite of food. It was definitely something I had never had before. I turned to Big Bill.

"What is this grub?" I asked.

"Grub," Big Bill answered.

"Well, yeah, but what is it?" I again asked.

"Grub," Big Bill again replied.

Willie leaned over and whispered. "It's grub alright. It's some concoction B.B. made outta worm-like larva."

Before suddenly losing my appetite, I noticed that everybody else's plates were on the ground and were still full.

"Stop," B.B. shouted as he entered the campfire area. Never before had I been so happy to hear that word. I quickly added my plate to the collection on the ground.

"I'd have thought ya'll would be hungrier after a day of drivin'," B.B. said kinda disappointedly as he went around gathering the dishes. "Tiny Bob had himself thirds."

"Well, it was only a partial day of driving," I said to keep B.B.'s feelings from getting hurt. "So we weren't too hungry."

A smile appeared on B.B.'s face. "It does give us plenty a leftovers fer lunch tomorrow, don't it?" he said. "Maybe even enough fer dinner."

Happy with the thought of once again serving his "Dilopod Delight", B.B. took the plates and exited.

"I ain't gonna eat no bugs," Willie said once B.B. was gone. "Save 'em fer Tiny Bob." There was unanimous consent on this.

"Boys, eat yerselves a big breakfast tomorrow," Pa said. "And I'll find a way to talk to B.B."

Thank goodness this ended the conversation. The talk turned to tomorrow's itinerary. Our camp was set on the banks of the West Fork Spring Brook, just outside the border of the Sam Houston National Forest. Pa hoped that the drive would be able to reach a little further than the midpoint of the Sam Houston, somewhere near Big Woods Hunter Camp and a distance of twenty miles, by the next evening.

I laid down and stared at the night sky, not realizing how tired I was. When you got right down to it, it had been quite a day. I had begun it a trivial repairer and ended it an important cog in a crucial endeavor. Along the way, I had experienced every emotion listed in Roget's Thesaurus. And still, one feeling lingered. Perhaps, because it was most foreign.

Before today, I had never really felt pressure. Sure, I had what I thought was pressure — to do well in school, to be liked, to make Pa and B.B. proud and to take care of my horse every day. These were a twelve year old's pressures, the pressures of natural progression with time as an ally. I now faced the pressure of having to grow up, quickly.

I felt the pressure of my role, the pressure of our future. Our success or failure would depend as much on me as it would on the others. So far, I was proud of myself. Willie had given me my first test, and I felt that I had passed. The demands were still there and I knew that tougher times lay ahead, but I felt something else creeping into the picture — confidence.

Even if the exigencies never slacked, if I gained confidence in my own ability, I could do the job. Then, perhaps, I could become a real cowboy, rather than just being excited because I dressed the part. Wouldn't that be something? To attain a permanent rather than a fleeting feeling of real cowboyness. To possess that special bond to John Wayne. That would make Pa and B.B. proud. And for the first time in my life, I realized that I wanted to make myself proud too.

It was quiet now. Just the sound of some crickets chirping and five thousand head of cattle chewing their cud. Orange sparks flew from the campfire upwards where they disappeared among the stars. A comet streaked across the heavens, so beautiful and absorbing that you forgot about the poisonous fumes it spewed forth.

Pa was officially announcing that Willie would be scouting and he would be bringing up the rear the rest of the way when I closed my eyes. I lost the stars, but not the peace and tranquility of the blackness.

10

"Breakfast!" B.B. shouted. "Come and git it!"

I'd been up for an hour, brushing and saddling You Romantic You when the call came. The reason I was up early was due in part to the fact that I had fallen asleep so quickly that I hadn't pulled out my sleeping bag. So when I awoke, I had lots and lots of bright red painful rock indentations on my body. But more importantly, I got up early because I was starving! My stomach had been growling all night and it hadn't stopped yet. Together with everybody else's stomachs, it sounded like thunder rolling across the plains. Needless to say, when B.B. called "breakfast", dust flew as a line formed right quick by the chuck wagon.

Willie stood first in line.

"Here ya go," B.B. said as he served Willie what appeared to be an omelet.

I guess on account of dinner last night, Willie stood there studying the egg. After a short while, he lifted part of the egg off the plate, carefully looking at the underside of what he had been given.

"Damn sakes, Willie," B.B. said. "It ain't gonna explode!"

Just then, an explosion rocked the campsite.

"It came from the direction of the horses," Pa shouted.

We all ran. There was no need to guess who was responsible, only the extent of the damage.

At the same spot where I tripped over him last night, Tiny Bob was standing as stiff as a neck trying to peek into the girl's shower at Grangerland Junior High. He was holding a magnifying glass in one hand and there was a smoking pair of reins near his feet, but nothing else.

"It ain't my fault," he said as we arrived.

"What happened?" Pa asked.

"It ain't my fault," Tiny Bob again replied. "Pa, I was layin' here 'cause I couldn't git up. And then I felt somethin' sniffin' me. And then I looked and saw it was Pokey. And Pokey musta gotten loose and thought I was food. And I told her to scat. I told her to scat a couple of times. But she kept on sniffin' me like I was a big weiner or somethin'. So I reached into my pocket and got my bug magnifier. Seein' as how it's a sunny mornin' and all, I was just gonna burn her a little to git her to scat. Pa, I only had the sunspot on her fer a couple a seconds. I swear it."

Little Ben studied the still smouldering reins. "Spontaneous combustion," he said. Big Bill stomped on the reins a few times to cool them off.

No, it couldn't be true. I quickly looked around in all directions. Raw Speed was nowhere in sight. The reins! Through the smoke I recognized them as Raw Speed's. It was true! My horse was gone! Tiny Bob had blown her up!

Now, I had heard of spontaneous combustion, when things just explode for no reason. I never really believed it happened, although Clem Spreg of Spreg Cattle Insecticide Ear Tag fame claimed he came home one day to find that his missus had spontaneously combusted. Now, while it's true that he was upset by the loss, he was also proud that he had the first recorded instance of a spouse spontaneously combusting. He was greatly disappointed, though, to learn that it was not going to be declared a true spontaneous combustion because the house had also blown up. And there was also a question about whether it might have actually been the dog that spontaneously burst first which then set off a chain reaction.

I went over and picked up the reins. Tears flowed from my eyes at the thought of zillions of Raw Speed's atoms now spreading out over the countryside.

"I'm tellin' ya, it was somethin'," Tiny Bob said. "One minute Pokey's thar with just a little bit of smoke comin' from a little brown point on her snout, then poof. And the wind from that thar poof done threw me to my feet."

I continued staring at the reins and crying. Everybody else had moved closer to Tiny Bob so that they could hear more of the details. I felt hurt and alone.

Pa saw me standing by myself and came over. He nodded in

the direction of the others. "Can't blame `em," Pa said. "It's not everday that ya have yerself a spontaneous combustion."

He put his arm around my shoulder and continued. "Look, Son, these thins just happen. And if we knew why and when, we probably wouldn't git so attached. That's the funny thin. We know somethin ain't gonna last forever, but we love it just the same. Now, it's okay to feel the loss, just so long as it don't interfere with ya bein' able to love somethin' again."

He then looked me squarely in the eyes. "And Son," he said. "Bein' able to love means bein' able not to hate."

I hugged Pa. I felt a lot better. Most of what he said made good sense, but I still hated Tiny Bob more than ever. While certain things may just happen, I didn't feel any of this would have if Tiny Bob hadn't heated up my pet. Oh, why couldn't it have been the Bob Mine that blew instead? I swore to myself then and there that one day I would get even.

We dug a small hole in which I placed the reins. Next to the reins, I placed the old green moldy slab of spam. We all stood around as Little Ben delivered a short eulogy on the noble qualities of the horse. He didn't really mention Raw Speed though, probably because he didn't feel many of the qualities applied. Big Bill filled in the hole, while I stuck in a gravemarker which read, "Raw Speed — Born May 2, 1967. Exploded September 24, 1987. May She Rest In Pieces."

We ate breakfast in silence. I guess that everyone was just too busy reflecting. I reflected on the tragedy which had befallen Raw Speed. The others, because of the way the sun hit their silver belt buckles, just plain reflected.

Willie finished before the rest of us and took off on Clint's Pickle to rescout the trail he planned on taking. This trail would lead us north across the Lawrence and Peach Creeks, where we'd enter San Jacinto County, across the Boggy and along Little Caney until we reached Nebletts Hunter Camp. There, we would head northwest a bit, crossing Winters Bayou and Black Brook before following Pumpkin Creek just about into Big Woods Hunter Camp. Willie had already scouted the trail earlier in the morning, but as you learn, a trail is not a stagnant thing. Right when you think its clear, things fall on it or move across it.

Breakfast over, everybody prepared for the day's drive. Clint,

Little Ben and Pa mounted and rode off to ready the herd. Big Bill carried Tiny Bob under his arm like a two by four over to Fido. There, he placed Tiny Bob on top of his horse and put the reins in his hands.

"Sit tight," Big Bill instructed Tiny Bob. "And I'll lead ya to the herd. Left the horses with 'em anyway."

"'Kay," Tiny Bob replied. "Can't move nohow."

Big Bill left Tiny Bob to retrieve No Olive Loaf. I thought,"If only I had a paper bag." Unable to move even his head, Tiny Bob was powerless. I could easily have strolled up, taken the magnifying glass out of his pocket and told him that I was going to see how likely it was for two horses to spontaneously combust on the same day. Then, while he was busy screaming, I would have walked around to the back of Fido and pretended that I was using the magnifying glass. After waiting a sufficient amount of time, I would have blown up the paper bag and then POP. Tell me that wouldn't have scared the living cow chips out of Tiny Bob.

But, I didn't have a paper bag. Funny the things you forget to pack. My revenge would have to wait.

Big Bill returned on his horse, and, soon, No Olive Loaf and Fido were loping off to join the herd. I helped B.B. pack up the chuck wagon, being careful to not wedge the chickens in too tightly. One chicken was so smashed that it now looked like a snake with a beak.

I had just finished up when I felt the ground tremble. I looked up and in the distance I saw the cattle running across the Atchison, Topeka and Santa Fe railroad tracks and entering the Sam Houston National Forest. Little Ben was on right point, Clint on left point and Pa brought up the rear. Big Bill was with the horses and Tiny Bob, well, he just kinda went along with wherever Fido decided to go.

B.B. doused the campfire with one more bucket of water from the brook and then climbed on the wagon. He looked my way and gave me a thumb's up sign. I took this to mean "here's to success", figuring that there just wasn't much point in B.B.'s hitchhiking in the middle of nowhere. Soon, B.B. and the wagon, including the thump, thump...thump,thump...thump, thump of the wagon wheel lamp cord, were out of camp, over the railroad tracks and into the forest.

I shook the reins and put You Romantic You into a slow gait. You couldn't have asked for nicer weather for the first full day of the drive. Not a cloud in the sky and you could see for miles. My job would certainly be easier under these conditions. Except for two dense wooded areas, the visibility on our trail would be very good. Because of this, I figured that I wouldn't be all that far behind the herd and wouldn't arrive at the camps too late for meals. 'Course, that's assuming that we weren't being served grub again.

I stopped You Romantic You as we reached the railroad tracks and looked in both directions. I recall Ma saying that there were three times when you look both ways- when crossing a street, when crossing railroad tracks and when watching ping pong. You just don't want to miss seeing a car coming or a train coming or a good match being played. 'Course, ever since Ma's Uncle Ned was killed by an errant ping pong ball over at the American Legion Hall in Grangerland, the last warning had taken on much greater significance than at first.

With no trains (or cars or ping pong balls) in sight, we crossed the tracks and entered the Sam Houston. From what I knew from my history and geography classes, the Sam Houston was named for, well, Sam Houston. He, of course, was the president of the Republic of Texas. Supposedly, he was loved by all Texans and saloonkeepers. As for the land, the first people arrived here around 7000 B.C. and they've been coming ever since. Most of the early ones were hunters or gatherers with some having a dual role of gathering hunters. The national forest, itself, was set up to control the different land uses, two of which are cattle grazing and driving.

The first two and a half miles into the forest were pretty uneventful, unless one considers trotting under a power line an event. There were a few nice trees, but nothing to write home about, assuming you have a home to write to. We had just started to cross a very small creek when I saw a very small stray.

"My first non-timber stray!" I thought as soon as I was sure that it did not have udders on top of it or "cow" written on its side. From the looks of it, a Red Brangus calf had wandered into some thickets along the creek's far bank and now appeared stuck.

It only took us a couple of seconds to cross the creek and reach the calf, mainly because a creek's far bank just isn't all that far. I dismounted You Romantic You and tied her to a small tree. I then walked over to the calf.

"You look mighty tangled there, Mr. Calf," I said as I studied the situation. The calf was pretty much surrounded by thickets, thick, thick thorny thickets. "Any ideas on how to get you out?"

I asked. The calf gave me a look which said, "No, but I'm not the human here, am I?"

I've never been much good with puzzles, especially when they deal with removing an intertwined cow from thickets. It would have been nice to have Floyd Thompson here. He was good at puzzles, like how to make televisions disappear from locked houses. But it would be impossible to contact Floyd now since he himself has disappeared, this time with Betty Jane Whomper's jewelry.

I considered using a rope to pull the calf out. Unfortunately, the calf would be sliced brisket by the time it was pulled from the prickly maze. I also dismissed cutting a hole in the thickets. All I had on me was my knife which was barely sharp enough to stir paint. And the roots of the thickets were much too deep for You Romantic You to have a decent chance of pulling the thickets clear.

Then it hit me. I would sing!

You don't know a thing about my singing, but let me tell you, I can clear a room almost as fast as one of Preacher Jim Earl's pauses. It usually takes but one note to get people up and running in the opposite direction. I'm not upset by the fact that I have a terrible singing voice. I know it's terrible and, sometimes, we just have to accept our limitations. That's why I even stopped joining in on "Happy Birthday To You" a long time ago, much to the relief of all those trying to celebrate.

The funny thing was, I was a member of the Grangerland Junior High School Choir. Before you get the idea that Wilber M. Boil, the choir director, must have been deaf, let me tell you that the Board of Education had a rule which read, "all students shall be in the choir". It so happened that Mr. Boil was deaf, but you see that under the rule, it didn't much matter.

But believe it or not, even through his deafness, Mr. Boil knew I was horrible. During our first rehearsal, he put his hand on my throat while I sang and said that my vocal cords didn't vibrate correctly or something. He said it felt more like a convulsion than singing. And he said that this was probably the first time in his life that he was truly grateful to be deaf.

Still, though, he didn't break the Board's rule and even went so far as to offer me a solo. Yep, he gave me my own room, right next to where everyone else rehearsed. He then honored me by naming me the understudy choir and told me that if everybody from the main choir could not perform, then I'd get the nod. It turns out that I almost got the nod once too. The entire main choir was almost suspended on the spot when, during the Christmas pageant, instead of singing "Onward Christian Soldier", they began to sing "Take This Job And Shove It". I guess they figured that Mr. Boil certainly wouldn't know the difference. Unfortunately, the rest of the horrified audience, including Principal Spud Twitty, did. However, the audience and Principal Twitty were even more horrified when they found out who the understudy was. The final outcome was that Principal Twittty gave the choir a good tongue lashing and told them to continue with the assigned program.

I turned my thoughts back to the calf trapped in the thickets. It dawned on me that not only was this calf my first real stray, but it was also my first captive audience. Poor, poor calf. I cleared my throat and began.

"Onward Christian Soldier," I sang not knowing what else to sing. The calf's ears shot up like a gusher, its eyes widened like a fat lady's in a bakery.

"Marching as to war," I continued. The calf kicked and jerked, starting to free itself.

Still singing, I quickly ran back to You Romantic You. I untied and mounted her, prepared for the chase soon to come.

"With the cross of Jesus," I belted. You Romantic You started to buck, so, thinking quickly, I grabbed some cotton out of my saddle bag and stuffed her ears. I looked over and saw the calf still stomping and wrenching, but almost out.

"Going on before," I continued as I shook the reins. Me and You Romantic You arrived at the thicket just as the calf backed out, clearing himself of the thicket.

The calf spun its head in all directions, finally landing its eyes on me. I tightened my grip on the reins, ready for the pursuit. But then a funny thing happened. The calf's eyes turned dreamy-like and the calf ceased all its wild movements.

"Isn't this something," I thought. "Well, come on, Mr. Calf, let's get you back to the herd."

Me and You Romantic You tried to get the calf to budge, but to no avail. I shouted, I got off my horse and pushed, I used my lasso and pulled, but nothing.

"Come on, you," I said. "Let's Go!...Or I'll start to sing again." Still, the calf wouldn't move.

"Alright then," I said as I again tightened my grip on the reins and picked up where I had left off, "Like a mighty army, leads against the foe, forward into battle, see his banner flow."

Immediately, the calf started to walk towards us! It was as if he was in a trance or something. Shocked to say the least, but still singing, I turned You Romantic You and began to walk her towards the trail. And would you believe it, that darn calf kept right on following us. I felt like some sorta Pied Piper.

I kicked my horse into a trot. I turned and looked back. There was the calf, trotting right along with us. I broke into a canter. So did the calf. I stopped singing. The calf stopped dead in its tracks. I smiled. This reminded me of a game I used to play as a kid, "Musical Cows".

I started singing again, and the calf resumed its walk towards me. This was certainly unexpected fun out on the range. As soon as the calf was near, I put You Romantic You into a gallop. I glanced over my shoulder and there was that obviously tone deaf calf keeping pace.

The terrain was fairly flat and the trail was clear, so we continued at this gait for a couple of miles. As we approached what I guessed was the Peach Creek, I looked back. There, running behind us, were three cows!

Well, I was so suprised that I totally forgot about Peach Creek and, more importantly, about slowing down as we hit it. You Romantic You left the south bank at full throttle. We barely made it to the north bank, or I should say, the horse made it fine, I was almost lost in transit. But with my arms wrapped around You Romantic You's neck, I managed to stay in the saddle. 'Course, in this position, I don't have to tell you where the saddle horn was sticking into. My first note upon landing was a high soprano.

It was now that You Romantic You finally had the sense to stop. She couldn't have stopped before the creek? So much for the expression "good horse sense". Anyhow, I turned and watched as the three cows jumped the creek with ease. I stopped singing and very, very slowly dismounted. My pickle and my pickle vats just weren't about to do any bouncing for awhile. I tied up the horse, and then very, very slowly and all hunched over, I walked back to the cows.

I guess that, except for the jump, I had been so busy having fun that I had stopped concentrating on drags. Where these other two had been hiding, I hadn't the slightest idea. All I knew right now was that, in general, cows must really lack appreciation for fine music. I inspected the calf first, who was fine, but a little tuckered out from the run and jump. I moved in for a closer look at the other two strays. They, too, were fine, but… they weren't ours! One was a sixteen hundred pound Pinzgauer with a RRRR brand on her white backside. I recognized this brand as being from the Quadruple R Ranch. The other new recruit was a tough looking, rust-colored Limousin bull with MOM branded on his rump. Looking at this bull, you had to wonder whether this really was a brand or whether it was possibly a tattoo?

All I knew was that I was almost shot once for rustling. Well, B.B was almost shot once. But no matter, I wasn't about to be accused again. I walked up to the calf and, since I was already in the leaning position, I put my mouth up to her ear.

"Onward Christian Soldier," I sang very quietly. And although she was still exhausted, that calf crept along with me as I began to walk while still singing sour nothings into her ear. Soon, we were out of the other cows' hearing ranges.

I gave both myself and the calf a little breather as I went and retrieved You Romantic You. My throat was getting a little dry, but I figured that we were about halfway to Nebetts Hunter Camp and the herd. I oh so carefully climbed into the saddle and tried to sit, but the vats were not yet ready to be disturbed. I figured that I'd just have to ride standing in my stirrups for awhile. So, standing not quite tall in the saddle while mutilating "Onward Christian Soldier" for the thirty-fifth time, me, my horse and the OM branded stray departed for Nebetts Hunter Camp. The nice slow walk got us within view of the camp around about noon. The only event enroute worth mentioning was that me and You Romantic You were almost run over on an unimproved road by some guy who was really hauling ass. But it turned out that because he was busy pulling his mules, he just didn't see us crossing. And once he realized what had happened, he immediately stopped and apologized.

We approached camp by way of the herd, where I dropped off the stray simply by not singing anymore. I rode off as the poor, bewildered calf came out from under my siren-like spell. I took the cotton out from You Romantic You's ears and placed it back in my saddle bag for future use.

I arrived in camp, a little hoarse on a big horse. I tied up You Romantic You with the other horses and walked over to where all the others, with the exception of Pa and B.B., were standing. No one seemed particularly happy.

"Hey guys," I said raspily as I approached. Only Willie looked up.

"Hey yerself," Willie grunted.

"I found myself a stray," I said. "Actually, I found myself three strays, but only one was ours."

"Good fer you," Willie grunted.

"What's wrong?"I asked.

"Lunch," Willie replied. "That's what's wrong."

"It's not grub again, is it?" I asked, curling up my nose.

"No, it ain't," Willie answered. "It's Bull's Tail Soup. B.B. couldn't find what he did with the grub. But lucky fer us, he said, he had kept the tail that had popped off of that thar bull. Yeah, real lucky fer us. Had I known that I was gonna be fed soup made from some tail that dragged Tiny Bob a mile 'fore poppin' off, I wouldn't a hid the grub!"

From behind the chuck wagon, Pa came walking over.

"It's all fixed, Boys," Pa said. "I talked to B.B. and I told 'im that while we all sure do appreciate his gourmet cookin' and his fine experimentatin', well, when ya get right down to it, we're all just a pretty borin' bunch".

"What'd he say?" Little Ben asked.

"Oh, he readily agreed," Pa said. "I said, `then thar's no sense wastin' yer gourmet meals on us. Why don't ya just cook us simple thins for simple people'."

"What did he say to that?" Willie asked.

"Cow Pucks!" Pa replied kinda sheepishly. "He said, `Ya'll just don't like eatin' bugs and tails. But I ain't 'bout to go wastin' my talents and bustin' my butt tryin' to prepare ya'll fer fine cuisine like ya'll find in New York. No, I'll stick to makin' ya grits and chicken fried steak and pork chops'."

Smiles broke out all around. I even saw a smile on Tiny Bob's face, but I think that was because they had leaned him up against a big old tree with some big old bark, and by shifting his weight from foot to foot, he found that he could have his back scratched.

"Now, it's gonna be a while 'fore lunch," Pa continued. "B.B.'s gotta dump that soup and start over." We all sat down on some logs that surrounded an ash-filled pit where many a fire had burned. Pa pulled out some chewing tobacco from his vest pocket, put some in his mouth and then offered it around. Willie, Clint and Big Bill took some. Little Ben was already busy chewing, so he declined. Then the pouch got to me.

I had never tried chewing tobacco before. I had always believed that it was only meant for real cowboys, and, before yesterday, I had never felt like a real cowboy. But I had always wanted to try it, although I didn't particularly like the color it stained your teeth.

I stared at the pouch, full of the brown shreds from which was derived such descriptive words as tobacco juice, spit, chaw and wad. I then looked at Pa. Pa smiled and noddingly gave me his approval.

"Just a pinch now, Bert Boy," Pa said.

"And put it 'tween yer cheek and gum," Willie said as Clint pulled down his lip to demonstrate, thus exposing his bluish black lower gum. It looked like it had been in a fist fight and had been beaten to a pulp. But in reality, it was the proud mark of a chaw chewin' real cowboy.

I carefully followed their directions, putting a little bit inside my mouth. Then, with a grin that would make a man check his zipper, I leaned back, tilted my hat and started to chew.

The first chew tasted like a combination of tar, sticks, hair, rubber and gum that had been dropped in dirt and oil, and I almost puked…But I liked it, I really did. Everyone was looking at me for my reaction, so I gave a little smile.

"Um, goo schtuff," I said as something yellow dribbled down my bandana.

Pleased, everyone else sat back to enjoy their snuff and wait for lunch. I took another chew. My stomach sent the signal to my mouth to send that stuff back from where it came, but I stubbornly kept my lips closed. I then took a couple of quick chews, hoping to outwit the taste.

Willie threw a tin can into the center of the pit. Everybody took aim and tried to hit it with their tobacco sludge. Everybody, that is, but me. I rolled my head around pretending to admire Nebetts Hunter Camp. Although my head was swarming and my eyes were seeing waves and fuzz, the camp looked like it was it situated in a big clearing in the middle of a fairly dense portion of the forest. About a hundred yards from the pit was a log cabin. I guess it was used for shelter in case of bad weather and for sleeping during hunting season. In front of the cabin was an old stone well. B.B. had pulled the chuck wagon up next to it. I noticed that, all around, the foilage was very green, and turning greener and greener with every chew.

"Ya okay?" Little Ben asked me.

"Fine, jes fine," I said closing my mouth after every word for fear of what might happen otherwise. "Goo schtuff."

The game of spit on the can went on for what seemed like an eternity. Finally, the sound of B.B.'s bell rose above the sound of the hocks.

"Lunch," B.B. shouted. "Git yer no taste butts over to the wagon."

Everybody got up and walked over, arguing over who hit the can the most. Well, I should say that almost everyone walked over. Big Bill carried Tiny Bob over. And as for me, when everybody was behind the wagon, I got up and ran a staggered path into the forest and did what I had to do.

Eventually, I was able to stumble over to the wagon. B.B. had prepared roast beef sandwiches. You could tell by B.B.'s disposition that he was none to pleased to be serving this meal.

"Ya got tobaccee juice all over yer shirt," B.B. snarled as he saw me approaching. "Clean yerself up, then take yer sandwich and git."

I shook my head. "I'm not hungry, B.B.," I said.

"Did ya hear that," B.B. shouted to the others as he put his arm around my shoulder. "Even Tinier Bert ain't hungry. He musta had his heart set on Grub and Bull tail soup. Ya all see what a little education could do fer ya!"

I didn't say anything. I just watched B.B. go in and out of focus.

I still felt woozy by the time we packed up and left camp. The only thing good about this feeling was that it had completely taken my mind off of my injured pickle and pickle vats.

I was grateful that my job called for me to lag far behind the herd. I would never had been able to explain why I had to repeat-

edly dismount You Romantic You on absolutely no notice and run
to the nearest pine or hardwood. And these turned out to be the
bright spots of my afternoon. I guess anyone whose horse exploded
first thing in the morning should have realized that today just was-
n't going to be his day. So much for the old adage about starting off
your day with a bang.

While still in the dense pineywoods surrounding Nebetts
Hunter Camp, we came across some of the wildlife indigenous to
the area. We couldn't have been lucky enough to cross paths with
some nice silent deer or quietly soaring bald eagles. No, we had to
run into a flock of red-cockaded woodpeckers. These birds immediately took a liking to me and You Romantic You and decided to follow us clear to Winters Bayou, making sure to peck each and every
single solitary tree enroute. Fifty or so busy little hammers and their
accompanying echos flying from tree to tree made my already
aching head feel like it was ready to spontaneously combust. I
yelled at them to stop, which resulted in a group bird laugh before
continuing with their mission to drill tiny holes just to annoy me.
They knew that they were an endangered species, so that there was
absolutely nothing I could do.

I don't have to tell you how happy I was to finally come out of
the dense forest and lay my still unsteady eyes on Winters Bayou.
That is, until I saw, standing in the middle of the Bayou and staring
into the water, that same stupid calf!

You may say, "Ah, C'mon Even Tinier Bert. All cows look
alike". Maybe to you, the layman or laywoman reader. But when
you've lived on a ranch as long as I had, you reach the point where
you can recognize individual animals. And throw in the fact that I
had spent a good portion of my morning and voice crooning this
cow, and I had no doubt about which calf this was.

You Romantic You and me approached my positively identified calf, who seemed somehow stuck in the shallow water and
mud. How any animal could get stuck in one inch of mud and three
inches of semi-still water was beyond me. I guess what we had here
was just one really stupid calf. So, as a smile crossed my face for the
first time all afternoon, I decided to name the calf Albert Einsteer.

"Well, Albert," I squeaked through my sore throat. "We know
what has to be done now, don't we? But how about a little varia-
tion?"

Albert remained staring into the water. I laughed because Albert probably thought he had found another calf in the bayou, unless of course, he was fishing for bass. I placed the cotton back into You Romantic You's ears.

"Oh when the Saints, come marching in," I strained as I turned You Romantic You and headed her to the far bank. "Oh when the Saints come marching in. How I'd love to be in their number. When the Saints come marching in."

I turned my head back and was quite surprised to find that Albert had not moved. But I was even more surprised to see a black bass hanging out of Albert's mouth.

"Well, if that doesn't beat all," I said to myself as I turned my horse around and headed back to Albert.

"Didn't you like that song?" I asked Albert. But Albert just stood there with that fish flapping in his mouth. Maybe he just didn't hear me, I thought.

"Oh when the Saints, come marching in," I sang again. "Oh when the Saints come marching in." No reaction whatsoever from Albert, although the fish seemed to take in the beat.

"Let's try something else," I said. "Happy birthday to you. Happy Birthday, dear Albert. Happy birthday to you." Again, no reaction from Albert, while the bass' face seemed to say "thanks for remembering, but my name's not Albert."

I sighed. I dreaded the inevitable. But I had no choice. So, I sighed again.

"Onward Christian Soldier," I sang dejectedly. Albert immediately dropped my much more well-rounded audience back into the bayou as the hypnotized gaze once again appeared on his face. Continuing with what was quickly becoming my least favorite tune, I turned You Romantic You and shook the reins. The road company of the Grangerland Understudy Choir and my sole groupie slowly exited the bayou and returned to the trail leading to Big Woods Hunter Camp.

It was going t o be a long, long afternoon.

11

BY THE TIME I APPROACHED Big Woods Hunter Camp early that evening, I was leading a procession of twelve cattle, with Albert at the front. All twelve cows were of different breeds, colors and ranch brands. It reminded me of some sorta cattle delegation to the U.N.

But I wasn't going to be worried about returning these cows now. Besides my throat hurting, I was tired, hungry, hurting, dirty and smelly. I was barely able to drop these cattle off in the back of the herd. Maybe overnight, they'd return from where they came on their own. And if they didn't, well, I knew that I wasn't a rustler. I'd figure out something. It would just have to wait until morning.

I tied up You Romantic You with the other horses and went straight to the chuck wagon. Slurps, chomping, gnashs and gulps emanating from the area surrounding the campfire told me that dinner was already in progress.

"Even Tinier Bert," B.B. said as I approached. "Ya look tired, hungry, hurting, dirty and smelly. But let me tell ya somethin', yer pa certainly got himself a grade A sperm thar when he sent you a swimmin'." I took this as a compliment.

B.B. dished out a plate of food for me. "Musta been one rough day lookin' fer strays," he continued.

I tried to answer, but only strange Cyrus H. Squirrel-like chirps came out. I pointed to my throat.

"Lost yer voice, huh?" B.B. said and then smiled as he handed me the plate. "Well, that's sorta good fer the rest of us since we're a plannin' on singin' 'round the fire tonight. But, here, this should help ya. It ain't grub, which I know'll disappoint ya, but its real good anyhow." I glanced down and on my plate were sweet potatoes, okra and what looked to be fried fish.

"It's black bass," B.B. continued. "Strangest thin I ever did hear. Eugene brought 'em to me. He said after crossin' some bayou, well, ever single cow had a fish in its mouth. 'Course, I had to throw most of 'em back 'cause I barely got me room to keep them bald chickens let alone five thousand cow-caught black bass. But, thar's plenty more here if ya want seconds."

B.B. looked at his watch and frowned. He raised his brows, then quickly looked in all directions, as if to see if anyone else but me was around. Certain that we were alone, he quickly set the hands of his watch back a few minutes.

"Go ahead and eat," he whispered. "And take yer time."

Sure that B.B. would not understand a Squirrel chirped "thank you", I just smiled. I took my meal and walked over to the campfire.

I could tell by the dispositions of the rest of the Old Miss company that they were extremely happy with the plain old fish dinner. They were carrying on about some forest ranger who had stopped them and had asked to see their grazing permit. In the meantime, Tiny Bob appeared to be able to bend a bit. He was over by the fire, sucking on red hot coals to see how big he could get his lips to swell.

"Even Tinier Bert," Willie said as I entered the light of the fire. "Ya almost missed yerself one fine meal."

"One fine meal," Clint nodded in agreement as a fish bone hung precariously from his chin.

"Cows caught 'em," Little Ben said.

"Did ya ever see such a thin?" Big Bill asked. 'Course, I had, but I wasn't able to respond.

"See, Pa," Big Bill continued. "Told ya he'd be speechless."

"Well, it was mighty strange," Pa said. "Anyway, Bert Boy, sit down and eat. Ya look awfully tired, hungry, hurtin', dirty and smelly."

I chose a spot near Clint, figuring that if I really did smell, he couldn't say anything about it until someone else did. I started eating like I was at the once a month Sunday buffet at Claudia's Beauty School and Culinary Institute, where the sign in the window read, "Gorge Yerself 'Til Ya Pop! $4.99".

"We were stopped by a Park Ranger this afternoon," Willie said, turning to me. "Said we needed a permit to take the cattle on through."

"To do anythin' nowadays ya gotta have a damn license or permit or certificate," B.B.said, entering the circle of cowboys seated around the fire.

"Does that mean I couldn't a been born without a birth certificate?" Big Bill asked. There was dead silence. I glanced over to Pa, who was looking around in the hopes that someone else would field this question.

Luckily, at that instant, Big Bill happened to turn in Tiny Bob's direction. "Gawd Almighty," Big Bill said. "Lookee at the size of them lips."

Sure enough, Tiny Bob's lips were now so large that he probably could have sucked in a whole chicken, although I wasn't about to give him any ideas. They resembled two boiled hot dogs which had burst open from overcooking. The only positive thing about them were that they had taken Big Bill's mind completely off of the subject of his birth certificate.

'Course, Big Bill's birth certificate, in particular, was kinda interesting. He was so large at birth that Doc Buford had him down as twins. To solve the problem, Ma and Pa named both twins "Bill". Now everybody understands that this was done just so they wouldn't have to tear up the certificate and write a new one. Not that Doc Buford was lazy, mind you, but Infant Bill had laid down the best footprints ever seen on a certificate and it would have been a real shame to waste them. Anyway, everybody understood why Ma and Pa did what they did, with the one exception of Big Bill. And unfortunately, to this day, Big Bill sometimes talks to himself thinking that he's talking to his twin brother.

"Bob Boy," Pa said. "Ya best put some cold water on them lips of yers."

Tiny Bob slowly walked over to the stone well, where he drew up the wooden pail and took a drink. Sssssssss! Steam came off his lips.

"So, Eugene, did the Ranger sell ya that damn permit?" B.B. asked.

"Bought that and a box of chocolate covered peanut butter Ranger cookies that he was sellin'," Pa answered. "Look, we just ain't gonna git in trouble with the law. Never have, never will. 'Sides, we might have ourselves enough trouble when E. Lester finds a good part of his collateral missin'".

"Well....I guess I agree," B.B. said begrudgingly. "But why'd ya buy the cookies?"

"Seems the National Forest Service's got this new fat spokes-animal named Woodsey the Owl who's cuttin' into some of their old mascot, Smokey the Bear's territory," Pa said. "The older Park Rangers ain't happy 'bout it neither, so thar secretly sellin' cookies to raise money fer a campaign to git rid of this stupid, make-believe Woodsey character."

"I see their point," Little Ben said.

"Yeah," Willie jumped in. "Who wants thar kids worshippin' a fake cartoon hero when ya got yerself a real live bear who wears a helmet and overalls?"

"And talks!" Big Bill exclaimed. I readily agreed, out of patriotism and my hatred of fictional characters.

"This calls fer cookies fer dessert," B.B. said, moved by the topic at hand. "We gotta help Smokey."

"I put 'em in the wagon," Pa said. "Under my sleepin' bag."

B.B. got up and walked back to the chuck wagon. I took my plate and followed. I helped myself to another piece of fish as B.B. watched.

"Look, time's up, Even Tinier Bert," B.B. said and then whispered. "So, why don't ya sorta wander off where I can't see ya eatin'? What I don't know ain't a gonna hurt me, right? But ya gotta promise not to tell anyone."

I smiled and nodded.

"And I'll leave ya a cookie when I find 'em, 'kay?" B.B. said as he winked and turned to search for the cookies.

Before I left, I grabbed my sleeping bag out of the wagon. In case I fell asleep, I didn't want to wake up with a fresh batch of painful red rock indentations all over my body. With sleeping bag and fish in hand, I wandered away from the campsite.

The moon and stars lit the way through the trees. I guess I had walked about five minutes out of camp when I found myself a nice grassy area. I propped myself up under a towering pine and ate my seconds, my brain unable to do much more than figure out the location of the fish on my plate and a way for my hand to lift it to my mouth.

I used the last bit of energy I had left to run a quick check for scorpions. Satisfied that the area was scorpion-free, I unrolled my sleeping bag and plopped down. It was only a matter of seconds before I fell asleep — just long enough to hear the Old Miss company starting to sing an old ranch favorite, "We're Gonna Get Cookies!"

12

"Rustlers!" B.B. shouted. "Rustlers!"

B.B.'s cries woke me immediately. I sprang out of my sleeping bag and started running toward the campsite. The sun was peeking out just enough so I could see where I was going.

"I saw 'em," I heard B.B. continue. "Three masked thiefs on horses. They took off with some of the cattle."

I then heard Little Ben say, "Let's git 'em". I quickly changed directions and started running toward the herd.

"To the horses," I heard Pa shout. I quickly changed directions and started running toward the horses.

"Put that thin down, B.B.," I heard Willie scream. "Yer too far away to shoot." I quickly changed directions and dove behind a nearby bush.

BAM!

The shotgun blast echoed throughout the woods- BAm Bam bam bam bam bam ba b — until it was no more.

"B.B.!" I heard Willie shout. "Ya almost winged me!"

"Ya almost winged me!" I heard Clint yell.

"No, yer bleedin'!" I heard Big Bill shout. "Don't ya feel it?"

"Yeah," I heard Clint answer.

"Then why didn't ya say ya were hit?" Willie shouted. Of course, Clint didn't know what to say.

"What's that Tiny Bob's got?" Pa shouted.

"It's a red-cockaded woodpecker!" Willie yelled. "Gawd almighty, B.B.! Ya kilt a red-cockaded woodpecker!"

"That's trouble," Little Ben shouted.

"What 'bout Clint's arm?" I heard Big Bill ask.

"We'll worry 'bout that later," I heard Willie reply. "B.B.'s done kilt a member of an endangered species!"

"How 'bout the rustlers?" B.B. shouted.

"We'll have to let 'em go," I heard Pa say. "We gotta do somethin 'bout the bird."

At that point, I figured I could be more useful than crouching behind a bush.

"Pa," I shouted, scaring myself with the strength of my own voice. I hadn't figured on my voice being back by today, but a sound sleep sometimes worked small miracles. Take Lulu Bell Davis for instance. Lulu Bell told a story that before she moved to Grangerland from up north, she lived with a very cranky, bitter old aunt. This wasn't by Lulu Bell's choice either. One day, her aunt just decided to quit the good life of trapping wart hogs and moved on in.

Anyway, one morning sometime thereafter, Lulu Bell awoke from a sound sleep to find that her aunt was gone. She had just plain vanished. Lulu Bell's prayers had been answered and the townspeople, who really couldn't stand the old wench either, proclaimed that a small miracle had occurred.

Now, it turned out that that same day, someone found bear tracks leading up to Lulu Bell's house. But the fact that the bear had chosen Lulu Bell's house rather than some other was itself a small miracle. And when it was found that the door to Lulu Bell's house had been left unlocked and slightly ajar, well, that too was a small miracle. Lulu Bell had never ever forgotten to close and lock the door in the past! So it was a small miracle that this night in particular she had had a mental lapse. Finally, when traces of honey were found leading into Lulu Bell's house, up the stairs and into her aunt's bedroom, the small miracle was declared a large miracle. You see, Lulu Bell's hobby happened to be house cleaning. So, this had to have been the one time in Lulu Bell's life when she had dropped honey in the house and had not cleaned it up immediately. Sound sleep and small miracles? I've believed in them ever since.

"Bert Boy, is that you?" Pa said.

"Yeah, Pa," I shouted. "I'm not too far from the horses. Why don't I go and check the herd."

"Good idear," Pa shouted back.

I got up and ran toward the horses. I now had the major task of determining how many head of cattle had been taken. Feeling the weight of this responsibility, I jumped on You Romantic You, then dismounted and untied her and jumped back on her again.

We loped over to the herd. The rustlers were now long gone with who knows how many cattle. Do you?

Neither did I, so I began the long count. I sectioned the cattle off into groups of five — four in a row, then one diagonally placed on top. I know it sounds crazy, but having one cow placed on top of the other four made for nice compact little cow bundles to count. Also, since you already know how uncooperative cattle could be, this way if one of the five decided to wander while I was counting, well, the whole bundle would have to wander, and it's a whole lot easier to see a wandering pile of cattle in the forest.

It took me an hour and a half to finish the count. And there were cattle missing alright. Nine to be exact. The rustlers had stolen the U.N. delegation!

I had totally forgotten that, in my exhaustion of the previous evening, I had left the nine foreign cows at the back of the herd, deciding that I'd figure out what to do with them when I awoke. Well, the rustlers had solved my problem for me!

Happily, I unbundled the cows and rode back to camp to deliver the news. I arrived to find the Old Miss company standing around a small mound of dirt. Stuck in the dirt was a make-shift tombstone. It read, "Here lies a Dead Bird. It was a Red-Cockaded Woodpecker, which was shot by accident and for which we are truly sorry. But, if it will make you feel any better, we also shot one of our own men." It was signed with the OM brand and dated September 25, 1987.

I felt sorry for the little bird. Then I remembered that it could have been one of the ones near Winters Bayou. This made me feel a little better.

Willie saw me walking towards the group. "I suggested just pluckin' the thin and writin' "chicken" on its side," Willie whispered. "I figured then we could fool 'em into thinkin' it was one a our birds…But ya know yer pa. That tombstone was his idear."

"How's the herd?" Pa asked.

"All accounted for," I said.

"Ya sure?" B.B. said with an extremely puzzled look on his face.

"I used the bundle system," I said.

"Ain't no mistakes then," Little Ben said.

"Well, hell, I know what I saw," B.B. snorted. "And my peepers don't lie. Them rustlers got some cattle!"

"Yes, they did," I said with a smile. 'Course, this statement confused just about everyone. The only one it didn't confuse was Tiny Bob, who was too busy taking some recently found tree sap, rubbing it on the top of his head and creating little hair spikes.

I looked away from my brother, whose head now really made him look like a Bob Mine, and explained the entire herd situation to the others. When I finished, everyone was laughing, except for Tiny Bob, who ran off thinking that we were laughing at him.

"Bert Boy," Pa said. "While I can't say that yer methods are the same ones my pa taught me, I gotta say that yer gettin' fine results. Yep, Son, yer developin' into one fine stray finder."

I turned bright red as all the remaining members of the Old Miss came over and slapped my back. The last one to do so was Clint. He had his left hand placed over a spot on his upper right shoulder, which was the same color as my face.

"How's the arm?" I asked him.

"Damn," Willie said slapping himself in the forehead. "Clint, we forgot all 'bout yer gunshot, didn't we?" Clint nodded.

"Give me a gander," Little Ben said. 'Course we all took this to mean a quick look rather than a male goose. The reason I mention this is that Doc Buford had a gander that was an expert in removing bullets. Whenever Doc Buford said that he was going to have a gander, you weren't quite sure what he meant, unless, of course, you weren't there to see him for a bullet wound. Although, last I heard, that gander was getting pretty good at delivering babies too.

Clint took his hand away from the wound. Big Bill carefully helped him off with his shirt. We all stared at the little hole in Clint's upper right shoulder. To me, it resembled a little oil gusher which hadn't been capped, except that the little gurgling oil was red in color.

"Should be capped," Little Ben said.

"I got an idear," B.B. said and ran off.

"We gotta do somethin to git the bullet out 'fore we can stop the bleedin'," Pa said. "Looks like ya lost a lot of blood already. Are ya feelin' weak?" Clint didn't answer.

"Yeah, I'm feelin' weak," Willie said.

"Yeah, I'm feelin' weak," Clint said.

"I wish we woulda thought to bring a gander," Pa said. "How could we have forgotten somethin so basic?"

B.B. came running back over. "How 'bout tryin' this?" he asked holding up a bald chicken.

"It's no gander," Little Ben said as he took the chicken from B.B. "But I'll try."

"Is it sterile?" Pa asked.

"Boiled the beak," B.B. replied.

"Okay," Little Ben said as he moved close to Clint. "Big Bill, hold Clint." Big Bill tightly wrapped his arms around Clint's stomach.

"When I say `now', imitate a worm" continued Little Ben turning to Willie. "Like the worm's in the wound."

" `kay," Willie said as he went and stood behind Clint's right shoulder.

"This might hurt," Little Ben said, looking at Clint. "Never used a chicken 'fore."

Little Ben pulled his bandana up over his mouth and moved the chicken's head close to the wound. Without the feathers, it was fairly easy to manuever this two-legged surgical instrument into position.

"Steady," Pa said.

"Careful," B.B. said.

I didn't say anything. I just watched the miracle of modern medicine at work.

"Now!," Little Ben said moving the chicken within a quarter inch of the wound.

Willie began to make undulating sounds from behind Clint's right shoulder. Little Ben squeezed on the chicken's stomach. "Look, worm!" he shouted.

All of us joined in, pointing and shouting, "Worm, worm, worm, worm, worm, worm!"

Little Ben squeezed a little harder, but it wasn't really necessary. That old bald bird had already zeroed in on its prey. It gave a mighty squawk and went right for the middle of the red oil field. One quick peck and it was over.

Now, the whole thing happened so fast that Clint wasn't sure if the chicken hadn't missed. You can understand his concern too. Chickens aren't known for having particularly great eye sight, or we'd probably have adopted the expression "chicken- eyed" rather than "eagle-eyed". And, we were dealing with a bird which was neither medically educated nor clinically trained. So, while I can't quite say the chicken was a quack, we were dealing with a bird of unknown skill.

But there it was for all to see. There was the chicken, just as proud as it could be, with a slug in her mouth.

"B.B., take Clint over to the wagon and dress the wound," Pa said.

"C'mon, Clint," B.B. said as he turned and headed towards the wagon.

"And Ben Boy," Pa said. "That was a mighty fine bit of doctorin'."

"Thanks," Little Ben said.

"And it looks like we found us a mighty fine bullet removin' bird too," Pa said. "Paint a red cross on her side and keep `er."

"Right," Little Ben said as he turned and left.

"And Willie, mighty fine worm impression thar," Pa said.

"Thanks, Mr. Henry," Willie replied.

"And Bill Boy," Pa said.

"Yes, Pa?" Big Bill responded.

"Ya did a mighty fine job holdin' Clint," Pa said.

"Thanks, Pa," Big Bill responded.

"But, Son, B.B. can't fix up Clint's wound as long as he's still here and yer still a bear huggin' `im," Pa said. "So, I think ya can let `im go now."

"Right, Pa," Big Bill said, releasing his grip on Clint. Clint turned and walked towards the wagon.

Pa then turned to me. "And Bert Boy," Pa said.

"Yes, Pa?" I answered, not sure why I was about to receive praise when I hadn't done anything.

"Ya told us a mighty fine story `bout the rustlers which got us to laughin'," Pa said, before lowering his voice. "Ya see, it was probably a blessin' that Bob Boy thought we was laughin' at 'im and ran off. Otherwise, who knows what coulda happened durin' surgery. Bob Boy mighta snuck up behind Clint and popped a bag right durin' a crucial moment and then we woulda had to be removin' both a bullet and a dead chicken's beak from that thar wound."

"Now, praisin' ya fer tellin' a fine story might seem like some sorta made-up praise to ya," Pa continued, returning to his normal tone of voice. "But ya know that I don't praise just fer the sake a praisin', even if I'm a praisin' everbody. No, Bert Boy, this is a sincere praise. Ya see, tellin' a mighty fine story is another characteristic of a real cowboy. Yer gettin' thar, Son, yer gettin' thar."

"Thank you, Pa," I said, feeling as if I had just gotten bingo at Preacher Jim Earl's Wednesday night bingo games to raise money to treat bingo addiction. I felt the same euphoria as if I had been the first to bolt from my chair and shout "bingo". 'Course, I realized this feeling wouldn't last (which was why people want to keep the feeling and wind up playing two, three, four even five cards a night), but it was lingering longer. No, this wasn't bingo, but life imitating bingo. Not until I filled every slot of my real cowboy card would I be able to retain my real cowboy feeling. Still, with Pa's comment, I felt that I had succeeded in filling another space. After a day and a half, I was making Pa proud and I knew that I had cause to be proud of myself too.

"Let's git a movin'," Pa shouted. "We gotta pick up some time. I'm gonna go find Bob Boy. The rest a ya pack up and head on out."

With the feeling of a real cowboy still with me, I dashed towards You Romantic You and took a mighty leap into the saddle. Well, I couldn't tell you where Tiny Bob was now, but I did find out where he had been. There was sap in the saddle! All real cowboy feelings vanished immediately. Obviously, I was still too immature to fill the space on my real cowboy card marked, "Foregoing Childish Revenge Against A Certain Sibling". No, this slot would have to be filled later. I trotted over to the wagon to see if I could be of any help, mainly because there wasn't much else to do, being stuck in the saddle. Clint had a bandana wrapped around his arm covering the wound and was using a piece of rope as a sling. I think that this rope was a little too heavy though, because Clint didn't seem to be able to lift his head, and his chin was deeply embedded in his chest. I didn't say anything about it figuring that it was best to leave the doctoring to Little Ben, B.B. and the chicken.

The only thing B.B. needed me to do for him was to douse the fire. It seems that because of the events of the morning, we weren't going to be having breakfast. But not to despair, B.B. told us that we'd be enjoying a fine brunch.

It cost me a good portion of the seat to some fine dungarees, but I was finally able to pry myself out of my saddle. As I walked over to the camp's well, I could hear Willie singing as he rode off to join the herd, "Nine hundred ninety nine thousand five hundred and ninety eight bottles of beer on the wall, nine hundred ninety nine thousand five hundred and ninety eight bottles of beer. If one of those bottles happen to fall…"

After dousing the fire, I walked back over to the wagon as Pa and Tiny Bob came riding through. I saw at once that Bob the barber had gotten hold of Fido's mane. Her beautiful hair had been shaped into ugly little sap spikes.

"How's yer butt?" Tiny Bob shouted. I shot him a look of total disgust, but I would have preferred to have just shot him.

Pa stopped Ma next to Clint.

"Ya okay to ride today?" Pa asked Clint. Clint tried to nod, but his chin was still stuck in his chest.

"I think he'll be fine to ride," B.B. said.

"Bleedin' under control?" Pa asked.

"Don't see how it could git much worse," B.B. replied.

With that, Pa and Tiny Bob rode off. Hot on their heels were Big Bill and Little Ben. I climbed back onto You Romantic You and looked down at B.B.

"B.B.," I said. "Besides the fact that in one and a half days, we've killed one bird, shot one cowhand and seen a horse explode, do you think things are going pretty well?"

B.B. shrugged his shoulders and tapped his lump. "Don't harp on the past," he said. "It'll make ya lazy for the future."

I rode off thinking about B.B.'s advice and how I was going to scrape the torn-off seat of my pants from the saddle.

13

RIGHT BEFORE WE LEFT the thick forest surrounding Big Woods Hunter Camp, we ran into another Park Ranger. Pa simply showed him our drive permit and bought another box of cookies and that was that.

As usual, I lagged behind the herd. But once out of the dense pineywoods and with the sun shining brightly on the relatively open trail, I felt that it was safe to close the gap a bit. I rode just behind the dust cloud, searching for strays and scratching sap off my seat. I tried saying this five times fast just to amuse myself. I was amused, but I think I would have been more amused had the sap come off.

Well, I did not see one stray all morning, not even Albert. When I had counted the cattle earlier, I had moved Albert to the center of the herd. My guess was that Albert was now wedged in among the throng of cattle and unable to escape. Remembering what it was like to fight the crowds at the Grangerland Woolworths during their "Back To Mulching Bargain Days", I kinda felt sorry for Albert.

We crossed the East Fork of the San Jacinto River. It made me think about the Old Miss, being situated on this river's western brother and all. I figured that by now, E. Lester had been by the Old Miss. I could just picture his Eeoogie face puffing up like a stewed tomato, except without the seeds, when he realized what had happened. And, believe it or not, I felt sorta guilty. It wasn't because we may have caused the Eeoogie to suffer a stroke, but because we had snuck away from the Old Miss. True, we didn't have much choice, but the idea to leave and not come back was mine and I had never considered myself a sneaky person before.

We stopped after the crossing, and, as promised, B.B. fixed us a fine brunch. As was usually the case with his brunches, there were a few more lunch items than there were breakfast. Otherwise, B.B. says, you'd have to call the thing a "leakfast". And it's not so much that B.B. objects to that word when spoken, mainly because it's pronounced "leckfast", but when you see it written, you have to explain that it's a meal, and not some kinda control problem with one's pickle.

As we ate, Little Ben told me that he had come across a stray. He tried singing "Onward Christen Soldier", but to no avail. He wasn't sure whether his voice just wasn't soothing to the cattle or whether he had just happened upon a cow of the Hebrew persuasion, but he ended up having to lasso the critter.

And speaking of ropes around their necks, Clint seemed to be holding up. Well, at least holding up everything with the exception of his head. And the way his chin was pressed to his chest, it made it look as if he were intently studying his navel. But the important thing was that, so far, his arm seemed okay. He just wouldn't be able to signal for a touchdown any time soon.

Not that we'd have any need for being able to signal for a touchdown now, but back at the Old Miss, well, we were right up there with most other Texans when it came to football. You're born with it in your genes. And that's probably why Texas is the only state whose constitution specifically enumerates the right to play football. 'Course, the legislature has also declared May 17th, the day some guy first stuck shoelaces through a pigskin, a state holiday. The story goes, however, that it was actually the fellow's wife's idea to use the pigskin. She had watched her husband and his friends attempt to toss the whole pig and catch the squealing projectile. But it was the noise the critter made upon being spiked after a touchdown that convinced her that there had to be a quieter way to play the game.

Football season was the only time of the year when it was tough living on the Old Miss. Like I've told you before, we couldn't pick up any t.v. or radio signals, and in Texas, there were as many teams to watch as there were people. (This was another enumerated right- one football team per person.) Now, someone in Grangerland once suggested that we could solve our problems by getting a satellite dish for the ranch, but B.B. said that we had enough old plates laying around as it was.

So, we had to be content playing tackle football among ourselves. The teams were always me, Pa, Big Bill and Tiny Bob against Little Ben, Willie, B.B. and Clint. And you know how on every team, there was that one person who would have been declared a spy if this were a war? Well, they had Clint and we had Tiny Bob. Even after a huddle, Clint could not remember the pattern he was supposed to run. So, he'd usually follow right behind Willie, often tripping him from behind by accident. We'd also only have to use one defender to cover the tandem receivers. As for Tiny Bob, he just liked the tackling part of football. He would tackle whoever had the ball no matter what team that person was on. And if he had the ball, well, he'd just tackle himself.

I have to tell you, though, that we would go in to Grangerland every Friday afternoon to watch the Grangerland High Nadswerfs play. The team was named for the first coach they ever had, Gipper Nadswerf, from whom, I'd like it known, the famous expression, "Win one for the Nadswerf" came. I was usually proud of the team and its name, except when it came to the cheer, "Go Nads". But since I was the only one who seemed to feel that there was something wrong with this, I kept quiet.

The reason I've gone into great lengths about football is that after brunch, as the herds crossed McCombs Creek, one of the lead cows picked up, as unbelievable as it might sound, a football that just happened to be sitting on the opposite bank and started running. That darn cow must have thought it was a Texas Longhorn.

The cow ran right past Clint, who took off after the crazy critter. Clint tried to use his Pickle to direct the ball carrying cow back onto the trail, but that cow just kept on running. This sorta put Clint in a pickle on a Pickle. With one arm out of commission, Clint couldn't hold the reins and toss his lasso at the same time. If only he could have lifted his head a little, he might have been able to wedge the reins in between his chin and chest. But since this was not an option, Clint had only one choice.

Clint jumped off of his Pickle and landed on the cow's back. He wrapped his left arm around the cow's neck and wrestled the fleet-hoofed animal down. As the cow hit the ground, she dropped the ball. Clint left the grounded animal and pounced on the ball. Little Ben, who saw the whole thing, rode over and declared the play dead. Little Ben's reasoning was that while it was true that

Clint had made a legal tackle, the ground had actually caused the fumble.

"That was a good call," said a gentleman stepping out from behind some thick brush. "Or should we have an official replay?"

Before we could respond, the stranger continued. "No, let the play stand! How do you do? I'm Bart Namath, and forgive my appearance, but I've been out hiking for a long time."

As we congregated around Mr. Namath, it was obvious that he was not kidding about his hiking. His clothes were torn and tattered, stubble grew from his face and caked-on dirt covered his skin and hair. To me, he resembled an adult Tiny Bob.

"How do, Mr. Namath," Pa said, dismounting Ma. "I'm Tex Henry and these are my boys and ranch hands." We nodded accordingly.

"Call me the Dodger," said Mr. Namath as he shook Pa's hand.

"Eugene," Pa said. "I was gonna say that it looks like ya've been out here awhile.

"Yes, and there comes a time when you just start to miss good football," Mr. Namath replied.

I reckon yer right," Pa said. "It just strikes me as kinda funny that a football was just lyin' in the middle of a National Forest."

"Oh, it's mine!" Mr. Namath said gleefully. "I've been kicking it all the way from New York."

"Yer from New York?" Willie asked.

"New York City," Mr. Namath said.

"That's where we're headin' with them cattle," Big Bill said excitedly as he pointed back to the herd.

"Heard it's a meat market," Little Ben said.

The meat market! A sudden tightness gripped my chest as Mr. Namath pondered the question. A cetain conversation returned to the forefront of my mind, a conversation which had taken place back at the Old Miss, where my good intentions won out over my gut instincts. Until now, until the mention of the term "meat market," I had completely forgotten that New York might not be a meat market at all, or, at least, not one in the sense that I led Pa and the others to believe. I thought that I had plenty of time left before the truth about New York and my well-meaning deception of Pa came out. I thought wrong.

Who could have figured a chance encounter with a New

Yorker in the middle of nowhere, a New Yorker about to set the record straight one way or the other. If he confirmed my silent doubts, then the drive was about to become stranded. Yet, wasn't there a chance that Little Ben was right? He had never been wrong about anything before, and I really didn't know anything for a fact. We had both been going on hearsay and gut instincts. And since Little Ben was over twice my age, wouldn't that make his gut instincts twice as good? Maybe New York was, indeed, the type of meat market the rest believed it was, a meat market where cattle fetched a good price.

Then why was I perspiring? Because Willie had nodded to me after I had confirmed the fact that New York was nothing but a meat market, that's why. That nod had meant something.

I quickly looked over to Willie. His face exhibited a clear expression of dread. Our eyes met, and I saw the remorse.

Complete and total shame washed over me as I knew that this New Yorker was about to end the fiction about our destination, end the drive, end the Old Miss and end the Henrys.

"New York's the biggest place to sell beef in the world," said Mr. Namath.

"Yee Ha!" shouted Willie. I almost fell out of my saddle.

"Land sakes, Willie," B.B. scolded. "Ya done almost got Even Tinier Bert thrown from his saddle."

"Sorry," Willie said, his expression doing a one hundred and eighty degree turn about. "But ain't it excitin' hearin' 'bout our destination from someone whose been thar?"

"Yep," said Little Ben, a big smile on his face.

"They got stockyards there for as far as the eye can see," said Mr. Namath. "And people who are just waiting to buy all the cattle they can. They come with wads and wads of money in hand."

"We were thinkin' 'bout grazin' the herds in Central Park," said Pa.

"The perfect place," Mr. Namath said. "As a matter of fact, that's where most people keep their cattle before they take them to market."

"Is the Lincoln Tunnel a good way into the city?" Willie asked.

"Or the Martha's Vineyard Ferry," said Mr. Namath. "Either one."

"I don't right recall that first option," Pa said.

"It's a cattle boat that will take you right across the Murnsey and into Manhattan," Mr. Namath said. "Of course, you might want to consider flying in on one of the shuttles. Depending where you want to end up in the city, the Pan Am Shuttle will fly you into O'Hare Airport, while the Trump Shuttle lands in Wrigley Field."

"New York has two airports?" Willie asked.

"Believe me, it needs them both," said a very serious Mr. Namath. "You just can't imagine how much livestock arrives on a daily basis."

"Wow!" exclaimed Big Bill.

Mr. Namath glanced over to the herd. "And if you're thinking of taking this many head on one of the shuttles, I'd strongly suggest reservations."

"I reckon that we'll probably stick to our itinerary and just walk 'em into the city," Pa said as Mr. Namath nodded his approval.

"Yes, the exercise will keep them fit for market," Mr. Namath said as he lifted his shirt and patted his stomach. "Look at me, and I still have some walking left to do."

"Where ya headin'?" asked Pa.

"To Houston," Mr. Namath replied. "To the Astrodome. To the Big Game."

"Which game is that?" asked Big Bill.

Mr. Namath pondered this question a few moments before answering. "I'm not quite sure, but the people who broadcast football have declared every game the big game and every play crucial. From the first whistle, whole seasons are hanging on the balance, careers are on the line, seasoned veterans lose their spices and, if you can believe it, there I was just sitting around and doing nothing. Nothing!"

"Well, not anymore!" Mr. Namath continued. "I've got to get to Houston where they desperately need my aid. I've got to stop the horror, the destruction. I must stop the quarterbacks from throwing "the bomb". And don't you realize that any game could end in sudden death?"

Whether he meant to or not, Mr. Namath displayed a sharp contrast to our way of thinking. Not that we understood them, but Mr. Namath's concerns were obviously more worldly than ours. Here we were, like most Texans, concerned with our own well-being, while here was Mr. Namath, the philanthropist. I could only surmise that Mr. Namath was representative of all New Yorkers and that all New Yorkers looked after their fellow man. I wondered where in the many miles that laid between the Old Miss and New York the change occured and whether it was a gradual or sudden change. I was humbled by the thought that, at a minimum, New Yorkers, and perhaps the rest of the country heading east, would rather help others than themselves.

I think Pa was humbled by the generosity of this noble man too. "We'd be honored if ya'd stay and have a bite to eat with us," Pa said.

"I wish I could, but I've probably spent too much time already," Mr. Namath said. "I'm needed."

"Well, is thar anythin' we can do fer ya?" Pa asked, picking up on Mr. Namath's philosophy.

"If you can just point the way to Houston," Mr. Namath said. "Then I'll be going."

"I can't tell ya 'bout the roads, but this here cattle trail'll take ya most of the way," Pa said.

"That's perfect," said Mr. Namath. "This trail will give me the room I need to kick my ball."

Not wanting to detain Mr. Namath any longer, Pa extended his hand and said, "Well, it's been a pleasure meetin' ya, Dodger."

"Likewise," Mr. Namath said, shaking Pa's hand. He then abruptly turned and began kicking his football down the trail in the direction from which we had come.

"A fine example, boys" Pa said as we watched Mr. Namath depart. "A fine example."

"It's nice to know that New Yorkers care 'bout others," Willie said.

"Perty friendly too," Little Ben said. Cowboys have always appreciated hospitality. And after meeting Mr. Namath, I now saw why. Hospitality flowed directly to the individual. I mean, no self-sacrifice existed with receiving. I could have been ashamed by the fact that I really enjoyed other's hospitality, except that we at the Old Miss had been raised believing in hospitality reciprocity. And it was nice, if not calming to know that miles from the Old Miss, after traveling for months on end, we'd be running into friendly, hospitable people.

"Yeah, friendly," Big Bill said. "And he liked football."

"Yeah, and he didn't brag 'bout the fact that he was a doctor neither," B.B. pointed out. And that was true too. Even as he was all but gone from view, I could still make out the printing on the back of his shirt which read, Bellevue Hospital.

Now, despite the newly exposed flaw in our nature, we couldn't have been more excited. Not because our character flaws particularly excite us, but because of Mr. Namath's confirmation of New York as a meat market.

Personally, I know that Willie felt much, much better. He was probably only sorry that he had doubted Little Ben in the first place. Me, well, I just sorta felt better. While it was true that Mr. Namath had taken me off the hook, there was just something that didn't sit right. But since I really couldn't fully articulate my concern, I thought it best not to mention anything and not lose any sleep over it. I mean, maybe in the east, it is perfectly normal for a doctor to be kicking a football cross country.

14

AN EXTREMELY CHEERFUL, carefree Willie was down to nine hundred ninety nine thousand four hundred and thirty three bottles of beer on the wall by the time we crossed Palmetto creek and left the Sam Houston. A large wooden sign read, "Ya'll Are Now Leaving The Sam Houston National Forest". We appreciated this notice, mainly because the tree cover had grown so sparce, we were starting to worry that we had made a wrong turn and were now in some sorta Sam Houston National Desert. In small letters underneath this farewell, it read, "yer tax dollars at work". I guess every once in awhile, people just like to see concrete examples of where their tax money's being spent. I've heard that politicians, thinking the same thing, wanted to order shirts with this line printed on them. 'Course, in my mind, they'd have to drop the "at work" portion or risk suit for false advertising.

Next to this large sign was a smaller wooden sign which read, "The Killing Of Red-Cockaded Woodpeckers Is Strictly Prohibited. Penalties Include Fines And/Or Prison." B.B. gulped. However, in small letters underneath this warning was written, "unless it was by accident and then it's okay". B.B. breathed a sigh of relief. As me and You Romantic You walked by the warning sign, I noticed another small handpainted sign directly behind it. This one read "Death To Woodsey" (and in small letters, "yer cookie dollars at work").

With the first of many hurdles now behind us, we decided to camp on the banks of the Palmetto for the evening. Actually, we were going to travel a bit farther, but decided to stay on account of Big Bill. He thought it would be an honor to stay on the banks of a creek which was named for his breed of horse. So, rather than explain to him that his horse was a palomino and not the pimento that he thought it was, neither of which are the name of the creek, we just stopped.

As far as I was concerned, I was glad that we did. The stacking of cows first thing in the morning did me in. I was mighty thankful that I didn't have to chase a single stray all day or I just might have fallen asleep in my saddle. Why there were no strays, I hadn't a clue. Maybe it was the heavy clouds rolling in that kept the cows huddled together all day. Or the more likey reason was that Tiny Bob had probably used sap on them too, and they had no choice but to stick together.

Fortunately, there'd be no more sap for awhile. We were out of the forest and at least a two day drive from the Davy Crockett. As we sat around the campfire eating dinner, it seemed strange to be back out in open territory. The sounds of the Screech Owls had given way to chirping crickets. The large, looming trees which had surrounded us the past few nights were no more. In a way, I felt a little vulnerable. We had only the cover of darkness, the fire and everybody's, except B.B.'s, marksmanship to protect us. I found comfort only in the fact that at least I was safe from Tiny Bob pouncing on me from the upper branches of a tree.

After dinner, we discovered that Tiny Bob had gotten into the red paint and had painted red crosses on all of the chickens. Since this made identification of our medical chicken impossible, we had to hope that we wouldn't be shooting any more of our own men. 'Course, we also had to hope that if someone figured out a way to tell the birds apart, B.B. hadn't just fried and served the one we needed.

A dense fog rolled in just as we sat down around the fire. This fog was so thick that the customary evening tobacco chew was marred by miscalculations and accidental spittings on each other. 'Course, the fog did allow me to sit back and pretend to join in with everybody else. For some strange reason, I still had not yet derived the same pleasure in chewing as the others, although the aroma no longer made me lose my appetite.

As the evening progressed and the conversation went from tomorrow's itinerary to what we were going to do with the new box of cookies, it became obvious that Clint's right shoulder was growing progressively worse. At first, we thought that the howling we heard was just Tiny Bob tormenting a wolf. However, even through the dense fog, it soon became clear that the howling was coming from Clint, who must have further injured his shoulder while tackling the cow.

Pa went to the wagon and returned with a case of Shiners. It was the only case that he had had time to pack, figuring that we'd stock up in Tyler. He had told us that he was going to save it for a special occasion. Now don't get the wrong idea. I don't think that Pa was considering Clint's learning to howl a special occasion. Knowing Pa, he was probably thinking that the alcohol in the beer would help Clint to forget the pain and also help us to forget Clint's pain.

Tiny Bob proceeded to pop open all of the bottles with his teeth and the drinking began. While we drank, Pa decided that until Clint was feeling better, I would be taking his point. This sudden and unexpected promotion made my head swim…or maybe it was the beer, seeing as I was not as big a drinker as the rest. No matter, in my mind, it showed Pa's increasing confidence in me which, of course, bolstered my own confidence one more notch. I chugged the rest of my beer and took another.

As thee nite wor on and i kkept uppp boddle fer boddle width thee ress of thee Ole Misssss peeples, I thoughtt bout mY tuff, newww respons…respons…respons…job thad i had ta do startin tamorrow. Butt dun't worrie, i did'ent thinkk two mush. Ether, id got alod moore foggie or i jest past out. Butt, thee lassed theng I remem…remem…remem…recalll wass hearin everbodie else geddin drunnk and singin,"Wee're Gunna Ged Cookiezzzzzz…"

15

PLINK…PLINK…PLINK…PLINK…PLINK…

"Stop it, Tiny Bob!" I shouted, which I immediately realized was a big mistake. The throbbing in my head went into a gallop.

Plink…Plink…Plink…Plink, Plink…Plink, Plink…

"When I open my eyes, I'm going to kill you," I whispered. I had yet to open them, but I figured that here it was, the middle of night, and my idiot brother was finding fun in waking me from my beer induced sleep by tossing wet pebbles on my head. He would probably find great delight in the fact that each one rang in my ears for what seemed like forever.

Plink, Plink…Plink, Plink…Plink, Plink, Plink…Plink, Plink, Plink…

"Prepare to throw your last stone on this earth," I said as I slowly sat up and attempted to pry open my eyes.

Plink,Plink,Plink,Plink,Plink,Plink,Plink,Plink,Plink…

As I opened my swollen lids and tried to bring things into focus, I realized that I was perspiring heavily. Too heavily.

"Even Tinier Bert," I heard B.B. shout. "Git yer fool self outta the rain!"

Rain!

I looked across camp. There was Tiny Boob, happily diving into newly formed streams of mud.

For once, I couldn't blame him for my misery. Believe me, that was a strange feeling.

"Bert Boy," shouted Pa. "Yer gonna float away if ya don't git over here."

I glanced down and saw that I was laying in about an inch of water. I wondered if I just might have fallen asleep in a lake.

Probably not. I think I simply had the misfortune of passing out on a flood plane during an extremely heavy rain.

I squeezed my hands on my forehead to keep the pounding from coming out. It was something Ma taught me that she said would come in handy for hangovers when I was older. The idea was, the harder you pushed on your forehead, the less your brain could sloosh around. Now, I don't know how Ma knew about this cure because I never ever saw her drink alcohol. 'Course, I do remember Ma disappearing for hours at a time, and I seem to recall that she did have fingerprints imbedded in her forehead.

With hands on head, I dragged myself over to a make-shift tent set on slightly higher ground where everybody except Tiny Bob was standing. Nobody said a word. They were all too busy squeezing their foreheads.

The tent consisted of a very large staked sheet and, luckily, had needed a good washing for some time. Somehow, the fact that it was relatively dry under the sheet did little to comfort me. It was just hard to get excited when it was impossible to get any wetter than I was right then and there. Big Bill spoke up and suggested burning the sheet to dry us off. We all just kept quiet and pressed our heads a little harder.

I peered out from the sheet and watched the rain fall from the milk pail gray sky. I realized that I had not seen this much water since Moses Jefferson's bath tub incident.

Moses Jefferson was Grangerland's professional "proofer". Anytime anybody needed something made resistant to certain elements, well, Moses was the man they'd call. He was the best. He would not only do the job he was hired to do, but he would also try to anticipate other possible troubles. For instance, Moses was hired to "noise proof" Butch Jake Laroo's mother-in- law's bedroom. Butch Jake's mother-in-law lived with Butch Jake and she would sit in her bed and scream and nag him for hours at a time. That's when Butch Jake, near the end of his rope, called in Moses. Somewhere during the course of the job, Moses realized that the work he was hired to do would only be a temporary solution to Butch Jake's problem. So, thinking ahead and without any additional cost, Moses made a few additions. When the job was complete, Butch Jake found himself with a room which was not only noise proof, but escape proof too. And from that time on, Butch Jake never had to listen to or see his mother-in-law again.

So, it was said about Moses that the only thing he couldn't proof one hundred per cent was his moonshine. Anyway, one day Moses got a call that his workshop across town was burning down. Moses was horrified, mainly because the workshop was supposedly fire proof and this would certainly be bad for business. Moses, who was about to take a bath when he received the news, ran out of his house in such a hurry that he forgot to turn off the water in the bathtub.

When he got to the shop, he was much relieved to find that it was the rest of the block that was burning down while his structure stood unscathed. He was relieved until he returned home and found that his water proof rancher was filled to the roof. 'Course, he was still happy because not one drop of water could be found leaking out of the house, but, still, how happy could you be to find your home turned into a huge fish bowl? I mean, you could see the guppies and goldfish that used to be sitting in the living room window now swimming by the kitchen window.

The local townsmen arrived at Moses's place soon after they had put out the town fire. By then, the walls were beginning to swell. But since the house was burst proof, no one knew for sure what would happen if they couldn't get inside to turn off the faucet.

Otis Plunk volunteered to walk right up to the front door, open it and let the water out. When someone pointed out to Otis that the rush of water coming out might be too much for Otis to outswim, Otis said not to worry, he couldn't swim anyway. I think if ever given a chance, Otis and Big Bill would have had some very close debates.

A group of men then tied a rope to the front door knob and tried to pull the door open from afar. The door didn't budge, mainly because it was burglar proof. However, the rope broke and the men fell on their butts. It turns out that the knob was "Group Of Men Trying To Pull Door Open From Afar With A Rope" proof.

The men tried throwing rocks at the shatter proof windows. They even tried turning off the water main leading up to the house, which might have worked except that the job was left up to Otis and the water main was fool proof.

At that point, everyone was prepared to just sit down and

watch the house expand from a one family dwelling to a two family dwelling to a three family dwelling and so on. That's when I realized that we had among us the one contingency that Moses could not have protected himself against, because no one could. I spoke to Pa who spoke to Moses. Moses showed signs of doubt, which was more out of fear of the unknown power than anything else. But since Moses, already the father of ten, did not wish to have more children just to fit the size of his house, he gave in. 'Course, he probably wouldn't have enjoyed living underwater either.

After a brief discussion, Big Bill went trotting up to the side of the house. He removed his hat and wiped his brow. Intently, he studied the entire side wall. He lifted a blade of grass and let it go. I was impressed by Big Bill's unexpected foresight in taking the time to determine wind direction. 'Course, I later learned that that blade had simply gotten stuck between his toes and he was just getting rid of it.

Big Bill placed his hat back on his head. He moved to the dead center of the stucco wall and stopped. He stepped forward until he was no more than an arm's length away. Slowly, he lifted his right foot in the air. You could see the determination on his face. His foot showed the tension of the moment. His hamstring quivered with excitement.

Then, with one loud shout, Big Bill brought his foot crashing into the wall. As I had expected, his foot went smoothly through the wall. It looked so easy.

Big Bill withdrew his foot and water immediately began to rush out of the foot shaped hole, but this, too, was expected. What wasn't expected was the tremendous creaking of the house as the water pressure built around the hole. Then, the house began to rock on its foundation and that's about the time everybody started to run.

From the base to the roof and running directly through the hole, Moses's house parted in two. A river carrying sofas, tables, lamps, beds and clothes gushed from the split rancher. And it didn't take long for the fast flowing current to catch up to us slow running people.

I was swept away by the swift running water. Luckily, thanks to swimming lessons at the Grangerland Recreational Quarry and Strip Mine, I was able to keep myself afloat. Tiny Bob, however, came barrelling by. He was totally submerged, tumbling head over heels, and, with the force of the water, unable to right himself. Thinking quickly, I reached my hand out to grab him. 'Course, he slapped it away, made some gurgling noises which I took to be some form of laughter and kept right on going.

Pa then came floating by seated on a Lay-Z-Boy recliner and chewing tobacco. He pulled me out of the water and sat me on one of the arm rests. Together we drifted until the water reached a sorta incline and stopped. This created a little lake, which is now a tourist attraction known as the Red Lake, and touted with the slogan, "If you can't make it to the Red Sea, come look at the other water of Moses." And people come from all over to behold the miracle of Moses and the only lake in the world that is naturally stocked with guppies, goldfish and furniture. People often leave with inner peace and great bargains.

Anyway, thank goodness nobody got hurt in the flood, although we were worried because we couldn't find Big Bill for awhile. It turned out that he was still up at the house and an even bigger hero than anyone first realized. Not only did he kick the hole, but he somehow managed to stand his ground during the onslaught of water. Then, with Moses's house totally in ruins, Big Bill stepped over what was left of the wall, waded through the rub-ble and turned off the faucet.

The town honored Big Bill with a Big Bill Henry Day and a parade where no participants could wear shoes. However, to show their appreciation, the whole town showed up barefoot too. It gave ninety-eight year old Lloyd P. Kasbart a chance to use his joke that since Big Bill succeeded in getting Lloyd P.'s wife barefoot, maybe he could also help in getting her pregnant. It was funny the first four or five times I heard Lloyd P. shout it. Actually, about the sixth time, Lloyd P.'s wife, Lucinda, popped Lloyd P. over the head with her pocketbook, which killed him on the spot. While most felt that it may have been too drastic a measure on Lucinda's part, it did enable those of us standing nearby to finally be able to hear the three piece marching band.

At the conclusion of the parade and after the removal of Lloyd P., Mayor Peeper Crud brought Big Bill up to the Coca Cola crate that we called a podium. Mayor Crud gave a speech describing Big Bill's heroism and the new golf course that the mayor was planning to build near Grangerland High. He then told Big Bill that to honor this act of bravery, he had ordered a gold faucet which he would later present to him. 'Course, we all knew that there was no golf course or gold faucet. Still, on this occasion, we didn't really care. We were all just mighty proud of Big Bill.

"Ain't gonna clear," Little Ben said, watching the rain. It seemed to be raining even harder if that was possible, which it must have been because it was.

"I ain't ever seen it rain like this 'fore," B.B. said.

"Could be a hurricane," Pa said.

"Yeah," Willie said. "Hurricane Eeoogie!" Everybody chuckled, then pressed their foreheads a little more.

"Don't make no more jokes," said B.B.

There was a moment of silence as everyone waited for their throbbings to stop. "We gotta start thinkin' 'bout movin' out," Pa said with a frown. He himself wasn't particularly thrilled with his own decision. I appreciated it even less as I remembered that I was switching places with Clint at left point. The first time in my life that I was going to be riding point and it had to be during one dilly of a storm. How was I going to be able to keep all the cattle to the right of me and You Romantic You in this blinding rain?

"We'll just take it slow," Pa continued, looking my way. I guess he sensed my concern.

B.B. removed ponchos from the chuck wagon and distributed them all around. I took one even though I knew it was way too late. They'd do a poor job of keeping the new rain out, while doing a fine job of keeping the old rain in.

We trudged through the mud over to the horses. It took a great effort as the mud tried to suck off our boots with every step. What was sorta amusing was the sound that our feet made each time they were pulled from the mud — Slurp, Slurp, Slurp. 'Course, part of this was also Tiny Bob, who was smacking on a fresh mud pie. Big Bill also seemed to be enjoying himself somewhat, wiggling his toes in the muck.

The horses, on the other hand, seemed miserable, and they didn't even have hangovers. I guess it was because they smelled bad, and they knew it. Usually, the smell of a horse is just that, a smell. It is a good smell, a rugged smell, a distinct smell. It is the smell of man's other companion. But the smell of a wet horse is not a smell, but an odor. It's sharp, it's foul and it lingers. It's the type of smell that Tiny Bob strives to attain, which is why the horses were so depressed.

I mounted the very wet and smelly You Romantic You. "You can't help it," I whispered in her ear, which I think made her feel better. I shook the reins and we slurped our way over to the herd.

The herd was still, wet and smelly. 'Course, unlike horses, cattle like to be smelly. A smelly, dirty cow is usually very popular with other cows. A smelly, dirty cow is also very popular with flies, which they proudly wear like our soldiers wear ribbons.

But, on a day like this, I was actually thankful for the smell. I'd need to use everything I could to keep a line on these critters. The clouds were so low and dense and the rain was so deafening that I could not even see or hear Willie and Pa as they approached.

"It's gonna be a tough one, Bert Boy," Pa said as he trotted up. I was so startled that I may have broken out in a cold sweat, but who could tell?

"I'm sorry that we gotta throw ya on point," Pa continued, raising his voice a little so that I could hear him. "But sometimes in the show we call life, the understudy's gotta go on with no rehearsal." Now, you might be thinking "Pa the Thespian," but Pa's analogy really came from just one trip to the theatre. (Well, one trip to Grangerland High's auditorium, but there was a show being presented.)

To raise money for a new police whistle and badge, Grangerland's two big civic groups, the Grangerland Improvement Society and the Grangerland Just Patch It Up And Keep It The Same League, once put on a production of the Monarch Note's version of "Romeo and Juliet". Ma was picked to play Julie's understudy, but since there was only one performance of the piece, she and Pa figured that there was no sense rehearsing the part. Wouldn't you know it, but Tola Mae Bumwheat, who was supposed to play Julie, came down sick opening and closing night. Well, Ma quickly learned one line, "Ray, Ray, where are ya, Ray?", which she repeated everytime Julie had a line. In the end, the play took seventeen minutes, which was two minutes more culture than the audience had planned for. Yet, thanks to Ma's brilliant performance, nobody complained. So Pa, being proud of Ma and all, came up with a profound saying to mark the occasion.

"All ya gotta do is keep the cattle to yer right and keep 'em movin'," Willie shouted above the rain. "Don't worry 'bout the few that'll wander to the left. Clint'll take 'em. Remember, ya gotta be thinkin' point, not stray."

"Ben Boy can handle himself on right point, so Bob Boy will be backin' ya up," Pa said. "And Willie can double back from scoutin' or I can come up from the rear if ya need real help."

"Ya can do it," he added with a nod. I smiled and nodded back.

"It ain't a great day for hearin' or seein'," Willie said. "So use yer sense of smell 'cause if ya ain't noticed it, the cattle stink."

"Now, it'll be 'bout five to ten miles of headin' due north 'til we hit Lake Livingston," Pa said. "Then we'll be a travelin' west 'round the lake 'til the spot Willie's found fer us to cross."

Pa looked over to Willie and then up at the sky before continuing. "And I think we'll stop thar and cross tomorrow. How far do ya reckon that is total, Willie?"

"My guess is 'bout twelve to fifteen miles from here to thar, Mr. Henry," Willie replied.

Pa winked at me. "So keep it slow, 'kay?" he said. "We ain't in no hurry." And it was true. Even if we just walked the herd, the trip would take no longer than five hours. Yes, it would be five cold, wet, woeful hours, but I wouldn't have near as much pressure on me as if we were going the usual twenty-five to thirty miles.

"Good luck to yer at point," Willie said as he wiped the rain off of his limp stringy moustache. He kicked Clint's Pickle and quickly disappeared into the herd.

"Head on over to the left and I'll git the herd goin'," Pa said. I followed Pa's instructions, turning You Romantic You's head to the west and shaking the reins. We were quickly at a slow canter and soon found ourselves on the left border of the herd. I then turned You Romantic You upherd, trying to position ourselves somewhere near the midpoint before Pa started them up.

"Albert?"

Yes, through the fog and monsoon, who did I spot but Albert. He was grazing alone at a spot west from the rest. And from the looks of it, his spot just about marked the smack dab middle of the herd. It made me wonder whether this was just a very strange coincidence, or if Albert could possibly have known that I would be filling in at left point. And if the latter, why cattle find us Henry men so attractive.

Albert lifted his head and saw me. His eyes immediately widened. He then opened his mouth and showed me his cud. I took this gesture as the proper cow etiquette for a greeting between friends. And I guess that as far as cud goes, this was a pretty nice chunk. Still, I had to turn the offer down.

"Thanks anyway, Albert, but I'm not particularly hungry," I said even though I hadn't eaten any breakfast. Albert approached anyway, which made me feel a little better since I had just rejected his hospitality.

"I'm riding point today, Albert," I continued. "So, I can't serenade you if you get lost. Besides, even if I weren't riding point, you wouldn't be able to hear me over the rain. If you want, you can tag along with me and You Romantic You. But, you've got to keep pace. We can't be waiting for you. Do you understand?"

Albert mooed. I didn't know whether that was a yes or a no moo, but I didn't have time to wonder. The day's drive was beginning.

It reminded me of the bumper cars at the Paid Well Firemen's Carnival that was thrown once a year by the two firemen of Grangerland to honor the fact that they didn't have to be volunteers. It starts with the cattle in the rear. Pa gets them moving forward where they quickly bump into the cattle in front of them who had no idea that they were supposed to be moving at all. These cattle are then pushed forward and bump into cattle in front of them, who are then pushed forward and bump into cattle in front of them, who are then pushed forward and bump into cattle in front of them, who are then pushed forward and bump into cattle in front of them. Assuming that you don't need any further explanation of the progression, this whole thing continues until the entire herd of bumper cattle are colliding their way forward. 'Course, I wouldn't swear on it because I'm not a farmboy, but I don't think that bumper crops work the same way.

Well, the cattle nearest me had just been bumped and pushed forward into the cattle in front of them, who were then bumped and pushed forward into the cattle in front of them...So, I shook my reins and we began to walk along side. I glanced back over my shoulder and there was Albert following right behind. It must have been a "yes" moo.

Despite the fact that the rain was relentless and the wind was growing colder, I was enjoying myself. Even my headache cleared as I cantered You Romantic You up and down the left side of the herd, keeping the cattle within a ficticious boundry that I had created. I called this boundary the Mexicattle Border and made up a little game to keep myself occupied. Any illegal alien (cow) that crossed the border would be chased back over by me, Even Tinier Bert, Head of the U.S. Border Patrol.

Whether it was coincidental or not, Albert appeared to be joining in my game. Every time I looked back, he seemed to be directing another cow back to the herd. As a matter of fact, after traveling about five miles down the Mexicattle border, I had only sent one cow packing, while Albert had lead seven cows back to the land of the peso. 'Course, with this success, I named him my trusty deputy agent and officially let him join my patrol.

In the meantime, the downpour continued, above which you could barely hear the sound of over twenty thousand hoofs trudging along — slurpslurpslurpslurpslurpslurpslurpslurpslurp-slu, each cow secretly waiting to take advantage of any small mental error on the part of the U.S. Border Patrol.

Now, Albert had just caught his eighth illegal alien and, after what I guessed was a short lecture on the virtues of a green card, was directing him back over the border when the sky turned bright white followed by the inevitable groundshaking explosion. No, it was not another case of spontaneous combustion. Lightning had struck nearby!

SLURPSLURPSLURPSLURPSLURPSLURPSLURPSLURP-SLURPSLURPSLURPSLURPSLURP

Stampede!

At once, the cattle were transformed into five thousand molecules, still colliding like before, but at a much quicker pace than the bumper cars. Yes, panic had set in.

You Romantic You bolted, but I managed to stay on, thanks in part to the fact that my zipper had somehow gotten stuck on the saddle horn. I yanked back on the reins as hard as I could, trying to get You Romantic You to settle down. I was afraid that once she realized that she couldn't throw me, she'd take off in the direction of the stampede. I pulled harder on the reins. My arms strained until I thought they would pop off like that bull's tail.

Finally, just as both my energy and zipper were about to give way, You Romantic You ceased her bucking. I took a moment to catch my breath, figuring this was alot easier to catch than the wild-eyed cattle that were still thundering by.

I lifted my head and looked around. Albert was nowhere to be seen!

"Albert," I shouted even though shouting was an effort in futility. "Trusty Deputy Agent!"

I turned my head in the direction of the stampede and tried as best I could to pierce through the rain and fog. I was squinting so hard that I must have resembled a hamster coming out from his wood chips into the bright light after a night's sleep, except I wasn't wiggling my nose.

There! Yes, there about 100 yards, now 110 yards, now 120 yards, now 130 yards...was Albert! His poor little head was bobbing up and down among the driving masses. As he was forced forward, he kept looking back, seemingly bewildered.

I spurred You Romantic You into a gallop.

Slurpslurpslurpslurslurslurslusluslusllslslsssssssssssssssssss

We were soon moving so fast that the ground could not take hold of the horse's hoofs. I did not know how to stop the stampede other than letting the cattle run out of steam. My real concern was that Albert would be trampled by bigger cattle before then.

The gap between Albert and me shortened. We were now traveling as fast as we could along the perimeter of the herd. Albert saw me. His eyes begged for help. I thought quickly. I knew that if I tried to get in the herd to Albert, I'd probably end up being squashed along with him. So, somehow, I'd have to get Albert out.

I looked back over to Albert. He was wedged as tightly as a Kraft American Single between two pieces of plastic. I looked down. There, tied to my saddle, was an old lariat.

Willie had given me this lasso and had attempted to teach me how to throw it. He had been a champion lassoer in the rodeo and could do all kinds of tricks with it. He could swing it and jump through it. He could swing it and have other people jump through it. He could swing people while others jumped and not use the lasso at all! Anyway, he told me that I should learn to toss the lariat because it was the best thing ever invented for catching livestock. Unfortunately, I was only able to catch deadstock and inanimate objects. So, I soon put to rest the idea that I would follow in Willie's champion footsteps. However, I did keep the lasso, mainly because it looked good with my saddle.

Anyway, aesthetics aside, I had nothing to lose by trying to use it now. I grabbed it. I quickly made sure that the slip knot for the noose was functional. I then gripped the rope firmly beneath the knot.

"Here goes," I thought to myself. In a slow circular motion, I began spinning the noose overhead. Had I been better at this, I probably would have thrown in a "Yee Ha" right about there.

My eyes shifted down from the lasso to the route ahead. "Holy Cow Pucks!" I shouted. Lake Livingston had come out of nowhere! The herd was heading right for it and were showing no signs of slowing down. Now I was sure that if Albert wasn't trampled, the cattle in the rear would push him and the rest of the cattle in the front into the lake, probably drowning about half of them.

Knowing that it was now or never, but not wanting to see the outcome, I closed my eyes and tossed the lasso into the thundering herd. I kept my eyes shut, wondering and hoping that the rope would suddenly become taut with an Albert at the other end. Then, at once, I felt a tremendous pull. I quickly opened my eyes and looked over and, while I hadn't nabbed Albert, I had roped a cow!

I guess it was the fact that I had roped something that made me so excited. Because, when I thought about it, the whole herd was still fast approaching the lake and I was holding onto the wrong cow. Had I not started panicking myself, I probably would have felt proud that I had roped the Muley running right along side of Albert and had only missed Albert by a matter of inches.

"What do I do now?" I thought as I kept pace with cattle. Knowing that what I wasn't going to do was to be dragged into the lake with the herd, I let go of the rope.

Well, the cow running along side of me immediately got his leg caught around the lasso's free flying open end. This slowed him down which caused the rope to be pulled tight as Albert's neighbor, with the noose end around his neck, was still in a lope. This caused a whole line of faster moving, unsuspecting cattle, who did not see the leg height rope as it was jerked taut, to trip over it and fall. Then, cattle behind them began tripping over the cattle who had already fallen, and, before you knew it, the entire back half of the herd were down and on the ground.

Now, all of the cattle in the front half of the herd, hearing all the noise from the rear, turned around to find out what was happening. 'Course, this immediately lead to these cattle tripping over each other since they were no longer looking at where they were going. Soon, every single Old Miss cow was down on the ground. Well, every cow but Albert, who, being in the dead center of the herd, was not tripped up by the rope nor the falling cows in the back nor the curious cows in the front. Albert proceeded to step over his fallen bretheren and walk over to where me and You Romantic You had pulled up.

I wiped the rain and sweat from my brow and looked ahead. I was staring directly at the banks of Lake Livingston. We had come within a few hundred feet of falling in. I glanced around. Mere words can not describe a four thousand nine hundred and ninety-nine cow pile up. And then there was Albert, who was grazing contently next to You Romantic You. It was all a truly amazing sight.

"What a truly amazin' sight," Pa said riding up from behind. "I've never in my life thought 'bout endin' a stampede by trippin' up the whole herd."

Little Ben and Willie came loping over.

"What in the hell happened?" Willie asked.

"Ya should a seen it," Pa said beaming with pride. "Bert Boy used his lasso and stopped the whole herd."

"The lasso that I gave ya?" Willie said, kinda shocked. "I thought that ya could only catch deadstock and inanimate objects with that thin, and that, sometimes, even them thins got away from ya." I smiled sheepishly.

"All I know is that one minute I'm tryin' to figure a way to stem the stampede and the next thin I know, I look over and thar ain't anymore cows runnin' next to me," Little Ben said. "So, I stopped and just happened to look down and thar I saw cow bodies everwhere."

"Wow," I thought. I must have really impressed Little Ben.

"Well, ya should a seen it," Pa said. "I was comin' up from behind and what I saw was some real quick thinkin'. Ya know, if the whole herd hadn't been tripped, we woulda had ourselves one big mess of water logged cows on our hands."

"Son," Pa continued looking directly at me. "Ya've done somethin' singlehandedly on yer first day at point that most men haven't done in thar lifetimes. And not only that, ya've made fellow members of the Old Miss proud to be workin' 'long side of ya." Willie and Little Ben applauded.

"And Bert Boy," Pa added. "Ya've made Ma proud."

Now, I knew that Pa could tell that he, Willie and Little Ben were proud of me, but how could he tell that his horse was also proud? I was about to ask him when I saw that he was holding a small jar in his hands.

"See, I told ya that yer son would make a fine cowboy someday," Pa said to the small jar, which I suddenly realized was not a jar at all.

"Pa, you brought Ma along!"

"When I sat down and thought about it, well, I a just wasn't about to leave her ashes in Texas," Pa said fondling the urn. "To be blown about by the first dust storm that hit. We'll find her a new restin' place when we git to New York." He opened the lid and gave Ma a wiff of fresh air and then placed the urn back into his coat pocket.

We were soon joined by Clint, Big Bill, Tiny Bob and B.B.. Pa told them of my quick thinking. He even brought Ma out to hear the story one more time. I was starting to feel a little guilty, mainly because it was more sheer luck than anything else. But, no matter how old you are, it's kinda hard to turn down praise, especially when it comes from your Pa. I mean, Pa got just as much joy in being able to praise me for doing something as I got in having Pa throw superlatives my way. Besides, Pa knew that I couldn't throw a lasso and the only reason I kept it was because it looked good with my saddle. I think he was proud because, at least, I reacted and did something. Who are we to belittle a little luck now and then?

Everybody, except Tiny Bob, offered me their congratulations. Actually, Tiny Bob did offer me his hand, but when I saw it was filled with burrs and slugs, I declined. Pa declared the rest of the morning, "Even Tinier Bert Henry Morning". He apologized for not being able to give me the whole day, but I understood. It was obvious that I would have to help them pick up dazed cattle sometime this afternoon.

Pa also said he'd get me a gold lariat to mark the occasion, and I believed he would because Pa was not a politician. With the ceremonies concluded, Pa placed a wad of tobacco in his mouth. "Now, Bert Boy," he said. "Ya stay here and enjoy yer mornin'. The rest of ya, let's start gettin' them dazed critters to thar feet. And B.B., ya can set up camp here. I don't think them cattle will be in any condition to travel anymore today."

"How `bout the itinerary?" Little Ben asked.

"It'll throw it a little off," Pa replied. "But a whole lot less than if we would have had to dredge the lake for these cows. 'Sides, if we tried to drive 'em now, it would be like Piñada Night at the Veterans Hall."

Pa didn't have to say anymore. The disaster of an evening that occurred once three years ago was called Piñada Night. It had been thrown by the Grangerland Little League Baseball team to raise money for new uniforms. All one hundred people who came were blindfolded and given a baseball bat. When the clock struck nine, they were told to start swinging at the one piñada hanging down from the ceiling. Now, even if Tiny Bob hadn't taken the piñada down at eight fifty, it still would have been a fiasco. When the clock struck nine, people began to wail away with their bats in all directions and they wouldn't stop until they hit something solid. Needless to say, even those of us who were still conscious at the end of the evening found ourselves dazed and bewildered. And I would say that the whole town walked around in a state of total befuddlement for at least a week. Maybe this wouldn't have been so bad if the event had turned out to be successful for the Little League team, but it wasn't. While it was true that they had made enough on the event to buy new uniforms, they now had to throw another fund raiser to get money for new bats.

So, all you had to do was remember the chaos of that week of dazed townsfolk wandering all over the place with absolutely no sense of direction or purpose, multiply it by fifty and that's what we'd be in for if we tried to drive the cattle in their present condition. Pa had made his point, and with that, he and the rest left to start picking up the cattle and putting them back onto their feet.

Me and B.B. stayed back. Before he started to set up camp, B.B. asked me what I wanted for lunch. He said that, in my honor, I could have whatever I wanted. I happened to be looking out at the herd at the time, and, for some strange reason, I told B.B. that I had a sudden desire for eggs over easy. With my decision made, I sat down in the torrential downpour to enjoy the rest of "Even Tinier Bert Henry Morning."

16

WE ENDED UP STAYING along the banks of Lake Livingston for a couple of days. Unfortunately, while Even Tinier Bert Henry Morning ended, the rain did not. On top of that, just after the last of the cattle had been righted, Big Bill slipped on an old discarded banana peel, knocking half the herd back over. That's about when Pa made the decision to stay.

"Bill Boy's slippin' on a banana peel's a bad omen," Pa said. "Especially one that old, black and crusty."

"Yeah," B.B. replied. "Usually them thins are biodegradable."

"Looks like a bad omen to me," Willie said.

"Looks like a bad omen to me," Clint said.

It did appear to be a bad omen. And we believed in bad omens ever since Old Lady Warble died.

Old Lady Warble was a one hundred and one year old spinster, although at her age, she did very little spinning and spent most of her time as a seamstress. As the story goes, one day, she was working on a particularly difficult seam when she heard a voice in her head say, "You are not long for this world." It turned out that Old Lady Warble's dentures had picked up the audio portion of a Houston based public t.v. program about U.F.O.s, and the show's narrator was doing nothing more than commenting on the length of an alien from outer space who had been discovered living in a retirement community in Miami. But, Old Lady Warble did not know this and, believing it to be a bad omen, panicked.

She ran out of her house screaming. And that's when it happened. Old Lady Warble's screams caused her dentures to shift, which in turn, changed the channel in her mouth from P.B.S. to M.T.V. It took only two minutes of Guns 'N Roses resounding in her ears and the Old Lady Warbled no more. Now, everybody took this to be a bad omen, but the older people in the community also took this to be their proof that Rock and Roll can have serious consequences. As for us younger folk, well, we just sat around and listened to Old Lady Warble's head for awhile. You see, while we had heard of M.T.V. before, we never knew anyone who could actually pick it up.

And ever since that time, we at the Old Miss have taken omens, if indeed it is decided that something is an omen, very seriously. You might disagree with us on this one, but a nonbiodegradable banana peel in the middle of nowhere and the sure footed Big Bill slipping were just too odd for us. Besides, the cattle that had fallen over again were now doubly dazed and a few days rest would certainly help Clint's arm.

Well, finally the time came to move on. Hurricane Eeoogie had rained itself out, the cattle had become coherent and the banana peel had disappeared. Willie believed that the peel had just been a late degrader, while I was very sure that Tiny Bob had eaten it.

Even though Clint's arm showed improvement, Pa thought it best that I stay on at left point for awhile longer. I surely appreciated his confidence in me, but just for luck, I kept my pal, Albert, by my side. 'Course, it didn't hurt any to have Albert around for Mexicattle Border duty either. We crossed Lake Livingston somewhere in Walker County. The crossing went without a hitch, which, under the circumstances, didn't really surprise us. You see, I don't think that the cattle realized that they were crossing a lake. The land surrounding the lake was so swampy and flooded that no one could tell where the land ended and where the lake began.

We then headed north, passing somewhere between the towns of Trinity and Glendale. Willie joked that the land had become like a young woman starting to grow up — some bumps here and there, but generally flat. 'Course, the analogy was completey dismissed by Big Bill, who insisted that young girls starting to grow up did not have trees and lush meadows growing out of them.

We set up camp that evening a couple of miles short of the towns of Lovelady and Holly. Once again, B.B. tried to sneak in a new dinner item — banana peel soup. Even with the promise of s'mores for any takers, we just didn't want to know. That night, we enjoyed the comforting warmth of the campfire and the stars for the first time in many days. At least, I did. I stared at the heavens and wondered just how significant our problems were in the realm of the whole universe. The rest of the Old Miss company worked on their tobbaco spitting.

The next few days were filled with the same, beautiful daytime skies illuminating beautiful East Texas landscapes. The early October sun quickly dried the ground. So quickly, in fact, that "slurp" gave way to "swoosh", the sound of five thousand tails brushing away the last of the summer flies. Soothing nighttime skies brought out our inner thoughts and more group spittings.

Some thoughts were cheerful, some melancholy. We tried to keep it a good mix. As a matter of fact, if the conversation was, say, too cheerful, Pa would ask Willie to play his harmonica, immediately putting us all in a pensive mood. Well, all of us, except Tiny Bob. Tiny Bob was too preoccupied with fly wrestling. To his credit, he had been interested in fly wrestling ever since childhood. But back at the Old Miss, all he had to wrestle with were tired, domesticated flies who had been buzzing around in a window sill for a week or more. Now that we were out on the trail, he was finding a real challenge with the flies of the wild. He'd sneak up on one sitting on the back of a cow, shout "ready, wrestle" and then jump it. He'd then give himself three minutes to pin the fly's front two legs down. If the fly won, Tiny Bob would let it walk undisturbed all over him and any food that he happened to be eating. If Tiny Bob won, well, he'd smush the loser. If you want my opinion, the whole thing didn't seem particularly fair to the fly.

Maybe that's why none of the rest of us ever took to the sport. But that's not the reason for our being pensive. We were moving further away from our roots and further into unknown territory. And even with all the maps in the world, we'd always know what we had found, but not what we'd find. Yes, our world had been condensed to foldable sheets of paper labelled AAA. And at this point, life was moving at one inch per day where one inch equals twenty two point five miles. And contrary to the map, that one inch, from point A to point B, was not some stationary entity. A million different things were happening every second within that one inch, none of which could ever be captured on a piece of paper.

Add up all the inches it was going to take to get us to New York and, perhaps, you'd feel a bit overwhelmed too. And feeling overwhelmed is just one of many routes you can take on the road to becoming pensive. 'Course, when we started to get too pensive, Pa would make everybody hold hands and start singing, "We Are The World" (which was a song that I had heard coming out from Old Lady Warble's head and had taught to the Old Miss company.) Like I said, we liked to keep it a good mix.

During these couple of days, we had, among other things, passed through the Davy Crockett National Forest. I was a bit curious as to why we did because, when I looked at the maps, I realized that we had traveled a bit out of our way to get to the 161,497 acre forest. Pa said that his reason for doing this was just to make sure that we all got one more chance to see things like native white tail deer, doves and quail. And we did get to see these things too, along with a paper mache Woodsey the Owl hanging in effigy at the exit to the forest.

Now, if you want my thoughts on why we took this sidetrip, which, by the way, exposed us to the risk of possible contact with a red-cockaded woodpecker just as Clint's arm had almost healed, I don't think Pa's giving us one last opportunity to see Texas wildlife was the whole answer. No, I think it had more to do with the fact that we were out of cookies. Pa had had Willie scout out a Ranger as soon as we entered the forest, and before we left, Pa had bought enough of the chocolate covered peanut butter variety to last us until Tyler. While I'm not complaining, mind you, I did think about approaching Pa and asking him if this was part of the reason for us going off course. But after I thought about it, who really cared? I decided instead to just stuff my face with cookies.

Once out of the forest, we had traveled northwest, following the Neches River until it hit Route 294. Route 294 was a dinky little road with a dinky little bridge which crossed over the not so dinky river. At one time, this road had been the only major thoroughfare out of Slocum, Texas, which, I guess, is why nothing more had been built than a dinky little road and a dinky little bridge. Before moving the herd across the bridge, Willie suggested that we camp out along the banks of the Neches for the evening. This, he said, would give him a chance to see how sturdy the dinky little bridge was, and if he found it to be too dinky, he could scout out the Route 84 or 79 crossings further upstream. We did end up camping along the banks of the Neches for the evening, but I don't think Willie gave a hoot about dinkiness. I just think he wanted a chance to check under the bridge for trolls.

And I guess you could say that the crossing went very smoothly, because there weren't any incidents (or trolls) to report. The next day and a half took us due north, passing as close as you'd probably want to get to towns like Maydelle, Ironton, Reese and Mount Selman. It's not that we had anything personal against these towns, but hailing from Grangerland can be tough at times. Now, it might seem a bit snobbish to you, but we just didn't think we'd have all that much in common with people who came from towns smaller than ours. And it's not that we wouldn't want to educate them, but you can understand that we didn't have the time just now.

We did, however, stop in the town of Teaselville on that second evening. The excitement was mounting because we were about a day's drive from Tyler, and to celebrate, Pa suggested stopping in town for dinner. 'Course, the fact that B.B. had underestimated our food supply and we had nothing left to eat played a part in the suggestion too.

So, we drove the herd down Main Street, Teaselville, Texas, which consisted of a gas station, a baptist church and a flashing yellow light, until we reached a fancy restaurant called "Eats". We left the herd in the parking lot and went inside.

"Can I help ya'll?" the waitress said as we entered.

Talk about your fancy waitresses. She was dressed in a white uniform and apron and there wasn't a new stain on her. She even had a writing pad and a nametag which read, "Flo." And her hair! I had never seen hair stacked so high on someone's head before. I think they normally call it a "beehive", but this one was more like "Beeworld, U.S.A.", a place that most bees could only dream about.

"Table for eight, Ma'am," Pa said.

I looked around the place. There was a long counter with swiveling stools in front. A real formica counter, mind you, with those fancy kind of metal stools with the green vinyl tops. Tiny Bob was so excited that he quickly plopped himself down on one of the stools and began spinning. Behind the counter, there were not one, but two griddles! A big gray metal jukebox which was playing Tex Ritter singing "Jingle, Jangle, Jingle" stood between two doors marked "Hens" and "Cocks." Some real formica top tables which were bolted to the wall rounded out the rest of this sumptuous restaurant.

"Ya got yerself reservations?" Flo asked.

"No, Ma'am," Pa replied.

"Then yer gonna have to wait a couple a minutes," Flo said.

"No problem, Ma'am," Pa said even though, upon closer inspection, we were the only people in the place. But we had heard of these high class places before, where they make you wait no matter what, so we were prepared for this.

"And yer gonna have to do somethin' 'bout them dogs," Flo said pointing to Big Bill's feet. She then pointed to a sign which read, "No Shirt, No Shoes, No Service."

Since the opportunity to dine at such a fine restaurant comes perhaps once in a lifetime, B.B. ran out to the chuck wagon to fetch his extra pair of boots. When he returned, we began the difficult task of trying to get the boots onto Big Bill's feet. It took us a good ten minutes of shoving and twisting and of Big Bill groaning and grimacing before the job was done. At that time, Flo informed us that our table was ready and that Tiny Bob, through the miracle of centrifugal force, had flown off the stool and was stuck to the wall in a state of discomtinybobulation.

Clint went to peel Tiny Bob off of the wall as Pa and Little Ben helped Big Bill to the table. I watched each painful, awkward step that Big Bill took as he struggled to reach the table. Like I said before, I can't remember ever seeing him in shoes before, and he looked about as uncomfortable as a saddle sore cowboy with the trots.

Finally, he made it to our table, where he practically dove into his seat. The rest of us were then seated, very much relieved to have made it this far, or so we thought. We couldn't have been sitting there for more than a minute when Big Bill suddenly started to break out in funny little red bumps and his left eye began twitching uncontrollably. Pa noticed first.

"Quick," Pa shouted. "An allergic reaction to shoes!"

"I'll git the bullet pluckin' chicken," B.B. said out of reflex.

"Won't do no good," Pa said. "Just git them shoes off!"

Willie grabbed one of Big Bill's feet, while Little Ben grabbed the other and both started yanking. By this time, Big Bill's eyes were rolling around his head like spin art.

I quickly grabbed Little Ben and Clint grabbed Willie and we started pulling too, but none of us seemed to be getting anywhere. It appeared that Big Bill's feet had begun swelling inside the boots. Flo, who had been watching this whole production for lack of anything else to do, came running over with some melted lard. She poured it around the top of Big Bill's boots and let it seep in some. It didn't matter that it had come hot off the griddle because Big Bill was in no position to feel anything. By this time, Big Bill's eyes were all white and his tongue was dancing around outside his mouth. It was really a shame that Big Bill was in so much trouble because his tongue seemed to be keeping perfect time to "Jingle, Jangle, Jingle." And this was from someone who had absolutely no rhythm!

We gave the boots another try, and, sure enough, they slid right off. Big Bill's tongue immediately stopped its dancing and his pupils came back from nowhere. Everybody breathed a sigh of relief, including Flo, whom I noticed was sweating a bit which was causing her hair to lean to the right. I hoped that she wouldn't topple over, especially in light of how she had helped Big Bill.

Pa and Flo then had a brief discussion as to what to do about the "no shoe" dilemma. We had our hearts set on a gourmet meal and understood that Flo couldn't break the rules, but we couldn't enjoy a dining experience of this sort without Big Bill. Flo, her whole body now leaning at a thirty degree angle to the right, came up with an idea. She opened a nearby window so that Big Bill could dangle his bare feet outside of the restaurant during dinner.

And what a dinner it was. We got to order off of real plastic coated menus stained with ketchup and coffee. There were real paper napkins in a gray metal dispenser so that we wouldn't have to use our arms. And the plates, glasses and silverware had less dishwashing spots than we were accustomed to, but that's to be expected when you're paying $2.00 for a chicken fried steak dinner.

As for the food, I splurged and started off with a thing called an appetizer. Maybe I'm wrong, but I think this was the same thing Ma and B.B. used to call a before-meal snack and which was strictly prohibited. But rather than figure out why it was that eating before your meal at home would ruin your appetite, while eating before your meal at a fancy place like Eats would stimulate it, I just ordered and kept quiet. For dinner, I had meat loaf in a basket. It was exquisite, even though the gravy quickly seeped through the wax paper and began dripping onto the table.

After dinner but before dessert, Pa excused himself from the table. He had seen a pay phone out front of the restaurant and thought he'd call Uncle Ray and Aunt Tammy Faye to tell them that we were running a little behind schedule on our itinerary. Pa went to get some change from Flo, but was informed that the call would be free. It seems that Southwest Bell had made the phone into an 800 number, believing that Eats had received a star in the Michelin Red Book. Not that they didn't deserve a star, mind you, but it seems that the fact that a Michelin tire salesman had once used the room marked "Cocks" at Eats had somehow gotten blown all out of proportion. Now, I can understand folks believing a mistaken rumor, but Southwest Bell? Since when did a phone company ever make a mistake?

Anyhow, Pa went to use the phone. I could tell that he felt mighty bad for Southwest Bell because a mistake of this magnitude might easily set them up for some severe ridiculing and take away all that public confidence that had been building over the years. Yep, Pa firmly believed that monopolies had feelings too. But I could also tell by his exit that he felt worse for Eats, mainly, I guess, because they didn't get a star.

Dessert came soon after Pa's departure. Flo placed our desserts in front of us, but we all just sat quietly and waited for Pa's return. That's when Flo praised us for our etiquette, but told us that if we didn't start eating, there was a good chance that some of the desserts would get moldy. So, under the circumstances, we began to eat. Well, all of us except Tiny Bob began to eat. Tiny Bob wanted his dessert moldy.

I was just about finished with my white mousse with fresh raspberry sauce when Pa returned. I realized that he had been gone quite awhile. At least he had been gone long enough for Tiny Bob's dessert to, indeed, grow mold. Pa sat down quietly.

"Is everthin okay, Eugene?" B.B. asked.

Pa slowly looked around the table. He then stared down at a hunk of pie that Flo had brought him, which had a slightly green tint starting to show.

"Boys," he finally said, before taking a long, dramatic pause. "E. Lester's a comin' after us."

17

EVEN WITHOUT A HARMONICA, we were in a fairly pensive mood that night at the campsite, which, by the way, happened to be the Eats parking lot. Eats management (a cook named Crawdad and Flo) gave us permission to camp out on their lot after no reservations seemed to be coming in on their Watts line. They also gave us permission to run an extension cord out of Eats and plug in the chuck wagon's wheel for the first time since the trip began. But even though we didn't have to build a fire and Eats said that they'd waive the valet parking charge couldn't take our minds off of E. Lester. So, we huddled ourselves around the wagon wheel fixture, which was now the brightest light in all of Teaselville, and talked about our predicament.

"So the Eeoogie's comin' after us," Willie said.

"Well, Ray and Tammy Faye think so, 'though they don't know no details yet," Pa replied. "Accordin' to them, E. Lester's in desperate need of our cattle. Seems some bank examiners want to shut him down 'cause he ain't got enough reserve funds to cover the bank's debts."

"That true?" Little Ben asked.

"Well, Ray and Tammy Faye think that the bank had problems givin' Old Man Wilkens a withdrawal, and they guess that had it been any other depositer, thar would a been a run on the bank," Pa said. I nodded my head in agreement because I knew exactly what he meant. Old Man Wilkens was confined to a wheel chair, so it would have been impossible for him to have a run on anything. 'Course, he could have started a "roll on the bank", but since those aren't the words that strike fear in a depositor's heart, E. Lester was very lucky.

"So, they figure that E. Lester's after all of his outstandin' collateral or else he'll be forced to declare bankruptcy real soon," Pa continued.

"Probably on the advice of Cyrus H. Squirrel," said Willie, bucking his teeth and wiggling his nose. We all laughed.

"Well, at least we got some thins goin' fer us," Pa said feeling a little more at ease. "Ray and Tammy Faye think that E. Lester didn't git out to the Old Miss 'til yesterday. Seems he got some sorta toe infection from bein' forced to walk without shoes on some broken toes when his car broke down in the middle of nowhere."

"Got us a nice head start," Little Ben declared.

"Yep," Pa nodded as he turned and looked in the direction of the wagon wheel. "Bob Boy, not too close now, 'kay." Tiny Bob was busy seeing how close he could come to sticking his finger in the one socket that didn't have a lightbulb in it without getting a shock.

Pa took a pinch of tobacco and continued. "Anyway, we got ourselves a good jump on E. Lester," he said. "And we also got some comfort in that E. Lester don't know where we are or where we're a goin'."

"And Uncle Ray and Aunt Tammy Faye would never tell him!" I declared.

There was no truer statement. To give you some idea of how good Uncle Ray and Aunt Tammy Faye were at keeping secrets, Uncle Ray once surprised Aunt Tammy Faye with a gift. Now, before he gave it to her, he had been keeping it at home, yet he hadn't said a word. The impressive part is that even after he gave her the gift and she opened it, he wouldn't tell her what it was. And even to this day, Aunt Tammy Faye doesn't know what it is…but she does know that it's sure starting to smell!

Now, Aunt Tammy Faye got a little perturbed at receiving something no one seemed to be able to identify, so she told Uncle Ray that she, too, had a little secret that she had been keeping from him. And when she wouldn't tell him what it was, Uncle Ray said that he also had another secret, this one pretty juicy, that just wasn't for Aunt Tammy Faye to hear. Aunt Tammy Faye then suddenly remembered another secret, this one juicier than Uncle Ray's and not to be divulged, but dating back to the day she was born. 'Course, Uncle Ray then informed Aunt Tammy Faye that he was just sorry that he couldn't talk about the juciest secret in the world which dated back to before he was born, whereas Aunt Tammy Faye countered with the juiciest secret in the universe, which she was not at liberty to reveal — this one occurring before Adam and Eve!

Well, it turns out that each one of them had about a zillion juicy secrets that they refused to discuss. And now Aunt Tammy Faye and Uncle Ray don't talk to each other at all anymore, or at least if they do, it's a secret. All of which goes to show that they are just about the two best secret keepers I've ever met, and why we all felt that our itinerary was safe with them.

"Well, that's all done and good," B.B. said. "But we got us five thousand head of cattle. Even if he ain't got our itinerary, it ain't gonna take that fat butted banker forever to git wind of our trail."

"Ya got a point, B.B.," Pa said. "Anybody got any idears on how we're gonna avoid bein' found?"

"Give 'im bad leads," Little Ben said.

Pa considered this a moment before speaking, "I guess we could tell people we're a headin' somewhere when we really ain't. So when he asks questions, he'll be sent the wrong way."

"How 'bout speedin' the pace?" Willie suggested. "Git them doggies to New York and sell 'em 'fore he catches up."

"Speed the pace," Clint said.

"What 'bout disguisin' them cows as goats," Big Bill said. "He won't be askin' fer no info 'bout no goat herds."

"Stand on a cliff and drop a big boulder on the Eeoogie," Tiny Bob said grinding his teeth. "And mush 'im."

"Tell people we're a headin' to Californee," B.B. said, raising his voice.

"Bad leads," said Little Ben.

"Speed the pace," Willie rebutted.

"Speed the pace!" Clint rebutted, but louder.

"Disguise 'em!" Big Bill clamoured.

"MUSH 'EM!" Tiny Bob screamed.

Seeing that the discussion was getting a might too heated, Pa chimed in. "I think we got too many cooks ruinin' the soup."

"But the more the merrier," B.B. countered, giving credence to Pa's theory based on Newton's third law of nature — for every cliche, there is an equal and opposite cliche.

"Boys," Pa said. "This ain't to say that all yer suggestions aren't good and welcomed. But sometimes, thar's just no point in causin' friction."

Pa stopped to watch Tiny Bob briskly rubbing his dungarees with his flannel shirt sleeves.

"Tiny Bob," Pa continued. "No point in causin' friction!"

"Sorry, Pa," Tiny Bob said sincerely as he ceased his rubbing. 'Course, he could afford to be sincere since he had accomplished what he had set out to do. Smoke was now coming from his pants leg.

"Now go and put out yer pants," Pa said to Tiny Bob before turning back to face the rest of us. "And everbody else, just sit back and enjoy the fine light fixture. E. Lester's a long way off, and Ray and Tammy Faye told me that if I called 'em every couple a days, they'd keep me posted."

"Did you pick a certain time to call them?" I asked. "To make sure they'd be home?"

"In all the years you've been alive have ya ever seen 'em leave home?" B.B. asked me.

"Yer such a worrywart," said a still smoldering Tiny Bob.

"Boys, thar just ain't no point in worryin'," Pa said. "Let's just wait and see what happens. The best solutions are usually those that just sorta pop up 'cause of circumstances."

Pa seemed to make sense as usual, so with that, I tried to settle down around the wagon wheel to enjoy the rest of the evening.

18

IT TURNS OUT THAT Pa's words couldn't have been truer. An idea on how to avoid E. Lester sorta came to us as a result of things that happened in Tyler...but, as usual, I'm jumping way ahead of myself.

Very early the next morning, we left Eats' parking lot, destination Tyler, Texas. We were going to have breakfast at Eats, but contrary to the sign posted in the window which said, "Open", it wasn't. We had a short debate on whether to consider this to be a bad omen, but figuring that Crawdad and Flo were probably just out bagging "Varmint Du Jour", decided that it wasn't. Pa filled out the little comment card Flo had given him, giving each and every item a check under the column marked "Very Excellent". Then, in the space marked "Additional Comments And/Or Human Interest Stories", Pa scribbled a quick note of appreciation and indicated that Eats deserved not one, but two stars in the Michelin Red Book. Big Bill wanted to take a couple of minutes and write down the story of Old Lady Warble and her radio mouth, but Pa thought it was time that we'd be leaving. So, as Pa slipped the card and a 20% tip under the door, B.B. unplugged the wagon wheel and Willie hit nine hundred eighty six thousand two hundred and two bottles of beer on the wall, we headed 'em up and moved 'em out.

It didn't bother me that we left without eating because I wasn't too hungry to begin with. E. Lester was coming, and even though I knew that he was hundreds of miles away, he was still out there, somewhere. True, it's a big country, but E. Lester's a big man. Any foe who could cover an acre without moving is a force to be reckoned with. I know that Pa told us not to worry, but when you're twelve, things like this are all you have to worry about.

But, I knew I had to put these thoughts on the back burner and concentrate on looking for strays. Clint's arm was feeling better, so me and Albert were going back to our original assignments. You may not believe it, but I think that we both felt kinda glad to return too. True, we had surprised even ourselves at point, but me and Albert were still a little too young for that kind of pressure on a daily basis. So, we were far from disappointed that Clint was able to resume his duties on the Mexicattle Border. Actually, because of the stress I had felt, I was starting to worry that if Clint didn't come back soon, my trusty deputy Albert was going to tender his resignation.

So, for the time being, I placed thoughts of the Eeoogie into the recesses of my mind and went about my job of bringing up the tail end of the Old Miss drive.

As we headed due north from Teaselville, the landscape started to change. There was more green and more rolling hills. And on top of the more rolling hills, were clumps of trees. And through the clumps, in the not too far off distance, I caught fleeting glimpses of what could only be the city of Tyler!

Each time there was a break in the trees, the immensity of this city became clearer. At first glance, it looked to be no more than a speck on the horizon. Then, slowly, like an amoeba, the speck divided again and again, until many distinguishable dots covered the area where the speck once stood. And with each step, these dots grew and divided. I could only marvel at the sight before me, and I knew in my heart that a town like Grangerland would just not feel the same again.

The excitement mounted as we came out from a fairly thick tree cover and found ourselves staring at a four lane highway- two lanes in each direction. Willie made sure that no traffic was coming and then swung the cattle onto the highway.

Me and Albert stepped onto the roadway last. I knew that we were only on the outskirts of town, but I still couldn't turn my head quick enough to take in everything. I was so absorbed that I totally forgot about watching for strays. But that was okay because the cattle were so absorbed that they forgot about being strays.

Directly to our right along the highway was a huge billboard which read,"Welcome To Tyler, Texas — Rose Capitol Of The World, And Welcome To The Texas Rose Festival". Across the highway was the tallest building I had ever seen, at least four stories high. In front of this building stood a large mounted sign which said, "Ramada Inn".

"For gosh darn's sakes," I shouted to Albert, being sure to omit all dirty superlatives. "It's a hotel! They could house all of Grangerland in this place and still have room left for the next generation." Albert mooed. It had to have been in awe. Underneath the Ramada sign was another sign which read, "Congratulations Rose Queen — Peggy Jean Elrepute".

"Could royalty really be in town?" I thought as my heart raced faster. Albert must have had similar thoughts because he seemed to have that starry eyed look, for no apparent reason.

I shook the reins and got You Romantic You to trot over to a street sign posted on the next corner up. I glanced over at the street name and, at once, was even more impressed.

"Broadway!"

Excitedly, I turned back to Albert who had trotted up behind us. "Albert, we're on Broadway! Can you believe it? Broadway! Even I've heard of Broadway, home of the American theater!"

Albert glanced around before indulging in a quick snack of grass over by the side of the road. I just don't think that Albert was as impressed as I was, but, then, what did Albert know about the theater…although he was quickly becoming quite a ham. ('Course, as a matter of semantics, Albert could never be a ham. At best, a prime rib or a steak…But I would never let that happen.) As we resumed our trot, I wondered whether Pa the thespian realized that we were on Broadway. Funny thing, though. I never knew that Broadway was in Tyler. But there was that street sign, plain as milk.

The herd continued on down Broadway. We passed a Catfish King, a Burger King and a Dairy Queen.

"Yep," I said turning to Albert. "There seems to be a lot of royalty around."

Then came the Ford and Chevrolet dealers. Then came dealers selling things called Mercedes, Volvos, Porches, BMW's, Jaguars and Saabs. I felt kinda sorry for these places. I couldn't see how they possibly expected to stay in business when none of them sold trucks. We Texans have always loved our trucks and this was true even before the state legislature declared the "Pick-up" the official state automobile. And, while these cars looked fancy enough, you just can't break entirely from tradition. Not in Texas.

We next passed block after block of stores, each store attached to the next. I had never seen so many stores in my life. Each specialized in something — from Videos to Greeting Cards to Videos to Wedding Gowns to Videos. Then there was this one group of stores called a mall. The mall had no windows, so I had no idea what they were selling in there. That is, except for one store called Dillards. Even someone raised in a smaller city can discern a fancy abbreviated name when they see it. I only wished that we had some time to see what species of armadillos they were selling.

I looked ahead and saw that Pa had the urn out and was showing Ma the mall. I don't think Ma had ever seen a mall, and, before her cremation, Ma was always in search of new places to shop. So, Ma probably would have loved this place. 'Course, that's assuming two things. First, I'm assuming that Ma wouldn't have minded the fact that the shops appeared inside out. I mean, here we were, outside of the stores. So, we should have been looking at some kind of storefront or windows. Instead, all we were looking at were bricks. You see, Ma had a major problem with things that were inside out. The only inside out thing that she could tolerate was an occasional belly button. But even then, Ma would try to correct the problem before she would concede that the thing was a permanent "outey".

Second, I'm also assuming there was a way into this place. For the life of me, all I could see were these brick walls and the posted store names. How did people get in and out? For that matter, where were all the people? As I glanced around, I noticed that there were absolutely no other people in sight.

The herd had stopped and it looked like everyone was meeting at left point. I left Albert in charge of the drags and quickly loped You Romantic You over to the others.

"Saw Ma out," I heard Little Ben saying to Pa as I approached.

"I wanted to show her the mall," Pa said. "I ain't sure if she'd like it, though. The stores look inside out and ya know how yer Ma hated thins that were inside out."

"I thought somethin looked mighty peculiar 'bout this place," B.B. said. "Thar ain't no damn entrances to any of them stores."

"I thought I saw an entrance 'bout halfway down the bricks," Willie said.

"One entrance?" B.B. replied. "Fer all them stores?"

"Maybe it's akin to one of them thar roach traps," Willie said.

"That would explain why thar ain't no people `round," B.B. said. "Shoppers go in, but they can't git out."

"That may be a good way to bring in business," Pa said. "But it don't seem quite fair to the shopper."

We all agreed that it didn't seem quite fair to the shopper, not one little bit. In Grangerland, all was fair, and a merchant couldn't sleep at night until he knew his customer was happy. Warranties were always extended and the only proof of purchase needed was a simple, "'Course I bought it here." As a matter of fact, things were so good between shopkeepers and shoppers that Grangerland's Better Business Bureau changed its name to the Can't Get Much Better Business Bureau. And as far as I know, the only complaints filed with them in the last ten years revolved around back scratchers purchased from the House of Back Scratchers.

It all began when Wilamina Trubulb bought the deluxe model back scratcher from the House of Back Scratchers. However, on account of her stubby little arms, Miss Trubulb's back scratcher still wasn't long enough to reach her "sweet spot" — that spot just out of arm's reach that produces a prolonged "aaaah" when finally scratched. So, she filed a complaint with the C.G.M.B.B.B. Well, Elmo Duncan, proprietor of the House of Back Scratchers, was so upset that he personally began coming over to Miss Trubulb's house to scratch her back.

Now, Miss Trubulb recently gave birth to a baby. The reason I'm telling you this is because the same exact thing happened to Miss Lang, Miss Crepton and Miss Mudd. They all purchased deluxe back scratchers from the House of Back Scratchers. They all complained that the scratcher's were too short and, after Mr. Duncan was kind enough to visit their homes personally to rectify the problem, they all had babies. 'Course, this caused quite a stir. People like Mildred Furball, mother of seventeen, immediately traded in her deluxe back scratcher for a regular model. But the point is that Mr. Duncan did whatever was necessary to keep his customers happy. That's what integrity's all about, and, to us, this mall thing showed a real lack of this.

"So, ya think all the Tyler folk are stuck inside the mall?" Big Bill asked.

"Must be," Little Ben said.

"Yeah," said Willie. "A nice October Saturday morn' and thar ain't a soul on the streets."

I wasn't about to disagree, but, somehow, I had my doubts. It was true that we had not yet come across a single, solitary person and this was very strange for a city this big. But I couldn't believe that an entire city of people were so dumb that they all got themselves trapped in a mall. I could tell from the store windows that the people were more sophisticated than that. I mean, everybody knows that people who travel abroad are usually sophisticated, right? Well, I had noticed that every single store window we had passed advertised "Visa". Now, to have that big a demand for visas, you must have an awful lot of travelers, and, therefore, sophisticated people around. So, I think the more plausible explanation for the lack of people was that they were all just out of the country.

"I don't know why no one's 'round," Pa said. "Maybe thar all further downtown. I do know that we gotta find someone and stock up on some supplies 'fore we leave."

"Darn tootin'!" B.B. said.

"Yeah, Tiny Bob, stop it," I said. Tiny Bob had been blowing into a discarded pop bottle right next to mine and B.B.'s ears for the last couple of minutes, producing the most irritating tooting noise.

"I can't get no helpful inklins when yer givin' me a headache," B.B. said to Tiny Bob.

"C'mon, Boys, let's git `em movin'," Pa said. We returned to our positions and continued the drive.

Still traveling down Broadway, we gradually headed out of what looked like the business area. But in between the stores and the houses barely visible in the distance, was a buffer zone filled with all types of restaurants. Just the type of area you don't want to travel through on an empty stomach, especially when every one of the restaurants was closed. We passed a number of pizza places-Pizza Inn, Pizza Hut, Pizza Barn, Pizza Here. It struck me as strange that each one of them advertized, "You've tried the rest, now try the best." We also came across places like "Fletcher's Original Texas State Fair Corney Dogs", "Jeb's Bar B.Q. Pit" and "What-A-Burger". I glanced down and realized that I was chewing on the strap to my cowboy hat. Thank goodness I caught myself before I chewed clear through or my hat would have blown off with the wind. Sighing deeply, I looked up just in time to see

Willie's, Big Bill's, Little Ben's, Tiny Bob's, Clint's and B.B.'s hats fly off their heads.

After a fast break to retrieve the hats and down a quick sandwich so the straps would no longer be endangered, we continued on once again. We soon came upon a great number of houses. The houses, themselves, were huge, each having its own private, fenced in watering hole. But, the houses were so close that you could peek in your neighbor's window if you were that kind of person.

"Tiny Bob, git away from that window," I heard Pa shout.

"But, Pa, thar ain't no one home," I heard Tiny Bob reply in a rather startled voice. He hadn't realized that Pa had been watching him noseying around.

"Don't matter," I heard Pa say. "Ya ain't that kinda person. Everone expects privacy in thar homes...even when they do live right on top of one 'nother."

This was my first glimpse at a housing area that, I believe, is generally referred to as a development. But, after taking a few minutes to look around and study the place, I would call it a regression. I learned in science class that all things tend toward a maximum state of disorder. (Me and Tiny Bob's bedroom used to be a good example of this principle.) Anyway, it's called entropy, it's part of nature and it's part of evolution. Here, we have people, who rather than spread out randomly, have moved closer together into equidistant little parcels of land. I'm sorry, but that's a step backwards. There is no development in that.

In Grangerland, to make sure people obey the laws of nature, they passed the Entropy Zoning Ordinance — no two people may build the exact same house, and all houses must be out of the sight, sound and smell of your nearest neighbor. 'Course, aside from evolutionary necessity, the ordinance also protects homeowners from tacky neighbors. It ensures that individuals do not have to look out their windows and be subjected to pink plastic flamingos or little men holding lanterns next door.

Tiny Bob slowly rejoined the drive. I don't think he was finding Tyler as interesting as I was. 'Course, I also think that his attitude would be different if Pa let him peek in a few people's houses, or even if Pa would have let him stop in the building full of dillos, I mean, dillards. All I know was that Tiny Bob's present disposition had all the makings of a volatile Bob Mine. And knowing who would get the brunt of the explosion, I left Albert in charge of the drags and quickly gaited over to B.B.

"Tyler's a lot different than Grangerland," I said to B.B. over the squeak of the wagon wheels and the thumping of the electrical cord.

"Even Tinier Bert," B.B. said looking over as I approached. "I knew ya'd be comin' by."

"An inkling?" I asked.

"Nah," B.B. said. "Tiny Bob looks mighty testy, so I figured ya'd wanta hide awhile. But that's okay 'cause I know ya woulda been by to say "howdy" at some point." B.B. grinned. He did, indeed, know me well (although, not well enough to know that I never say "howdy").

"What do you think about the big city?" I asked.

"Don't like it none," B.B. said as a look of disdain crossed over his face. "Everwhere ya look, it breaks the Entropy Zoning Ordinance! And that just ain't natural."

I nodded my head in agreement as B.B. gestured to his right.

"And looky at that that," he continued. "Even when someone decides to make a change, well, ya got yer basic "Monkey see, Monkey do" Syndrome."

Again, B.B. was right. I hadn't noticed it before, but the style of houses had changed from ranchers to colonials. I don't know where the change occurred, but now all the houses around us were colonials. Not a single rancher was in sight. Someone, somewhere behind us, had made the switch and then everybody else had followed suit. And up ahead, I could see the colonials coming to a fast halt, giving way to cottage after cottage after cottage.

"Nope," B.B. said, shaking his head. "I don't like it. I don't like it at all."

"But, I'll tell ya somethin," B.B. continued, now on a roll. "I don't think all them cityfolk are stuck in that mall back thar. I don't right know where they are and why thar ain't no traffic, but I got myself a real strong inklin' that we're a gonna be findin' out."

As B.B. scratched his lump, trying to fine tune his inkling, I told him my theory.

"All out of the country on visas, huh?" B.B. said after some consideration. "Maybe. But, my inklins tellin' me that thar somewhere in town and thar all together."

"Then maybe they are all trapped in the mall," I said.

"Or maybe they saw us comin' and now thar a hidin'," B.B. said. "Maybe thar 'fraid of foreigners."

"A case of xenophobia?" I asked.

"No thanks, ain't thirsty," B.B. replied. "But thanks fer as as as as as as as as as as k k k k k k k k k k k k kin'."

The street had suddenly gone from asphalt to red brick. Any further conversation between me and B.B. seemed kinda pointless. I looked ahead and saw that Tiny Bob was seated on his saddle horn and enjoying each little jolt caused by the bricks. Figuring that I was safe for the time being, I said "goo goo goo goo goo goo goo goo good b b b b b b b b b b b bye" to B.B. and headed back to Albert.

We continued down the brick street for about ten minutes. Why anyone would want to build a street out of brick was beyond me. 'Course, these were the same people who just might be stuck in a mall…

Now it's true that the brick street was somewhat pleasing to the eyes. But that's about the only part of the body that did find it pleasing.

My thoughts immediately turned to Pa. Pa had himself a little poem that we heard countless nights over the dinner table,

Any type of berry
in a crust will make a pie.
But an airplane made of concrete,
ain't never gonna fly.

'Course, it would have been a whole lot less confusing if Pa had just said that ingredients are interchangeble, while building materials aren't. At least, that was my interpretation of the poem. Everybody else, on the other hand, always thought that it meant that we were going to have pie for dinner. But if my interpretation was correct, I could only imagine what Pa thought of this brick road. He was probably thinking that this was one crazy city and that he wouldn't be surprised if we should soon come upon some houses made of asphalt.

I also knew Willie's opinion of building brick roads. He once told me, "Bricks are like the woman you decide to marry. Stacked, but never laid."

Well, my thoughts were interrupted as the drive made a left

hand turn onto a street made out of real asphalt. Albert stopped at the intersection, obviously because of a sign that said "No Left Hand Turns 6 a.m. – 10 a.m." and it was 9:50. Proud of my cow's intelligence and law abiding nature, I trotted back and pointed out to him that he could make the turn since the sign was only in effect Monday thru Friday. And sure enough, Albert then continued on…well, after nature called, that is.

"My God! People!"

Up and down West Front Street and on both sides, what looked to be the entire city of Tyler were standing en masse. They were cheering wildly and waving little Texas flags. Most were tossing roses of all sizes and colors into the air. Albert caught a pink baby rose in his mouth, which made him look quite debonair, until he ate it.

One thing I knew, B.B.'s inklings were, once again, on the mark. These people weren't trapped in a mall, they were out here all this time. But why? Why were they cheering, waving flags and tossing roses at cattle? Could they have spotted us coming? Could this be a surprise welcome for us? Or could this be a trap set up by E. Lester?

The mind! Just when you're convinced that you've forgotten those darn old troublesome thoughts, they pop right back out. I'll tell you, it makes you wonder how truly tormented people ever function.

I stood in my stirrups to survey the potential Eeoogie trap. In front of the herd were two differently outfitted groups of girls tossing batons. Both groups wore cowboy hats, but one group had on banners that said "Apache Belles", while the others wore banners which read "Rangerettes". The two groups appeared to be trying to see who could toss their batons higher and still catch them. The crowd seemed more delighted when one of them dropped a baton than when they set a new height catching record.

In front of the baton twirlers, I could hear the faint strains of "Everything's Coming Up Roses". Squinting, I was able to make out the Red Raiders Marching Band. They were only a little off beat, which was sorta amazing. Our high school's marching band was very much off beat and all they had to do was march and play. These Red Raiders also had to be on the lookout for wayward batons. As a matter of fact, just as the song ended, the tuba player missed a duck and caught a baton right square in the noggen. 'Course, the crowd applauded, I'm sure because they appreciated the mostly on beat rendition they had just heard and not because the tuba player was knocked unconscious. Unfortunately, if they had caught the errant baton, I think the Rangerettes would have had themselves the new record.

Obviously, this was not an Eeoogie trap, but a parade. I couldn't say how large it was because of some sorta float directly in front of the marching band. It was just so big that it blocked all view of the street ahead. It appeared to be covered with about a ton of red roses. A large white canopy covered the top of the float and billowed in the wind. I think I saw a few people seated underneath the canopy, dressed completely in white, but, then again, I might not have.

By now, I thought the parade was for us. Everybody was waving to us. And the cattle seemed to be soaking it all up. If they had fingers, I bet they would have waved back.

Through the cheers, I heard the unmistakable echo of a P.A. system in the not too far off distance, "And on this float...representing household condiments...is the Duchess of San Antonio... dressed as a bottle of ketchup. Actually, there are absolutely no tomato products covering her costume...but over one hundred red roses. Representing mustard...the Duchess of Corisicana's outfit contains over two hundred baby yellow roses. The Duchess of Beaville and the Duchess of Highland Park depict for us the ever popular salt and pepper...by their use of white and dead roses respectively." A polite applause went up from a crowd somewhere.

I looked around for the source of the P.A. and applause as I saw the big float turn right and the rest of the parade follow.

"And look...here come the Brothers of the Fez Lodge...riding in tiny little cars. Even though they might look silly now...when the brothers take off their tassle hats...they are actually upstanding members of this community. By the way...those tassles they are wearing on their hats...have all come from discarded high school graduation caps. Had the brothers not saved them...those tassles would have met a much less fortunate fate." The crowd errupted into a wild and sustained applause.

As the herd turned the corner, I was at once gazing at Rose Stadium, a massive oval structure complete with a large metallic rose affixed under its name. The big red rose-covered float clambered into one of the stadium's mammoth portals and disappeared.

"And now entering the stadium are the last of our Ladies-In-Waiting...Gloria Prescott from the House of Prescott. Gloria...a sophomore at S.M.U. and majoring in fraternities...is wearing an all white lace gown...with a white lace veil...which helps Gloria to keep her lovely complexion...Victoria Huisman...from the House of Huisman...is in her sophomore year at U.T. and is majoring in trying to make it to her junior year...You'll notice that Victoria's dress is a white silk gown...accentuated with a white silk trail...where over two thousand rhinestones have been hand-sewn...the pattern forming the State of Texas. Over five hundred rhinestones alone went into the panhandle...And Rebecca Yearson...from the House of Yearson...is a sophomore at T.C.U...but plans on taking a leave of absense and living off her trust fund for awhile...You knew she had to be wealthy, though. Beauty, body and grace certainly didn't get her the position of a Lady-In-Waiting...which is why Rebecca wants us to inform you that her daddy is the wealthiest of all and that her white gown cost the most." A respectful applause followed.

The herd was quickly approaching the stadium. Willie turned in his saddle and looked back to Pa. Pa signalled for Willie to stay on our present course. So, as the remainder of the parade continued toward the portal, the herd followed. I guess that Pa was thinking what I was thinking, and if the parade was for us, it would be downright inhospitable not to go into the stadium and thank our hosts.

"...Jefferson High Red Raider Marching Band...And, indeed, everything is coming up roses...Tyler General tells us that Todd Poret, the tuba player, suffered only a mild concussion...and has fully regained consciousness." A mighty cheer ensued.

The massive portal loomed before us, like a large mouth on a toothless giant. It had already swallowed the rest of the parade and looked very capable of accommodating five thousand head of cattle for dessert.

"...And traditionally last, but never least...the famous drill and dance squads...the always wholesome Kilgore Rangerettes... and just as pure...from our own Tyler Junior College...the Apache Belles. Girls...men all over Texas thank ya for keeping those skirts short and those leg kicks high."

Into the portal we went. The tunnel leading to the field was very long and very dark. It reverberated with the echo of thousands of hoofs clopping on its concrete floor. The applause of the crowd was barely audible. The faint speck of light coming from the other end of the tunnel was our only guide. Wondering what we would find, it very much reminded me of being led by the Star of Bethlehem. It was exhilarating — to be in my first parade, and to have it be in my honor and to being led by something like the Star of Bethlehem.

"And there you have it. The Texas Rose Festival's Celebration of Spices and Condiments. Queen Peggy Jean Elrepute and her Court thank ya'll for coming to the Rose Festival Parad…What the hell?"

I was momentarily blinded by the light as me and You Romantic You stepped onto the field. I covered my eyes to block the sun and then quickly glanced around. The stands, which completely surrounded us and looked like they went clear up to the ozone layer, were packed! And everyone of those people was waving little Texas flags. On the field were at least ten huge rose covered floats, twenty marching bands, thirty drill teams, forty members of the Good Sam Club, fifty grown men wearing silly cone-shaped hats with tassels, sixty people on motorcycles, seventy clowns and eighty women selling Mary Kay Cosmetics. And now, five thousand cows, who, at once, found the football turf delicious.

"Ladies and Gentlemen…Umm, there appears to be, umm, an addition to the program…Umm, ahhh, umm…I guess, um, to honor the condiment, umm…yes, that must be it! …Here are some real live Texas cattle to honor beef bouillon cubes!"

Well, you can imagine my surprise at the standing ovation we received. I was so taken that I dismounted my horse. Everyone was on their feet, applauding. I even heard people banging on their metal seats and chanting, "Bouillon Cubes! Bouillon Cubes! Bouillon Cubes!".

Albert came running towards me. At first, I thought he merely wanted to share the moment with me. Either that, or he was seeking my protection, fearful of one day becoming a beef bouillon cube. But when he suddenly tripped, I was able to see for the first time a private field-level viewing box in the direction from

which Albert was coming. In the box, some sorta commotion
ensued. A small group of very fancy dressed men and women
were involved in a bitter argument. After a few seconds, three of
the men stormed out of the box and onto the field. Actually, two of
the men stormed, the third just followed. No matter, the storm
appeared to be heading in Pa's direction. Albert must have meant
to warn me of the impending danger.

After making sure that Albert was okay and that he had suffered no more than a possible sprained ankle, I mounted You
Romantic You and rode over to Pa. The rest of the Old Miss company, me and the three men all converged on Pa at just about the
same time.

Before Pa could get out a "howdy" (Pa is the one who says
"howdy"), the fattest of the three men was on him. "What the hell
do ya think yer doin'???" the fat man screamed, his eyes and veins
bulging causing his bowtie to pop off. "Yer right in the middle of
the Rose Festival Parade!!!"

"Ya know," Pa said, his expression changing from a big old
smile to a big old frown. "I shoulda known that this here parade
wasn't fer us. But I figured we had to stop in just in case."

"Parade for you???" the oldest of the three yelled, causing his
chicken neck to vibrate.

"Just who are ya?" the third man chimed in, only because I
think he was trying to impress the other two.

"Well, fellas," Pa said, making extra sure to draw things out
nice and slow. "We're from the Old Miss Ranch, outside of
Grangerland."

"Well, go back, git out, leave!!!" warbled the obese one, his fat
dancing like fresh caught catfish under his shirt. "'fore ya ruin everthin'".

"What have we ruined?" Pa asked.

"The purpose and integrity of the Rose Festival!" the fat man
spat.

"My daughter's big day!" the chicken neck squawked.

"Well, the field," the third man said as he shuffled his feet.

"I like it best when the oldest guy yells," Tiny Bob said.
'Course, that got the chicken neck fluttering again, which pleased
Tiny Bob to no end.

"We didn't ruin nothin'," Little Ben said, stepping in.

"Ya didn't???," the oldest man said, his neck now shriveling with every word. "See that float right thar, the one yer goddamn cows are nibbling on. That's my daughter! Queen Peggy Jean Elrepute from the House of Elrepute!"

"Well then don't tell us we're ruinin' the integrity of yer shindig," Willie said. "Not when you crown a queen who comes from a house of ill repute."

"Elrepute!!!" the oldest man shouted. "The House of Elrepute. Fifth generation Texan."

"They're all fifth generation Texans," spat the fat man. "Fer people like ya'll to gaze at and admire. This is a society event! These are society women! Born and raised to be debutantes! This is not for you!!!"

"How 'bout Gerty?" Little Ben said.

"Yeah, then how 'bout Gerty?" Clint repeated.

"She's a sixth generation Texan!" Willie proudly proclaimed.

"Born and raised to be a champ," Big Bill bragged.

"A pure blooded Red Brangus!" Willie added.

"This ain't fer cows!!!" the fat man snapped.

"Then how'd that fat thin git to be in it," Willie said, pointing to the float that had been in front of us in the parade, and, in particular, to the obese Lady-In-Waiting wearing the most expensive gown.

"That is my daughter!!!" belted the fat man.

"Gerty weighs less," Little Ben stated.

"And Gerty's won sixteen blue ribbons," Big Bill said. "Bet that heifer of yers ain't won a thin."

The fat man's whole body quivered and quaked like a volcano about to blow its top. I took a step back so as not to be splattered with any gray matter.

"Ya just insulted Tyler's wealthiest citizen," the third man stated meekly.

"That ain't true," Willie said. "Big Bill here insulted his daughter."

"That's cause he insulted Gerty," Big Bill said. "Sayin' that she ain't good 'nough to be in yer festival."

Smoke was now pouring from the fat man's ears. So much so that you would have thought a new Pope had just been elected. The billowing bulk of fat turned to the third man and in a screech that made hair disappear back into its follicles said, "Yer The Goddamn Mayor, Do Somethin!!!!!!!"

The Mayor let the ringing in his ears stop and gave his arm hairs a chance to pop back out of their pores. He then spent a couple of minutes clearing his throat and trying to find his spine before he turned to Pa and spoke, "Look, yer all gonna have to leave.

"Pa broke his silence. "Can't do," Pa said. "Has to do with somethin said before, 'bout integrity. Obviously, our Gerty qualifies fer yer festival, but ya still ain't a gonna let her in. Well, ya can't go 'round havin' thins that are only opened to those of yer choosin'. I just can't condone exclusive types who make it seem that thar better than others, 'specially when, from what I've seen, yer all 'bout as special as the daily specials over at Elmo's Diner, which haven't changed in forty years. So, we ain't 'bout to leave, not 'til Gerty is allowed to participate."

"Ya warned 'em," gobbled the chicken neck turning to the Mayor. "Have 'em arrested!"

Before the Mayor could even consider hemming and hawing, a fiendish smirk broke out on the fat man's fat face. With much strain on his heart, I'm sure, he rubbed his pudgy hands together and said, "Or else, Mr. Mayor, my bank won't sponsor this here festival anymore and ya know how much Tyler's economy depends on it. And if our economy goes bust, the first person people are gonna blame is you."

"I knew he was a goddamn Eeoogie," B.B. said. "Should'a brought my rifle."

The Mayor looked around, maybe for a constable, or, maybe for a rock to hide under.

"Now ya'll might want to put us in jail," Pa said as calm as could be. "But that'll be yer mistake." Then, right before my eyes, Pa began to chant, "Bouillon Cubes". It took a few minutes before we all caught on and joined in. And before you knew it, the entire stadium was once again resounding with the banging of metal and the deafening shouts of "Bouillon Cubes! Bouillon Cubes! Bouillon Cubes!"

Pa turned to the mayor. "Them people know what's a goin' on. Ya could tell the minute we walked into the stadium. They relate to us, not to them stuffy floats or the people that think thar high falootin'. So, if ya really want to shut the festival down fer good, arrest us. I reckon the bad publicity and hard feelin's would close this here event a lot quicker than a shortage of some Eeoogie's money. 'Course, if ya opened up the festival to everyone, then you'd probably be able to make back the money that's a bein' pulled out. But, seein' how yer the Mayor, ya probably already thought of that."

The Mayor rubbed his brow, totally perplexed by reason.

"Have 'em arrested!" demanded the banker.

"Now, just hold on, Chester," the Mayor said. "I'm contemplatin' here."

"Don't be a weasel," whined the chicken neck.

"Well, he is a politician," B.B. said, which was the first thing that everyone, except the Mayor agreed with.

"I'm not a weasel," the Mayor said, "But, I'm just not so sure anymore that allowin' everyone to participate in the Rose festival is such a bad idea."

"What 'bout all of the tradition?" moaned the Eeoogie.

"Well, the tradition is sorta important," the Mayor said, turning to Pa.

"You'll be startin' a new tradition," Pa said.

"Ah, a new tradition," the Mayor chirped.

"But it won't have the same prestige if ya let poor people sit on the floats," Chicken Neck protested.

"True, it won't be the same with poor people on the floats," said the Mayor turning to Pa.

"It'll be better," Pa replied. "Prestige comes from power which comes from bein' strong. And ya git strong from liftin' things! And yer gonna be liftin' somethin…the prohibition against certain folks participatin' in the festival. That'll make ya stronger, which'll give ya more power and'll make this event even more prestigious."

'Course, this was the type of mumbo jumbo that only a politician could understand. "Makes perfectly good sense to me," the Mayor said, nodding in agreement.

"You are a weasel," the fat banker said, shaking his head in defeat.

Except, not to be a total weasel, at not least in his mind, the Mayor stated, "But, I still think the festival participants should be limited to humans," he said.

"Well, let's talk 'bout it," Pa said. And, as everyone stood around to negotiate, I turned You Romantic You away and gave her a slight kick. With the still deafening sounds of "Bouillon Cubes" rising from the stands, I headed for the fifty yard line and the biggest float of all.

Half-eaten red, then white, then pink roses spiraled around and around and up the gigantic float. The spiral ended at a rose covered canopy perched on top. And there, sitting on a mighty gold throne, was her majesty, Queen Peggy Jean Elrepute!

She was striking. Her buffont of blond hair looked as soft as mashed potatoes, with eyes as blue as dungarees. And here she was, sitting before me, in her white lace coronation gown and jewel encrusted tiara, her left hand clutching her scepter as her right hand was engaged in a perpetual wave. Her red popsicle colored lips opened and closed, constantly forming the words, "Hi, Ya'll".

I was just standing there in awe when suddenly, from nowhere and without warning, Albert streaked by me, jumped on the float and bolted up the little staircase which lead straight to the throne.

"My God, the Queen must be in trouble," I thought immediately. Even with a possible sprained front ankle, Albert, sensing danger, was reacting instinctively. Yes, he was going above and beyond the call of duty of a Deputy Agent. Fearlessly, he was rushing to the Queen's rescue.

Queen Elrepute, on the other hand, was oblivious to her peril and what was happening. She was facing the other direction and waving.

Realizing that Albert might need my assistance, I hopped onto the float and ran after him. All the while, I hoped that we weren't too late.

As Albert reached the throne, his ankle gave way and he tripped on the top stair. With her hand in a half-wave, Queen Elrepute immediately turned her head in the direction of the noise. She looked at Albert as he righted his front torso.

"Hi, Ya'll," Queen Elrepute said, marking my spontaneous and winded arrival. "I think it's real cute that ya'll trained this here cow to bow fer me."

"Thank you," I said, thinking to myself that if that was what she believed, so much the better. I saw no need to scare the Queen. As I caught my breath, I glanced around to find the cause of

Albert's concern. Well, be it a royal subject about to make an attempt on the Queen's life or some other act of festival terror, Albert must have succeeded in thwarting the plan. Everything appeared normal and calm.

The Queen, still impressed by the fact that Albert had been taught to bow, tapped him on both of his shoulder blades with her royal scepter. I was not about to correct her misconceptions, mainly because I believed that Albert, indeed, deserved to be dubbed by her Royal Highness. Little did she know that she now owed her life to this hero.

Following the rules of proper royal etiquette, I bowed to the Queen before leading Sir Albert down the steps and off the float. He was hobbling a bit, but he did not appear to be in too much pain. Once we we reached You Romantic You, I stopped and turned to Sir Albert.

"You are so brave," I whispered into his ear before I hugged him around his neck.

"'Fore ya git too lovey dovey," Tiny Bob said, appearing from out of the blue on top of Fido. "Pa wants ya back."

Tiny Bob turned Fido in the direction of Pa and the others before looking back over his shoulder at me with my arms still around Sir Albert. "Ya know," he added. "I gotta say that that thar cow of yers can really move when he gits a good slingshot to the rump."

"You keep away from my cow!" I shouted after Tiny Bob as he trotted away. "You have no right to touch royalty, you peasant!" Seething, I hopped off of my horse and petted Sir Albert until I had cooled down enough to join the others.

Me, You Romantic You and Sir Albert returned just as they were completing the negotiations. Pa had acquiesced about limiting the festival to humans, so long as the Mayor promised that all humans had the equal right to participate. And Pa believed him, despite the fact that he was a politician, mainly because he agreed to read any agreement they reached over the P.A. for all to hear.

In return, the Mayor had also agreed to stock us up with the supplies we needed if Pa agreed to get the drive moving. 'Course, we weren't planning on staying in Tyler anyway, so we had definitely come out way ahead on the bargain.

The crowd reacted to the Mayor's announcement with wild

enthusiasm. This was a great relief, especially because there was a near riot when the Mayor came on the P.A. and interrupted the "Bouillon Cube" chant. Then, even though the parade had been over for awhile, the entire crowd stayed, to show their support and appreciation and to ensure that we got what was promised to us. Our supplies were delivered to us right quick too. I'm sure the Eeoogie was responsible for this. There's no doubt that he wanted us gone.

During the time it took us to get the supplies, the crowd was entertained by, or should I say, subjected to fourteen renditions of "Everything's Coming Up Roses" with lyrics sung by the Good Sam Club. Fortunately, a spontaneous tug-o-war broke out between the Brothers of the Fez and the Mary Kay women which helped to break the monotony. The Mary Kay women won decisively, despite an appeal by the Brothers that their tassles got in their way.

A procession of police vehicles delivered the supplies. Sheriff Slim Thiggins, in his Tyler cruiser, lead the procession. Overseeing the whole transaction was Sister Dorothy Lertz, a neutral observer. So you could say that the chances of one side cheating on the deal were on the order of Slim to Nun.

Once B.B. assured us that the provisions were in place and that we were completely restocked, we returned to our drive positions. Willie began to turn the herd around as Sheriff Slim's men prepared to lead us out. The crowd gave us a long, sustained standing ovation. Queen Elrepute threw Sir Albert a rose, which he promptly devoured. And Gerty, who I guess got wind of everything that had transpired, worked her way to the front and appeared as if she was all set to lead the herd with a baton in her mouth.

I was just starting to mentally prepare myself for the transition from parade back to work when Pa came trotting over. He was followed by Sheriff Slim and Sister Dorothy.

"Bert Boy," Pa said. "The good Sister here wanted to speak to ya fer a minute." Pa and the Sheriff then stepped back to talk.

Perplexed, I subtly inspected her hands for raffle tickets. "Pa is holding all my money," I said, thinking that I had, indeed, seen something.

The Sister opened her hand, displaying Rosary Beads. I would have felt really awful had the Sister not been hard of hearing and missed my comment entirely. She stared at the beads for a few seconds before she looked up and began to stare at me. Finally, with a look of total bewilderment on her face, she said, "Yes, Young Man?"

"You wanted to speak to me, Ma'am?" I asked, stepping down from You Romantic You.

Sister Dorothy scratched her head.

"That's what you told my pa," I said.

She shrugged her shoulders and began to whistle. I was just thinking that this whole thing was a might odd, when, suddenly, Sister Dorothy stopped whistling.

"Young Man," she said. "I wanted to talk to you."

"Yes, Ma'am?"

"I'm here on behalf of my Order...Our Ladies Of Fleeting Recall...

Sister Dorothy's face went blank. After a moment, she began to hum.

Now, I hated to interrupt, but I knew it wouldn't be long before we'd be leaving. "Ma'am?" I said.

Sister Dorothy ceased her humming and gave me a very stern look. However, that quickly passed. "Young Man, I wanted to talk to you," she said.

"About Our Ladies Of Fleeting Recall?" I asked.

From the look on Sister Dorothy's face, she must have thought that I could read minds or something. "Well, we used to be Our Ladies Of The Knighted Cow, but we never thought we'd see the likes of a Knighted Cow, so we gave up the cause," she said before returning to oblivion.

I was beginning to understand how this Catholic ended up in Baptist country.

"Young Man, I wanted to talk to you," she said.

"Cow," I replied.

Sister Dorothy rolled her eyes. It took about a minute for a synapse to connect. "So it's just amazing that from nowhere, a Knighted Cow appears. And since you seem to be friends with him, me and the girls were wondering if we could take a group shot with him...for old time sakes."

Sister Dorothy returned to space. I waited patiently.

"Young Man, I wanted to talk to you."

"Ma'am?"

"Yes, we're holding a raffle to raise money for the convent," she said. "Five tickets for a dollar. How many would you like?"

"Group shot," I said.

Sister Dorothy's face went through a few painful twists. "So, could you introduce us to your friend, so we can take the group shot with him?" she asked.

"Sure, Ma'am," I said as I rushed her over to Sir Albert. I sped through the introductions and ran over to Pa before Sister Dorothy had another chance to fleet.

"That's my orders," Sheriff Slim was saying to Pa. "To escort ya to the city limits in any direction ya wanna go."

"If ya can take us to Highway 20, I reckon that that would be fine," Pa said.

"I'll take ya there, but I hope ya weren't plannin' on usin' it," Sheriff Slim said.

"Why?" Pa asked, appearing perplexed. "Is somethin' wrong with the highway?"

"No," Sheriff Slim said. "But, if you were thinkin' 'bout drivin' the herd on it, no can do. All highways is now strictly for vee-hickles."

"Is that just in Texas?" Pa asked.

"As far as I know, everywhere in the whole dang Union," Sheriff Slim said.

I couldn't believe my ears. This was the worst news possible. Our entire itinerary wiped out in a flash! Without the highways to travel on, how would we be able to continue to the place Dr. Namath called the biggest meat market in the world? Was the drive about to come to a screeching halt? That'd mean that we'd be stranded on the outskirts of Tyler. I mean, the only other option was to return from where we came. Either way, E. Lester would have little trouble finding us.

Poor us. Poor Sir Albert. I had become so absorbed in this shattering new development that I had forgotten about Sir Albert. I looked back to find nuns crawling all over him. I ran as fast as I could.

"Oh Blessed Knighted Cow," one nun said as she crossed herself in front of Sir Albert.

"Giddyup," another nun said as she sat on Sir Albert's back.

"Good posture, Young Man" said yet another nun as she hit Sir Albert's behind with a ruler.

"Why are we here?" asked another.

"Excuse me, Sisters," I said as I believe I saw a look of relief cross Sir Albert's face. "I think we're going to be leaving."

The good sisters all looked in my direction, and then, in unison, their faces went blank.

"Raffle tickets," I said, thinking quickly. Then I added, "The Mayor".

One by one, in an Orderly stupor, the nuns left Sir Albert and, with raffle tickets in hand, headed for the Mayor.

Sir Albert lowered his head and came up with a clump of grass — obviously a royal gesture of appreciation.

"Anytime, dear friend, and no thanks are necessary" I said. "And, unfortunately, we have serious problems to attend to."

I relayed to Sir Albert what I had overheard. In the background, Sheriff Slim's siren began a slow "wah wah" building into a full-fledged wail. A host of other sirens joined in, sounding like some sorta ugly mating call. The flashing reds and blues completed the sound and light extravaganza.

Slowly, the herd began to move. I looked at Sir Albert, but there was nothing to say. All around us, the crowd continued their ovation. It was now such an irony, but I couldn't fault them. How could they know that their cheerful applause was sending us to the sad conclusion of our dream? I knew how an old timer at an old timer's ball game must feel.

19

SHERIFF SLIM AND his boys left us on a vacant grazing field just over the Tyler city line. The sheriff accommodated us as best he could by taking us east. Unfortunately, the spot itself conjured up the feeling of being in a candy store without any money. No more than a hundred yards in front of us ran Highway 20, the no longer viable route to New York.

B.B. fixed a late lunch while the rest of us sat around listening to Pa explain what I already knew, our latest present predicament. I sat quietly and watched the traffic speed down Highway 20, that is, until the darndest thing came chugging along. It had four wheels and Winnebago embossed on its side, but I don't think I'd quite call it a vehicle. Rather, I'd call it a living room.

The living room was still in sight when Pa concluded. By now, it had picked up ten cars in its wake. These cars were honking their horns, and I wondered if this was some kinda signal of admiration.

The Old Miss company just sat there, sorta stunned. Not so much because a living room had just driven by, but because of what Pa had said. Pa's words were so disheartening that even Willie couldn't think of anything to smile about, and I happen to know that he had pulled a practical joke which he was dying to tell us about- something to do with the fat banker's daughter and Gerty's feed bag.

"Lunch," B.B. cried. Slowly, we proceeded over to the chuck wagon. B.B. had prepared a wagon special, pinto bean sandwiches. I don't know whether B.B. had consulted his inklings before choosing the menu, but this couldn't have been a better choice. One medicinal quality of beans that is often overlooked is their ability to make you really concentrate and think. Hence, the expression "That's using the old bean". 'Course, new beans work too.

"So we're stuck," Little Ben said as he took a sandwich and sat back down.

"Just sittin' here waitin' fer E. Lester," Willie said munching away. "Good bean sandwich, B.B."

B.B. didn't say anything. Not that he didn't appreciate the compliment, but his beans already had him thinking about alternatives to our present fate. In anger, he began to wave his serving spoon in the air, flinging little bitty bean pieces everywhere.

Even Big Bill's beans helped a little. "By the time E. Lester gits here, maybe I'll have the money to pay 'im off," Big Bill said, displaying a hand full of the Order of Fleeting Recall raffle tickets.

"What's the prize?" Willie asked.

Big Bill studied the tickets. "It don't say," Big Bill replied.

"When's the drawin'?" Little Ben asked.

"Thar ain't no date on these thins," Big Bill said dejectedly.

"Well, I hope ya didn't pay a lot fer them," B.B. said.

"Didn't cost a cent," he said suddenly perking up. "The Good Sisters forgot to ask me to pay." All in all, I felt that some sorta status quo was reached.

During this exchange, I had prepared myself three four scoop bean sandwiches. These were mighty hefty sandwiches by anyone's standards. Yet, for the good of the Old Miss and for the good of my stomach, I finished them all off. I then sat back and let the beans do their thing.

At the end of the field stood an old farmhouse and barn. From where I was sitting, they looked long deserted. I swung my head and glanced back to Highway 20. I wondered if any of the people driving by could tell of our dilemma, or would they think that we just belonged here?

Think we belonged here?

This statement echoed in my head. I could feel bean power rushing to my brain. The highway was too far for the people to see that the farmhouse and barn were empty. To them, we must have looked like typical ranchers with a typical herd out for a typical graze. So, what if…

"Pa," I shouted.

Bert Boy?" Pa replied through a mouthful of beans.

"We make it look like we belong," I said, immediately realizing that I was concluding before I was beginning. I took a deep breath to slow myself down and to give Pa a chance to swallow.

"We can't travel on highways because we aren't allowed," I continued. "And it's not likely that people will let us go traipsing across their properties, again, because we aren't allowed there... unless, of course, they don't realize that. So, we make it look like we do belong there."

"I'm sorry, Bert Boy," Pa said. "I ain't digested the number of beans that ya ate, so I'm a havin' a little trouble followin'."

"We move the herd from grazing field to grazing field, or anywhere else Willie finds other cattle," I said excitedly. "We move them at night and, during the day, we leave them as close as we can next to the other cows...'course, making sure that the two herds don't mix. Then, we all sorta hide out until night. That way, during the day, whoever passes by will just be looking at a mess of cows, some that belong and some that don't. But since everyone, including the owner of the land, is expecting to look out and see cows, nothing will seem wrong."

Pa took another bite of his sandwich. With every chew, the corners of his mouth turned more and more skyward. With a satisfied gulp, he turned to Willie. "Willie, ya think ya can find us herds big enough to hide our cattle among?" he asked.

"If I can't, I don't deserve to be a scout no more," Willie said confidently. Beans or no beans, this was the thinking everyone needed to hear. I know that I felt the spark of optimism spreading.

"It'll mean drivin' in the dark," Pa said. "And that'll make it tough keepin' the herd together."

The chilling thought of a nighttime stampede crossed my mind. Yet, I didn't say a word. I didn't want to douse the spark.

"It'll mean sleeping during the day," Pa continued, turning to Big Bill. "Do ya think ya can handle it?"

Big Bill had real troubles sleeping when there was any light around. Me, on the other hand, had problems for some time sleeping with the lights off. Anyway, after Big Bill's problem refused to go away, Old Doc Buford examined him and found Big Bill's eyelids were defective. It seems Big Bill was born with meagerorb-coveritis — eyelids that were half the thickness of normal eyelids. Maybe some of the skin meant for his lids went to his feet instead.

In any event, Doc Buford described it as akin to having clear plastic over your windows to keep the sun out. Two recommended treatments were an eyelid transplant or a dark mask to wear over the eyes when sleeping. Big Bill opted for the second.

"Sure Pa," Big Bill said. "I brought my mask."

Pa nodded approvingly, before turning back to the rest of us. "Travelin' at night'll also mean no more campfires," Pa said. "Which'll mean no more s'mores."

My eyes widened. I had not fully comprehended all of the ramifications of a night drive. But, what other choice was there?

"Sacrifices gotta be made," Little Ben said.

One by one, Pa looked into each of our faces. Well, all except Tiny Bob's, who had somehow succeeded in getting his face stuck in a groundhog hole. We all agreed with Little Ben.

"Well, I guess that's it then," Pa said as he slowly rose to his feet. "Git some rest. We'll be a leavin' tonight. And Bill Boy, don't put yer mask on 'til after ya find a place to rest. Remember how ya almost fell off a cliff once."

Everybody except Big Bill and Tiny Bob scattered in search of napping spots. Big Bill went to the wagon to get his mask, and Tiny Bob, with his face still stuck in the hole, just sorta slumped over. It looked mighty uncomfortable, the way his neck bent at a ninety degree angle, but who was I to tell a Bob Mine how to sleep.

I found a nice little shaded place under a large tree. It came complete with a nice breeze created by the traffic whizzing past on Highway 20. I made myself comfortable, lowering the brim of my hat over my eyes. All beaned out, I quickly fell asleep.

I dreamed it was dusk and we were about to start up the drive. The surroundings were very green, pines and oaks, so we weren't in Texas anymore. Maybe Kansas. There were two herds of cattle, one ours, one I didn't recognize. The entire Old Miss company was coming over and patting me on the back, saying that we never would have gotten so far if it hadn't been for me. Pa said he was so proud of me that he'd let me take lead which lead to a congratulatory clomp on the back from Sir Albert. Excitedly, I crossed over a small bayou and retrieved You Romantic You from among the oak tree where she was tied. Mounting her, I heard a voice above me.

"Yer different, Even Tinier Bert…or, so I thought. But, this was yer idear! Never figured ya'd be as deceivin' as the rest of them Old

Missers. Did ya really think ya could hide from me? Well, Even Tinier Bert, I've found ya and since this was yer idear, you'll be the first to suffer the consequences."

I quickly looked up. Poised and ready to pounce was E. Lester!

I sat up like a sprung mousetrap. I yanked off my hat. A cold sweat covered the brim. I shot a glance skyward only to find the branches above me void of any Eeoogies.

"Ya okay, Bert Boy?" Pa said. I snapped my head around and saw that Pa was sitting next to me.

"Hope it wasn't me that startled ya," he said as my heart continued to pump quicker than a dehydrated man at a deep well. "But I figured I'd come over here while ya were a sleepin'… just in case. While them beans are good thinkin' material, they can also lead to some mighty funny dreams."

A strange thing, the mind. You go to sleep content, only to have those darn old troublesome thoughts pop up in your dreams. Grangerland's own Wilheim Godfrig, PhD., tried to tackle this problem and sat down to invent a spigot to turn on and off the brain. This was definitely a noble and challenging undertaking by the local gym teacher (PhD. is Grangerland's abbreviation for physical education). Unfortunately, the project failed and now Mr. Godfrig has to walk around with a metal pipe protruding from his head.

Pa removed his pouch and helped himself to a wad of tobacco. "I'd offer ya some, but I know how ya probably don't want any since ya still got beans in yer system," he said as he winked at me.

I smiled. I couldn't even keep my hatred for the stuff hidden from Pa. How did he always know? I figured that B.B.'s lump helped him to know me inside and out. But Pa, well, it was different with him. He not only knew me inside and out, but upside down, downside up and any other way I happened to be. Sure, he was my pa, but I'm not sure that all pa's connect on this level. I think the fact that he had also been Surrogate Ma played a part.

The two of us sat there in silence, interrupted only by Pa's occasional "phtooey".

"Pa," I finally said as a look of concern crossed my face. But before I could get out another word, Pa raised a finger to his lips.

"Bert Boy," he said. "A man's gotta do what a man's gotta do. A woman's gotta do what a woman's gotta do. A dog's gotta do what a dog's gotta do. A cat's gotta do what a cat's gotta do." He stopped, figuring that I got the point.

"But it's kinda deceitful, for us to go hiding out and sneaking around and all," I replied.

Pa took a chew and studied my face. "Do ya think the cattle drive is wrong?" he asked.

"No," I said without hesitation. "You, us, your pa…we've all worked hard for those cattle. It's bad enough that we had to lose the ranch."

Pa spat. "Well, then Bert Boy," he said. "Sometimes when ya truly believe yer right in the long haul ya gotta do thins in the short haul which might not seem exactly right." I pondered this for a few minutes.

"Like at the Rose Festival?" I finally said. Pa nodded affirmatively and suddenly everything made sense.

Pa spat. "Bert Boy, ya ain't deceitful. Ya got integrity and ya make me proud. It wasn't just them beans 'fore. Ya got yerself one good head on them shoulders. Keep on usin' it and ya'll be goin' far. Ya might even end up a runnin' the New Miss when I'm gone…'course, that's once we have a New Miss."

A branding iron couldn't have had more of an impact. "But Pa, Big Bill's the oldest and Little Ben's the smartest," I said.

"Don't go lookin' so stunned," Pa said. "I ain't a gonna be gone fer a long while and ya still need a lot more maturin'. But who ever said that ya gotta be the oldest or that ya ain't as smart as anyone else? Don't sell yerself short. Ya got the leadership qualities ya need right now. You're articulate. Ya got heart. And ya got smarts, the book smarts and the smarts to know yer limits. Ya see, then ya can take yer determination and yer book smarts and yer limits and y'articulate what has to be done. Older people are already listenin' to what ya have to say."

I remained quiet for sometime, while Pa continued to chew. The ground rumbled slightly from the vibrations of Tiny Bob's underground snoring.

"Pa," I eventually uttered. "How do you know all these things about me when I don't even know these things about me? Is it some sorta inklings?"

"No," he replied with a big brown smile. "I was just like ya when I was yer age.

20

ALL WE NEEDED WAS Pa and we were ready to depart as dusk settled over the Tyler metropolitan area. I watched the last ray of sun as it lingered on the horizon. Soon, all but our newfound hopes would be dark. The drive had met with more obstacles than the Grangerland miniature golf course, yet we had surmounted each one. 'Course, we hadn't met with any windmills yet. There's no denying that the drive had been stalled on more occasions than we would have liked, but we had yet to reach the six stroke limit.

Because of the change in circumstances, Pa had spent the afternoon mapping out a new route...one over sparsely populated areas and farmlands. Roughly, Pa now had us traveling through Southern Arkansas on a northeast course heading into Mississippi. Once we were clear of Memphis, we'd then swing north into Tennessee. Between Nashville and Knoxville, we'd again turn north and steer for Kentucky. We'd traverse the blue grass state bearing northeast until we hit West Virginia. From there, we'd continue in the same direction, crossing into Western Maryland and Pennsylvania. We'd follow the Appalachians and Pocono Mountains into New Jersey, and, at that point, the map showed a straight shot east into New York City.

Anyway, Pa had gone to call Uncle Ray and Aunt Tammy Faye to give them the new itinerary, even though it was extremely general and subject to change depending on where other herds could be located. While waiting for Pa's return, we discussed the new itinerary. Only B.B. expressed disappointment — the only state left of any interest to him was West Virginee.

Willie had taken off right after Pa and had returned a few hours later with a positive scouting report. He had located a large herd of cattle about three miles northeast of the town of Judson. Altogether, this was approximately twenty-five miles away and happened to be exactly enroute. Everyone congratulated Willie, who tried to downplay his scouting ability, claiming that it was still fairly easy to find cattle in Texas and that his real test was soon to come. Still, the news was good and the comradery got the blood flowing, so who really cared?

In preparation to leave, Little Ben tried to explain to Big Bill that putting headlights on the cattle would sorta defeat the purpose of our night drives, while Clint and Willie attempted to exhume Tiny Bob's head from the ground. Each had a leg and they tugged and pulled until it became disgorged with a POP. There was momentary panic as Tiny Bob played "the old head in the shirt" trick, but even if his head had been left behind, I honestly believe that he would have gotten use to it.

It was about then that Pa came galloping back into camp. Pa rarely galloped into camp, so we knew that something was up. He appeared troubled, and I am reasonably sure that it had little to do with Tiny Bob almost losing his head.

"Somethin wrong, Eugene?" B.B. asked as we all gathered around.

"How are we fixed fer movin' out?" Pa responded in his let's-see-what-the-situation-is-like-here-first-before-I-explain tone.

"All ready," Willie said. "Even got tomorrow's camp scouted."

"Good," Pa replied, changing into his now-I'll-tell-you tone. "I talked to Ray and Tammy Faye. 'Course, what they heard is all just rumors and ya know what I think of rumors." Pa hated rumors. He hated rumors so much that when we were growing up, he forbid us from playing the "telephone game", where a phrase is whispered from person to person with the goal being to see how the phrase changes as it makes its way down the line.

"So thar's no cause fer alarm," Pa continued. "But thar's a chance that when E. Lester left town, he didn't leave town alone. He mighta left with a possee and a gunslinger named Moe."

Possee! Gunslinger! My mouth dropped involuntarily. My nightmare had been vivid enough, caused by the subconscious fear of a single solitary Eeoogie on our trail. And now I was hearing that an Eeoogie was being joined by not only a possee, but a gunslinger. This was no longer one man's search for his collateral. This had escalated into a full-blown, out and out, picture on a milk carton, cow and manhunt!

"Now see, some of ya are startin' to worry," Pa said, trying not to look directly at me. "Like I said, it's just hearsay. 'Sides we still got a good head start and a good plan to git us cross country. And we'll be in touch with Ray and Tammy Faye, who, by the way, think the itinerary is just fine. But it still don't hurt none if we git a move on."

"And even if it's true, we'll be ready fer 'em," B.B. said tapping his lump, which was a comforting thought, but also pointing to his rifle, which was not.

"We'll worry 'bout guns later," Pa said. "And we'll worry 'bout worryin' later. In the meantime, let's git out thar and concentrate on the drive."

I bolted over to You Romantic You, but only because we were in a hurry. Before I mounted her, I found myself checking the branches overhead. Finding them empty, again, I realized how silly I was being. Despite its vividness, the dream had been just that, a dream. Pa was right. I was worrying about something which I'd have no control over even if it turned out to be true. So what if E. Lester was out there? So what if he had a possee? So what if he even had a gunslinger named Moe? I just wasn't going to let it worry me!

B.B. climbed into the wagon as everybody else, including Tiny Almost Headless Bob, mounted their horses. And so began our first of what we hoped would be many night drives to come. (Oh, please don't let the rumors be true...)

21

IT WOULD HAVE BEEN nice had the moon been out for the first night, but, fortunately, no one had the time to contemplate whether this should have been taken as a bad omen. Actually, had we stopped to think about it, I probably would have voted to consider this a good omen. With no moon to light the landscape, I had to use all of my energy just to concentrate on the drive. This completely took my mind off of E. Lester…Well, almost completely. But I didn't really see the point in worrying about an Eeoogie that I couldn't have seen if I tried, which is difficult with a person of his hefty size. It was so dark out that I couldn't describe anything we might have passed. I think, though, that we passed near the towns of Big Sandy and White Oak. I ended the first night with a couple of scratches on my face, so I must have passed a few trees too.

For a while, I had Sir Albert by my side helping me watch for strays. Not that either of us could have seen one anyway, mind you, but I did enjoy the company. Fortunately, the cattle were a little intimidated by the pitch blackness and remained more like a swarm than like a herd. Unfortunately, I lost Sir Albert somewhere in the swarm a few hours before sunrise.

After traveling throughout the night, we came upon the herd of cattle that Willie had scouted out. I couldn't see what the breed was, but I could tell by the resonance and quality of the moos that this was a large herd which was happy to see some new friends. We quickly moved the Old Miss cattle into position next to this other herd, where we realized at once that it was going to be nearly impossible to keep the two herds totally separated. So, we decided that we would have to work under the premise that we were going to lose a few of our cattle enroute, but that we'd try to keep our losses to a mimimum.

Exhausted, we left the cattle and found a fairly secluded wooded area nearby to set up camp. Clint climbed a tree and took first watch over the cattle as the rest of us found places to bed down. Spectacular streams of multicolored haze fanned the horizon as I quickly fell asleep.

I awoke around two in the afternoon to the smell of barbequed ribs. I now knew why every dream I had had centered around the fine art of licking. The truth was that the Old Miss had the best ribs in Texas, bar none. To honor their creator, the Grangerland City Council voted to drop the "Q" and adopt the name, "B.B. ribs". No matter what you called them, the sauce played a symphony on your tastebuds while the sweet, tender meat danced around in your mouth.

The minute B.B. rang his little triangle, I leapt from my sleeping spot and joined the others in a race to the food. "Ya boys all that hungry?" B.B. said with a smirk as everybody, except Pa, pushed and shoved and jostled their way into a bunch.

"If ya'll can't form a line, then B.B. just ain't a gonna fix this no more," Pa said in a very disappointed tone of voice. And it was sad, but true that all semblance of manners fell to the wayside when B.B. ribs were in town.

Half-hearted replies of "Sorry Pa" and "Sorry Mr. Henry" were forthcoming as Pa moved to the front of the line and we continued to secretly push and shove and jostle behind him. I ended up dead last behind Willie.

"So what's the occasion?" Willie asked as B.B. placed a slab o' ribs on his plate.

"Thought ya'll deserved a treat," B.B. said. "Our first night's done, we got here with no problems or signs of E. Lester, and my inklins told me so long as I kept the fire low, we weren't a gonna be discovered." B.B. pointed to the barbeque pit he had contructed where a small, controlled fire burned. 'Course, a low fire was one of the key ingredients of B.B. ribs, so this was nothing out of the ordinary. Puffs of smoke rose from the flames, dissipating and disappearing in the surrounding trees.

I smiled broadly as B.B. served me up my slab, mainly because that's all I could do. He understood that for me to open my mouth now could be a disaster. As I stared at my plate, I could feel my tastebuds tuning up.

I sat down under a tree and began to indulge, feeling at once a special closeness to our primitive ancestors. I ripped each rib from its slab o' brethern. I stared and admired the reddish brown and black charcoaled beauty, each rib a single unit of pleasure. My own gnawing joined in with the others, adding a new dimension to the sounds of the woods. I laid back to enjoy my remaining ribs and to suck on all those conquered bones, hoping that I had missed some precious meat. I became blissfully covered in sauce, and I loved it.

I was sad, but content when I looked down and saw nothing but marrow. Dejectedly, I took my plate over to the chuck wagon. Before putting it away, I literally licked it clean then walked over to Pa and told him that I would go and check on the herd. He understood my melancholy, the one unfortunate side effect of B.B. ribs which always follows the immoral words, "thar ain't no more".

I mounted You Romantic You and slowly rode off into the late afternoon sun. Yes, hours had passed, yet we had been on rib time, where time is not measured in seconds, because usually there aren't any. With rib time, the standard fluctuates depending on what's left- the less ribs left to be eaten, the faster the time moves.

I was careful to be sure that no one spotted me approaching the cattle. I could see now that the herd we had left our cattle with were also Red Muleys. So, unless someone had come by and noticed the OM brand, we couldn't have been safer. Yet, I still felt a tinge of wistfulness left. I needed a dose of Sir Albert.

I first checked our herd. There was no sign of him. I then found the inevitable break in the barbed wire fence and checked the other herd. Again, there was no sign of him. I did find a few of our cattle who had also discovered this opening and had strayed through. However, since we were now anticipating loses, I figured it was better to leave them than risk being caught roping cattle on someone else's property. The last thing I wanted was to be shot as a rustler. That would definitely put a damper on the ribs.

I made one more sweep of our herd. Nothing. No Sir Albert. Where was he? Suddenly, a horrible answer came to mind.

I raced over to You Romantic You, leaping into the saddle. Willie probably would have been proud of the mount, but that didn't matter now. I disregarded the fear of discovery and galloped back to camp, racing through a field which was totally exposed.

Pa met me as I arrived in a cloud of dust. But before he could reprimand me, I dismounted and ran over to B.B. "B.B.," I said in a shakey, breathless voice. "Those were pork ribs we had today, right?"

"Nope," B.B. said as he finished placing the cooking utensils back into the wagon. "Beef."

"Did you bring them with us from Grangerland or did you get them in Tyler?"

"Even Tinier Bert, ya know better than that. Meat'll spoil. I found myself a nice sized calf this mornin' and…"

That was all I heard as I flew past Pa, whose mouth now hung open, and remounted You Romantic You. We were quickly in a gait heading back to the herd. A wave of nausea passed through my body as one all consuming thought stuck in my mind — we've eaten Albert!

"Albert," I shouted upon arrival. "Sir Albert, where are you?" Had I been thinking straight, I would have realized that, again, I was placing us at great risk. But, in my dread-filled mind, they were risks I had to take. A memory of a friend might keep you company, but it can't play fetch.

I rode through both herds, shouting for Albert and then waiting in anxious silence for a familiar reply. Nothing. How could this have happened? And how could I ever live with myself? Cannibal, that's what I was. And not only had I participated in eating my best and royal friend, but I had enjoyed it! And even that wasn't quite accurate — I had enjoyed it immensely! I looked down at the sauce-covered sleeve of my shirt and began to cry.

When the tears finally ceased, I closed my eyes and prayed that Sir Albert was now being well taken care of elsewhere.

I knew that I eventually had to head back and properly bury whatever rib bones I could find. Yet, for now, I could do no more than sit in the saddle and listen to the faint sounds of a church organ over the herds. The music had a soothing healing effect, and sounded vaguely familiar — perhaps because the organist repeated the same song over and over. I became strangely drawn to find the source of the music and thank whoever was responsible for its timely play. I shook the reins, and we headed in the direction of the melody.

After half an hour, led on by the only song the organist knew, we came upon Judson Baptist Church. It was a small white wood building on the far outskirts of town. It came complete with a large black felt poster board, a huge white steeple and a cow standing on its front steps. A cow? A cow! It was Albert! He was not in my stomach being subjected to enzymatic juices at all! He was here, alive, standing in front of this church! Then, as my grief vanished, it struck me just what song was drifting out through the open church windows — Onward Christian Soldier!

I jumped off of You Romantic You and ran over to Sir Albert. I hugged him so hard that had I continued, I might have processed his innards into hot dogs. Sir Albert momentarily came out of his dazed state and curled his cow lips, obviously, a smile. Quickly, I removed my socks and stuffed them in his ears, then roped him and swiftly led him away.

About a mile or so from the church, I freed Sir Albert and a joyous reunion was had by all. I told him what had happened and how I thought he was gone forever. He nodded as if he understood, but I doubt that he heard anything with those socks in his ears. But, it really didn't matter — we were together. As Pa always says, "What counts are family, friends and mathematicians".

I tried to keep this in mind as I rode back into camp with Sir Albert. I was expecting to get chewed out by Pa for my careless actions. So, I thought I'd introduce Pa to Sir Albert, tell him about my friend and then quote Pa's own motto. Well, I did and did and did.

"It's good that ya care 'bout yer friends," Pa said, patting Sir Albert. "And I never told ya who yer friends should be and it don't matter if thar different. I mean, that's sorta what we were standin' up fer in Tyler."

"But," he continued. "We coulda all been found out by the landowners if ya woulda been seen, and while I told ya not to worry, we still gotta be careful 'bout E. Lester. So, I ain't sayin' ya didn't do the noble thin, but sometimes ya gotta make a vowel with yerself to sidetrack yer impulses, even if it's just fer a second, and think thins out. The difference between motions and emotions is that vowel."

"I'm sorry, Pa, but I panicked."

"Well, a panic turns into a picnic when ya remember to keep the basket and the case separate," Pa said. While this one flew over my head, by now I understood the gist of what Pa was getting at.

"Anyway, I think ya understand, so I ain't gonna say no more, 'cept that ya can probably take yer socks out of yer cow's ears now," Pa continued. "But Bert Boy, don't feel too bad. Yer still mighty young and yer gonna make some mistakes. That's what maturin's all about." Pa patted Sir Albert one last time before he turned and walked off.

I removed the socks and stroked Sir Albert. I wondered if I'd ever be able to eat meat again. But rather than rush into an emotional response, I figured that I'd just wait and see.

22

"CIRCLE 'ROUND, BOYS," Pa shouted. From all directions, we turned our steeds and converged upon Pa.

"Somethin wrong, Mr. Henry?" Willie asked as he brought Clint's Pickle to a halt.

"I just wanted to let ya'll know that we just left Texas," Pa replied solemnly.

I hadn't seen an emotional moment like this since Eunice Dumkin married Siamese twins and then was arrested on her honeymoon for bigamy. The judge refused to hear the pleas from the community that her husband came as a pair.

True, we knew this moment was going to come sooner or later. And, often, the anticipation far outnerves the actual event. But this was one time when it had been impossible to gauge how we would feel at this moment.

"Pa, I feel sick," Tiny Bob said.

"I know how ya feel," Pa said. "I think we're all a feelin' the same way. But, Bob Boy, it would help a little if ya took that lizard outta yer mouth." Tiny Bob took the tail of the lizard he had been chewing on and pulled it out from his mouth like a piece of spaghetti. He placed it on the ground and it immediately scampered back across the Arkansas border into Texas. Perhaps it knew that it was now safe there.

It felt too strange to describe, but, yes, we were out of Texas and now in Arkansas — the place Big Bill pronounces Kansas except with an R in front.

"Thought it'd take longer," Little Ben stated somberly. He was referring to the fact that Texas was such a big state that none of us thought we would be here this quickly. The only states any larger weren't nearly as important.

But, the time factor for crossing Texas depended on your starting and end points. In some cases, it could take days if not weeks
before you walked across one of its borders. 'Course, if you lived on
the border, it might only take minutes. We hadn't had to traverse or
vertically cross the entire state. We only had to cover part of East
Texas, just enough that when plotted on a map, our path to date
had formed two thirds of a "Y" or the way I used to draw birds.
And even that had taken days. So, all in all, Texas was lots of miles,
lots of smiles.

"Willie brought us here in real good time," Pa said.

"Too good," Willie muttered under his breath. This was only
our third night of night travel and daybreak was still an hour or two
away.

"Why don't everbody get off thar horses?" Pa suggested.
"And B.B., why don't ya rustle up some beers?"

We all dismounted as B.B. walked around to the rear of the
wagon. Big Bill walked back to where Pa believed the Texas line to
be. After staring into the darkness for awhile, he lifted his right
barefoot and placed it back into Texas. Just as quickly, he brought
his foot back into Arkansas. He continued setting foot back and
forth in Texas for a couple of minutes.

"Doin' the Hokey Pokey?" B.B. asked upon his return.

"He's just torn about leavin'," Pa said. "We've left our home-
site, our hometown and, now, our homeland."

Silently, B.B. handed each of us a Shiner's. Pa popped his bottle top, then turned toward Texas. He lifted his bottle and held it
high. The rest of us followed suit before breaking into a spontaneous hum of "The Yellow Rose of Texas." Choked up with emotion upon the finale, I could see Pa attempting to put a lifetime's
worth of feelings into words.

"Good bye, Texas," Pa finally toasted.

"Good bye, Texas," we echoed.

Pa turned one hundred and eighty degrees.

"Hello, Arkansas," he said.

"Hello, R Kansas," Big Bill said.

We downed our beers and threw the empties back into Texas.

Now, you know me, Mr. Sentimental. For some reason,
maybe it was the beer, I was taking this moment very hard, and I
hadn't even lived in the state as long as everybody else. Anyway, I

turned back around, and with tears forming in my eyes, gazed back into Texas.

"It's a damn shame," B.B. said stopping and joining me. I could do nothing more than nod in agreement.

"Yep," he continued. "Leavin' all them five cent deposit bottles just a sittin' thar on the ground. A real pity." He turned and left as Pa approached. Pa appeared surprisingly content.

"Bert Boy," Pa said putting his arm around my shoulder. "I can't tell ya it ain't okay to cry over spilt milk, 'cause sometimes ya just can't help it. I'm a guilty of it too. But I can tell ya that ya'll feel a lot better when ya realize that the spilt milk soured."

He let that sink in before continuing. "How's yer cow, Sir Albert?"

"Fine," I sniffled.

"I saw that bandana ya tied 'round his neck," Pa commented.

"Just making sure there's no more chance of mistake."

"Good idear. 'Sides, it makes 'im look very stylish."

I turned from Texas and looked back at the herd. There, standing in the rear, was Sir Albert. His three hundred pound red frame was complemented not only by the black birthmark located dead center of his forehead, but now by the yellow bandana. Indeed, the bandana looked so sporty that I would say it went way beyond a fashion statement and would have to be called a fashion exclamation.

As I continued to look in the direction of Sir Albert and the herd, I couldn't help but smile. Pa saw this and removed his arm from around my shoulder. "And that's the direction of our future now," he said. And, as if on cue, Sir Albert lifted his head and nodded. One state down, nine to go.

23

THINGS WENT SO SIMPLY the first couple of nights in Arkansas that there's not much to tell you. So, why don't you take the rest of this space to tell me what you've been up to.

24

It was late in the afternoon of our sixth day in Arkansas. We were camped out in the thick underbrush that engulfed the Bayou Bartholomew. The closest town was a spot on the map called Grady. This was much improved over the campsite we had chosen for the previous evening. Not that the actual site was horrible, mind you, but it was situated close to a town no one wanted to be near named Pansy. And it wasn't that we had anything personal against the townspeople, but real cowboys don't want to be associated with a name like that. As a matter of fact, real cowboys won't use the "p" word even if it's just in reference to the flowers of the same name. You'll often hear conversations between real cowboys where they'll say they just gave their gal an assortment of cultivated violets bursting in vibrant colors, just to avoid the "p" word. But that's what happens when you grow up in a place where both cows and men are branded, if you get my drift.

I had already finished preparing for the night's drive and since Willie had not yet returned with the scouting report, I took the opportunity to just sit by the bank of the bayou and relax. For the first time, I noticed the spectacular foilage. Back in Grangerland, most things stayed green. That is, all except the Evergreens, which had some sorta root rot infestation and were now all Everyellows. But here, all around me, were the many hues of autumn which I had read about, but never seen. Reds, yellows, oranges, browns-nature's M & M's.

The land itself had become a terrestial hodgepodge of fields, valleys, hills and mountains. I couldn't figure out if God had a master plan in creating this geography or whether he had just used leftovers from other areas. 'Course, the master plan might just have been an attempt at a terrestial hodgepodge, so who knows.

I took a deep breath. Fueled by the cool, crisp air, my sinuses popped open like our old Dodge truck's carburetor. We were over three hundred eighty miles northeast of Grangerland and you could feel the difference. But this was to be expected considering Pa's rule of tudes — a slight change in any "tude" can have its effects. Here, we had a profound effect with a slight change in longitude, latitude and altitude. 'Course, the rule also works with attitudes, especially when the person is affected to begin with.

I took another deep breath and sat down among some oaks. It was all so peaceful that I, that I...

"Yer different, Even Tinier Bert," a voice said from above.

I glanced skyward and, there, in the branches of the tree sat E. Lester, poised and ready to pounce. I was so stunned that I could not move or talk.

"Which is why ya gotta go," E. Lester continued. "Yer too dang smart, which makes ya too dang dangerous."

"Now I know ya ain't about to pounce on 'im, are ya, E. Lester?" The voice was cold and commanding. My eyes shifted to its origin. Perched a few branches above E. Lester was the ugliest, grubbiest, facially stubbiest hombre I had ever laid my eyes on.

"No, no," E. Lester quivered. "Of course not, Moe."

"Didn't think ya would," replied the gunslinger with the black hat. He withdrew a pistol from underneath his black leather vest with the black leather frills and pointed it directly at me.

"Ya pay me fer a job," Moe continued. "And I aim to please." E. Lester chuckled nervously.

"Wasn't no pun intended," Moe said. E. Lester shut up faster than a fly trap on a fly.

"I think we should take 'im into town and hang 'im," a host of voices chimed in from a host of branches. Instinctively, my eyes searched the tree. And by the time my attention returned to Moe and his gun, I had counted ten other cowboys sitting in various locations throughout the oak.

"Why is it that possees always wanna string people up?" Moe asked rhetorically. "Is it some kinda character flaw that demands that everthin' ya do be public? If ya'll have this subconscious need of bein' onstage, of displayin' yer conquests, of this overwhelmin' desire fer an audience, then ya'll got some deep-rooted inferiority complex and a need fer intense psychotherapy."

A few moments of silence passed.

"It's just that hangin's are such a sociable event," one of the possee members said meekly.

"It's a chance to get together with old friends and make new acquaintances," said another.

"But, to prove to ya that we ain't deranged, we'll forgit the public hangin' and hang 'im right here," offered a third possee member.

"Fine," said Moe. "After I shoot 'im."

"I say we hang 'im first, then shoot 'im," said a fourth possee member.

"No, I shoot 'im first," Moe demanded.

As the bickering continued, it wasn't hard to see that no matter who won, I lost. A cold sweat suddenly drenched my body…

I opened my eyes and found myself staring into empty branches. A darn dream! And this time, beans were not the cause… But it all seemed so real, those twelve men sitting in the tree, the sweat. Hestitantly, I touched myself and found that I was soaking wet!

A sudden splash of water followed by my second drenching removed all doubt as to whether I was awake, dreaming or in some sorta in between, twilight state. I turned my attention to the shallow blue waters of the bayou. Tiny Bob was busy indulging in rock diving, but to him it meant diving into rather than off of other rocks. It appeared he had again missed the rock he was aiming for and had landed in the water. Still, generally speaking, he looked scraped and bruised and happy.

While I was mighty glad to be woken, I wasn't about to let Tiny Bob, of all people, know it. So, I considered going over and reprimanding him for getting me wet, mostly because it's what he'd expect. But deciding it wasn't worth the effort, I simply shook the remaining, soggy, dripping cobwebs from my head and continued to watch.

Tiny Bob climbed out of the bayou and muttered something about the damn water. He scurried back up the banks of the bayou where he assumed his stance in preparation of diving head first into a boulder the size of a small barn. I guess that he was making absolutely certain that he wasn't about to miss for the third time and end up in the water.

And there he stood and stood and stood. Five minutes and counting. Frozen, eyes buldging forward, he had all of the grace and beauty of a gargoyle.

"Perhaps this was a delayed concussion," I thought to myself. Out of curiosity, I then stood and walked over to investigate.

I searched the area around the Bobsicle, a frozen Tiny Bob. When I failed to discover anything out of the ordinary, I looked at the water below. Finding nothing unusual there either, I approached Tiny Bob and gazed over his shoulder.

"Nice rock you've picked to crack your skull on," I commented. There was no reply.

I saw that only epoxy could have affixed his eyes better to the boulder in front of him. So, I took another glance at it. Squinting, I now noticed something brown, tubular and coiled situated on top of it.

While you might have thought that Tiny Bob didn't know the word fear, or any other word over three letters, remember, there was one thing that Tiny Bob was deathly afraid of — rattlesnakes! "What should I do?" I immediately thought.

I recalled my heartstopping experience with Sir Albert and my discussion thereafter with Pa. "Don't let emotions rule," I said to myself. "Remain calm and think things out."

I pondered for a while, thinking about such things as Raw Speed exploding, Sue Sue Watkins and sap in my saddle. I even distinctly recalled my promise of revenge. Yet, no matter where my thoughts began, they always ended at the same end...saving Tiny Bob. Believe me, I tried to come to some other conclusion, any other conclusion, but there really weren't any. At least none that would placate Pa.

"I could push Tiny Bob off of this ledge and out of the path of the snake," I thought, but then dismissed it. I sat down on the grass to consider other plans of action. Fortunately, at this point, I had two things going for me. One, despite the lack of beans, my mind still felt sharp and I knew, in time, I would come up with something. And two, the snake was rubber.

Yes, I had recognized the snake as belonging to Willie's collection of practical joke snakes. Willie usually employed these rubber classics when he wanted to come across as a hero to a certain petrified individual. He'd appear from nowhere and remove the varmint. This always resulted in a shower of hugs and kisses from the unsuspecting victim.

Willie's favorite prey were the members of the Grangerland Women's Poker and Garden Club, who must have believed that their headquarters stood on top of the world's biggest snake den. A meeting wouldn't go by when at least three or four of these critters would turn up, followed soon thereafter by Willie the Bold. But I honestly believed that Willie had retired the snakes after Jethro Yam, Candy Yam's husband, discovered one of the snakes while waiting for his wife in the Club's parlor room. The Yams were one of those couples that may have begun life as distinct individuals, but after forty years of marriage were now interchangeable. Both weighed in excess of two hundred pounds, had gray thinning hair and breasts. Anyway, on this occasion, Willie mistook Jethro for Candy and saved the petrified Yam, who took Willie in his arms and showered him with hugs and kisses. 'Course, Mrs. Yam ended up divorcing Mr. Yam now that his secret was out. And to this day, no one quite understands why Willie would have wanted to play this joke on Mrs. Yam to begin with. Willie could usually do much better than a two hundred pounder with thinning gray hair and breasts, man or woman. The postscript is that Willie still receives an occasional postcard from Jethro, who moved off to San Francisco.

I figured that Willie must have gone this way and dropped the snake by mistake. I mean, I can't believe that he was hoping to save Tiny Bob and be showered with hugs and kisses. Lucky for me that my relationship with Tiny Bob was such that I didn't have to worry much about any hugs or kisses. I'd be lucky if I got an appreciative grunt.

I decided on a dramatic encounter with the snake. I figured that if Tiny Bob did not realize that he was fooled, we'd all be better off. I could only imagine the wrath of a Bob Mine who discovered that he was the butt of a practical joke, even if the joke was purely accidental.

Slowly, I rose and began to stalk the snake. I darted then stopped, then darted again. I zigged and zagged, then zigged some more. I noticed that the Bobsicle's eyes were now following my every move.

I was now no more than two feet away from the snake and standing perfectly still. "Good snake," I hissed. And it hissed back!

This had an immediate impact on my bladder and I throughly soaked my pants. My first controlled response thereafter was that here was a real live rattlesnake and here I was standing two feet away from it like an idiot.

But it couldn't be real! I knew Willie's snakes. And this one looked like the Deluxe Rubber Rattler. I recognized the coloring, the pattern, the inscription. How many wild snakes had a marking which read, "Acme Novelty Co., Peoria, Illinois"? So, as I forced my foot forward a step, I prayed I was right, and I prayed that somewhere close by someone had been letting air out of a tire.

Steadily, I crept forward. My pulse pumped like ketchup from a squeeze bottle. My trembling hands were now just inches away. Was this, indeed, a fake snake or was I soon to be a new project for a deadly serpent- something that he could really sink his teeth in to?

Slowly...slowly...slowly...NOW!

I sprang. It may have only taken a second, but it was if time had slowed down to where I could have counted the miliseconds. My right arm was released from its cocked position. My fingers opened, briefly revealing my sweating palm, then disappeared as I rotated my hand around. My fingers closed in a vice-like grip around the snake's head. And I felt rubber!

I screamed. True, it was for joy, but Tiny Bob did not have to know that. Promptly, my mind and body went off red alert status, and it was time for the theatrics to begin.

I yanked the snake off the boulder, immediately grabbing its midsection with my left hand. I proceeded to wrestle with it, pretending that the snake was putting up quite a battle. I brought its head close to my face and desperately struggled to keep its deadly rubber fangs from sinking into my flesh. Three times the rubber snake attempted to strike. Each time I was just barely able to ward it off. Finally, I broke its will, and, with one more mighty scream, I flung the beast as far as I could downstream. It landed on top of a large log. And there it lay, unmoving, all stretched out- a dead Deluxe Rubber Rattler.

The Bobsicle remained still for about ten seconds before defrosting and turning to me. By this time, I was doubled over, feigning sheer exhaustion.

With hands on hips and breathing like my lungs had holes in them, I somehow found the energy to lift my head. Tiny Bob's face was one of extreme puzzlement. His eyes blinked as if a hoard of gnats had just flown into them. He began shifting his eyes back and forth from me, downstream to the snake, then back to me in such rapid succession that it appeared that his eyes were one elongated pupil. His lips began to twitch, followed by his chin, cheeks, nose and forehead. It was a very busy face.

Finally, after about ten minutes of facial fireworks, his mouth formed a cockeyed frown. "Don't think I'm gonna shower ya with hugs and kisses," Tiny Bob strained through an obviously dry mouth. "Ya ruined my plan. I was gonna handle that critter myself. Make 'im think I was a statue 'til he fell asleep. Then I'd grab 'im fer B.B., to make soup outta."

THE NERVE! THE INGRATE! Not even a grunt of appreciation! At least my theatrics were good. Who was he kidding? No matter how you looked at it, I did save him from something!

"Then why don't you go and get him now," I huffed, pointing to the snake downstream. "He's still there."

I could see a lump forming in Tiny Bob's throat. "'Cause we can't eat it now," he gulped. "Don't ya know that ya can't debone a dead snake?"

Tiny Bob shot me a look of disgust. As he turned and walked away, I heard him mumbling something about snake bone's getting caught in people's throats and them choking.

Then, it hit me. "Debone a snake?" I thought. "DEBONE A SNAKE!"

"Snakes don't have bones, you ninny!" I screamed, but Tiny Bob was already out of sight. I was disappointed in myself for the outburst, but, fortunately, no one was around to see it. I waited a couple of minutes for my temper to cool. Calmly, I then climbed down the bank of the bayou. Hopping from rock to rock, I eventually arrived at the final resting place of the Deluxe Rubber Rattler.

I stared at the snake long and hard. "Yep," I finally said to myself. "Mature or not, I don't think a rubber snake could survive in this wilderness...especially one from Peoria." With that, I gathered up the snake and headed back to camp.

25

ME AND THE SNAKE arrived back in camp to find that Pa had checked in with Uncle Ray and Aunt Tammy Faye. They had given him an update on E. Lester. Rumor had it that E. Lester's possee had grown in size. Just how big, however, nobody knew.

"Oh great," I thought. "I'll have thirty men sitting in a tree in my next dream."

Also, a distant cousin of Uncle Ray's (actually, a first cousin who just lived very far away) reported to Uncle Ray that he thought he had spotted E. Lester in Louisiana, but it turned out that it was only Elvis Presley. People called in further sightings of a bulky banker, his possee and a gunslinger named Moe from Yosemite to Loch Ness, but all were unconfirmed. E. Lester's whereabouts remained a mystery.

Yet, no one else in the Old Miss Company sensed immediate danger, probably because they were too smart to listen to rumors and let E. Lester interrupt their dreams. 'Course, the fact that B.B. swore by his inklings that E. Lester was nowhere around helped too. Now, B.B.'s inklings had never been wrong, but who really knew the range of his power? Even the best radars could only sense objects up to a certain distance away. So, E. Lester and Company could be a day or a week away. And couldn't even the best radar detectors be beaten? Think of the consequences if E. Lester had himself an inkling detector. He'd know where we were and could sneak right in and…

The mind! I put my imagination aside and decided to try remaining calm like the others…but it couldn't hurt to keep myself on some sorta alert status.

"Pa," Little Ben said, appearing from out of some thick underbrush. He kept peering back in the direction from which he came. He had a fairly unsettled look on his face, which brought a fairly unsettled look to my face since he was on watch.

"What's wrong?" Pa asked as we quickly huddled around Little Ben. I listened intently to see if my state of alert should be upgraded from a fairly unsettled look to a cold sweat.

Rather than wasting time developing a shorthand explanation, Little Ben motioned for us to follow him. Silently, we entered the brush and crept behind him. We stole along the banks of the Bayou Bartholomew until we reached a point that I recognized as the place where I had recently given a Tony Award winning performance [the prize given by the Grangerland Academy of Pretentious Arts for the best actor in town and named after the brilliant performer, Tony the Tiger] in front of a typical comotose critic. Here, Little Ben gestured for us to look out through the brush surrounding the Bayou.

As I quietly parted the thickets and peered out, my state of alert dropped as I learned the answer to at least one question from the snake encounter. An elderly man and woman were sitting in the front seat of an old Oldsmobile. Steam, billowing like a cloud and hissing like a snake escaped from under the hood.

"If I told ya once, I told ya a hundred times to check the radiator," the elderly woman was screaming.

"Ya didn't just tell me once," answered the elderly man. "Ya say everything a hundred times. Ya never shut up."

"But ya didn't check the radiator, did ya?" asked the woman.

"Wasn't it enough that ya had me checkin' the lugnuts on the wheels?" said the man.

"Now we're gonna miss our great granddaughter's weddin'," said the woman.

"Gonna?" replied the man. "It was yesterday! We missed it 'cause ya had me checkin' out so many dang pieces of this car!"

"Well," the woman huffed. "We still coulda made the reception!"

"Not if I taken the time to check the radiator," the man snipped back.

"So, now we're just gonna sit here until we die," said the woman.

"Reminds me of the time I was stuck on a deserted road, deep behind enemy lines with the Kaiser breathin' down our throats, thinkin' I was gonna die," said the man. "Did I ever tell ya about that?"

"About a hundred times," answered the woman.

The man pointed a finger at the woman. "Thar's a big difference between naggin' and tellin' a good story over and over."

"Then next time, let the Kaiser check the radiator," said the woman.

Each member of the Old Miss slowly withdrew from their respective viewing spots. We all huddled back at the Bayou.

"Well?" Little Ben said, shrugging his shoulders.

"Well, we gotta help those that are in distress," Pa said, once again conjuring up the image of Bart Namath.

"Yep," Willie said. "We gotta git them on thar way. We gotta save the marital bliss."

"What we gotta do," said B.B. "Is save the peace and quiet of this bayou."

"Figured that," said Little Ben. "How?"

Pa pondered. "That's an interestin' point, Ben Boy. I guess if we step right out thar to help that sorta ruins our not bein' seen, unless them people are good at keepin' secrets."

"I don't think they come close to Uncle Ray and Aunt Tammy Faye," I said. Pa nodded his head in agreement.

"Both got thick glasses," Little Ben said. "Could be blind as moles."

"So yer thinkin' that even if they saw us, they wouldn't be able to identify us?" Pa asked. Little Ben shook his head affirmatively.

"That lady could see a piece of lint droppin' outta a navel, said B.B. "Good naggers always got good eyesight."

"Not if they aren't looking," I said.

"Sounds like the introductory line to a plan," Willie said. "Let's hear it."Everyone gathered around me. I was a little nervous because this was the first time after Pa had pointed out to me that older people listened to what I had to say that, well, that they were listening to what I had to say. And after I finished explaining my plan, even Tiny Bob liked what he was hearing. So, maybe Pa was right, and I did have smarts too.

It didn't take long before everyone was ready with the pieces in place. Willie and Clint had brought over George, the bull who was in love with Pa, from the herd. It then took all of Clint, B.B.,

Little Ben and Big Bill's strength to keep him quiet and hold him back, not so much because he was a mean, ornery bull, but because once he feasted his eyes on Pa the tasty tart, he really wanted him and wanted to let the world know. George calmed a bit after Pa afixed a wallet-sized photo of himself to the tip of George's nose for George to look at. Maybe George thought that Pa was interested after all.

In the meantime, I snuck around to the bushes on the other side of the road. My role was to create a diversion so that this couple's attention would be directed my way, as Willie and the rest proceeded with their part of the plan. I found two large sticks and crouched down low. The fact that I not be seen was crucial.

I didn't have to wait long before I heard Willie's signal, the common mating call of a brown tailed whip-poor-will. At once, I began the diversion. I jiggled the bushes good and hard with the sticks creating your standard rustling effect.

"What's that?" asked the woman, looking over the dashboard.

"Could be a diversion," said the man.

"Ya still got World War I on yer brain," said the woman. "The Kaiser and his men ain't in R Kansas."

"If it ain't a diversion, then what in the Sam Hill is it?" the man asked, peering out the front window.

"If ya bothered to listen, it sounds like the common mating response of a brown tailed whip-poor-will," answered the woman. "And if ya bothered to watch, ya might just see it comin' out from behind that rustlin' bush yonder."

Willie had already taken the end of the rope that was not tied around George's neck and made a slip knot. And he had been twirling this make-shift lasso in the air for a few minutes when the woman spoke these last few words. Figuring this was the perfect moment, he tossed.

Willie, the ex-rodeo champion, had lost none of his skill. His throw caught the Oldmobile's front fender. As he pulled the rope taut, he gave the nod to Tiny Bob. Tiny Bob leaned back then swung a piece of wood about the size of a baseball bat. It landed squarely on George's rump with a tremendous whack. Simultaneously, the others relinquished their grips on the bull, who they had positioned in the direction of the road.

Well, George took off like a shot. He streaked by the car,

pulling the rope tight and jerking the car forward. My one fear concerning the plan was that, at this point, the rope might snap. But it didn't, and soon George, the car and its occupants were speeding down the road. And as the bull-powered car faded into a dust speck on the old dirt road, you could still hear the old man yelling, "I told ya it was a diversion. I told ya."

Figuring that it was now safe, I got up and ran across the road to join the others. 'Course, everybody was standing around, waiting for me.

"Ya done it again, Bert Boy," Pa said as he patted me on the back.

"Smart plan," Little Ben said.

Everybody else then came up and offered their congratulations. Even Tiny Bob mumbled something about a temporary truce seeing as how he got to whack something.

"Think them folks'll make it to town?" Willie asked.

"George just ain't gonna stop so long as he think's he's got Eugene in front of `im," B.B. said.

"Ya gonna miss George, Pa ?" Big Bill asked.

Pa shook his head. "I told `im a long time ago, I just wasn't interested."

All in all, everything seemed to work out for everybody. I was going to miss old George, but Pa was right; George should have taken the hint a long time ago. But, in case you're thinking that this whole thing didn't seem quite fair to George, well, you have to remember that George did end up with a wallet-size picture of Pa for all time. Since that's the best he was ever going to get, like I said before, everything seemed to work out for everybody.

26

THE DRIVE TOOK A TURN. Not for the worse or anything, just a turn. It happened our third night in Mississippi. We had passed Looxahoma which is near Thyatira, and, figuring that we were now far enough southeast to avoid Memphis, we changed direction from due east to northeast. B.B's inklings had proven right so far as we had not come across any evidence that E. Lester was around. Still, I remained on alert status, alternating between looking for signs of strays and looking for signs of E. Lester.

It had taken us fourteen days to travel through Arkansas and part of Mississippi to reach this point. We could have made better time, but we had experienced some delays. For instance, we were going to cross the Arkansas River near the city of Moscow, but decided against it because we had heard about the tight security around this famous city and had no desire to be detected.

Once across the river, the drive passed between the towns of De Luce and Ethel. Here, for some unknown reason, Willie spent an afternoon in search of towns named Fred and Ricky. Unsuccessful, we ended up bedding down for the day near Crumrod, a town situated close to the banks of the Mississippi River.

The Mississippi. The mighty Mississippi. I stood along the shoreline, with my hands in my pockets, and tried to comprehend the vastness of this river. I gazed at this tremendous body of water which seemingly went on forever in all directions. I felt like a bug in a bathtub.

The Mississippi. The Old Miss. I felt pangs, then fangs. My right hand grasped the Deluxe Rubber Rattler which I still carried in my pocket. Since the bayou incident, I had often thought about leaving the snake in Tiny Bob's sleeping bag. However, the fact that

I had on my person the most effective Tiny Bob repellant known to man turned out to be a very comforting thought. And as I stared out at the river, the proud river that our once proud ranch had been named after, I needed this little bit of comfort.

The crossing of the Mississippi, itself, began with the launching of the "S.S. Hope It Floats". We spent that afternoon removing the chuck wagon's wheels and then placing the whole wagon on a makeshift log raft. B.B., who swore to God that he was an atheist, was on his knees praying as we pushed the trusty, hopefully amphibious vessel out to river. I quickly lost sight of the chuck craft, which was last seen drifting downriver, while curse words drifted upriver.

As B.B. headed off to the Gulf of Mexico, Willie commenced the crossing of the herd. The evening was unusually warm and it didn't take much coaxing to get things moving. A few well placed "yahs" were soon drowned out by the sound of thundering hoofs and splashing bodies. All animal forms roared down the dirt incline and into the Mississippi. With Sir Albert by my side, I sat poised on You Romantic You along the bank, waiting until the last of the cattle were in the river. In the moonlight, I could see thousands of cattle, horse, chicken and human heads going up and down with the current, just like bobbing apples.

It took us eight thousand six hundred and forty bottles of beer on the wall before we got all of the cattle across the river. But we had crossed. With an extremely hoarse voice, Willie informed us that all of the cattle had made it. He also informed us that he was so sick of the beer bottle song that he no longer cared if all the bottles fell or not. But Willie was no quitter, and I knew that it was only a matter of time before the countdown resumed.

We were all a little nervous when B.B. failed to show up that next day. Perhaps E. Lester squashed him, or the possee hung him, or Moe shot him? Only Tiny Bob was more concerned about missing "B.B. the Cook" than "B.B. the Friend". To relieve a bit of the anxiety, we set up camp near a town named Little Texas. While Pa, Willie and Tiny Bob went off in search of B.B., the rest of us remained to gather anything we considered edible. 'Course, Pa took Tiny Bob along mainly because he was afraid of what Tiny Bob might consider edible.

Now, not only did our find have to be edible, but also non-natural. Real cowboys hate eating anything natural. A feast of nuts and berries was a contradiction in terms. A good defense for a charge of assault and battery was that the defendant was served a breakfast of granola, whole wheat toast and yogurt by the plaintiff. If it isn't fried in lard or doesn't have fat attached, they won't touch it. The most natural thing real cowboys eat is naturally aged beef jerky.

It turned out that B.B. had washed ashore near a town named Bobo. B.B. in Bobo. Not quite Alice in Wonderland, but it did have a sorta ring to it. Anyway, had the local Bobos not helped B.B., we might never have seen him again. When B.B. landed, which, from all accounts, was the best docking of a floating chuck wagon the townspeople ever witnessed, he was at an immediate disadvantage. The wagon was still on logs, which even Big Bill knows would be harder for horses to pull than if the wagon were back on wheels. 'Course, that was assuming that B.B. had some horses, which he didn't. And B.B. couldn't think of calling A.A.A. for roadside service. As I understand it, he had let his membership expire. He cursed out his lump for that one.

So, the Bobos or the Boboers or the Boboites or whatever they liked to be called, helped B.B. to remove the raft from the bottom of the wagon and to replace the wheels. Still, B.B. was without horses, and the Boboians, being a community of cotton pickers, had no large animals to lend. They called a quick town meeting to discuss B.B.'s lack of a means to pull his wagon and voted to donate the use of their pets' services. I guess they figured that a bunch of little animals would equal a big one.

The people of Bobo returned to the wagon with dogs, bunnies, cats, sheep, fish, mice, ant farms, gerbils, hampsters, possums, turtles (snapper, box and dead), sea monkeys and chia pets. The animals were strategically strung together so that when they looked ahead, they saw a food group in front. And, if they looked back, well, then they felt like someone else's dinner.

B.B. tethered the Old Miss chickens to the canaries and parakeets, all of which were tied in front of the cats. Then, when the last of the pets had been attached, B.B. climbed onto the wagon and shook the reins. 'Course, there was no way these tiny critters could pull the wagon, wheels or not. But you can imagine the scene Pa, Willie and Tiny Bob came upon as they rode into town. A mile long chain of barking, snarling, wailing, snapping, howling,

snorting, hissing, squawking, squealing, growling, whining, quack-
ing, yelping, screeching, croaking, squeaking, yapping, shrieking,
warbling animals, frazzled beyond repair attached to an immobile
wagon.

'Course, if it hadn't been for the tremendous ruckus, Pa,
Willie and Tiny Bob might never have found B.B. again. So, in that
respect, the Bobos were instrumental in the reunion. Pa wanted to
thank the townsfolk personally for sending out this distress signal,
but by this time, all of them had fled into the fields to stuff their
ears full of cotton.

Seeing as their job was done, Pa quickly detached the
A.S.P.C.A.'s worse nightmare from the wagon. Pa wanted to then
untie each of the half-crazed animals, but they all took off immediately. When last seen, Pa said the line resembled one of those pulse
graphs, with the birds giving it its peaks and the frogs, its blips. To
this day, I wonder whether this all-in-one petting zoo is still roving
around loose in Mississippi or whether there's just a lot of empty
rope and some very fat dogs.

Naturally, Pa and Willie were happy to have located B.B.,
despite the fact that the Old Miss chickens were now clucking in
parts unknown. And, I hate to say it but, thanks to Tiny Bob, they
were probably faring better than a lot of the other animals because
of their prior chain gang training. Pa hitched up some extra horses
he had brought along to the wagon, and they returned to Little
Texas.

That was two days ago. Now, here it was, our third night in
Mississippi. The drive had settled into its normal routine since
the joyous reunion in Little Texas. As this night was coming to an
end, we were quickly approaching a large farm northeast of Tyro
that Willie had scouted out enroute to Holly Springs National
Forest.

Through the peeping purple rays of dawn, I could make out
the silhouette of the farm. By now, the dropping off of cattle for the
day had become second nature. You left them, hid, secretly took
turns watching them and then retrieved them. I was preparing for
the "leave them" phase when the herd came to a halt, still a good
thousand yards from the farm. Not sure what was going on, I left
Sir Albert in the rear and rode around the herd to the front. Willie
and Pa were on top of their horses, talking.

"I swear it, Mr. Henry," I heard Willie say to Pa as I approached. "Thar weren't no pigs here earlier today."

"I believe ya, Willie," Pa replied as the rest of the Old Miss hands converged. "Yer the best. But it looks like we now got ourselves a heap o' trouble. Thar ain't no way that we'll be able to keep the cattle and them pigs separate."

A few hundred feet in front of me lay a grazing field. Beyond this grazing field stood a fenced area containing a herd of cows with a farmhouse way off in the distance — the typically perfect drop off setting which Willie had been finding for us day in and day out. But, dotting the entire length and width of this outer and supposedly vacant grazing field were thousands of squat, grunting torsos which were turning pinker by the minute.

Pa looked to the fading stars in the sky, searching for his favorite constellation, Puppis the Poop, before continuing. "Can't find Puppis no more," he said. "Means we got ourselves less than a half hour 'fore the sun's out. Do ya remember seein' any other farms or fields nearby?"

"I ain't sure," Willie answered. "Once I found this place, I thought it would be fine." Willie turned up his moustache, obviously disgusted with the pigs who had invaded his find.

"We'll all head in different directions," Little Ben said. "To find 'nother place."

"Ain't enough time," Pa said. "Accordin' to Puppis."

"Where's the Forest?" Little Ben asked.

"Too far," Willie replied. "At least ten miles."

"Well, we can't just stay here," B.B. said tapping his lump. But we didn't need his lump to know that. With our herd standing on County Road 305 , we looked, well, exactly like we were — a cattle drive with a bit of a problem. What we needed was to look like a grazing herd and fast.

"Then we'll pick a direction and hope fer the best," Pa said.

"Then I reckon our best bet is east", Willie stated. "Ya got some bigger roads to the north and south and I ain't sure how traveled they are. To the east, thar ain't much that I can recall 'fore the Forest."

"Could travel into mornin'," Little Ben suggested.

"Well, I wouldn't wanta push it," Pa said. "Don't want us gettin' spotted."

"No," Big Bill said. "Remember what it was like when I had the measles?"

"Let's move 'em east," Pa said, pretending not to have heard Big Bill.

"Who's out there?" a voice from behind some bushes asked. All eyes quickly turned to the bushes.

"Who's back thar?" Pa replied.

"Asked ya first," responded the voice.

Willie slowly withdrew his gun. B.B. started for his gun, but Little Ben stopped him.

"That ain't you E. Lester, is it?" Willie asked.

"Or the possee or Moe?" I blurted.

"No," said the voice. "Ya ain't the sheriff and his deputies, are ya?"

We sorta chuckled with the thought, which made the voice behind the bush very uneasy.

"Why ya'll chuckling?" continued the voice, now beginning to quiver just a little. "Ya ain't robbers, are ya? 'Cause if ya is, me and my daughter ain't got nothing ya'd be interested in taking."

"No, we ain't robbers," Pa said. "But I can tell ya that I've never had this long a conversation with a bush before. So why don't ya'll come on out so we can see who we're a talkin' with?"

There was a moment of silence followed by the rustle of leaves and branches. Slowly, two figures emerged. I could barely see the outline of a tall man and a smaller girl. It's not that there wasn't enough light. It's more like there wasn't enough people. What I mean is that, usually, when something gets closer, it gets bigger. These two, well, I couldn't tell if they were approaching or not because they were skinny, so skinny, perpetually skinny, that they'd appear the same whether they were up close or far away.

"I thought ya'll said ya ain't robbers," said the man. I was so startled that I jumped in my saddle. See, they were so skinny that I didn't even realize that they were both now standing about three feet away, and the man was pointing a stick, no, his arm, at Willie.

"Willie," Pa said. An equally surprised Willie placed his gun back into his holster.

At this distance, I was able to make out a little more of the pair. The man stood well over six feet tall, was dressed in overalls and wore a battered straw hat. He needed a shave, which was sorta amusing in that his face, even though it was too thin to deflect light, was throwing off a five o'clock shadow. 'Course, I kept this observation to myself, knowing that Big Bill would argue that it was impossible to have a five o'clock shadow now that it was six o'clock.

The girl looked to be about my age. I felt kinda sorry for her, with her straggly hair, her torn peasant dress and old, beat up shoes. She tried to stand behind her father, but that was impossible.

"If ya ain't the law and ya ain't robbers either, who are ya'll?" the man asked. "Ya ain't, um, the landowners?" He pointed his arm towards the grazing field and farm.

"No, we ain't," Willie said. "But I thought maybe ya'll was."

"No," the man said. "Don't own no land no more. Well, I do own land, but I ain't on it. Actually I don't know if I own land or not anymore, but if I don't, then I used to. The name's Vern Sowbelly and this is my daughter Nellie." Nellie Sowbelly curtsied, reminding me of a rubber band pushed in from both sides, then released.

"Eugene Henry," Pa said with a nod, before pointing to each of the rest of us. "That's Willie, Little Ben, Clint, Big Bill, Even Tinier Bert, B.B. and…" Pa quickly searched around, finding who he was looking for over by the shoulder of road, sitting in a discarded tire and biting off chunks of an old exhaust pipe for his rust collection. "…and Tiny Bob."

"Glad to meet ya'll," Vern said, before adding in a neighborly tone. "Looks like a mighty fine herd of cows ya got there."

"Thank ya," Pa replied. "Looks like a mighty skinny…,um, mighty fine…, um, mighty fine bush ya'll found to hide behind."

"Thank ya kindly," Vern said. "Now, I don't mean to be nosey, well, maybe I do, well, you'll tell me if I'm being nosey or not, but what are ya'll doing walking all these cows down a road at this time of the morning and worrying about whether I'm the landowner or not?"

Pa hesitated before answering. "Well," Pa finally said. "We're sorta on a secret drive."

"Really?" Vern said, his eyes lighting up. "Us too!"

"Really?" Pa replied, half curious, half surprised.

Vern raised his boney arm, once again directing our attention to the grazing field and farm. "See them pigs," Vern said proudly. "They're mine, well, they're sorta mine, well, I still got them. Nellie and me brought them all the way from Coon Rapids, Iowa. A banker wanted them, but we left before he got them. We decided to come down here, to Mississippi, because we'd heard that there were a lot of porkers down here. We'd drive the pigs at night and then leave them on grazing fields near other pigs during the day."

"Just like us, Pa!" Big Bill exclaimed. Pa nodded, amazed by what he was hearing.

"Only we haven't found much of a pig market, just a lot of ugly women," Vern said turning somber. "And we're sorta running low, well, we're sorta outta, no, we're definitely outta supplies."

"We've got of supplies," Pa said without hesitation.

"Hold on a sec," Vern said. "I didn't say what I said just so I could get a handout for my poor, starving daughter and me. Well, maybe I was trying to get a handout. Yes, a handout would be greatly appreciated."

I looked at Nellie, still standing behind her pa. I hadn't noticed her eyes before. They were big and brown, hungry and afraid. Yet, they twinkled with the dawn of the new day. They showed a hope, a dream, a faith in her pa that could not be doused. I had never seen so much of a person's inner self shine through their eyes before, and it touched me deeply.

"We're on our way to New York City," I spouted. "We heard it's a big meat market."

"New York City?" Vern replied, with a wrinkled, inquisitive face.

I was obviously on the spot. "Yes, Mr. Sowbelly," I said, quickly plodding my course in my mind. "We were told that they deal in cattle, but a market that big must be able to accomodate pigs too."

"Well, we haven't had much luck here," Vern said, sorta contemplating to himself. "Actually, we've had no luck."

As Vern mulled this over, I turned to Pa. "If they joined us, that would solve today's problem," I said. "We could leave our cows with the pigs."

Pa shot me an immediate smile, then looked to the pig farmer. "Would ya join us, Mr. Sowbelly?" Pa asked. "We'd be helpin' each other out."

Vern took another moment to think things over. "Only if ya call me Vern," he finally replied.

"And ya call me Eugene," Pa said as the two men shook hands. "Willie, Clint, Bill and Ben Boys, quick, take the cattle over and introduce 'em to the pigs. We've only got 'bout ten more minutes 'fore light."

"Puppis the Poop?" Vern asked looking skyward.

"Yep," Pa replied, no longer surprised by anything Vern might say. "Bert Boy, I don't reckon that we'll all be able to fit behind this here bush. So find us a bigger daysite."

Pa gave me one more big smile, before turning to B.B. "And B.B.," Pa continued. "Rustle up some vittles and clothes fer Vern and his daughter."

Everyone scattered like shooed flies out of compost. Me and Sir Albert found a nice large wooded area only about a quarter mile away which afforded a safe view of the grazing field. We were back within the half hour, just as the sun spilled out from the clouds, drenching what looked by all appearances to be an extremely content herd of cows and pigs grazing by their farm.

By this time, Vern and Nellie were just about finished eating. B.B. had fed them slabs o' leftovers, which they had devoured at once, and they were now working on ears of corn. Vern was working on his ear at breakneck speed. He didn't stop for a breath as he went back, forth, back, forth, back, forth, while rotating the ear upon a completion of a row. He moved so fast that I was sure that at any moment the kernels would start popping right on the ear. Nellie, too, was moving at a pretty good pace, although holding the ends of the ear with her pinkies extended, she looked more refined.

Now, B.B. had laid down the rules of eating just prior to feeding Nellie and Vern. But, being so hungry, they finished well before B.B. could think about saying, "stop". The slabs o's had been reduced to dregs o's and shreds o's, and the thoroughly ravaged ears of corn were still steaming five full minutes after Vern and Nellie had discarded them on the ground.

"If yer all through, we best be headin' to the site," Pa said. Vern nodded and both he and Nellie rose from the log on which they had been sitting.

"I got first watch," Little Ben said before turning to Vern and smiling. "I'll use yer bush."

Little Ben stepped off the roadway and disappeared behind

the bush from which the Sowbellys had first appeared. The rest of
us took our horses by the reins and, with me leading the way, began
the short walk to the campsite.

"Fine vittles, Mr. B.B.," Vern said wiping food away from his
mouth, chin, cheeks and hair. Vern had eaten so quickly that he had
missed his mouth on more than one occasion. But as Pa had always
said, "Only wings can make food fly faster than hunger."

"Thank ya," B.B. replied.

"I really mean it," Vern said. "When some people are hungry,
they're glad to get their hands on anything they can. Me and Nellie,
on the other hand, would rather starve than eat a less than quality
meal. Well, maybe not totally starve. Well, we definitely wouldn't
eat as much. But, believe me, I know my quality food. Back in Iowa,
I used to weigh well over three hundred pounds."

Looking at Vern now, this was hard to believe. There wasn't an
ounce of fat on him, or an ounce of muscle or an ounce of anything
else for that matter. Actually, that's not altogether true. There was
an ounce of crumbs that he forgot to wipe away over by his left ear.

"It's true," Vern continued. "My wife was a quality cook before
she passed away from acute salmonella. I'd be out in the pens dishing slop into the troughs, and, quite often, my mind would drift off,
thinking about what we were having for supper. And always the
best leftovers in Iowa too. That was the problem. See, your breakfast, lunch and dinners will only take ya a total of three hours a day
to eat, which leaves ya twenty one hours for leftovers."

"Yep, it wasn't the meals that got me, but the nibblin'," said
Vern as he patted the area where his stomach probably was.

"See, boys," B.B. said with his usual air of authority. "That's
just why I have the rule against snacking."

"And it's a good rule, Mr. B.B.," Vern said. "You don't want to
be over three hundred pounds, but I did kinda wish we would have
run into more quality food on our way down. Well, some quality
food. Well, any quality food. Pigs just ain't quality. Well, some parts
of them are quality, for awhile, until ya get sick of eating them day
in and day out."

Vern's eyes suddenly widened. "Say, Mr. B.B., you don't have
any relatives in Iowa, do ya?"

"Nope," B.B. replied. "Born and raised in Grangerland,
Texas."

"Oh," said Vern, a bit disappointed. "It's just that we lived about sixty miles from a place named Beebeetown, and I thought that you, being such a quality cook and all, might have come from there. Or maybe, your relatives came from there. Or maybe, your recipes came from there. But, that's not to say that quality cooks can't come from Texas. But, I really wouldn't know one way or the other because I've never been there. But, there must be at least one because you're from Texas and…"

Thank goodness Nellie tugged on her father's overalls. "Yes, Nel?" Vern said, turning to his daughter. He bent down just a bit so that she could whisper in his ear. As Vern nodded his head in reponse to his daughter's undertones, I realized that Nellie had yet to speak out loud.

Now, there had been a family in Grangerland, the Sennetts, with four kids who were so shy that when they were in public, they'd all hold onto their mama's apron as they'd walk along behind her. It got so that when people saw them coming down the street, they'd say, "Look, here come the Sennettpedes." The whole thing became downright embarrassing when the kids reached their thirties. And it became downright sick when, after their mama had passed away, the kids still walked down the street clinging to that apron. Now, I'm not saying that Nellie was this shy, or shy at all because, for all I know, she was quietly informing her pa that perhaps he shouldn't run on at the mouth so much. But I'm just pointing out that it was kinda strange not to have heard her speak yet.

"Mr. B.B.," Vern said as Nellie released her grip on her pa and moved a few steps away. "My daughter'd like to know if ya got any soap? Ya can tell we're a bit soiled…well, dirty…well, odious and repulsive, and she wants to try to find a stream and tidy up a bit before she puts on the clean clothes ya gave her."

Vern smiled and shrugged his shoulders as he added, "Ya know women."

"I'll see what I can do," B.B. said with a grin. He disappeared around the back of the chuck wagon.

"Pa," I said. "The site's right up here." I pointed off the road and up a hill. The bottom of the hill was sparsely covered, but as the incline grew steeper, it became dense with oaks. From afar, the hill resembled the hair style of a boxing promoter whose picture I had once seen.

"Dense with oaks," Pa said, his eyes studying the hill. "Good site, Bert Boy."

"The site's up yonder," Pa announced to the others as he pointed up the hill.

"Here ya go, Miss," B.B. said as he returned with the soap. Now, B.B. had heard that the guests of fine restaurants and hotels were expected to remove the toiletries when they left. Accordingly, as a sign of class, he had taken the liquid soap dispenser from "Eats". He now handed the bulb-shaped, plastic dispenser to Nellie, who responded with a smile.

"Wow," said Vern, admiring the dispenser. "I wish we could have afforded to eat in fancy restaurants...well, any restaurants... well, just afforded to eat something of quality...something besides pigs."

"Nel," Vern continued, turning to his daughter. "We'll be right up this hill, okay?" Nel nodded. Then, with her soap in one hand and clothes in the other, she spun around and began to skip away.

"We don't have to worry about her," Vern said, watching his daughter skip away. "She's got a great sense of direction."

We all stepped off of the road and headed up the hill. Just once, I looked back to see if I could see Nel, but the oaks were blocking my view. It had been the skip. At first, I thought it was kinda silly for someone my age to be skipping. 'Course, I had to keep in mind that she was a girl. Now had it been a boy, well, a real cowboy caught skipping should make his next skip town.

But there was just something about her skip, the way her narrow hips seemed to sway in the breeze, even though there was no breeze. It had been carefree, yet determined. It displayed excitement in the quest for rejuvenation of the mind and spirit. 'Course, if she was skipping along because she was holding a fancy soap dispenser, then I stand corrected.

We reached the peak, which did afford a safe, secluded view of the herds. If you squinted, you could even make out the Sowbelly's bush near the field. I tried to find Little Ben hidden in the bush, which sorta reminded me of the "spot the hidden objects" game they used to have in my "Highlights" magazine, but to no avail.

After the horses were tied, everybody went about the daily grind of setting up camp. Vern, talking about quality people from Iowa, helped B.B. unload necessities from the wagon. The more they talked, the more B.B. seemed to recall ancestors who may have hailed from Iowa, and it soon became entirely possible that Beebeetown was named for him. I left the conversation to begin my chores just as B.B. was struck with the notion that his great great great grandpa probably founded Iowa.

As usual, my task was gathering kindling. Clint or Little Ben, depending on who didn't have first watch, was then delegated the assignment of finding real wood as Big Bill dug a small pit with his feet. Pa still prohibited large campfires, mainly because he felt that the smoke might lead to our detection. But, under a fairly dense tree cover, he would allow very small fires. This way, since the weather was turning colder, we would at least be able to have a hot cup of coffee to keep us warm.

It must have recently rained because all of the kindling that I was finding was wet. So, I walked down to the bottom of the hill where, since there was more exposure to the sun, there would hopefully be some dry twigs. Traveling along the bottom of the hill, I quickly found one fist full of kindling.

Now, I guess I was probably about a half mile away from the campsite when, suddenly, I heard the most horrifying shriek I had ever heard. Naturally, being kinda startled, my kindling went in every which direction. I stood my ground and waited until the sound of my heart pounding ceased so that I could perhaps hear where the shriek came from. At that moment, a piercing after-shriek, the slightly less intense scream that follows the first major earth shaking shriek, filled the air.

At once, I began running in the direction of the cry — across the road, down an embankment, through the woods, into a tree, up off of the ground, around the tree, through more woods, until I finally hit an opening. I stopped and peered out.

Standing there, in the middle of a small stream was Nellie. And she was shaking like a blender, either totally terrified about something or extremely cold because of the fact that she wasn't wearing any clothes. NO CLOTHES! I could feel the force on the back nerves of my eyes straining to keep my peepers from popping out of their sockets.

I tried to move, but my muscles totally ignored all brain signals. "Move, don't stand here, do something," I thought, but to no avail. Then, Nellie — Oh God, Move, Please Move, Please, Please,

Please Move- turned and saw me standing there, with my mouth at full gape and eyes halfway out to New York.

Nellie began running towards me. I tried to at least turn my head away, but my neck refused to budge. I was already beyond embarrassed. I mean, I'm not the type to just stand and gawk, but I wasn't doing it on purpose. I mean, I was trying not to look and I only looked in the first place because of the scream, but she doesn't know I'm not the type who would never look in the first place except under circumstances like this and here she comes and HOLY MACKEREL!

"Hold me pleath," Nellie begged as she flung her arms around me.

At once, she tightened her grip around me, as I tried not to get excited. I felt more ashamed about myself than ever before. Here she was, terrified and pleading for comfort, and all that crossed my mind was that a stark naked girl was clutching me. I had never seen a naked girl before, never! Sue Sue in the barn had been the closest to naked and she had all her clothes on! Now, here was a naked girl, holding me no less, her body tingling in the chill, her skin dripping and moist, her hair illuminated in the early morning light. Urges... I wish I knew more about them-like why have the few that I've experienced always come at the wrong time?

"Hold me pleath," Nellie once more requested. "Thereth a wild animal out there. I heard it in the busheth!"

No, the only wild animal out there was me, and I wasn't proud of it. Actually, Nellie probably did hear an animal rustling around in the bushes near the stream, and that animal was either a Tiny Bob-o-link or a Tiny Bobcat.

"I'm thscared," Nellie cried. "Hold me, Pleath."

Very, very slowly and, shamefully not for all the right reasons, I found myself suddenly able to lift my arms and place them around the shivering girl. My hands, they touched naked skin! I almost fainted. Did I dare tighten my hug or would she then really know who the wild animal was? The urges said, "squeeze, SQUEEZE, SQUEEZE!" But then I heard Pa's voice in the back of my head saying, "No, Bert Boy, ya ain't a pervert!"

"Bert, take your mind off of what's happening," I thought to myself. "Do something, anything. Hum "Onward Christian Soldier". NO!, then Sir Albert would come over, and he'd think you're a pervert. Not to change the subject or anything, Bert, but had you noticed that she has a cute little lisp? You didn't realize that before, did you? Maybe that's why she doesn't talk much. And you know, with a little meat on her, she'd be really pretty. And now that she's clean, Bert, if you'd bother to lift your eyes up from her breasts, (Oh, God, is that where my eyes wondered?) you'd see just how pretty her face and hair are. And now that you are holding her, comforting her, bringing a feeling of safety to her soul, Bert, do you realize that her pa would kill you if he found you like this?"

Now, I can't quite say that I flung her away, but it might have been a lot harder than a slight nudge. All I know is that when I looked into her big, brown eyes, there was a look of shock and hurt.

"I, I'm sorry," I said. "B, But I think it best that you put some clothes on."

Until that moment, I don't think she had even realized that she had been standing naked in front of me. She dove for the fresh clothes B.B. had given her which she had left by the side of the stream. She hastily buttoned one of Little Ben's hand-me-down shirts, before awkwardly stepping into my old pair of jeans. She then slowly, painfully, brought herself to look up at me.

"I'm, I'm, I'm tho embarrath…I, I, I don't know what to…" she tried to say, but I put my finger to my lips and smiled.

There was a moment or two of silence. Then, Nellie began to smile. And we just sorta stood there, looking at each other for awhile. Finally, I said, "You know, if, um, you want me to hold you now, I will." And that was fine by her.

27

Trying to drive pigs and cows was like trying to drive oil and vinegar. The pigs wanted to go one way, the cattle the other. It was obvious that the pigs hated the drive and would do whatever they could to try to disrupt it. Often, these mischievous scamps would engage in the fine art of cow tipping. They would charge an unsuspecting cow, knocking the cow over in one fell swoop as if the cow were made of porcelain. Since the cow was now stuck on its side, with its legs dangling nowhere in particular, we'd have to ride over and right the critter. The pigs, they'd stand around, squealing with laughter.

But if that wasn't bad enough, we had new lyrics for an old favorite of Pa's:

> Pigs and horses,
> Pigs and horses,
> Go together like
> Love and divorces.

The pigs would purposely run through our horses' legs in an attempt to trip them up. And since the majority of the pigs were so low to the ground that the horses had difficulty seeing them, the pigs usually succeeded in their endeavor.

Tiny Bob took a special liking to the pigs. The rest of us, well, we had our work cut out for us. This was especially true for Willie, who now had to scout out farms with both cows and pigs.

But on we went, still with no sign of E. Lester, his possee or gunslinger, although, one day, Big Bill gave us quite a scare. He came running into camp claiming that he had found evidence of E. Lester. After inspecting Big Bill's find, Pa took it upon himself to explain to him that even someone as large as E. Lester could not leave bear prints. Even so, Big Bill wanted Pa to call Uncle Ray and Aunt Tammy Faye.

Uncle Ray and Aunt Tammy Faye still had no first hand information on E. Lester. However, they now heard talk that E. Lester had offered a reward. 'Course, this meant that more people would be joining in our hunt which gave us all the more reason to press on quickly, but quietly.

So, as the day's grew shorter, the drive grew longer. Vern now usually rode with B.B. in the wagon, and the two of them would whisper up a storm. It didn't take long before B.B. had made Vern an honorary Texan, and Vern named B.B. an honorary fighting Jay Hawk.

It turned out that Vern had come from a long line of Sowbellys, and, with a name like that, there wasn't much choice about whether you went into pig farming. He did have a uncle who had tried to open a financial planning service, first under the name E.F. Sowbelly, then under Merrill Sowbelly, but both failed. So, everybody else stuck to their pigs.

Vern's herd was made up of three different breeds of pigs-Berkshires, Cheshires and Hampshires. Being hospitable, I pretended that this information interested me. But, to a real cowboy, one pig looks like another.

Vern also began helping B.B. with the meals. Pretty soon, we were feasting our eyes on such delicacies as hog jowl, chitterlings, pigs' knuckles, pigs' feet and headcheese. I saw why someone could easily lose weight fast if they stuck to eating pigs.

But not Nellie. She began filling out. And she was beautiful. During the drive, she'd often ride along side of me and it was awfully tough trying to keep my attention on the herds. We giggled a lot. I'd whisper in her ear, she'd lisp back. And I think her pa liked me. See, it did pay to listen to stories about pig breeds.

Well, even with the obstreperous pigs, who certainly demonstrated why they're also known as swine, and the uncomforting thought that there was now a price on our heads, there were no major incidents to report until around about three quarters of the way through Tennessee. That's when we lost Sir Albert again.

We had been traveling through the Crab Orchard Mountains, and when we stopped for the day along the banks of the Emory River, I realized he was gone. I immediately went to B.B., who swore that he hadn't B.B.Q.ed him. B.B. said that he knew Sir Albert was protected property and that the only way Sir Albert could been any safer was if we were in India. B.B. did have an inkling, though, that Sir Albert was not lost in the mountains as I had feared, but had wandered northeast. With this information, me and Nellie took off to find him.

For two hours, we rode northeast along the Emory, while singing "Onward Christian Soldier" at the top of our lungs while trying not to be too conspicuous. Nellie had a very pretty voice too, at least for the first hour and a half. At that point, our voices began to have more cracks than peeling paint. And at the two hour point, well, our vocal cords had been reduced to twines. The only thing we felt fortunate about was that we were near the town of Wartburg. Tired, since we had yet to sleep, as well as depressed, hoarse and thirsty, we readily justified our cautiously wandering into this town and splurging for a soda pop.

We tied up You Romantic You outside of town and walked down Route 27 until it turned into Main Street. By now, it was mid-morning, yet, as we entered the city, both the street and the city appeared surprisingly deserted.

"Tyler revisited," I whispered to Nellie, who did not understand what I meant. "Keep your eyes peeled for a shopping mall or a stadium."

"Why?" she whispered back.

"Because that's where the people are," I said.

"No, they're not," Nellie responded. "They're at the end of the threet." And sure enough,at the end of Main Street, at the end of Wartburg, stood a mass of people.

Still thirsty and now curious, Me and Nellie cautiously began to walk down Main Street. Nonchalantly, I checked for "Wanted" posters on lamp posts and in store windowns as we headed towards the crowd. But even had I seen one, it wouldn't have mattered. The crowd's attention was fixed on something in the road. Yes, they were definitely surrounding something, but the crowd was so dense that we couldn't tell what was happening. And there was no sense asking the people standing in the back what this was all about. As we approached, they were all rubbing their necks, attempting to relieve their muscles strained from trying to see over those in front. Obviously, none of them had succeeded in learning the source of the excitement because they had resorted to the next best thing — opinionated conjecture based on triple hearsay.

"Dead, eh?"

"Poor Mr. Martin."

"Ain't Mr. Martin. Heard it's a martian."

"Well, that's good, er, I mean for Mr. Martin. Always liked him, don't particularly like martians."

"Hear that? Someone don't like marchin'!"

"Must be a communist."

"Winston, they're sayin' there's a columnist up there."

"Probably from Knoxville. Well, ain't that typical. Everybody crowding around, wanting to be interviewed by some hotshot from the big city."

"Someone from the city's been shot?"

"Is he dead?"

"Ain't Izzy, heard it's Mr. Martin."

"Poor Mr. Martin."

"Ain't Mr. Martin. Heard it's a martian."

And so it went, and I easily understood why Pa hated rumors. But rather than stand idly by and listen to the gossip, I put Nellie on my shoulders to see if she could get a true fix on what was going on.

"If you can thtand on your tip toeth, I think I'll be able to thee," she said, almost peering over the crowd. I arched my feet.

"Good, good," she exclaimed.

"Can you see now?" I grunted, sorry that I didn't have more of the genes in me that went into forming Big Bill's feet.

"Juth barely…It lookth like, it lookth like there'th a cow in the middle of the crowd, lying on the road, and, and…No, it can't be!"

"What? What?"

"That cow. It lookth like it'th Thir Albert!"

I was overcome with horror. These were certainly words I didn't want to hear. 'Course, the people around us, they picked up on the "cow" right away, which soon became "Moscow", which lead right to the communist, then columnist and eventually back to poor Mr. Martin.

Nellie immediately jumped down off my shoulders. She, too, was terror-stricken. I grabbed her hand, and we ducked, darted and crawled our way through people's legs as we headed for the center. I tried not to think of what we'd find, but my brain kept imagining the worst case scenario. A zillion miles of footage I've accumulated in my cerebellum over the years containing wonderful, joyful images, and, here was my brain, stuck in a single horrifying loop.

Both my and Nellie's pants legs were torn to shreds and our knees a little bloody by the time we finally popped our heads out and saw light. But our battle wounds were inconsequential — we had made it to the center. And here, in the eye of the crowd, in the midst of the throngs, the cause of the commotion was, indeed, a three hundred pound Red Brangus complete with a black birthmark on his forehead and yellow bandana around his neck, lying still in the middle of Main Street.

I crawled out from my vantage point, which happened to be between the legs of someone who probably wouldn't have worn those pants had they known about the embarrassing rip in the seam and, forgetting about our danger, ran towards Sir Albert. Nellie followed right behind. We were about three yards away from him when we were intercepted.

"What have we got here?" said a policeman as he grabbed me.

"Oh God, we've been caught." Why did I have to be so young and impulsive? And it won't take a genius to figure out that if we're here, the rest of the Old Miss contingent can't be too far away. Thanks to me, they'll be captured within a few hours, then we'll all have our choice of being shot, hung or squashed.

As tears swelled in my eyes, I couldn't even lift my head to look at Nellie.

"Look, I'm gonna have to ask you to move on," said the policeman, relinquishing his grasp. "I have a lot of other people here straining to see what's going on."

Somehow, and I wasn't about to question just how, he didn't recognize us! Me and Nellie could just walk away with the policeman being none the wiser. But, we could never leave without Sir Albert. I know he'd risk his life for us. This was going to have to be an all or nothing situation. I knew that Nellie understood what I had to do. So, I ran through a quick prayer, crossed my fingers and said, "But he's my cow!"

"It'th twue, it'th twue," Nellie shouted hoarsely.

"Check his rump," I said.

"I ain't gonna do no such thing!" snapped the officer.

"There's an OM brand there," I added. Hesitantly, the policeman bent down and inspected. I quickly dropped down near Sir Albert's face. But before I could bring myself to go any further, I looked up to the policeman.

"Is he, is he, de…de…dead?" I sniffled.

"Dead?" the policeman chuckled. "Not quite. Drunk as a skunk is more like it." At that point, Sir Albert stirred. He slowly and painfully lifted one eyelid and burped.

"Albert?" I was shocked and appalled.

"Yer cow caused quite a ruckus," the officer offered. "From the look of things, he musta broke into the "Good Old Times Bar and Grill" and helped himself to quite a few Kahlua and creams."

I moved closer to Sir Albert. "Why?" I whispered in his ear. Sir Albert struggled to open his eyes. When he finally succeeded, it looked like he was trying to focus on Nellie. He then gave me what sounded like a forlorn "moo".

"Then," the policeman continued. "It appears he kicked the jukebox until it played "The Way We Were". Sometime later, he stumbled out here, passed out and was discovered by a passer-byer."

I fully understood. I knelt down next to Sir Albert's head and gave him a hug. "You're still my best friend," I whispered. "And if I've spent less time with you lately, I'm sorry, but I thought you'd understand. It's not that I like Nellie more, it's just that I like her differently. Maybe, one day when you find a heifer that you really like, then you'll understand. But don't be jealous of her. We can all be friends. She really cares about you, you know."

Sir Albert's big old cow lips parted as if to say to me, "I'm sorry. I've been a foolish cow." I stroked his head.

"Please get him out of here," the policeman said. "He's been blocking the street and holding up traffic, and supposedly some bigshot communist from Mars is on his way here."

There were no arguments from me. The policeman got all of the other officers to help him right Sir Albert. With his head throbbing and legs wobbling, Sir Albert mooed bloody murder. One of the officers placed his mirrored sunglasses on Sir Albert, which helped a little bit. The officers then parted the crowd, forming a lane from which we could exit.

So, we ended up leaving town without our soda pop, but not

without Sir Albert, my lovable, overly jealous, staggering cow. 'Course, maybe I should have gotten Nellie something to drink while we were in town. In her exhaustion, she thought that she saw Tiny Bob standing on the steps of the Good Times Bar and Grill, holding aloft two empty bottles of Kahlua and laughing.

Girls, what imaginations!

28

HOURS HAD TURNED INTO days, days into weeks into months, back into weeks, to days and hours. On Thanksgiving Eve, we crossed into Kentucky. We set up camp in the Daniel Boone National Forest. Pa surprised us by announcing that we'd be taking the next night off so that we could celebrate Thanksgiving properly. I assumed this was to honor the fact that back in Texas, the Indians and the Henrys had gotten along well for generations. We had always respected them and now that we had our land snatched out from under us, we could relate to them better too.

And while we didn't have a football game to watch, we did have beer left. So, celebrate we did. We decided to play our own football game, reverting to the original style of tossing the whole pig. We found the only real problem with this was getting the ball to stay put on the line of scrimmage while the teams were huddled. My team ended up winning on Big Bill's fifty yard field goat. No, it's not a typo. The pig ran late in the fourth quarter, which was strange because we had called a passing play in the huddle. Anyway, we were penalized for offsides because the ball was ours and it had crossed the line of scrimmage to make its escape. Then, we were penalized for delay of game as we went off in search of a new ball. Well, Big Bill returned with a wild goat, which, due to the accumulation of penalties, was placed on the fifty yard line. With less than a minute to go, I snapped the goat, Nellie held, and Big Bill, the original barefooted kicker, booted the goat up and through the uprights. Big Bill would have been presented the game ball had one been left — once it hit the ground, the goat took off in the same direction as the pig.

After the game, we just sorta sat around and talked about

Thanksgiving while waiting for the traditional dinner. Big Bill wasn't sure about the meaning of Thanksgiving, so Pa read it to him from his pocket Webster's. We then all gave our thanks. Pa was thankful that the drive was going so well. B.B., as always, was thankful for his inklings. Vern was thankful that he and Nellie had met up with quality people. Big Bill was thankful that Pa always carried his pocket Webster's. Willie was thankful that we were taking the night off because he was already on his seventh beer. Clint was thankful that we were taking the night off because Willie was already on his seventh beer. Little Ben was thankful that Big Bill had made the field goat because he had been in charge of holding the pig down when it escaped. Tiny Bob was thankful that he was Tiny Bob. And, Nellie and me, we were sorta thankful for each other. 'Course, we took a good bit of razzing for that one. 'Course, me and Nellie were also thankful for Sir Albert.

Dinner was as traditional as you could get without having turkey, gravy, cranberries, stuffing, jello squares with marshmallows, pumpkin pie and sweet potatoes at your disposal. B.B. did mold some ground beef into the shape of a turkey and covered the outside with chicken feathers. He then dug out a cavity in which he placed some pinto beans as a substitute for giblets. Lastly, a Y-shaped twig was inserted in front so as to appease Big Bill's plea for the traditional wishbone.

After dinner, me and Nellie visited the herd, and, in particular, Sir Albert. Since the incident in Tennessee, I hadn't seen him drink, and I think he's come to know first hand what I meant about different types of friendships, although he sorta walks away whenever I broach the subject. I think it's shyness.

It seems that when we brought Sir Albert back from Wartburg, well, he was just another royal cow. This time, when we dropped him off with the herd, he was wearing not only his sporty yellow bandana, but also his newly acquired mirrored sunglasses. Add to that his stagger, which looked hip despite the fact that it was due to his hangover, and, I swear, the heifers couldn't take their eyes off of him. And now I've seen Sir Albert and Gerty standing side by side an awful lot. Like I said, Albert won't talk about it, but I think that they're an item. To me, this would be a match made in heaven since Gerty should have been named Rose Queen and, therefore, was technically nobility.

Me and Nellie arrived back in time to see Pa settling a dispute between Big Bill and Tiny Bob over the wishtwig. Big Bill was holding a partial Y-shaped piece of kindling in his hand, while Tiny Bob held a log. Tiny Bob's log must have been about five feet long and weighed sixty pounds, yet he was claiming that it had broken off from the wishtwig that had been placed in the poultry loaf after a fair and square pull with Big Bill. And since he was obviously in possession of the longer piece, he felt that his wish should be granted. Miraculously, our wish was granted and Tiny Bob disappeared as Pa ruled in Big Bill's favor.

Since we were well-hidden within the dense underbrush of the Daniel Boone forest and because it was rare to have a night off and it was Thanksgiving, Pa allowed us to build a small campfire. And B.B., he surprised us with s'mores. Willie brought out some Lone Star beer from his private collection, Pa passed around the chaw and we all sat back to enjoy the warmth of the holiday fire.

"Have some tobaccee, Vern?" B.B. asked as he placed a wad in his mouth and handed the pouch to Vern.

Vern took a pinch. "I don't think I've had chaw in a long time," he said. "Actually, I don't think I've ever had chaw. Well, come to think of it, maybe it's chewing gum that I've never had."

"It's good fer ya," Willie slurred through a chocolate covered mouth and a moustache caked with marshmallow. "Yer teef are too white and yer gumbs are too pink." As I had predicted, Willie had resumed his "beer bottle on the wall" song. And tonight, every time he'd sing about a bottle falling off the wall, well, he'd look in front of him and discover a new bottle of beer. Now, with a seven beer base to begin with, Willie figured that the bottle in front of him was the one which had just fallen off of the wall, and, rather than let it sit on the ground where someone might trip over it, he'd drink it and then dispose of the empty. Willie, always the good samaritan. At the pace he was going, Willie's song was rapidly counting down as the empties were rapidly stacking up. 'Course, part of the reason was that Willie kept on forgetting where he was in the song, and, therefore, was losing tens of thousands at a time. But one thing about Willie, he knew his limit. He'd stop drinking the moment he passed out.

Willie puckered his cheeks, preparing to show Vern the fine art of spitting. After a good build up, including some of the best sound effects he has ever had, Willie spit out the entire wad. Willie stared at the wad on the ground for awhile, and then started singing something about chaw on the wall.

"Nellie," Vern said. "Remember our Thanksgivings back in Iowa, back when yer mom was still alive?"

"Yeth," Nellie replied. "They were very thpecial timeth." Nellie had become more talkative around the rest of the Old Missers. Perhaps it was because with every day, with every meal, she was looking all that much more attractive, which, in turn, gave her confidence. Or perhaps, she knew in her heart that I was there to protect her. But more likely, she realized that there was absolutely nothing she could do or say that could be more embarrassing than Tiny Bob.

"They were some good times," I said dreamily. "Family times."

"Still are," Little Ben said.

"Not all the family," Pa said with just a hint of melancholy in his voice, and I knew this wasn't on account of the fact that Tiny Bob was not with us. A feeling of emptiness swept over me.

"The Hades it won't be all the family," Vern said suddenly perking up. He quickly retreated from the fire, returning a few seconds later with a jar.

"We brought Mrs. Sowbelly along," Vern continued, placing the jar which you could now see was filled with ashes on the ground in front of him as he sat back down. "And she's going to celebrate Thanksgiving with us!"

Well, a chaw-filled smile appeared on Pa's face. He excused himself, returning moments later with Ma's urn. "Yer right, Vern," Pa said. "No reason not to have the little ladies join us fer the holiday."

After a brief introduction, Pa placed Ma's urn next to Vern's jar, I guess so that the two containers could get to know each other.

"Wonder where we'll be for Christmas?" Vern asked.

"New York," B.B. replied , his eyes fixed on the fire. It was kinda spooky the way he said it, as if he knew the question was coming. And by the tone of his voice, there was absolutely no doubt as to his answer.

"Them inklins sure have been strong of late," Pa said.

B.B. continued to stare into the fire. "Central Park on

Christmas day," B.B. said in a deep, monotone. He was in such a trance-like state that I don't think he had even heard Pa.

"Thar are children fer Nellie and Even Tinier Bert," B.B. the zombie continued.

A shocked Vern whipped his head around to face us. "Ya kids doing something ya ain't suppose to be?"

Just as shocked, me and Nellie shook our heads vehemently, denying that anything much was going on. I mean, everybody knew we were courting. If we were doing anything more, it wouldn't have been called such a nice sounding word. B.B.'s inklings were enabling him to see far, far into the future, something he had never done before. But rather than figure out how or why this was happening, I concentrated on the fact that one day I'd be doing more than just courting.

"Vern will take his wife on a long vacation," B.B. stated, but I wasn't sure whether this meant some new woman or the one in the jar. "Eugene is back in Texas…land spreading out so far and wide, keep Manhattan just give me the countryside. Then thar's Ben and Willie's ice cream…sorta been done, and becomes a big hit when renamed "Brooklyn's Best", but is actually imported from Sweden…Clint, t.v., a job repeating fer the hard of hearing…Big Bill, goats are out to git ya…Tiny Bob, a presidential contender."

And then it got really eerie. "Faster than a speeding bullet," B.B. continued. "More powerful than a locomotive. Nothing can stop Superman except, except, except, except…"

"B.B.!" Pa said shaking him. "Snap outta it."

"Huh?" said B.B., his concentration broken. He swung his head back and forth to clear the cobwebs.

"Ya were soundin' like a broken record," Pa said. "And besides, I think I'm speakin' for the rest of us when I say it was a gettin' sorta scary." I couldn't even nod my head in agreement.

B.B. placed his hands up to his forehead and rubbed his lump. With all that activity, it must have been plumb tuckered out. He then looked back to us.

"Are you okay?" I asked. B.B. turned his head in my direction. He didn't say a word, he just grinned.

Three days later, B.B. was dead.

We found him lying in the wagon at our campsite near Krypton, Kentucky. He knew. His inklings had told him that night at the campfire, but he hadn't let on. And, so, three days later, he had quietly excused himself after lunch and gone to the wagon. He fished out his best Sunday outfit that he had packed away and put it on. He then climbed onto the wagon, laid down, folded his arms and waited. Big Bill became curious after B.B. failed to yell "stop" at the customary time, and, in his search, discovered the body.

B.B. had left no will or notes or messages of any kind. Had it been Willie, not being able to spell and all, we would have understood. But B.B.? Whereas he was gruff in life, he was quiet in death. I just thought that he would have gone out with more of a fight. But, then again, his inklings were never wrong, so what was the point of battling destiny? Like Pa always said, "The two things that are fruitless are waging winless wars and barren apple trees".

Pa immediately rode into Krypton. He wanted to call home to find out if B.B. had left a will there, and, if so, if there were any special requests as to funeral arrangements. It seemed obvious by his dress and the position we found him in that B.B. was opting for a burial over ending up in a jar or an urn. We just weren't sure if there was any particular site B.B. had in mind.

Pa first called Cyrus P. Squirrel only to find out that he had been run over by a car. Pa then called Uncle Ray and Aunt Tammy Faye. They hadn't heard anything about a will, but they had heard new rumors concerning E. Lester and Company.

Uncle Ray had heard that E. Lester now had an idea of our general location. Aunt Tammy Faye then corrected Uncle Ray, believing the new news to be that E. Lester had simply located a General. Uncle Ray declared this to be old news, stating that E. Lester already had a General out hunting for us, but now the General's entire National Guard unit had been recruited. Aunt Tammy Faye then insisted that it wasn't the National Guard, but Scotland Yard, plus the F.B.I. and the C.I.A. now assisting E. Lester.

Well, it soon sounded to Pa like every military, paramilitary, law enforcement organization and even some Y.W.C.A. members were out searching for us. Pa, tired of rumormongers, politely ended the phone call.

Still without a clue as to B.B.'s last wishes, we all tried to put ourselves in B.B.'s place. Where would he liked to have been buried? We unanimously decided to take the body with us and bury it in West Virginee.

29

I_T WASN'T UNTIL_ West Virginee and the funeral that the loss of B.B. really hit me. It was the finality. It was the fact that, from this point on, we would be leaving B.B. behind. Even though he was dead, B.B. had still been with us, at least in body, these last few days. And it hadn't really seemed much different than those times when B.B. got really mad and wouldn't speak to anybody for three or four days. 'Course, he would give you dirty looks back then, while now he was sorta stuck with just one expression.

We would no longer have B.B.'s inklings to warn us and protect us from E. Lester. We were bidding a final farewell to someone who was as close to family as you could get without sharing common ancestors. Someone who had spent more time on the Old Miss than I had. Someone who was often brittle on the outside, but soft on the inside.

Perhaps, that was why s'mores were his favorite. That's exactly what he was, a flaming marshmallow. Not flaming in any sense that a real cowboy would feel mighty uneasy about, but hot, seething, bubbling, in temper and in emotions — raging. Yet, the real B.B., the part that rarely showed, was sensitive and concerned. But because he was a real cowboy, these qualities had to bewell-hidden beneath a graham cracker, chocolate bar and toasted outer cover. Now you might be thinking, well, isn't the chocolate bar sweet? But if you take the s'more as a whole, that, too, is found on the inside.

These thoughts filled my mind as all but Tiny Bob stood in a circle around the pile of dirt that looked more like a pitching mound than it did B.B. Pa began the funeral service. I felt that very soon the dams which had been holding back my tears were about to burst.

And I was afraid that once the flood gates were open, I wouldn't be able to stop the flow. I closed my ears to Pa's words and glanced around at B.B.'s last resting place.

The spot we had chosen was on a hill top about ten miles over the West Virginia border. It overlooked the nearby town of Dingess. Pa had studied the atlas in the hopes of finding towns with names like B.B.ville, Cook or even Grangerland, but had no such luck. Dingess was the best we could do. Dingess was what B.B. called his "thing" — you know, the thing that separates cowboys from cowgirls — and he had always been awfully proud of his. So, at least he could spend eternity near something which had given him great pleasure in life.

Big Bill had struggled hard through two feet of solid rock to dig out the grave. Willie had carved a tombstone out of a tree stump, but no one felt much like arguing over the misnomer. He offered to inscribe it, but Pa felt that Little Ben had neater handwriting, and, besides, Pa thought that each of us should be involved in some way. 'Course, if the truth be known, Pa was probably afraid that Willie would misspell "B.B.".

Pa completed his eulogy and Vern was the next to speak. I shifted my watery eyes to the tombwood and read the epitapht,

> God Above
> The Final Ump
> Watch Our B.B.
> And His Lump.

Underneath, burned in for all time, stood the OM brand. And now, buried beneath this fine piece of craftmanship and poetry was B.B., wrapped in the burlap that he had removed from the sofa from the Old Miss's den. We had lowered the burlap-wrapped body of our dear B.B., which we affectionately tagged "Mummy Dearest", into the grave. The final task of refilling the hole fell on Clint and me. I apologized with each scoop of rocks and dirt that I threw onto B.B.

"And while I only knew him a short time, it was quality time," Vern was saying as I returned to the ceremony at hand. "Well, most of it was quality time. I'm not sure if when you're sleeping counts as quality time or not. If it does, then the entire time was quality time. If not, then I'm not too sure how ya figure it because you've also got to take into account time spent dozing and daydreaming too...Well, maybe let's just play it safe and stick to 'knowing him a short time' and then we don't have to get into a complicated mathematical formula for figuring quality." Vern finished and lowered his head.

"Bill Boy, ya got anythin to say?" Pa asked turning to Big Bill, who was standing next to Vern.

"'Bout figurin' out quality time?" Big Bill replied. "Pa, ya know I ain't no good in math."

"No, Son," Pa said. "'Bout payin' yer last respects to B.B."

"Well, I'm gonna miss 'im," Big Bill said, looking at the gravesite. "And I'm gonna miss the burlap." As a final gesture of respect, Big Bill lifted a stone in between his big and index toes and placed it on the grave.

It suddenly struck me — why were we here? I mean, what was the purpose of the drive? Was it to live life on the run, to become increasingly paranoid and ill-tempered from remaining on a twenty-four hour state of alert, to work ever colder nights, to bed down on the hard, unforgiving ground with sleep coming only out of sheer exhaustion?

And where had all of this gotten us? B.B. was dead. We had nothing more than what we had started with. We had arrived nowhere. No, that's not altogether true. We had arrived at Dingess, West Virginia. Dingess, a town you couldn't see if you squinted. And this was the place we were burying B.B. We were laying him to rest far from the place where he had spent all but the last few months of his life. Sixty plus years he had never left Grangerland and now he was buried in a place he'd never been except in death, far from home, far from friends. Sadder still, we'd be moving on. Would we ever pass this way again? Would anyone come to visit his grave? Ever?

The drive had been my idea, my idea from the start and no one else's, and it was entirely possible that the drive, my drive, had caused B.B.'s death. That made me, at least, partially if not wholly responsible. I'm sure the others made the connection, and for that reason, I guess I couldn't blame them if they now resented me.

The only conclusion I could reach was that the drive had been more than an awful idea, it had been a terminal mistake. Somehow, I felt that if I hadn't suggested the drive at all, B.B. would still be alive. We'd be back in Texas, and we'd still have B.B.

But had we stayed, we would have lost everything else. Still, how could everything else come close to in comparison to B.B.? Yet, was that the point? To stay in Texas meant remaining for the sake of remaining. There was nothing left for us there. I'm not talking about material possessions either. We were being stripped of our past, and there was no future. There was no life, no purpose.

The drive gave us a purpose. It gave us a hint of hope, an ounce of optimism. It gave us a reason to move forward rather than languish in the past. That's all the Henrys have ever needed, a purpose. It didn't matter how sketchy or faint it might be. If you gave us a reason, gave us a goal, we'd do more than just survive; we'd succeed. We'd been doing it for generations, and there was no reason to stop now.

It's just sad that in life there will always be losses. I hadn't realized until now how great the loss could be. I guess everybody else did though. They understood the circumstances and what was at stake, yet they reacted to the suggestion of a drive with complete and total enthusiasm. Even B.B. Yes, even B.B.

Perhaps, that was why he went so quietly. Not that he wanted to die, but he saw it coming, and after balancing the death of one man over the death of a way of life, I don't think that there was one among us who wouldn't make the supreme sacrifice. No, not if it meant the others could continue on.

I had no doubts that the drive was the right decision after all. Still, I'd miss B.B. I'd miss him alot. But, he wouldn't really be dead. I'd be carrying too much of him with me.

"Bert Boy," Pa said as he looked at me, next in the circle. "Ya wanna say yer `so long', Partner?"

I thought that I had come to terms with this event, or at least, some sorta internal truce. So, my mouth should have opened and words should have come out. I thought that I had sent out the right brain signals to get these responses. But I should have known that, in my present condition, my internal wiring had more cross connections than Grangerland Telephone — where it used to take three calls to reach the right party, but since switching over to optic fibers, it now takes four calls, yet no one complains because the wrong parties sound much clearer. Anyway, the signals my brain sent missed my vocal cords completely and just barely hit my lips, causing them to tremble rather than part. Yes, the signals sent by-passed their intended target and went straight for the tear ducts. And with a direct hit, well, those ducts sorta blew open like swollen water balloons dropped on a sidewalk.

Before anyone saw this, I turned and ran from the gravesite. Acceptance did not mean I wouldn't grieve. And through my tears, I wasn't even sure where I was going. But as the gusher from my eyes diminished to a trickle, I saw that my legs had taken me over to the chuck wagon.

This was, or, at least had been, B.B.'s territory even though it was soon to be Vern's. Here, still stacked neatly away were his pots and pans. And here were his cooking utensils, with names like mashers, shredders, peelers, grinders and cleavers. I even found his favorite, the spatula. He could toss pancakes a mile high with it. 'Course, it probably woulda been nice had he been able to catch too. Then, again, the fact that the kitchen ceiling had only been a half mile high helped in that only about half of the pancakes tossed ever returned. The rest became part of the ceiling for all time.

Holding the spatula was sorta calming for me. It was more than just an extension of B.B.'s throwing arm, it had been a part of B.B. Yes, I thought as I returned the spatula to its proper place, a major part of B.B. would still be coming to New York with us. And this part of B.B. was something tangible, something that could be held and which could soothe when the memories became too much to bear.

Beneath the spatula was a box of graham crackers, a bag of marshmallows and chocolate bars. I lifted the box of grahams and smiled.

As I turned the box over and over in my hands, I noticed some very small handwriting on its side. Curious, because the handwriting was in script and unless the people who packaged these cookies also wrote "Babar", I brought the box close to my face and read.

"Even Tinier Bert," it said. "If ya found the spatula first, then yer probably in a perty good frame of mind right now. Well, at least in a better frame of mind then when ya first had to come to grips with this whole thin durin' the funeral. Now, I figured that ya'd be the one to find this box 'cause sooner or later, ya'd figure that I was sorta like a s'more — ya know, how I was like a burnin' (not flamin') marshmallow. And how after you'd find the box, I figured that you'd a start reminiscing, probably turn the box over a couple of times, and be the first to find this here note. And that's good 'cause this note's fer you. But just in case yer weren't the first to find it, well, it don't matter 'cause no one else can read script."

"Anyway," it continued. "I just wanted to let you know, in my s'more-like way, that I'll be missin' ya the most. Ya were sorta the son that I never wanted. I mean, ya know that I didn't want no children of my own, but ya were sorta my son anyhow. I saw great thins in the future fer ya through my lump. Thins that will make everone proud, although I was already pleased with the way ya turned out. 'Course, yer Pa is too. That's my soft side talkin'. Now, my gruff side says don't do nothin' that'll ruin what I saw. And don't snack between meals! I'm runnin' out a room, so I best be endin' this message. Ya realize now that you ain't to blame fer this. This drive was our destiny. You keep this wrapper and pull it out when ya miss me, but don't tell no one that I wrote this to ya or they might get hurt feelins, 'kay? Actually, I shouldn't have to worry 'cause I always know that a secret's safe with you." And it was signed, "Wee B.".

I carefully removed the wrapper. I glanced at it one more time and noticed a very tiny postscript beneath the signature. It read, "p.s. Life's a S'more."

"You okay, Bert?" Nellie asked, stepping around the corner of the wagon.

I hadn't heard her approaching. I quickly folded the wrapper and placed it in my pocket before wiping the beginning of a tear from my eye.

"I'm okay," I said.

She sat down, and then took my hand and gently pulled me down next to her. "You can cry," she said softly. "It'th okay not to be what you call a "real cowboy", ethpecially around me. And that'th what matterth, right?"

"Yes," I said with a sniffle.

"Good," she said, tightening her grip on my hand.

We sat there for a little while just holding hands. I could tell that Nellie was giving me all the time that I needed. Nellie, who suddenly and unexpectantly entered my life while B.B. had suddenly and unexpectantly left it. Nellie for B.B.? Was it some sorta trade? Maybe that was what B.B. meant by "life's a s'more" — that in my life, sweet chocolate had replaced bitter-sweet.

"You're pretty understanding," I said.

"I know how it can be. My mom didn't path away all that long ago. And having her in perthon and having her in a jar just aren't quite the thame thing. Thtill, I'll pull out the jar and talk to it now and then becauth I alwayth feel better afterwardth. You think that'th thilly?"

"No, I don't think that's silly."

"That'th why you're different. You've never even kidded me about my lithp."

"You have a lisp?" I said, feigning shock.

Nellie smiled. "Yep," she said. "And people teathed me about it...until I retaliated. I began uthing more "eth" wordth, talking louder and right in their face. Then I could really thpray them."

"I'm sorry you were picked on to begin with," I said, sorta taking the blame for the way the rest of mankind acts sometimes.

"Actually, I kind of enjoyed thpitting in their face. But after awhile, I began feeling guilty."

"You?"

"Yep. I felt thorry for them. They were all trying to feel big. The majority of them were tho ugly or fat that they could have entered themthelf ath their own 4-H project." The words "sorry for them" echoed in my ears.

"Now don't go getting touched or anything," Nellie continued. "Although, that ith one of the thingth that maketh you different."

"What do you mean?"

"You're not a real cowboy," she replied point blank.

"I'm not?" I said, stunned and hurt and unable to hide either. My whole life, especially the last few months, I had been striving to reach real cowboyness. And I truly felt that I had been making progress. Now I was being told by the girl who I had grown to like a whole, whole lot that I wasn't making it.

"Real cowboyth are followerth," she said, studying my reaction. "They think they have to fit thome mold and they're afraid if they don't."

Nellie turned and looked me squarely in the eyes. "Bert," she continued. "You are a real cowman. Keep on being yourthelf. Don't be afraid to be different. I didn't have a choice, I learned and I'm proud."

I sat and pondered for a moment. "How come you didn't talk when we first met?"

"I was embarrathed."

"But didn't you just say that you didn't care what people thought of your lisp?"

"Who thaid anything about a lithp???" Nellie responded with a vengence. "I looked pothitively horrible! I wath thin and dirty and wearing a ragged outfit and, well, there you were! You have an awful lot to learn about women, Even Tinier Bert!"

"I hope you're willing to teach me," I said, knowing it sounded sappy, but no longer caring if anyone overheard me saying it to Nel or not. It was how I was feeling and that was all that was important.

"I am becauth you're different," she replied as a grin replaced her scowl. "And together, we're going to accomplith great thingth." Secretly, I reached back into my pocket and clenched B.B.'s note. I knew that Nellie was right, about everything.

30

Six days later, I again found myself reaching back into my pocket and clenching B.B.'s note. We had stopped for the day on the outskirts of a West Virginia town by the name of Newburg. Well, newburg, or I should say, tuna fish newburg happened to be one of those dishes that B.B. would prepare for special occasions. 'Course, Willie leaving enough sherry to cook with qualified as a special occasion in and of itself. Even Tiny Bob looked forward to this meal, knowing that he'd get to drink the packing fluid out of the empty tuna tins.

Anyhow, the name got me to missing B.B., so much so that I needed the consolation that the note had to offer. Grasping the graham cracker label firmly, I walked away from the campsite. I followed a small bayou until I found myself a secluded spot about a quarter mile away. I had to be alone, but it wasn't for fear of becoming emotional in front of the others. I no longer had any problems with that since accepting the fact that I could get all gushy and still feel manly. Yet, I had to be alone. B.B. had asked that I not let anyone else know of his note, and I was going to abide by his request.

Safe among the towering oaks, I unfolded B.B.'s message and read. The words were like the patter of rain on a roof. They were soothing to the ear and to the spirit. Yet, they were also sad and some, unbelievably deep.

Life's a S'more.

Yes, the longer I contemplated B.B.'s analogy, the more I came to realize that B.B.'s insight went way beyond his inklings. For awhile, he had me stumped. I was stuck on the notion that B.B. only meant it to relate to himself, Nellie and me. But, no, he was thinking in broader terms than that.

Yes, he and Nellie were ingredients, so were Pa, Sir Albert, the ranch hands and my brothers, even Tiny Bob. There were also all the people who we had met and all the places we had been. All these things were smushed together to form the s'more called life.

And like a s'more, life could be sweet, or at times, too much. It could crumble and fall apart, yet it could be built anew. And despite its awkwardness, there was that glue, that melted marshmallow, that somehow held it all together.

And yet, all s'mores eventually come to an end.

Yes, s'mores imitated life. Ah, B.B. the wise. I'd really miss his insight, an insight which I had never fully appreciated until this moment. And now, he was no longer around.

As tears formed in my eyes, I heard a voice, "Yer different, Even Tinier Bert."

"I know I am, Nel," I said, startled as I hadn't heard her approach. I didn't wipe my eyes, I scrunched up the note and shoved it into my pocket, which I don't think she saw because my back was to her. Now, I didn't want to tell her about the note, but I didn't want her thinking that I ran off for reasons that no longer existed. As I tried to figure out how to explain the situation, I turned to face Nellie.

And there was no one there!

But there had to be. I had heard a voice. And that voice... Flashes of recognition shot through my gray matter. That voice, these trees, what was said, triggered something. Had I been here before, was this deja vu? No, I had never been here. I'd never been out of Grangerland. More flashes. Grangerland, that voice, oak trees, a bayou, "Thought ya were different", A horse! There had been a horse...on one occasion. Yes, You Romantic You. I had tied her to a tree in a place that looked just like this...but then another time, I was in a place like this without a horse, and I went to lie down and...and then what happened? Nothing happened, none of it, I'd never been here before! So then why were chills going up and down my spine as if I had? Dream? Dream! I dreamed that I'd been here before...twice!...same place, different dream. That's why things clicked when I heard...

The sudden realization. They had been dreams, and they had been horrible dreams. And that voice...

In the same instant, I recoiled and shot my eyes skyward. My worst nightmare come true was right there, not induced by beans or worry this time around, but live and in massive person. Sitting on a tree branch overhead was E. Lester Shapes!

"So, I finally caught up to ya'll," E. Lester wheezed, exhausted from climbing the tree.

And certain that the only reason he had climbed that tree was so that my nightmare would come true, I pleaded, "Please don't jump down and smush me, Mr. Shapes, or have your possee hang me or gunslinger shoot me. I have a lot to live for."

E. Lester seemed amused by my response as he began to chuckle. 'Course, this caused the whole tree to rock and the few leaves that had been left on the tree to fall. "Stay right where ya are, 'cause I'm a comin' right down," E. Lester directed.

With no time to run, I closed my eyes. What else could I do but await the fate foretold in my premonition. I was helplessly destined for destiny. I hadn't even had the chance to say good bye to Pa, to all my brothers except Tiny Bob, to Nellie...especially to Nellie. The only consolation was that B.B. would soon have company.

I heard a branch spring from its bent position as a tremendous weight was lifted from it. My heart was in my throat as I heard the sound of a very heavy object, trapped by gravity, quickly descending towards earth. And it was all over as I felt the rush of air followed by the THUD.

And the first thing I thought about death was that it was silent and very peaceful. But, strangely, I didn't feel dead. Not that I would have had experience in feeling dead, mind you. But stubborn old Jester Lucas came back from death and said it was wonderful, with bands playing and food and even rides. Turns out he had just returned from Disneyland, but he insisted that he had been in heaven. You see, while in Disneyland, he ran into a mouse wearing red pants and suspenders. Now, Jester swore that he had killed just such a mouse a couple of months before. He even recalled removing the pants and suspenders to give to his granddaughter for her doll set before disposing of the critter. And so there he was, once again, facing what he knew to be the dead mouse. This was despite the fact, as was pointed out, that the mouse was now five feet tall. 'Course, even the mouse tried to explain that he was really a human, but stubborn, old Jester told the rodent that he didn't believe in reincarnation. Finally, because Jester wouldn't let anyone near the mouse until the situation was resolved and, by now, there was a hoard of screaming children who Jester kept on pushing back, the mouse admitted that he, indeed, was the mouse who had been struck down and accepted Jester's apology for killing him and stripping him naked.

Anyway, I also didn't feel dead, because I pinched myself and it hurt. But, not only did I not feel dead, I didn't even feel crushed. As a matter of fact, as I ran things back over in my mind, it seemed as if the thud had occurred somewhere behind me rather than on me.

Not feeling shot or hung either, I dared to open my eyes. If this was heaven, there were no bands or food or rides or five foot tall mice. If this was heaven, it looked exactly the same as where I just been. Little by little, I found the courage to turn around.

And there, laying in a newly formed crater, no more than a few feet behind me, was E. Lester.

Somehow, miraculously, the Eeoogie had missed me. I quickly glanced into the tree and saw no signs of a possee, gunslinger, Scotland Yard or any other group, including the Y.W.C.A. It suddenly dawned on me that in each instance, I had woken up before my nightmare ended. Perhaps, this was the way things were supposed to work out...me, standing here healthy and alive with E. Lester unconscious.

At that moment, a figure walked out from behind the tree from which E. Lester had just jumped. Moe! My heart skipped a beat and would have kept on skipping more than My Lou My Darlin' ever could have had the figure not come quickly into focus. Tiny Bob! And in his hand, he was holding what appeared to be a saw.

Well, that certainly explained a lot. It explained how something as big as E. Lester could have missed something as small as me. And the fact that he missed was nothing more than luck. Tiny Bob certainly wouldn't have gone out of his way to save me. No, I just happened to be standing at the right spot when Tiny Bob's natural inclination to cause trouble arose and he saw the opportunity to cut a tree branch from under a fat man.

Tiny Bob stepped toward me. Even though it was a saw he was carrying, the name Lizzy Borden still sprung to mind. He stepped on top of E. Lester as if he had just conquered a mountain. He jumped up and down a few times on E. Lester's bulbous belly before stopping and, seemingly, feasting his eyes on me.

Before I could react, though, Tiny Bob parted his lips, making his tongue dart in and out of his mouth, between his lips...like a snake. Then, to my total shock, he said, "I owed ya that one."

With that, he hopped off of E. Lester and sprinted away. Well, I ran this over a few times in my mind before concluding that I could probably spend years wondering if Tiny Bob had really realized I was in trouble and had saved me as a return favor for saving him from the snake. Besides, more pressing and less confusing was the fact that E. Lester had somehow found us and that he wouldn't stay unconscious forever. Fortunately, he was somehow alone, but it would only be a matter of time before his entourage knew we were here. I took off immediately for camp.

"Pa, Pa," I panted, running into camp a short time later at full speed. "E. Lester's here."

'Course this caught everybody's attention. I bent over to catch my breath as they all circled around me. Seeing me winded, Big Bill uprooted a small shrub with his foot which he then thrusted in my face. You probably could figure out why, but Old Doc Buford had once told Big Bill that plants were a source of oxygen. Maybe it's just that people don't go into enough details with Big Bill.

"Now that's certainly a noble gesture thar, Bill Boy," Pa said. "But I won't be able to hear yer brother through that thar bush if it's in front of his face."

Big Bill removed the shrub, allowing me to breath again.

"Where'd ya see 'im?" Willie asked.

"I le...le...left him un un unconscious about a quarter mile from here."

"Anybody else with him?" Vern asked.

"Not that I saw."

"Wonder how he found us?" Little Ben asked.

Pa thought for a moment as I slowly rose. "All them long distance phone calls I made to Ray and Tammy Faye," he said. "He musta traced 'em."

This made perfectly good sense, although it was no consolation to our predicament. "So what are we gonna do, Mr. Henry?" Willie asked.

Pa pulled out the deluxe map of West Virginia, which contained smatterings of Kentucky, Virginia, Ohio, Pennsylvania and Maryland. Pa studied the smatterings.

"I'm sorry ya'll that this had to happen," Pa finally said. "I shoulda been thinkin' when I called Grangerland, knowin' how mighty ornery E. Lester is. But, what's done is done, but that don't mean it's over. They mighta found us here, but that don't mean they knows where we're a goin'. B.B., if ya can hear me, I'm a gonna use an idear of yers to fix this here situation." Pa looked at me and winked. I should have figured that he would know that I knew of B.B.'s great insight too.

Pa turned his attention back to the map and back to business. "Willie, you'll drive most of the herds to here," Pa continued, pointing at one of the smatterings. "Northeast to Barrelville, Maryland and wait. You'll take everbody with ya `cept Vern and Bill Boy. Me, Vern and Bill Boy will take a few cattle and a few pigs southeast, towards Virginia. We'll git everbody to follow us."

"How we gonna do that?" Vern asked.

"We'll cover up thar tracks before we leave," Pa said. "So all E. Lester's gonna find are ones headin' south."

"And ya know that he won't know the difference between ten or a thousand hoof prints," Willie said. "And he'll convince the others that he's followin' the whole herd." Well, it was true that things could have been worse than being chased by a banker.

"He don't realize we got pigs," Little Ben said.

"I wonder if he's been thinkin' that them little hoof prints belong to midget cattle," Willie said.

"But won't E. Lester see it ain't midgets when he's followin' us?" Big Bill asked.

"Well, we don't actually let him catch up, Bill Boy," Pa explained. "We'll be a movin' much quicker than they will be." Now there was another reason why things could have been worse than being chased by a group led by a fat banker.

"We'll find a farm somewhere down here in the mountains," Pa continued, pointing to the map. "And we'll leave our critters thar fer E. Lester and Company to find. In the meantime, you, me, and Vern will gait north to Maryland."

"To Barrelville," Willie said with a grin as the plan came into focus.

"Now we just gotta think of a spot to meet up at," Pa said, raising his eyes from the map.

"How 'bout Barrelville," Big Bill said.

"That's good, Bill Boy," Pa said. "Now we're a lookin' fer somethin more specific."

"Well, how 'bout specifically Barrelville," Big Bill said, as proud as a kindergartener who thinks that what he drew is art.

"How many days ya reckon it'll take ya to git up to us?" Willie asked, turning to Pa.

"Figure that we'll head south fer, say, three and a half nights," Pa replied as he resumed studying the map. "That's 'bout the same amount time it'll take ya to git to Barrelville. And after we drop off our little herd, we can perty much travel day and night since we don't gotta worry 'bout bein' caught drivin' any animals. So, figure that's another two days. All together then, I reckon we'll git up thar sometime in the evening of the fifth day."

I looked at the map. "Then Pa," I said ready to join the planning. "Why don't we meet at the first place on Route 36 that's open in the evening?"

I pointed to the road and traced its route. The road ran northeast, passing directly through Barrelville. "That's just what we'll do," Pa said without hesitation. "We'll join up in five nights at the first place that's open on the way into Barrelville. Everbody got that?"

Everyone understood except Big Bill who felt that an unnamed place on Route 36 was less specific than specifically saying Barrelville. But that's why Pa always made sure that Big Bill was with him.

With that, we quickly broke down camp and prepared to depart. There was no time for praise or kudos mainly because no one knew how much leeway we had with an unconscious Eeoogie. 'Course, as a whole, I think the plan was a mighty good one.

31

THE REAL HERDS ARRIVED on the outskirts of Barrelville in the middle of the fourth night without incident. So far, the plan seemed to be working. We had crossed over the West Virginia line into Maryland on the second night and almost fell into Deep Creek Lake on the third night before finding refuge in the Savage River State Forest. On the fourth night, we drove the herds to a farm approximately three miles out of Barrelville along Route 36. And that was it. All we could do was wait for our designated rendezvous with Vern, Pa and Big Bill.

Little Ben and Clint spent the next day and a half taking turns watching the herd, while Willie passed the time watching Tiny Bob. First, Willie took Tiny Bob with him for an up close look at the region's most famous horses, the Baltimore Colts. They returned to camp dejected after learning that the horses had been moved to Indianapolis in the middle of the night. I wondered what other similarities the horses' move to Indianapolis had to our cattle drive.

Next, Willie took Tiny Bob up to the Pennsylvania line. Being less than five miles away, Willie thought the short trip could prove to be well worth it in the long run. And once there, he found what he was expecting to find. Just over the Pennsylvania line was a large sign which read, "WELCOME TO PENNSYLVANIA — THE KEYSTONE STATE". Well, with paint and brush in hand, he blacked out some letters and added others until he was left with, "WELCOME TO PENNSYLVANIA — banKErS wE hATE." Willie felt that if E. Lester happened to pick up our trail, this would act as a second line defense. 'Course, Willie couldn't pass up the opportunity at a practical joke, so upon his return into Maryland, he stopped at their welcome sign, where he changed it from "WELCOME TO MARYLAND — THE MASON-DIXON LINE" to "alLCOME fOr pARdons — THE richard nIXON LINE."

Now, Tiny Bob was having himself a grand old time. I mean, how often was it that a kid got to pal around with an adult who was pulling hijinks. 'Course, Willie's hijinks were of the good natured variety, so there was always the chance that Tiny Bob would grow bored. But, if Tiny Bob did start acting up and getting too out of hand, Willie himself had a secret weapon. Just before leaving Newburg, I had returned his missing rubber rattler to him. Willie had thought that his Ohio bred snake was gone forever and was understandably grateful upon its return. Anyway, he was now carrying it in his vest pocket, in a sealed paper bag upon which I had inscribed, "Break open and fling in case of emergency." That way, he could differentiate it from the bag containing his sandwich because, somehow, I don't think that flinging a ham on white bread would have quite the same effect on an unruly Tiny Bob.

While all this was going on, me and Nellie followed Route 36 east to the Barrelville city line. Along the way, we took in the scenery this part of the country had to offer. I would have to describe the whole area as a starter set. It seemed to have everything, but on a sorta smaller scale. Lakes were more like oversized ponds, and the mountains were so little that I wondered who looked after them, a park ranger or a babysitter. Now none of this was to say that the area wasn't beautiful and rugged and all, but you gotta remember that, being from Texas, I was used to vast open space, perhaps a tree, then more vast open space. Here, scenery was like the state itself, sorta small and compact. I mean, right now we were situated in what appeared to be Maryland's panhandle, but if you compared it to Texas's, well, you'd have to say it was more like a spoon handle, an itty bitty teaspoon handle at that.

As we continued along Route 36, we discovered remnants of the state flower, the Black-eyed Susan. 'Course, being December and all, Susan's eye trauma had spread long ago, leaving us with nothing but black Susans, and very stiff black Susans at that. Still, not knowing if I'd ever be this way again, I picked, or rather broke off a bunch of them, which I then presented to Nellie. She was so touched by the gesture that I sorta wonder what would have happened had there been live flowers on those stalks.

Crossing the Barrelville city line, we began to scour for the first place we could find that had evening hours. After looking for "wanted" posters and finding none, we began checking a number of posted hours on doors and in windows of restaurants and shops. We discovered that the first place open in the evening was a restaurant advertising Maryland steamed crabs called, "Our Crabs Don't Itch." Our task completed, we returned to camp to tell the others and to wait. As we walked into camp, I noticed that laying on the ground was Willie's emergency snake bag. It had been ripped open and discarded. I glanced around and saw Tiny Bob standing frozen with the rubber rattler at his feet. I didn't have to ask questions, though, as Willie approached me. Half his mustache was missing.

Willie had only been asleep for five minutes before Barber Bob struck. And now Willie had a dilemma on his hands, or should I say, on his face. He had to decide whether or not to cut off the rest of the mustache that he had been wearing since the age of five. After taking some time to consider all of the alternatives, he decided to keep the remaining half and to simply paint in a mustache on the other side until the real one grew back.

Finally, the time arrived to travel back into Barrelville. We all dressed nicely for the rendezvous. Seeing that we had to sit in a restaurant anyway, we figured that we might as well have ourselves some dinner. All the men wore ties, while Nellie wore a dress she had sewn out of our remaining burlap. She looked positively radiant in her new dress, upon which she had pinned a corsage. At first glance, the corsage appeared to be nothing more than a bunch of dried twigs. But I was moved, knowing that it was a corsage made from the Black Susans I had given her earlier.

Now I, myself, had to borrow the tie that Nellie had knitted for Sir Albert. Not that ties were required, mind you. The restaurant wasn't as fancy as "Eats." But that's not to suggest that it wasn't nice either. I mean, I don't believe this place would allow Big Bill in without shoes. So, I guess you would refer to it as casual dining. But, as Pa always said, "The difference between "casual" and "casualties" are the "ties". So, even on this occasion, we wore ties, even if we didn't particularly understand Pa's saying.

Still, Sir Albert's tie did make me look sorta dapper, and for my first dinner out with Nellie, I had wanted to do something special, even if the entire remaining Old Miss crew, including Tiny Bob, would be at our table.

Yes, we decided to bring Tiny Bob along. We figured that there would be enough of us in the restaurant to watch him. Also, he had been standing like a statue for thirty-six hours straight with the snake still at his feet, and we thought that it was probably time that he ate something. Lastly, no one wanted to stay back to watch him, missing a rare dinner in a restaurant.

Anyway, as the sun set over the toy mountains, Willie, with his half-painted mustache, led the rest of us out of the campsite. After the short hike up Route 36, our party arrived at the front entrance to "Our Crabs Don't Itch."

The first thing I noticed, which I hadn't noticed before, was the crab mallet hung in the dead center of the door. It hit me that we were, indeed, in Maryland.

As we entered, a burly man in a T-shirt approached us, carrying menus. "How many for dinner?" the man asked.

"Six now," Little Ben replied. "We're expectin' three more."

"Well, I'll seat you at a table for nine," the burly man said counting his fingers, before pointing to a large table nearby. "That's your table and your waitresses' name is Dixie."

As we walked by, he handed each of us a menu. "Thank ya," Willie said, taking his menu and leading the way to the table.

"Much obliged," Little Ben said, taking his menu.

"Much obliged," Clint said.

Tiny Bob didn't say much of anything, seeing as he immediately placed the menu in his mouth.

"I like your Black Susan corsage," the burly man said to Nellie as she walked by.

"Thankth," she replied.

I stopped when I got to the burly man. "I like your crab mallet on the door."

"Thanks," said the burly man. "But it's a gavel, not a crab mallet."

And, indeed, as I scanned the restaurant, it looked and sounded like they were having a judges' conference. At each and every table, people were banging away with gavels of their own. But not just to make noise, mind you. Each table was covered with newspaper, and on top of the newpaper, piled eye high, were these bright orange critters. I assumed that these were the crabs, and it was these crabs upon which the people were testing their judicial skills.

I walked over to our table and sat down in between Nellie, and as luck would have it, Tiny Bob. He already had a gavel in hand and was whaling away on the table. Seems I had just missed the plastic salt shaker taking a Tiny Bobardment, but the resulting carnage was all over the table.

"Tiny Bob," Willie said. "Hold up 'til we get some of them orange critters." Tiny Bob actually ceased his hammering. 'Course, he knew that, soon enough, he could legitimately pound away as much as he wanted to. It would be like giving a prisoner the keys to the jail, but there wasn't much we could do about it. He knew it, and that's why he sat there, content, for the time being.

"What will you all have?" said an apron-clad woman as she approached our table. Obviously, this was Dixie.

"Them orange varmints," Little Ben said.

"Yeah, them thins look perty good," Willie said, pointing to a nearby table. "Why don't ya bring us some."

"Will you have a pitcher of beer with your crabs?" Dixie asked.

"Sounds mighty tempting," Willie responded.

"Well, it's sort of a state law that you drink beer when you eat crabs," Dixie said. "Lots of beer."

"I think I like this here state," Willie said with gusto. "Sure enough, Ma'am, a pitcher of beer. We wouldn't wanta break yer laws. Matter a fact, better bring a couple a pitchers just to show ya that we're very law abidin' citizens."

"Ma'am," Little Ben said. "How do ya eat crabs?"

"It's pretty easy," Dixie said. "You pull off the claws, then you use the gavels to crack the shell and then eat the meat that you find in the claws. And to get to the meat in the body, there's this little tab-like shell on the bottom that you pull off. Then the crab opens up like the hood of a car."

"Where does the beer come in?" Willie asked.

"These things are pretty spicy," Dixie said. "You'll want to have some after every bite." This suggestion excited Willie.

"One more thing, the spices come off and end up on just about everything, especially your fingers," Dixie said.

"We use our hands?" Little Ben asked. Dixie nodded, at which point, I think I fell in love with the state.

"Anyway, the whole thing's pretty messy, especially for first timers, so if you'd like bibs..." Dixie said before being interrupted by Willie.

"Ma'am," Willie said sternly. "We're real cowboys."

I stared down at Sir Albert's tie. It was so nice and clean, and it was certainly generous of him to have lent it to me, well, for Nellie to have lent it to me. I shifted my eyes over to Nellie, whose own eyes were fixed on my tie. And from the expression on her face, I could tell she was thinking what I was thinking.

"Ma'am," I said with all the courage I could muster. "I'll take a bib." Well, there was some hemming and hawing and a few raised eye brows, but when the dust settled, seems like everybody at the table had changed their minds and was asking for bibs. Well, everybody except Tiny Slob.

"Real cowman," Nellie whispered in my ear. A warm feeling swept through me.

"Will that be all?" Dixie asked.

It hit me that we had ordered, but I was so used to not having much say in what I was eating that I hadn't even looked at the bill of fare. Quickly, I opened my menu and perused. On one side of the menu were entrees, while on the other side, were the beverages. Well, it didn't take long to peruse, because the only thing listed under entrees was crabs, while the sole beverage was beer.

Sorta confused, I asked, "What else could we order?"

"Soft crab sandwiches," Dixie replied. "When they're in season."

She could tell by my expression that I had no idea what one was, so she continued. "It's a crab that shed its hard shell and is growing back a new one when it's caught. You fry it, then put it between white bread with lettuce, tomatoes and mayonnaise."

Dixie chuckled. "When folks see someone eating them for the first time, well, because the legs hang out from the bread and all, well, they think you're eating a big spider."

Spiders! They were next to scorpions on the list of things that I hated most. I shut my menu and quickly replied, "Nothing else for me, thanks."

"That's okay," Dixie said as she collected our menus. "They're not in season anyway." Dixie then turned and walked away, disappearing into what looked to be the kitchen.

"Smart waitress," Willie commented. "Ya realize she memorized our order."

It didn't take long before we were staring at a mound o'crabs. Dixie left so many of them that I could only see the top of Clint's head across the table. At once, we started in on this mammoth pile. Well, all except Willie, who was busy proving that he was a law abiding citizen.

Gavels crashed. Shells smashed. Teeth gnashed. Beer splashed. Willie's trashed.

"Tiny Bob, the varmint's dead already," Little Ben said to Tiny Bob, who wasn't as interested in getting to any meat as he was into completely crushing the shell with his gavel. Tiny Bob temporarily stopped his major assualt on the crab and began eating the shell fragments. I hoped that this would keep him occupied for a while.

As this was going on, Pa, Vernon and Big Bill walked through the front door. They were right on schedule and not all that worse for wear. Little Ben waved to catch their attention, but they could only see those of us not hidden by the crab pile.

"Ya'll made it," Little Ben said as Pa and the others approached.

"And yer all here," Pa said. "I worried for a second thar, not bein' able to see over all them orange critters."

"Hiya Sweetpea," Vern said to Nellie as he gave her a kiss on the forehead. "I missed ya out there."

"I mithed you too," Nellie replied.

"And don't think I don't notice that fine Black Susan corsage you're wearing," Vern said, giving me a wink. Big Bill, Vern and Pa sat down.

I saw at once that Big Bill's feet had been painted black. Big Bill saw me staring and whispered, "Pa didn't want the same thin to happen that happened at "Eats.'" And in this dim lighting, he did, indeed, look like he had shoes on.

"Dixie, 'nother three pitchers of beer," Willie called out, before turning to Pa. "State law."

Dixie soon appeared with the pitchers. "Would you like to see a menu?" she asked, placing the pitchers in front of Willie.

"Naw," Big Bill replied. "Saw one 'fore at 'Eats."

"I think I'll just join in on them orange critters." Pa responded, watching us picking at the meat.

"Soft crabs in season?" Vern asked.

"No," Dixie answered.

Vern shook his head. "Then no sense looking at the menu," he said. "I'll just have steamed crabs."

"Sounds like you've had these critters 'fore," Willie said to Vern.

"Used to eat them all the time. Well, some of the time. Iowa's a big place for steamed crabs. No, wait, that's corn. Iowa's a big place for corn. I guess maybe I ain't ever had crabs before."

Dixie handed bibs to Pa, Vern and Big Bill. Vern tied his on right away. Big Bill looked to Pa. Pa simply nodded his head as if to say that it was okay for Big Bill to wear it and still be a real cowboy because everyone else had one on.

"How was yer trip?" Little Ben asked.

"Well," Pa replied, as he helped himself to a crab. "It was interestin'. We got them pigs and cows all the way down to the Shenandoah Mountains."

"That's perty far," Little Ben said.

"Wasn't hard when the only music they played in West Virginia was songs by Jimmy Dean." Vern said. "I'd never seen those pigs so spooked. Well, actually, I did once. During the radio program "War of the Worlds. Or, maybe, that was my wife. No matter, let me tell you something, pigs who no longer saw their future as black and white, but as link or patty, had no trouble in whipping those cattle into a frenzy. So, by the time everybody ran out of gas, we found ourselves down in the mountains, just shy of the Virginia line."

"Is that where ya left 'em?" Willie asked.

"Actually, we didn't leave 'em," Pa said. "We gave 'em to the town of Spadesville/Spaidsville, a little tiny place way up in the mountains."

Pa placed a lump of crabmeat in his mouth and continued. "Strange place. Town couldn't decided on its name 'cause half the town has the last name Spade and the other half has the last name Spaid. Not that it mattered 'cause everybody seemed to be related anyway. People were introducin' their spouses as also bein' their mother and half sisters. Anyway, everybody was outside playin'

banjos when we rode into town. And when they saw us, they imme-
diatley put down their instruments and started squealin' like pigs."

I anxiously awaited as Pa chewed his lump of meat. "'Course,
our pigs were in no condition to be upset not more, so lucky we had
Bill Boy to go over and talk to these people on their level. And it
turns out that the townsfolk just loved farm animals and assured
Bill Boy that they had plans fer 'em if we left 'em there. Well, since
we were lookin' to drop 'em off somewhere anyway, this seemed to
be a perty good arrangement."

"Assumin' Lester followed ya'll," LIttle Ben said, "Won't them
folks tell how they got the animals and yer direction?"

"Well," Pa replied slowly. "Supposedly, E. Lester did follow
our trail and did find the animals. But 'fore he could ask any questions, one group of Spades, I ain't sure which spellin', started
chasin' him down Main Street, while squealin' like pigs. I reckon
they mistook him fer a large hog. And supposedly, at the pace
E. Lester was hightailin' it South, he could be halfway to Florida by
now."

"What about the possee and gunslinger and the Y.W.C.A. and
all?" I asked. Pa shrugged his shoulders.

"So our trouble's behind us," Little Ben said. "At least fer the
time bein'."

"I don't know 'bout that," Willie said. His head was turned
and he was staring at a large man wearing a white T-shirt who was
seated on a stool over by a small bar area in the back of the restaurant. The man was staring back and snickering.

"Could it be Moe?" I whispered.

"Don't think so," Willie said. "He ain't wearin' black."

"Willie," Pa said. "We don't need no trouble."

"I hope thar ain't gonna be no trouble," Willie said. "But if he's
snickerin at us, well, ya know we gotta do what we gotta do."

"And I can appreciate that," Pa said. "Just make sure that it's
important enough and not just the state law a talkin'."

With that, Willie rose from his chair and swung around until
he faced the bar. The muscles in his face tightened, his shoulders
lifted and he locked his arms by his sides as he cocked his elbows
into perfect right angles. His fingers twitched in nervous excitement as we watched the transformation from Willie the crabeater to
Willie the ex-rodeo champion sharpshooter. 'Course, Willie was act-

ing out of reflex or on account of phantom signals being sent from his brain because he had left his guns back at camp.

"Mister," Willie bellowed, his voice echoing throughout Our Crabs Don't Itch. "Ya ain't snickerin', are ya?"

The large man slammed down the mug of beer he was drinking on the bar's counter and stood slowly. "Yep," he replied, still snickering.

"I hope ya ain't snickerin at anythin' over here," Willie said.

"I am," the man replied.

Willie lowered his eyes momentarily, before returning his gaze to the man standing about ten yards away. "Mister," Willie said. "Let me tell ya that where I'm from, I'm considered a real cowboy. And bein' a real cowboy, I'm tellin' ya that thar ain't nothin' wrong in wearin' a bib, comprende?"

"No," the man answered. "I don't speak Spanish."

"I asked if ya understood," Willie said.

"Yeah," the man responded. "But I ain't snickering at the bibs. Matter of fact, I wished I woulda wore one 'cause now I've got crab spices all over my good T-shirt."

"No," the man continued. "I ain't snickerin' at the bibs. I'm snickerin' at the silly painted on mustache you're wearin'."

By now, the rest of the diners had ceased their eating. They were now pounding on the tables with their gavels and chanting, "fight, fight, fight,..." 'Course, the tumultous noise caught the attention of both Dixie and the burly man by the door. Both of them came running to the confrontation.

"I think you've had enough," Dixie said to Willie.

"It ain't the beer talkin'," Willie said definitively.

"I'm talking about the crabs," Dixie said as she began removing uneaten crabs from Willie's place at the table. "Some people just don't know their limit. And they get downright ill-tempered when they're too full."

"Yeah, it's a real shame when you see two people who can't hold their crabs," the burly man interjected. "I just hope there's someone to drive you two home after the fight."

The burly man turned to Willie. "While you're waiting for your friends to finish, you may as well punch it out," the burly man said as he shrugged his shoulders. "Not much else going on."

With that, a few tables and chairs were pushed aside to create a small arena. Dixie and the burly man stepped aside, removing the last two obstacles from the area. Now, finally, the two combatants were fully able to size up the competition. It was impossible to even guess what was going through their minds, be it uncertainty, fear or even strategy. They stood stoically, exhibiting no emotions. The only movement was the pointless twitch of Willie's trigger fingers.

After a while, the dinner crowd began to grow restless. 'Course, there was nothin in their menus concerning entertainment, so I really couldn't understand their problem, especially when you consider that this entertainment was going to be free. Anyway, be it the general impatience or the fact that a few of the diners and begun to pelt the two fighters with crab shells, the men sensed that it was the time for action.

Slowly, cautiously, they stepped toward each other to begin their bruhaha, although there was nothing funny about it. By the time they reached dead center and stopped, they were pretty much nose to nose. Neither had squared off yet to do battle. Instead, they stared unyieldingly into each other's eyes.

This tense scene went on for about a minute before Willie said, quite assuredly, "Ya blinked!"

"Did not," his opponenet growled.

"Did too."

"Did not!"

"Did too!"

"Ya know, now that I'm up close, I can see that it ain't your painted mustache that made me snicker. It's your real one that looks silly."

"You've just insulted somethin' that I've had since the age of five," Willie seethed, as his face turned dark red and veins no medical expert had ever documented began popping out.

"Willie's mad now," Little Ben whispered to Vern.

"I ain't never seen so many veins," Vern whispered back. "Looks like he has a plate of spaghetti under his skin."

"No five year old ever had a mustache." the man retorted, before a strange look suddenly crossed his face. "'Cept at the Acme Orphanage."

Willie's face dropped. "The Acme Orphanage outside of Fred, Texas?"

"Yeah!" the man replied as his face dropped. "You know of it?"

"I was there!" Willie exclaimed.

"Me too!" the man replied excitedly. "And there was this kid named Willie…"

"That was me!" Willie shouted. "I was…I am Willie!"

"Hot damn, Willie," the man shouted. "It's your old pal, Orel!"

Well, Willie's spaghetti immediately receded back into his face and neck as he and Orel shook hands and exchanged back pats. I was moved by this unexpected reunion of two childhood friends. 'Course, the crowd sighed in utter disappointment and went back to eating.

Willie and Orel continued to stand in the center of the restaurant and talk. "So what happened to ya after ya left the orphanage?" Orel asked.

"I stayed in Texas," Willie replied. "Traveled the rodeo circuit fer awhile 'fore takin' a job with the Old Miss Ranch. Matter of fact, we're on a drive now, up to New York City."

"Yeah?" Orel replied. "Heard it's a meat market up there."

"That's what we're hopin'," Willie asked. "And how 'bout ya Orel? What's ya been up to?"

"Well," Orel answered. "I wanted to learn a trade after I got outta the orphanage. Wanted to be a baker, but I wanted to make more than just yer basic white and rye breads. Now, I had heard that there were places in the east that were famous for types of breads that we couldn't get in Texas. In particular, I heard that West Virginia was famous for its inbreads."

"So, I moved there," Orel continued. "I married one of the Spaid girls. Caused a bit of hostility too because I was the first outsider ever to marry into the family. But I guess, after all this time, they finally feel that I fit in. And now my wife and I have our own tar paper shack and bakery."

"Up here?" Willie asked.

"Nah, still down in West Virginia," Orel replied "Spadesville/ Spaidsville, West Virginia. I'm only up here 'cause of some guy we've been chasin' after and sqealin' at."

"You're one of the ones chasin' after E. Lester?" Willie exclaimed more than questioned.

"Ya know the guy?" Orel said, startled.

"He's a banker from Texas," Willie said.

"Oh, we thought they was filmin' a sequel to 'Deliverance'," Orel said disappointedly. "But how'd you know he was bein' chased?"

"Mr. Henry, thar, heard 'bout it," Willie answered, turning back and pointing to the table. "Thar the ones who left those cows and pigs with yer town."

"I was out deliverin' bagels and croissants," Orel said. "But I heard about their generosity."

A sudden look of worry crossed Willie's face. "but why are ya up here if yer chasin' E Lester?" Willie asked. "Mr. Henry heard that E. Lester was runnin' south as fast as his stubby legs would take 'im."

"Well, that banker, he's an ornery one," Orel answered. "He made a U-turn somewhere down in North Carolina and was seen heading back north."

More than a couple of ears perked up at our table. "Hear that, Pa?" Little Ben asked.

"Yeah, I heard," Pa replied wearily.

"It doesn't seem that we got much of a breather, does it?" Vern commented. "Actually, we didn't get no breather."

"Ya see any of the people who are travelin' with E. Lester?" Willie asked.

"Might have," Orel answered. "Then again, might not have. He's so large and all that I couldn't tell."

"We best be movin' on." Little Ben said.

"Looks that way," Pa said. "I'll get the check."

Pa called over Dixie, asked her for the check and for her to wrap up the remaining crabs to go. While we were waiting, Willie and Orel went over to the bar where they proceeded to drink lots more beer, first a couple for old time's sake, then for new time's sake. Naturlly, this led to their singing Acme Orphanage songs. And, by the time the bill was paid and we were ready to leave, both men were guffawing over the half mustache Willie had drawn on Orel.

Willie saw us stand up from the table. "Welsh, Orel," Willie slurred. "Looksh like we'sh a headin' out."

"Guessh I'll be headin' back too," Orel slurred back. "Sheeing as how it'sh jusht a banker and not Ned Beatty."

"It waz good sheein' ya again." Willie said. "Give my regardsh to yer wife."

"Will do," Orel replied.

"Where?" Willie asked as he looked around on the floor, perhaps thinking that he had an embarrassing accident.

"Nah," Orel answered. "I mean that I'll give her your regardsh."

"Oh," Willie chuckled, relieved.

"And you have a shafe trip up to New York." Orel said.

With that, the two old friends attempted to shake hands, but missed. Then they turned and parted, probably to never see each other again. 'Course, it was debatable as to how much they actually saw of each other after they had started drinking for future time's sake.

32

"Do do do you you you thi thi think E. Lester's ah ah around?" I asked Nellie. No, I wasn't speaking this way out of fear. I was talking like this because I was freezing, and my chattering teeth were causing me to stutter. Add to that Nellie's lisp and we could have graduated from high school the couple most likely not to be understood.

The nights had been fairly cold since we left Kentucky, but since we were usually moving at night, we were too busy to really notice. Besides, the days had always brought relief. Yet, this was no longer the case. The days were now just as brutal, especially up here in the Blue Mountains of Pennsylvania. As a matter of fact, for the last week or so, it was hard to differentiate day from night. Low gray clouds had hung over the mountains through which we had been traveling, competely blocking out the sun and dumping a good two feet of snow on us.

We had snow once in Grangerland. No one had ever seen it before, so Preacher Jim Earl immediately declared the day "Passover, the Sequel," swearing that it was God dropping manna on us. He then sent us out to eat the stuff, much like the Hebrews had. Well, it turned out to be a good thing because we were able to clear many of Grangerland's major throughfares. 'Course, a couple of kids were upset at having to eat their one opportunity to ever go sled riding. So, they made up for that by not missing their one chance at making snowballs, with which they proceeded to pelt the good Preacher. I think all those boys are still up at Boys Town.

But, here we were with enough snow to feed the State of Texas. Yet, in spite of the snow and the cold, we pushed on. As a matter of fact, since no one particulary wanted to stop for fear of freezing, we kept driving until total exhaustion set in. As such, we were making better time than we would have had it been nice out, so go figure.

But, like I said, there were times when we just couldn't go any farther, and now was one of those times. Me and Nellie huddled close together, which was pretty much the only positive thing about these respites.

"I I I don't kkknow iff E. Lethter'th a a around or not," Nellie finally answered, her vocal cords needing time to defrost. "Bbbut he could be. He hath alot of fa fa fat to keep him wa wa warm."

Nellie saw that this thought, coupled with the miserable weather, certainly didn't bolster my dispostion any, so she added, "Bbbut I have a way of fffinding out for thure."

"How?"

"Ha Ha Have you ever heard of "Ouija" ?"

I cringed as I recalled the numerous times that Tiny Bob had snuck up behind me and pulled my underwear up as high as it would go. 'Course, he always escaped with ease since I never felt quite like chasing him afterwards. I mean, it's awfully hard to chase someone when you're laying on the ground in the fetal position and turning various shades of green.

Nellie watched my facial contortions and chuckled. "Not "Wedgee'", she said. "Ouija!"

"Oh," I replied, feeling sorta relieved, although not having the faintest idea on earth why since I had no idea what one was.

But pleased that whatever it was, it seemingly had nothing to do with underwear, I asked, "Wh wh what's an Ouija?"

"I br br brought one from Iowa with me. I'll thow you."

Nellie left me to brave the chill alone. She returned carrying in one hand a board filled with all of the letters of the alphabet, the numbers zero through nine and the words "yes" and "no". In her other hand, she held some sorta triangular shaped pointer. She sat back down next to me and placed the board on the ground in front of us.

"Th Th Thpirith will communicate with me and you through the board and will anthwer any quethtion we athk," she said, pointing to the board.

I was immediately skeptical. Underwear I could relate to, but spirits? Like Pa always said about spirits, "Why try talkin' with the dead when people can't even communicate with the livin'."

"Th Th The board, you thee, it hath anthwerth on it," Nellie continued as she began to demonstrate. "Na na now, we'll place the pointer on the board and put our fingerth on the pointer and then one of uth will athk a quethtion."

"Tha Tha Then what happens?"

"Wa Wa Well, the pointer will point to the anthwer."

"I I I don't understand why we have to put our fingers on the pointer."

"Be Be Becauthe we have to move the pointer to the right anthwer."

"Ba Ba But then aren't we answering our own questions?"

"Na Na Not we. The perthon with the motht powerful fingerth anthwerth the quethtion."

"Sa Sa So the person with the strongest fingers pushes the pointer to the answer they want," I said as I shook my head in total confusion. "Sa Sa So where do the spirits come in?"

"Wa Wa Well," Nellie answered, sorta grinning. "Ta Ta To do it the right way, you've got to be in the right thpirit."

Nellie proceeded to place tin foil on each corner of the board. "Fa fa for better reception," she explained, as I then followed her lead and placed my fingers on the pointer. "Wa Wa We're ready. Now, go ahead and athk about E. Lethter."

Regardless of real cowman or real cowboy, I didn't say a thing because I, personally, felt totally silly talking to spirits and all.

"Ga Ga Go ahead," she prodded.

"Who da da do I direct the question to?"

"Ta Ta To the thpirith!"

What we don't do for love. I cleared my throat and said, "Spa Spa Spirits…Is E. Lester around?"

Then, with fingers perched on the pointer, we waited. After about a minute, I said, "Now what?"

"Wa Wa We wait a little longer to make it theem more mythtical, then we thlowly puth the pointer to…Uh oh."

"Wha Wha What's wrong?"

"Fa Fa First we were thuppose to athk if the thpirith are around. I mean, it'th thilly athking thpirith a quethtion if they aren't even around to anthwer. Go ahead, athk the thpirith if they're around."

Humoring Nellie as best I could, I asked, "Spa Spa Spirits, are you around?"

THE POINTER FLEW FROM OUR FINGERS! It moved rapidly in every which direction around the board, pausing only momentarily on certain letters before moving on. The heat generated by the pointer skating across the board warmed our hands. 'Course, the rest of our bodies were now shaking more than ever, but no longer from the cold alone.

By the time the pointer finished, it had spelled out, "Even Tinier Bert, is that ya? It's me…B.B.!"

As my eyes and fingers stayed glued on the pointer, all I could think of was how wonderful a wedgee would have been instead. Yep, a good, old fashioned wedgee. I wanted to wake up from this dream and find that my underwear had been pulled up to my ears, and the oxygen left my brain and I was just hallucinating.

The pointer again came to life, sending my and Nellie's hands all over the board.

"Even Tinier Bert, ain't that ya?", the message read.

All I could think of was that if my eyes popped out now, I would surely lose them in the snow.

"Ba Ba Ba Ba Ba Ba Ba Bert!" Nellie whispered, taking at least a minute to get it out.

I guess I took about a minute to whisper back, "Wha wha wha wha wha wha what?"

"It it it's na na never done this before." She was so scared that she forgot to lisp.

"Wha Wha Wha What should we da da do?"

"Ma Ma Ma Maybe we we should answer it."

"Oh Oh Oh Okay."

I felt the pointer slowly begin to move under my fingertips. I watched as it painstakingly crawled across the board until we had pushed it to the word "yes".

Immediately, the pointer skipped across the board, moving from place to place, reminding me of one of my only fancy childhood game, "Etch-A-Sketch".

"Hot Damn!" the pointer spelled out. "I was hopin' that, sooner or later, you'd try reachin' me. Now, don't be afraid or nothin'. Just keep on rememberin' that it's me, yer old pal, B.B."

I took a gulp of air and then spelled out, "How are you?"

"Not bad, considerin' the circumstances," the new message read. "They got me a cookin' up here. But with this many folks, well, sometimes the food gits a little cold, so ya know where they gotta send it to heat it up."

"By the way," the pointer continued. "Them scoops of rocks and dirt that ya threw onto me in the grave, well, I know how you were worryin' that ya were a hurtin' me. So, I just wanted to let ya know that I didn't feel a thin. And, I'm also glad that ya found my s'more message — Wee B."

Well, I can't say I still wasn't a little scared about what was happening, but who wouldn't be? Yet, I had no doubt that, somehow, I was talking with B.B. And if given a choice, I'd rather be a little scared.

"How are you doing this?" I spelled out.

"My lump!" came the reply. "Still got it with me. Turns out to be a fine transmitter here too, especially with that thar tin foil 'round the corners."

"Let me get Pa," I spelled out. "He'd want to talk to you."

"Ya know what yer pa says 'bout spirits," the pointer pointed out. "He'd think this was one of Willie's jokes. 'Sides, I can't stay long. Lotta people waitin' fer this line. So, I just wanted to tell ya…"

The pointer came to a complete halt. Me and Nellie anxiously watched and waited a good minute for some sorta continued action, but nothing happened. Finally, when the tension was as thick as cowhide, I pushed the pointer and spelled out, "B.B., what did you want to tell me?

The pointer streaked across the board. "Sorry, your call cannot be completed as dialed. Please check your number and dial again."

Well, I wondered what Preacher Jim Earl would think of this. He'd always preached that Heaven was a utopian setting. Yet, this sorta showed that there will always be a phone company around to ruin God's perfect plan.

I was about to try placing my call again, when the pointer jumped from my fingers. "Collect call from B.B. Will you accept the charges?", the message read.

I looked to Nellie, who had the same questioning expression on her face. So, I moved the pointer around until I had spelled out, "What are the charges?"

"Depends," was the reply. "Could be a lamb, could be a virgin, it all depends on your race, creed, religion or origin."

"I'm a cowboy from Texas," I spelled out.

"Cowman," Nellie corrected with the pointer.

"Then you must sacrifice a beer," came the reply.

"Does it matter that I'm a Baptist?" I spelled.

"Yes," came the answer. "It will cost you two beers."

"But I don't have any handy," I spelled.

"A Baptist Cowman from Texas without beer? That's pretty hard to believe. I'm sorry, Sir, but this call cannot be…"

The pointer took a sharp turn. "Ma'am, it's important and I don't get paid 'til the first of each decade," it spelled out.

"I'm sorry, Sir, but I must disconnect you at once."

"But Ma'am," the pointer pleaded.

"Sorry, but this call is…"

"Roseland."

"…now terminated!"

With that, the pointer came to an abrupt stop. Operators! The one group of people you were sure were destined for eternal damnation, only to find that not to be the case. Oh well, another popular misconception put to rest.

But more important now, was to figure out what B.B.'s last message meant. Roseland. Was it a warning, was it a sled? Maybe it was a code name for Tyler. Perhaps the Rose Festival council had joined in our pursuit.

We kicked the word around for sometime, thinking that maybe there was something cryptic in it and about the best we could come up with was "renal sod", which meant less to us than "Roseland". Yet knowing that it was important, we thought it best to ask Pa and the others about it. And knowing what we knew, we figured it would probably be even wiser if we just sorta brought it up without going into any details.

We found everybody sitting on a fallen tree over by the herds. Well, everybody except Tiny Bob. He had found an entrance to a large cave over which hugh icicles had formed. Tiny Bob was standing directly underneath the icicles and tossing stones at them. Everybody else were staring at brochures Willie had picked up somewhere.

"Pretty strange state, Pennyslvania," Vern remarked.

"I'll say," Little Ben said, before holding out a brochure for all to see. "Look at this one. It advertises an Amish Smorgasbord. Now, who'd want to eat an Amish?"

"How 'bout this one on the Poconos," Willie said. "This place talks 'bout how popular it is, but if ya look at the pictures of the rooms, thar ain't no one in 'em." Willie handed the brochure to Pa.

"Well, no wonder," Pa said inspecting the brochure. "They say they got whirlpools in every room."

"My Goodness!" Vern said, taking the brochure. "All those poor unsuspecting guests just sucked into oblivion. You'd think they'd give ya more warning than just a little footnote on a brochure."

Little Ben took the brochure from Vern. "And look at this," he said. "Mirrors over the bed. I think that would make it perty difficult to brush yer hair."

Pennsylvania was a strange state and the sooner we left, the better. "Pa," I said, feeling it was the right time to enter the conversation. "Did you ever hear of Roseland?"

"Ain't that a sled?" Big Bill replied.

"Sounds like a nickname for Tyler?" Willie answered.

"I think that's where Elvis is buried," Vern said.

"I've never heard of it," Little Ben said. "But if ya switch the letters around, ya get "renal sod'.""

Pa, who had been thinking, spoke, "Wasn't that President Jimmy Carter's wife's name?"

"I think you're right," Vern said.

"Yeah, that's it," Willie said.

"Yeah, that's it," Clint said.

"Who's President Carter?" Big Bill asked.

"I think ya got it, Pa," Little Ben said.

Pa then turned to me. "Any reason ya wanted to know?" he asked.

"Just wanted to know," I said as I contemplated just what could have been so important about President Carter's wife that B.B. would have sacrificed two beers to tell me if he had had them.

33

NEW JERSEY. THE GARDEN State. Except the farther we traveled into the state, well, quite honestly, the less things resembled anything close to a garden. 'Course, this was the East, and maybe around here, a pile of junked automobiles did qualify as a garden. And if not, maybe the fine folks of this state would put to good use the prime fertilizers being left by the herds.

We crossed into New Jersey three days after my conversation with B.B. Me and Nellie had thought about again trying to ring him up or conjure him up or whatever you do with a Ouija board, but there was just no time. With the snow still falling and the relentless cold wind blowing, we were so busy moving the herds that even analyzing the significance of an ex-President's wife had to take a back saddle.

We were no longer stopping, even for a moment's rest. We were all totally exhausted, my eyelids as heavy as extra fatty whipping cream. But Vern's warnings on hypothermia and the need to keep the circulation constantly moving had us all a might worried. He knew first hand the dangers extreme cold could bring, seeing as he had lived in conditions like this all his life, at least during the winter months. He told us a tale of a whole herd of pigs that had frozen to death in bitter cold weather. Then, when the cold finally subsided, he had to defrost the pen like a freezer and discard the pigs with the most severe cases of freezer burns.

We had distributed the winter gear back in Pennsylvania when it became obvious that the weather was not about to let up. We were now bundled up in wool-lined coats, hats, ear muffs and long johns. I felt like a sheep on parade. 'Course, only the constant scratching did anything to really warm me up.

We just weren't use to such extreme cold. Where we were from, they considered anything under 50 degrees a cold spell. Stores would close, schools would let out early. The reason behind this was a reported case of frostbite. Seems that someone was walking behind Old Doc Buford's office one blustery 49 degree day, when they overheard Doc Buford diagnosing someone for frostbite. Soon the word spread, frostbite reported in Grangerland. I happened to be in the second grade at the time and I remember the ensuing panic well. Now, it so happens that it had been one of my classmates, Lilford Dilson, whom Doc Buford had been treating. And, if the truth be known, Doc was treating Lilford for overbite. 'Course, a bunch of dumb second graders weren't about to set a bunch of hysterical parents straight, especially when they were demanding that the school close on days below 50 degrees, so we kept quiet.

And now it was at least forty degrees colder than the tolerated limit in Grangerland. So, there wasn't much Vern had to say to convince us of anything and that was probably best for all concerned. This included the herds, who I guess had also listened to Vern's tale of pig woe because I had never seen them so cooperative. The cattle traveled in front, packing down the snow so that the pigs could see where they were going. And by the time all the animals had traipsed over a certain spot, they had created a nice, wide, hard packed trail for the chuck wagon.

'Course, the fact that we were fast approaching our final destination also helped to keep things moving. Be it good or bad, there was just something exhilarating about being close to the end of anything. And here, even if you couldn't read a map, you knew we were on the last leg of the drive- Willie was down to his last couple of thousand bottles of beer on the wall.

Yet, I also had feelings of anxiety mixed in with my exhilaration. As we trudged on through continuous snowfall, passing by New Jersey towns with names like Brass Castle, Pleasant Grove, Ralston, Mendham and Florham Park, I felt as if the country was growing narrower. Over the piles of snow and through now limited visibility, I could see the outlines of civilizaton. The farms were becoming fewer and fewer, giving rise to factories, oil refineries and lots of toll booths. Willie was still able to scout us out a trail to follow, but the land was no longer a wide open space, void of signs of human habitation. Towns were popping up like Spring grass, and we weren't sure how much longer we could avoid them. In fact, it was probably only because we were the beneficiaries of what we later learned was the earliest blizzard in the history of the East that we weren't discovered.

It was crazy, but here I was, I had been constantly surrounded by thousands of animals, but only now did I feel suddenly claustrophobic. Why did all these people congregate into such a small area when there was all that country sitting behind us? Who would want to? Was it strength in numbers? Complacency? It couldn't have been the scenery.

We crossed Interstate 280. The map had warned us of major traffic on this highway, so we had planned on crossing ten animals at a time, and I don't have to tell you how long that would have taken. But, with all roads completely buried in snow and the animals in four hoof drive, highways were literally no different to cross than were fields. They had as many rocks, holes, divets, craters, bottles and trash as the fields had.

On the other side of Interstate 280, the herd came to a sudden halt. I know the herds overheard Vern's chilling tales, so the reason for them stopping must have been extremely important. To find out what was going on up ahead, I leaned over and asked Sir Albert if I could borrow his sunglasses. He seemed to lodge no objections, so I took them and placed them on. They were a bit stretched out, but they did enable me to see through the blinding snow.

"What ith it?" Nellie asked, as she and her pa pulled up in the wagon.

I peered through the twirling gusts of snow. Up ahead, in front of the herds, was a large green metallic sign. The posts of the sign were buried beneath the snow, but the sign, itself, was clearly visible.

"Oh my…," I started to exclaim before catching myself.

"What do ya see, Bert?" Vern asked.

"Well," I stalled, not wanting Nellie or her pa to worry. "With all the snow flying, I'm not quite sure. I'm going to ride up to find out."

Without waiting for a reply, I shook the reins and put You Romantic You into a trot. Through the snow we went, toward the front of the herd. That was where the sign was, the sign that I strained to see, the sign that said, "Roseland", the sign on top of which a snow-covered individual sat. And that snow-covered individual had little resemblance to President Carter's wife.

Pa, Big Bill, Little Ben, Clint and Willie were all off of their horses and standing around the sign as I approached.

"Gotta give ya some credit," Pa said, shielding his eyes from the snow while looking up at the individual on top of the sign. "Can't figure how ya found us."

"Well, when ya left the different grazin' spots, ya'll were in such a hurry that, I guess, ya'll decided that ya couldn't round up all the cattle each time," E. Lester replied from the top of the sign. "I mean, ya really didn't have much choice in the matter. But, what ya left me with was sorta akin to leavin' bread crumbs fer me to follow- a trail of OM branded cattle stretched from here back to Texas."

"I did sorta have two problems though," E. Lester continued. "I had to go 'round Pennsylvania 'cause it seems that bankers aren't welcome thar. And the other was down in West Virginia. Crazy people down thar chased me a couple hundred miles, squealin' the whole way. Don't know why, but I do know that all that runnin' took off a good hundred pounds." And even though E. Lester was bundled from head to toe, he did look like he dropped down to Eeoog size.

"Anyhow, I was able to pick yer trail up again in West Jersey," E. Lester said.

"But we didn't stop no more," Willie said.

"Well, I guess ya'll were so tired and it was snowin' so hard that ya couldn't see the couple of cows that wandered away from yer herd," E. Lester said. "So, I followed 'em, got an idea of where ya'll were headin' and then got in front to head ya off. Ya know, I ain't sure if I woulda been able to do that 'fore I lost them hundred."

A sick feeling went through my gut. It had been my job to look for strays and it was the strays that brought E. Lester to us and us to E. Lester. I had failed miserably. And in doing so, I had let everybody down. I was personally responsible for the end of the Old Miss, for the end of a heritage, an era, our livelihood. I was a real cowchip.

Pa glanced down from E. Lester over to me. "Bert Boy," Pa said. "I know ya and yer probably feelin' responsible. Don't.

Ain't nobody livin' who could see strays through this snow and wind."

"Yer pa's right," E. Lester said. "I didn't see them strays either. They would spot me and come over. Guess I still gotta couple more pounds to lose 'fore cows stop takin' me fer one of thar own."

"'Sides, Bert Boy," Pa said, sorta on the side. "I don't know how ya knew, but I think ya tried warnin' us 'bout this here place."

I think I would have been feeling much better, being vindicated and all, had it not been for the fact that no matter who was to blame, the end result was still the same. Roseland, New Jersey had become the end of the line, our final destination, our Alamo. And because of this, those vagabond blues wouldn't drift away.

"So," Pa continued, returning his attention to E. Lester. "I guess ya want to call in yer possee and take back yer collateral."

"What possee?" E. Lester asked.

"We heard ya had a possee," Willie said.

E. Lester laughed. "Ya must mean Pete," E. Lester said, lifting a shivering, furry, tan marisupial. "I always bring my pet possum 'long when I ain't gonna be home fer a couple of days. Funny thin is while I've been a losin' weight, this critter's been growin' in size."

"What about a gunslinger?" I asked. "Didn't you leave town with a gunslinger named Moe?"

Again, E. Lester chuckled. "At the bus station, I ran into a mudslinger named Gogh. Right away, he started badmouthin' everthin and everbody. Not the kinda person who should be workin' in public relations, but go figure. Lucky fer me that he wasn't headin' east 'cause I don't know how much more I coulda taken of him callin' his momma a 'tramp'."

"Ya didn't offer rewards?" Big Bill asked.

"I did have awful warts," E. Lester grinned. "But I had 'em removed in Kentucky."

"Boys, now ya see the pitfalls of listenin' to rumors," Pa said, which only sorta relieved me a little because I was still staring up into the face of a two hundred pound fact. Even with our lives spared, it was still the end.

"Now," E. Lester said. "'Bout that collateral."

"Thar all down here fer ya," Pa said with a heavy heart.

"Don't want 'em," E. Lester replied, quickly and simply.

Everything had been silent before the reply, mainly because

snowy days seem to have that effect on the outside world. But now, well, it was even more silent, if possible, than before.

Finally, Pa broke out of his stun, "Ya say ya don't want yer collateral back?

"That's what I said," E. Lester answered. "I don't want the cattle."

I know Pa was wishing it was warmer out because I knew he was just dying to take his cowboy hat off and scratch his head over this one. Instead, he had to settle for scratching his hat. "Well, then," Pa said. "Why were ya followin' us?"

"I wanted to join on," E. Lester said. "I want to work with the Old Miss crew."

"What 'bout yer bank?" Pa asked. "We'd heard that ya needed our cattle back to keep it a runnin'."

"What I needed was some missin' money returned to some bank accounts," E. Lester said. "The government came in and audited the bank books and found that the figures just didn't add up. Seems thar was some money missin'. And it seems that my trusty bank treasurer was the one who took it."

"Not E. Lester, Jr.!" Pa exclaimed.

"Kids," E. Lester nodded his head affirmatively and sighed. "'Cept, besides that Tiny Bob of yers, yer kids seem different, better. Matter of fact, I mighta tried tellin' Bert that very thin not too long ago. Then again, I might not have, it mighta been a dream. See, thar was a couple of lost days in thar where all I know fer sure was that I thought I had been talkin' to Bert when the next thin I knew I found myself a lyin' in the woods with a head and stomachache."

"So where's E.Lester, Jr. now?" Pa asked, quickly changing the subject before anyone was put into the position of having to 'fess up to anything. "Can't ya git the money back?"

E. Lester shook his head. "Got a post card from 'im," he said. "He took his mother and sister, sold 'em and then took all the money and bought a football team."

"That's sorta why I need the job," E. Lester continued. "I wanta buy my wife back...my daughter, too, if she's learned to behave herself."

"I just don't understand how if yer son took money from yer bank that ya can't git it back at all," Pa said, sorta pushing aside the issue of a job. "Weren't ya insured?"

E. Lester again shook his head. "I left that up to my trusty bank treasurer," he said. "And figurin' that without insurance, I was personally responsible fer all that missin' money, well, I sorta left town fast. I left lookin' fer ya'll, figurin' ya'll would understand."

Now, even if I didn't personally like E. Lester, I was starting to feel sorry for him. He was right. We had pretty much done the same thing that he had in a similar predicament, so we could sorta understand his thinking. 'Course, the one difference was that he was the one who was responsible for our predicament. Still, we had always lived by Pa's saying concerning bygones, "When you wanna forget the pain, the hurt and make amends, as to those incidents, pretend you have amnesia and then..."

And Pa was doing just that. He closed his eyes as he remembered to forget, as well as to mull over the prospect of offering E. Lester a job. In the meantime, E. Lester turned to me. "Bert," he said looking down to me. "Was it a dream or did I talk to ya somewhere down in West Virginia?"

Weren't we finished with this topic? It happens everytime you think you've successfully weaseled out of a bind. Somehow, the topic comes back around and you end up squirming all over again. Do I tell him that we did talk, that he was cut down from a tree, that I allowed him to stay unconscious on the ground as Tiny Bob used him as a spring board? Or do I keep on letting him think that I am somehow better than E. Lester, Jr.?

"I coulda sworn I was up in a tree," E. Lester said, as it looked like I was soon going to have to come clean. "Yes, I had seen ya comin', so I climbed a tree to wait fer ya. And I was sittin' thar when..."

No, he didn't suddenly forget what happened. He stopped because the Roseland sign on which he had been sitting began to sway, creak and groan and then collapsed. A proud Tiny Bob appeared from nowhere, once again armed with his saw.

We all went over to the snow bank into which E. Lester had fallen. You could tell by the size of the hole that he had formed upon impact that he was definitely losing weight.

"E. Lester," Pa said, peering into the hole. "Are ya alright?"

There was no response. "He's unconscious again," Little Ben said as he looked over Pa's shoulder.

"Well," Pa said with a sigh. "Job or no job, looks like we're a bringin' 'im along."

"Ya boys get 'im out of thar and we'll put 'im in the wagon," Pa continued. "And Bob Boy, ya did what ya thought was a noble thin. But, whether we like it or not, E. Lester's travelin' with us now. And since he's still got some weight to lose, I think it would be a lot easier on everone if he stayed conscious, understand?"

I don't know if Tiny Bob understood or not, but I understood that I had weaseled out of trouble for yet another day.

34

BELIEVE IT OR NOT, having E. Lester with us created more of a dilemma than before. It seems each of us was feeling the same way about the East. It wasn't just cold feet either, although we all had them.

No, it had nothing to do with the fact that a bunch of herds-men and a banker-turned-honest-worker were soon to drive their animals into what was supposedly the biggest city in the U.S.A. It had to do with the fact that the East was just such a dismal place. I mean, when we passed a place called "The Meadowlands", it hardly resembled any meadows that we had ever seen.

And now that neither E. Lester nor a possee nor a gunslinger nor even the Y.W.C.A. was chasing us, well, there was no longer any urgency or even the need to get the cattle to market. We now had time to change our minds. And after we reassessed the situation, who knew? Maybe we'd turn around and head back to, say, Maryland.

Still, New York was nearby, and Pa's opinion was that it might be easiest just to take advantage of New York's big, old meat market, the world's biggest as promised by Dr. Bart Namath. In the back of my mind, I still harbored a slight suspicion that something wasn't right, that we could be setting ourselves up for a great disap-pointment if we continued on to New York. Yet, we no longer had to head east, did we?

If we turned around and headed back, while E. Lester was no longer a problem, we would still be leading an unsanctioned drive and would still have to worry about getting caught by the authori-ties and charged with trespassing. 'Course, if we turned around, we'd also have to go back through Pennsylvania and risk possible encounter with their whirlpools.

So, as we were about to drive the herds across an empty, snow covered bridge over the Newark Bay, I faced a dilemma: Should we continue on or go elsewhere, or should I tell Pa my lingering doubts about New York and hope that he forgave me, realizing that what I did, I did for him?

I desperately needed to talk to someone, someone whom I had confided in my whole life and who had confided in me. Someone who had great insight and could probably impart even wiser advice now that he was no longer directly involved.

Now, I wasn't sure if it would work or not, but I "borrowed" two bottles of beer from Willie's private stock and Nellie's Ouija board and pointer and stole off to a large soot covered snow drift behind the chuck wagon. There, I placed the board on the ground and then the bottles on the board.

"I'm a baptist from Texas," I spelled out with the pointer. The two beer bottles began shaking and continued rattling unmercifully for about a minute before becoming suddenly still.

"B.B.," I continued, rapidly moving the pointer from letter to letter. "It's me, Even Tinier Bert. I'm hoping that you're there, but I can't stop because I don't know how much time two beers buys me on this line and that's all I could risk taking from Willie's private collection. Now, I don't know if you know what's been happening and it's a pretty long story, but E. Lester is now traveling with us, which means that we don't have to go to New York anymore which might help me out because I've never been too sure whether New York's a meat market in our sense of the term even though that's what me and Dr. Namath told Pa. Luckily, everybody's confused about what to do. Now, I know you're probably busy cooking and I know how you hate to be interrupted, but if you can just answer one question...should we head east into New York or should we head somewhere else, somewhere less dreary, less dirty and without the medical waste that I've read about?"

I lifted my fingers from the pointer and stretched them before they developed Ouija's cramp. Then, I quickly placed them back onto the pointer and waited, not even sure if B.B. had received the message. I waited anxiously. Finally, after what seemed like forever, the pointer began to move. It traveled slowly and succinctly, as if making sure that I acknowledged each letter before moving on. The pointer concluded its deliberate work, emphasizing its message with an exclamation point, "Go East, Young Man!"

So, that was it. That was the answer. I felt tremendous relief. B.B. would not have instructed us to continue east if New York was the meat market in the sense everyone else believed, would he?

I quickly pointed out, "Thank you, B.B.", but there was no response. I picked up the two bottles from the board and, not surprisingly, found them empty with the caps still on. I buried them deeply in the snow. Hurriedly, I left the snow bank and, after placing the Ouija board and pointer back in the wagon, met the others at the foot of the bridge. They appeared as perplexed as ever as they balanced the pros and cons.

"The chores," Big Bill said.

"The stores," Vern said.

"Fresh air," Little Ben said.

"Times Square," Willie said.

"Just so long as we don't go to West Virginia," E. Lester said.

I hesitated for awhile, along the perimeter of the circle, watching Pa. I really wasn't quite sure of how to approach him, but then decided to walk straight to him. And as I reached him, I pulled him aside. "Pa," I said. "Can we go for a little walk?"

"Sure, Bert Boy," Pa said. The two of us strolled off until we were out of the hearing range of the others.

"You know that I'm just your son and all and that you're my pa," I said.

"Yep, that's the way I see thins. This here sounds like a lead in."

See, he knew me like the front of my hand, which I was personally more familiar with than the back. "Yes, Pa," I said. "I wanted to talk to you about the choices."

"Well, don't ya wanta join in and discuss the pros and cons with the others?"

"No! I'm sorry, Pa. You know I'm not usually so abrupt, but I just want the two of us to talk."

"Ya got somethin stuck in yer craw?"

"Well, I know that there's probably a zillion reasons to turn around and head somewhere else, but I think we should continue on to New York."

"'kay, why?"

"Well, I think it's best if I don't tell you."

"I see. But ya think we should continue on."

"Well, I don't think, I know."

Pa was awfully quiet. He studied my face, which I made to look as determined as I could. I had never demanded nor really even asked for anything my whole life. And here I was, being pretty adamant over something about which I couldn't even offer a basis to back up my conclusion. This was as close as I had ever come to actually telling, not asking, Pa what to do. And I wasn't sure if he was now respecting me for speaking my mind or if he was thinking that I was getting a little too much like E. Lester, Jr.

"Bert," Pa said with a long drawl, forgetting the "Boy" and probably ready to disown me.

He waited another minute before continuing. "I've gained great respect fer ya durin' the course of this here drive. Like I said before, one day, I expect that you'll be the one a runnin' the Old Miss or New Miss or whatever we decide to call it and wherever it might be. That's 'cause yer different, Bert, and that's why I ain't mad at ya now. Yer fightin' fer somethin ya believe in, even if ya think ya might offend me. 'Course, it helped that you were tactful 'bout it."

"So, you're not angry?" I asked with much relief.

"I know ya and yer not an E.Lester, Jr.," Pa said. "And ya ain't challengin' my authority, yer just givin' me yer opinions. See, I know that even if I said we ain't a goin' to New York, ya might not be happy, but you would still be with us. And givin' me yer opinion of thins means yer thinkin', somethin I wish some of yer other brothers would do."

"But," Pa continued. "It so happens that I'm a gonna trust yer instincts and we're a gonna go to New York. And I'm a gonna respect yer right of privacy on how ya got them instincts, even if the basis fer 'em was talkin' with B.B. on an Ouija board."

Could Pa know?

Pa put his arm around my shoulder. "Now, I think we should tell the others 'bout the decision 'fore they git too debated out."

"You're absolutely right, Pa," I said. "I agree with you on that point."

Pa chuckled as we started to walk back. "One more thin you'll learn is that if ya stick to a certain position, ya gotta be prepared to take the responsibility," he said.

I suddenly felt a great weight on my shoulders. "You mean, if New York doesn't work out, I take the responsibility?" I said.

"Nah," Pa said with another chuckle. "New York'll be my decision. I'm a talkin' 'bout takin' responsibility when Willie finds out two of his beers are missin'."

And then he added, "That is the goin' rate for a Texas Baptist, ain't it?"

35

WELL, EVEN IF NEW YORK turned out to be the wrong decision, I think all of us would have been disappointed if we had turned around and later found out that we had missed the sight presently before us. According to our calculations, we were somewhere between Weehawken and Guttenberg, overlooking the Hudson River. And, there, across the river, our eyes were fixed on the most massive skyline we had ever seen…New York City.

We stood, staring in awe. Even from our vantage point peering through the relentless blizzard, we figured the buildings to be at least fifteen stories tall! And somewhere, in the midst of all those structures, was Central Park, home of the New Miss, and the meat market.

The only obstacle left was the river in front of us and we had formulated the plan for crossing it back in Grangerland. Figuring the cattle's natural aversion to water and the fact that the river was going to be too cold to swim, we planned to enter the city via the Lincoln Tunnel.

"Where's that tunnel?" Little Ben asked as he peered across the river.

"South along the river a couple of miles," Willie answered.

"We overshot it," Vern said, looking at the map.

"Looks that way," E. Lester said, glancing over Vern's shoulder. "Shame too. Looks like now we gotta head south, then north again when that thar park is somewhere straight in front of us."

"Overshootin' the tunnel ain't half our problem," Pa said with grave concern. "Back thar in Grangerland, back when we planned on usin' the tunnel, we didn't know what we know now."

He paused for a moment. "They ain't a gonna let us drive our herds through thar."

"But we've been usin' other public roads and bridges lately," Willie said.

"That's true, Willie," Pa said. "But that's 'cause they've been closed 'cause of all the snow. Now a tunnel underground ain't got no snow on it, so people might be usin' it."

We all mulled that over and realized that Pa had a point.

"Well, then," Vern said, still looking at the map. "How 'bout usin' the George Washington Bridge? That's gotta be closed."

"Thought we weren't gonna take that bridge," Willie protested much to our chagrin. We thought we had straightened Willie out back at the Old Miss, or, after traveling over a thousand miles, you would have thought that Willie would have at least forgotten. But no, here he was, once again fearing that trolls resided under that bridge.

"But we can't use the tunnel, Willie," Pa said. "Nobody's done seen us yet 'cause we're the only ones out in this here storm. Now, if thar are people in the tunnel, they'll see us and since we ain't allowed to be here to begin with, that might just spoil everthin'. And I think ya'll agree that we've come too far to risk that." Pa showed great diplomacy in avoiding the subject of trolls. Since Willie was still haboring this fear, it might have developed into a full-fledged phobia. And as Pa always said, "Don't belittle someone about their mental illness."

"How 'bout that Martha Vineyard's Ferry that Dr. Namath told us 'bout?" Willie asked.

Pa studied the map. "He musta meant the Staten Island Ferry. But it don't look to me that anythins a crossin' that frozen river."

We peered out and saw that Pa was absolutely right. The river looked frozen solid, which would explain why not one ship had passed by the entire time we had been standing here.

"How 'bout takin' one of them Shuttles?" Willie asked.

"Dr. Namath said we'd need reservations, and we didn't make none," Pa replied.

"Well, can't we wait 'til dark, and then sneak into the tunnel?" Willie pleaded. "We been sneakin' in and outta places ever since Tyler!"

"Well, I just ain't sure that we can sneak into this here tunnel, even after dark," Pa said.

"Pleeeeeeazzzze," Willie begged.

"Tell ya what," Pa said in a compromising tone. "'Fore we

drag the herds anywhere, I'll go down with Clint and scout out the tunnel, and Ben Boy, ya take Bill Boy and scout out the bridge. Fair?"

"Oh, yes, Mr. Henry," Willie said. Willie attempted a smile, but the weight of his snow encrusted half mustache allowed only the bare half of his lip to turn skyward, resulting in a half grin. 'Course, it was a very appreciative half grin.

As Pa and the others loped off, Willie crossed all his fingers, including his two thumbs, and remained that way until they all returned a short time later. Willie ran to meet them as they appeared from the dense gray clouds, Little Ben and Big Bill riding in from the north and Pa and Clint coming from the south.

"Well?" Willie asked with a great deal of nervousness in his voice.

"Sorry," Pa said, dismounting Ma and tying her to a tree. "Looks like yer finger crossin' didn't help. The tunnel never closes. We can't ever just sneak in thar." Pa leaned back to rest.

Willie kicked the snow and was about to do some heavy duty cursing, but Little Ben interrupted. "Don't do no cursin'. Got news 'bout the bridge…Can't use it either."

"Then my finger crossin' did work," Willie said to Pa as he struggled to uncross his fingers, which was difficult since they were now sorta frozen together.

Vern saw Willie straining to pull his fingers apart and said, "Ya shoulda been more worried 'bout the real threat of hypothermia than 'bout yer silly trolls."

"Shhh," Pa whispered in Vern's ear before turning to more serious matters. "Ben Boy, what do ya mean we can't use the bridge?"

"It's closed," Little Ben said. "But people are still watchin' it from itty bitty booths…"

"TOLL booths," Big Bill stressed, turning toward Willie.

"Bill Boy, ya know what I say 'bout mental illness," Pa said sternly before returning to the subject of the bridge. "It don't seem to make one bit of sense havin' someone sit and watch a bridge that's closed. At least the tunnel was open."

"Well, I asked 'em why," Little Ben said. "Seems they git paid, even if thar's no work. Union rules."

"Unions," Pa muttered. Pa had had his fill of unions back at the Old Miss. Before I was ever born, a union organizer came to the ranch and tried to get the ranch hands to unionize. When the hands asked what the union could do for them, the organizer said that the union offered the most efficient way of collecting dues. 'Course, the plan to unionize was defeated because the hands prefered not to pay dues to anyone and because the organizer had failed to propose any inefficient ways of collecting.

"Yep, they're thar twenty-four hours a day," Little Ben said.

"'Course thar ain't much fer 'em to do now 'cept sip whiskey and git paid fer it," Big Bill said. "Perty good whiskey too."

"Ya boys didn't drink none, did ya?" Pa questioned.

"Well," Little Ben said, sorta at a loss for words.

"Well, Pa," Big Bill tag teamed in. "Them people looked sorta confused when they saw us ride up."

"Don't think they were expectin' to see anyone," Little Ben said. "Or they didn't know the charge fer horses to cross, and thar union forbids 'em from thinkin'. They gotta clause holdin' thar performance at a low primate level."

"Anyhow, Pa, it turns out them people just thought they were seein' thins," Big Bill said. "So, to show 'em that it wasn't the whiskey talkin', we joined 'em fer a drink."

"Boys," Pa said, sorta upset. "We got a drive goin' and ya know how I feel 'bout drinkin' and drivin'.'"

"Just bein' hospitable," Little Ben said.

I think everybody was starting to realize the ramifications of the recent developments and that's why everyone was getting a wee bit testy. We had come so far only to fall short, all routes to New York seemingly cut off. And there below us was the river which separated us from journey's end, a seemingly invincible river with the haunting skyline of New York in the background. A feeling of despondency swept over me.

"Why don't we just walk the cattle 'cross," Clint said, breaking the long silence. "Seein' as the river is frozen."

It was brilliant! And yet the solution was so simple that it had been overlooked. Yes, the route home had been in front of us all along and we had failed to see it, making each of us feel a little like Dorothy from the Wizard of Oz. What's more, according to the map, it was the most direct route to Central Park. All we had to do was drive the herds straight ahead and we'd eventually hit it. What's more, if we got a move on, we could use the snow as cover and possibly arrive at the park before dark. But what's most, was whose idea it was.

We were so caught up in the solution to our predicament that we lost sight of the fact that Clint had suggested it. But, when we finally realized it, well, with all the whooping and hollering, you'd have thought that a Lone Star Beer truck had just appeared from nowhere. Willie suggested that something be done to commemorate this historic event. We all agreed, seeing as no one knew when Clint would ever have an original thought again, especially one of such far reaching magnitude. Vern suggested a plaque, for which Big Bill offered to scrape his teeth.

Then, a light bulb went off over Pa's head. "Bob Boy, stop throwin' them light bulbs from the wagon wheel," Pa said. "We might need 'em later."

But the bulb that exploded when it hit the tree where Pa was leaning gave him an idea. We hung a light bulb inscribed with, "Clint's First Original Idea — December 24, 1987" from one of the branches. Pa wanted to express the hope that as a tree may grow, so, too, may Clint's original thoughts. 'Course, we hoped that Clint appreciated the symbolism and didn't realize that this particular tree from which the bulb was hung was dead.

After the bulb-hanging ceremony, we quickly returned to our drive positions in anticipation of the river crossing. I patted Sir Albert while I exchanged smiles with Nellie as the cattle and horses followed by a shoal of shoats and the rest of the pigs slowly made their way down the steep bank to the Hudson.

Right at the shoreline, the herds again came to a complete stop. There was no need for concern, however. Pa just wanted to be certain that the river was, indeed, frozen. He had E. Lester walk halfway across the river and back. Satisfied that the ice had not so much as creaked under the strain, he had Willie start up the drive.

As the herds took their first few steps onto the ice, it was evident that we did have a problem. It wasn't the weight, E. Lester had been a pretty accurate measure of that. The problem was that the hooved animals, which pretty much included all but us humans, had no traction whatsoever, and those poor critters were slipping and sliding every which way on the ice. Their legs would skitter like a cat in a fry pan, resulting in positions that I thought only Pokey of clay horse fame could achieve.

Seeing that we had a problem, we quickly huddled, which I must say, also offered a little warmth.

"Reminds me of Fiasco On Ice," Pa said woefully as he watched the first couple of animals hit the frozen river. The reference was to an ice show that was once staged in Grangerland. Unfortunately, there is no such thing as natural ice in Grangerland, so thousands of ice cubes had been placed in a roller rink. Well, both the show and many of the performers fell flat as their skates wedged themselves in the space between the cubes. 'Course, things might have gone better had the spectators not started removing cubes from the rink to chill down their soda pops.

"So, what are ya gonna do now?" E. Lester asked.

"Why don't we take 'em back up the hill," Willie said. "Then let 'em race back down, hit the river on a dead run and let 'em slide on into New York."

Pa pondered a moment. "Problem would be if one of the critters fell," he said. "Could result in a couple thousand animal pile-up."

"No," Pa continued. "I know what's gotta be done." With that, he pulled out Ma's urn.

"Ma," he addressed. "Look yonder, that's New York City."

Pa held the urn in the direction of the city. I thought I detected the glimmer of a tear forming in his eye, and his voice quavered as he continued. "We weren't sure we were a gonna make it, but we're almost thar. I wanted ya to see it 'cause as I needed ya in life, I'm a gonna need ya now."

Pa was gushing from the eyes as he kissed the urn. It was a moving moment. While the others might have thought it weak, I had always known from where my "real cowman" qualities had come.

Pa removed the urn's stopper, then slowly began sprinkling the ashes onto the ice. After showing his horse that the ashes prevented slipping, Pa and his mount stepped onto the ice and started laying down a trail of Ma. Vern was so taken by the gesture that he brought out his wife and joined Pa.

Soon, the two women were stretched clear across to the other side. And it turns out that it was a good thing Vern offered his wife's services too. Ma, being a little woman, never would have made it alone. Actually, she wouldn't have come close without the help of Nellie's obviously portly ma, some of whom was even left over.

As I sat and stared at the completed trail, I thought that, per-haps, sometime later, after all of the ice melted, Ma and Vern's wife would float down the Hudson into the Atlantic. Then I hoped that they would stay intermingled so at least they'd have each other. But for right now, they could take comfort in the fact that without them, we'd have no safe route into New York.

Right before we were about to start the herd, I jumped off You Romantic You and ran over to the river. There, I raised my foot and stepped onto some ashes that I knew to be Ma's with my boot. 'Course, I meant no dispect whatsoever towards Ma by my actions. I just wanted to be sure that no matter where I traveled, I'd always be carrying a piece of Ma with me. And it didn't matter to me that she'd be stuck to the bottom of my boot. I'd know that she was with me and that was what was important.

36

ONE DAY, JUST OUTSIDE of Grangerland, I stumbled upon the entrance to an old cave. Now, to my knowledge, this was the first cave ever discovered near Grangerland, which was why I thought it strange that Grangerland had a Spelunking Society. 'Course, no one else questioned its existence since its members were so good at fixing clogged septic tanks. Anyhow, because every boy is a spelunker at heart, I entered the cave to explore.

The cave was kinda small and smelly, which, perhaps, explains why the Society felt at home in septic tanks. And while I didn't discover any gold, which I think is every boy's fantasy, I did unearth some writing on one of the walls. Based on my reported find, Carl Slocomb bought the property to use as a tourist attraction.

Carl billed the place as "the world's smallest cavern", but it wasn't the fact that everyone knew it was just a cave that caused the project to fail. See, even if the writing on the wall turned out to be of Caveman or even Indian origin instead of just a fairly recent limerick with a phone number attached, nobody and I mean nobody was about to pay good money to go into any natural underground wonder that didn't have a stalagmite organ. So dubbed "Carl's Bad Cavern" by the locals, the place soon went back to being just a cave.

Anyway, despite the writing on the wall, I still felt as if I had been the first one ever to set foot in that cave. True, the cave had been around a long time, but that did little to displace the aura of a virgin find, even when I knew that it was a virgin find many times over. And the decision to explore it filled my mind with limitless possibilities of adventure and discovery. This is the way I felt as we climbed up that embankment from the Hudson River on the New

York side. 'Course, this feeling of mine was reinforced when we reached the top of the river's embankment and saw, on the opposite side of the Henry Hudson Parkway, a large concrete wall covered with writing.

As we crossed the snow-covered Parkway, I glanced around and noticed that as in New Jersey, a cloister of abandoned cars was considered a garden. But like I said before, who was I to criticize another's culture? For all I knew, they replaced the overgrown weeds with flowers in the spring. Perhaps these cars were some sorta oversized planters. 'Course, it was still a mystery how the horticulturists drove these cars here to create these gardens in the first place. They all seemed to be missing important pieces like doors, steering wheels, tires and engines.

After crossing the Parkway, we stopped briefly to huddle and examine the graffiti covered wall.

"Looks like what ya found in Carl's Bad Cavern," Big Bill said to me.

"Ain't Willie's writin'," Little Ben said. "It's more primitive."

"Think it was left by cavemen?" Big Bill asked.

"Probably," Vern said, closely studying the scrawlings.

"Looks Neanderthal," Little Ben commented. 'Course, I thought it best not to bring up the fact that, somehow, I just didn't believe that cavemen had access to spray paint.

"Hey, ya'll, is this it?" E. Lester asked. "Is this Central Park?"

Sure enough, as I glanced around, it did seem as if we were in some sorta park. Off to our right, there were basketball courts without any hoops attached to any of the six backboards. Perhaps the point of the game in the East was to simply hit the backboard with the ball.

Turning and glancing through the trees to my left, I saw a large, prism-shaped, wrought iron object. I think this would have been a swing set had there been any swings attached.

Perhaps the answer to all of this was that in the East they provided the basics, then you supplied the rest. Although it was probably a bother to hook up your own swing or attach your own rim every time you want to use a basketball court or a swing set, it probably saved the taxpayers money and that makes everybody happy. And to think that I used to take these things for granted back in Grangerland.

"This ain't Central Park," Vern said, looking at the map. "It's Riverside Park."

"Well, I think it's way too small fer all the herds," Pa commented. Indeed, with our perimeters fixed by the Parkway on one side and a small stone wall on the other, we had ourselves a very cramped camp.

And it was as if some of B.B.'s great insight, rest his soul, had rubbed off on Pa because no sooner had Pa spoken than we heard a loud pop. It seems that the animals were packed so tightly together that, well, I'm not going to tell you one actually popped. But, what did happen was that the pressure surrounding one of the pigs built to such a point that the poor sow shot straight up like a bar of soap through wet hands.

After this, none of us had to be convinced that the herds were a little too big for this park. The only one who had a reason to stay was Sir Albert, but that's because he was the only one who happened to bring along a swing. 'Course, even I had to do a double take when I saw Sir Albert with a swing hanging from his mouth. It's one thing to underestimate the intelligence of your pet, but it's another to discover secret hobbies of theirs that you would have sworn were physically impossible. But that's a cow for you.

"Gather up that popped pig and let's git a move on," Pa said, pointing to the upper branches of a nearby oak. "'fore any more critters are sent into orbit."

At Pa's direction, Clint shimmied up the tree to rescue the squealing ex-projectile from its landing place. As Clint climbed higher and higher, I was truly amazed at the height that this pig had attained. In fact, it disproved the notion that pigs are not aerodynamically sound.

Upon Clint's return, I resumed my position in the back of the herd in preparation for departure. That's when I heard Tiny Bob's voice from where I had last seen Sir Albert.

"Let me swing!"

Klunk.

"Hey! It's my swing!"

Klunk.

"Hey! Watch where yer swingin' that thin!"

Klunk, Klunk.

"Hey! Cut it out!"

Klunk, Klunk, Klunk.

I immediately cantered back over to the swing set where I found a bruised Tiny Bob laying in the snow as Sir Albert was wildly flailing the swing, which still hung from his mouth.

"I found that swing in the bushes," shouted Tiny Bob as he sat up and pointed at Sir Albert. "And I put it in his mouth to see if the frozen chains would stick to his tongue."

"How could you!" I screamed.

"It ain't my fault it worked," Tiny Bob said as he got up from the ground and touched a large bump protruding from his head. "Ouch!…But ya figured that since the thin was stuck anyway, the least the critter could do was let me swing from its mouth."

I jumped off of You Romantic You and ran over to Sir Albert. "That cow of yers is crazy," Tiny Bob continued as he backed away. "Thar ain't no way I'm gettin' near him. No way!" Rubbing an assortment of black and blue marks on his face, Tiny Bob turned and walked off, muttering about my insane pet until he was out of hearing range.

Poor Sir Albert. Poor, tormented Sir Albert. His wild, thrashing head movements subsided enabling me to approach. I softly stroked his head as I tried to figure out how I was going to remove the swing from his mouth. Thinking it best to first examine the amount of metal actually stuck on his tongue, I gently opened his mouth. And the swing fell right out! Then, I swear, Sir Albert winked at me.

Well, I thought it best to just keep the entire incident to myself as I remounted You Romantic You and returned to the rear of the herd. 'Course, whatever the explanations, Sir Albert was emancipated once and for all from Tiny Bob's tyranny.

Willie led the herds out through an opening in the stone wall which surrounded Riverside Park and onto Riverside Drive as the drive began once more. I was hoping that as soon as I was out of the park, I would enjoy my first unobstructed view of the entire city. But, even without the falling snow, the buildings lining Riverside Drive blocked all views in front. I scanned this street only to get the sense that I was looking at a bar graph. The buildings were all box-like, some higher, some lower. Neither me nor Nellie was too impressed with this style. We couldn't figure out what was so interesting about a bar graph. I agreed with Nellie, who would have much preferred a pie graph.

Willie turned off of Riveside Drive and onto 85th Street, the first one way street heading east. On Riverside Drive, the buildings had been continuous, breaking only for the numbered streets. Here, on 85th Street, there was an occasional space between the buildings — not the wide open spaces that we were used to, but itty bitty spaces, all of which were blocked off by thick iron gates covered with barbed wire. Now I understood the boring architecture. Why build anything fancy when you're just housing a bunch of prisoners?

As we reached the corner of 85th Street and West End Avenue, a man wearing an oversized coat and wool hat appeared from nowhere and tried to squeegee Willie. But even in this bitter cold weather, Willie was able to react with real cowboy reflexes. Figuring this to be some sorta Eastern ambush, Willie whipped both guns out and had barrels pointed before you could say, well, even before your brain could think up a word for you to say. And let me tell you, that wool-hatted hombre hightailed it out of there faster than a Jack Turtle…who was the man caught sleeping with the Grangerland Police Chief's wife over at the Bronco Buster Motel.

While I wasn't about to confront Willie, I wasn't sure about the wisdom of his actions. That man was the first person we had encountered in New York City, and we had forgotten to ask Dr. Namath about the East's customs. So, he might very well have been part of the welcoming committee. I mean, no matter how much we had hoped that we weren't discovered until we had reached our destination, if someone did happen to see us, well, it was sorta obvious that we were from out of town. And, perhaps, the traditional welcome around here was to have a surprise squeegee. I just didn't know, and neither did any of the other members of the drive, which was why I just thought it best not to act too hastily.

Still, I was surprised that anyone else would be out in this blizzard. I had thought that people would be out in weather like this only out of necessity. So, you can imagine my surprise upon reaching the next intersection.

The street was packed with people!

I looked over to the street post and saw that this fairly large boulevard intersecting with 85th Street was named "Broadway". I shook my head in disgust. Wasn't one enough? Did they have to go and copy Tyler's?

Anyway, this Broadway, with all the people running to and fro in the snow, sorta had a carnival atmosphere to it, literally. On this street, the people were engaged in basically the same game as the milk bottle toss in Grangerland with some minor variations. Here it was bricks instead of softballs and storefront windows rather than milk bottles. But, after a direct hit, they'd get the same ringing bell. And then, they weren't handed a prize, but had a more effecient system. They climbed into the windows and helped themselves. Now, I could only assume that the whole thing worked on the honor system, but an awful lot of people came out of those stores totally loaded up with prizes.

We cast aside lingering fears and trepidations as we realized that, despite the horrible weather, these folks were just like Dr. Namath. Most of them seemed genuinely interested in us. Some people were kind enough to offer to hold our money, others asked us what our problem was. Some were so personable that they talked to themselves. And one individual asked us if we had any spare change, and since we did, we declined his generous offer.

One prize winning gentleman climbing out of a store window even went so far as to sell Vern a two hundred dollar camera he had just won for twenty bucks. If that's not friendly, I don't know what is. This same man wanted to sell me another one of his prizes, a brand new tape recorder, but I declined since we already had Clint.

Pa figured it was time to move on when Tiny Bob started to hound him about playing the brick tossing game. Pa told him that he could come back after we had set up camp, and this seemed to placate him. So, the herds crossed Broadway and continued up 85th Street.

At the corner of 85th Street and Amsterdam Avenue, we encountered "The Original Famous Guy's Szechuan Hunan Wok", while at the corner of 85th and Columbus Avenue, we saw "The More Original Famous Guy's Szechuan Hunan Wok". This made the ninth and tenth Chinese Restaurant we had passed in the space of four city blocks (six of which were the Original Guy's, the More Original Guy's, the Famous Guy's, the Sorta Famous Guy's, the Completely Unknown Guy's and Guy's Mother's), and the thirty-third restaurant overall. Vern stopped to take a picture of both of these last two "Guy's" for a photoessay he had started entitled, "What Do New Yorkers Do But Eat? ('Course, he later changed the title to, "Well, What Do New Yorkers Do But Eat Food And Toss Bricks?" and then to "Well, Is New York Food Quality Food?")

We continued on down 85th Street. And, well, it seemed like only seconds passed before we were standing on the corner of 85th Street and Central Park West, staring into what had to be Central Park!

I guess it was a combination of the low gray sky, the snow in our eyes, and the fact that blocks in this city just weren't like blocks back home that caused it to sneak right up on us. As a matter of fact, we had come upon it so suddenly and without warning that Pa wanted to check the map before we crossed the street to enter. 'Course, this was fine because we had to wait anyway until Willie reached zero bottles of beer on the wall.

"Willie, might as well go ahead and finish singin'," Pa said as he pulled out the map. "Just let us know when yer finished." Willie quickened his tempo, as the rest of us gathered around Pa.

"I just wanta make sure this is Central Park," Pa said, studying the map. "I mean, we hit it right quick."

"Think Willie done made a U-turn somewhere by mistake?" E. Lester asked.

"Not Willie," Little Ben said sternly. "He's seen the `No U-turn' signs." We all sorta got on the defensive when an Old Misser's talents were questioned, especially when it happened to be Willie's talents and especially when he was so busy singing that he couldn't defend himself.

"Guess I'm sorta bein' an ingrate, and I'm sorry," E. Lester said. "I ain't doubtin' Willie. It's just that, well, this here park don't look much different than that other one."

'Course, from what I'd seen so far, all of this city looked the same. And, indeed, this area was no exception. Where we were standing, we were again surrounded by bar graph buildings facing a park which appeared no different than the park through which we had already traveled. In fact, it was probably the fact that this park was also stone walled that had us stonewalled.

"Well I'll be danged," E. Lester cursed out of surprise as he determined our location on the map. "Looks like this here place is Central Park."

Pa simply grinned and then pointed to a break in the stone wall across the street. "Looks like we can enter yonder," he stated.

"And accordin' to the map, halfway through the park is a big grazin' area called `Sheep Meadows'. We might wanta build camp thar and let the animals mix."

"Put the pigs and cows with the sheep?" Vern questioned.

"Well, this here city's nicknamed the Great Meltin' Pot," Pa said. "And I think we should see if it's true."

"Then later, do ya think the city'll let us use that thar big old vat to make fondue?" Big Bill asked.

Afraid that the one circuit leading to Big Bill's brain was already overloaded, Pa simply replied, "We'll see."

"…No More Bottles Of Beer On The Wall!" belted a winded Willie, before wiping his brow and turning to Pa. "Ready when ya are, Mr. Henry."

"Just head due east," Pa replied as the rest of us congratulated Willie on finishing the most monotonous song ever written."

Willie waited until we were back to our positions before turning Clint's Pickle towards the park. While holding the reins in his right hand, he slowly raised his left arm and motioned across the street. "Head 'em up and forward ho!" he bellowed.

And then, in deference to a nearby sign, he added, "Keep 'em movin', fight gridlock."

Willie spurred Clint's Pickle and the drive surged forward on its way across Central Park West, the last frontier. I felt as if I had accomplished something as my turn finally came to ford the white blanketed street. We had arrived. I'll never forget that special moment, a moment forever captured in mind and in pictures, thanks to Vern.

Through the stone wall we went, passing by an area called "Strawberry Fields". Perhaps, beneath all this snow and after the spring thaw, there would, indeed, be some growing. After what I'd seen, I doubted it. But I could hope.

No, the farther we traveled into this park, the more it felt like we belonged. Surrrounded by ice topped trees and the hushed sound of muffled hooves plowing through fresh powder, the city ceased to exist. And as the snow fell and the crystalline park shimmered at dusk, one could have easily believed that we were back at the Davy Crockett Forest.

I wondered if the others were thinking similiar thoughts. Probably not. They'd argue that this couldn't be the Davy Crockett because it never snowed there. 'Course, that's the problem with asking a real cowboy to pretend.

"Sheep Meadows," Willie cried out as we exited the trees and entered a vast open area. His voice carried over the meadow and echoed through the far off trees.

We left our stations and loped to the middle of this great expanse. And after taking some time to look around, Vern captured what seemed to be the reality of the situation. "Don't see no sheep," he said.

"Maybe they're blendin' in with the snow," Little Ben said.

"'Course, this is a perty big place and it is gettin' kinda dark to see," E. Lester said.

"I think yer all right," Pa said. "Best we look fer 'em in the mornin'. In the meantime, when yer settin' up camp, be extra careful not to go settin' it up on top of any hidden critters."

"We're gonna set up here?" Big Bill asked.

"Well, this here is the place we were a shootin' fer, and even with them old concealed sheep, thar seems to be plenty a room," Pa replied, before taking the last few moments of shrouded twilight to glance around. "Besides, I can't believe that this here place resembles a tundra all year 'round."

"Yep," Pa continued with a big, old grin. "Say howdy to yer new home, Boys."

Who knows how long we could have celebrated under other circumstances, but our jubilation was tempered by sheer exhaustion. The events of the day had taken their toll. As a matter of fact, true to B.B.'s prediction, we had arrived by Christmas, but there would be no presents except safety and comfort that when we awoke Christmas Day, we'd be staring at the beginnings of the New Miss.

Quickly, before we collapsed, we corralled the herds into the Meadows. Then, drained of all energy, most members of the drive tied up their horses but fell asleep in their saddles even before they had a chance to dismount.

Me, on the other hand, well, I was fascinated by our surroundings. In the distance, in all directions, thousands of city lights peeked through the trees. And like cinders rising from a hot wood fire, they flickered beneath the cover of snow and darkness. Everything was so calm and tranquil that I prayed that it would always be this way.

Secluded, yet accessible, I hoped that we'd find our new homestead an eternal oasis rather than the eye of a hurricane.

Just before I dozed off, I performed one last act. It was something I had noticed on the way in and I wasn't sure if it was an Eastern custom or a city rule or what. But just to feel a part of this new place, to feel like I belonged, and to demonstrate to whomever might come across us that we desired to fit in, I constructed a sign which I hung around Sir Albert's neck. I then sat down. But before I closed my eyes, I took one last, admiring look at Sir Albert. There he was, glistening under the snowflakes, standing proudly, standing confidently, wearing his sign which read, "No Radio".

And all felt right with the world.

37

EVEN WITH THE SNOW still falling, me, Nellie, Sir Albert and Gerty had ventured out of Central Park on an early morning mission. We had left the others back at the Sheep Meadow, where they were deciding on the day's agenda. The choices boiled down to staking a claim and starting construction on the new ranch, finding the meat market, searching for hidden sheep or just plain resting up after our four month journey and celebrating Christmas.

Well, the weather was still a little too nasty to start chopping down trees. And as for the sheep, we felt they were either suffering from zenophobia or a case of snobbery, and if they later decided that they wanted to be sociable, they knew where we were. Two options thus remained, and since none of us knew either the location of the meat market or the calendar of Christmas Day events in New York City, it made sense to scout out a newpaper, no matter what our final decision turned out to be. So, our little foursome volunteered to round one up.

After strolling out of Central Park, we soon came across a green wood shanty laballed "Newsstand". We spent a good ten minutes searching through a display of candies, sodas, batteries and cassette tapes. There were also lots of magazines, the likes of which I had never seen before. Even Sir Albert, whom I always believed to be an extremely open minded animal, seemed totally repulsed by one called "Young Calfs Of Sweden". He lowered his head and refused to look up...until he calmed himself with some snow-covered cud.

Frustrated and repulsed, I finally asked the man inside the shack if he had any newspapers. Sorta perturbed for no reason I could guess, he reached over the counter and pushed aside a pile of post cards, lady's jewelry and umbrellas. He got even angrier when some of the umbrellas fell off the counter and, if you can believe it, broke in the snow. He mumbled something about how they weren't suppose to break until they were used once, but his words were lost in the paper's headlines.

"HOLY COWS! screamed the headlines of a newspaper called the Post.

The article in the New York Times appeared on page B23, under the caption, "Cattle Discovered In Central Park".

I immediately grabbed a copy of the Post as Nellie picked up the Times. With Sir Albert and Gerty looking over our shoulders, we hadn't more than a moment to scan the papers when the man behind the counter said, "This ain't no lounge."

I paid for the two papers, but refused to pay for the umbrellas. The transaction completed, I stepped back to read the Post.

HOLY COWS!

A report that thousands of cows were seen heading towards Central Park last night can no longer be dismissed as udder nonsense. "There were lots of them, and they definitely were on the moo-ve," said Manhattan resident Jason LaFlock, who "herd" the animals as they made their way up 85th Street. When asked his reaction, Mr. LaFlock, a professional dancer who currently waiters at Pregundo's stated, "I was shocked at first, but as a dancer, I always appreciate the chance to see real, live hoofers." Willie Jones, who spotted the cattle on the corner of Broadway and 85th, had a similar reaction. "I dropped a t.v. on my foot when I seen all them cows comin' at me," he said. "I thought I was gonna get 'creamed'". Sustaining a toe injury, Mr. Jones, who has no beef with the cattle per say, is still at the corner of Broadway and 85th awaiting Emergency Medical Services response.

It is still unknown where this excellent source of "cowsium" came from, but details will be reported as they become available, as the Post promises to milk this story for all it's worth.

After finishing this article, we turned to the one in the Times.

CATTLE DISCOVERED IN CENTRAL PARK

Informed and anonymous sources rendered varying accounts of domesticated bovines meandering within the delineatory confines of Central Park. More big words to follow.

Not that we were planning to keep our prospective ranch at Central Park a secret, like our drive, but the fact that we were the lead story in one of the papers was a bit disconcerting. Even Sir Albert seemed rattled, although it might have been because he had been accused of meandering. You see, I believed Sir Albert was a domesticated bovine with a definite purpose.

We figured we best hurry back to tell the others the news that we now had at hand, literally. So, we first had to wipe the print off our palms and fingers with snow. Newsprint running off onto one's hands had never been a problem back home which supports the Grangerland Daily's position on the continued use of clay tablets.

After cleaning our hands and folding the papers (which you can also do with clay tablets, after heating), we went bounding through the snow, across the street and into park back to the Sheep Meadow. I wondered what the reaction would be to our discovery. If the general masses acted in any way similar to the man at the Newsstand, I would have to warn the others to avoid all contact with umbrellas.

Well, approaching camp, I saw the answer. A huge crowd had gathered at the Sheep Meadow. I don't want to hazard a guess at how many people there were, but suffice it to say that even after leaving a fairly substantial buffer zone between themselves and the animals, they still completely encircled the herds. They were obviously here because of the news stories, as even from our position in the rear, you could tell that their hands were dirty with newsprint.

Now, their purpose in being here was an entirely different question, but one that we learned quickly. Someone standing in the back of the crowd turned and saw us exiting the tree cover and before we had a chance to even say "howdy do", we were engulfed like volcano-side vegetation by flowing molten lava. "Reston from the Daily News," said a man rushing over, holding a pencil and paper. "Who are you, and why are you here?"

But before I could answer, a woman came up and body-checked Mr. Reston out of the way and into a snow drift. "Jones from the Post," she said. "Can I quote you as being from Cowifornia? How about Cowgary?"

"Graham from the National Enquirer," shouted a man behind Jones from the Post. "Are you from Mars? We'll pay you for an exclusive."

"Von Webb monetarily engaged by the Times," said a man pushing Graham into Jones. "We'll publish a special series...on cattle...using pretentious words."

"Lankon, World News Tonight," said a lady to my side as a cameraman moved into position. "Is this a protest against recent political developments in India?"

"Letterman," said a lady pushing her way up along my other side. "Why don't I book you for Tuesday evening's stupid pet tricks?" Sir Albert swooshed his tail, swatting the woman in the process.

Behind me a mustached man was speaking into a camera, "...Christmas publicity stunt or a satanic cult worship?"

"Do your animals drive and if so, is their favorite vehicle a 'Cattlelac'?" yelled Jones from the Post as she tried to regain her position.

"Zicky, Village Voice," said a bearded man stumbling up on my right. "Hey dudes, what's happenin'?"

"ESPN," said a woman shoving her way up on my left. "You must be a Longhorn fan."

"How about you?" said a man thrusting a microphone in Sir Albert's face. "Any comment?"

Before Sir Albert could even part his lips, a woman hugged him. "G.Q.," said the woman. "Definite cover material." Gerty bit her.

"I promise non-run ink," stated Von Webb from the Times.

"Is this the line for Springsteen tickets?" shouted a voice from the rear.

A man stepped over the woman from G.Q., who was on the ground holding her wound. "PETA," said the man to Sir Albert. "How are you being treated?"

Sir Albert mooed.

"Did you hear that?" screamed a heavy set black man standing nearby, who was wearing a large gold cross and a beehive hairdoo. "I call for a `Day of Outrageousness'!"

Well, that was it. Enough was enough.

"Can I ask a question?" I shouted above the others.

Quite puzzled, everyone fell silent. After a few moments, someone finally said, "Sure."

"Why are you all here?" I asked.

Everyone looked at each other.

"Curiosity," said Reston from his snow drift after a few more moments of silence. All of the others nodded in agreement.

"Behold the plethora of individuals," said Von Webb waving towards the crowds around the Sheep Meadow.

"They're all from Mars," Graham from the Enquirer interjected just before being pelted with snowballs.

"You and your alien concepts," admonished Jones from the Post.

"Son, let me tell you who those people are," said Lankon of World News Tonight. "They're all New Yorkers. Typically callous, self-involved New Yorkers. Do you have any idea what it takes to get this many New Yorkers to take an interest in anything but themselves? Young man, this could be the story of the decade."

"So, will you please answer a few questions?" asked Reston. "Before we really get pushy." I could see the reporters digging in for the second offensive.

Why this would make the story of the decade was beyond me. I think the more interesting story would be where the sheep were hiding.

So I said, "I think it's best that I talk with my Pa first." As if on cue, Sir Albert and Gerty sprang forward, bowling over all who were in their way as they began clearing a path through the crowd. Me and Nellie stayed right on their tails, taking full advantage of their excellent blocking, as we made our way toward the herds.

The majority of the crowd just seemed interested in finding out what was going on. We did, however, pass a few people waving signs — "Democrats for Cattle", "Democrats for Republicans", "Elsie for President", "Dwarf Supremists Unite", "Bowler's Strike Force", "Beasts Against Beastiality", "Heterosexual Gays Against Leather", "Woodcutter's Against Splinter Groups", "The Indecisive Society Against _____", "Manhattanites Against the Outer Boroughs", "Army Against Navy…7-0 First Quarter" and "Abacus Programmers Against Computers".

We finally reached the front of the crowd, where we immediately met a line of blue-uniformed policemen. They had formed a human linked fence between the crowd and the herds. Thinking back, this would explain why the reporters hadn't already talked to Pa. 'Course, this also explained why the crowd had not collapsed on the herds. Not that the New Yorkers, themselves, would have meant to, but how could they avoid it with those pushy reporters shoving from the rear?

We approached one of the policemen. "Excuse me," I said. "But that's my Pa and her Pa and my brothers and E. Lester and Willie and Clint and our cows and horses and her pigs behind you."

Now, maybe it was Gerty's flashing the policeman her teeth, but for whatever reason, he believed us and let us pass without any questions.

"New Yorkers sure are trusting," I exclaimed as we stepped into the buffer zone, but Sir Albert failed to hear me. I guess he was feeling a tinge of jealousy over the policeman's reaction to Gerty's obvious attempt at a smile. And he continued brooding as we made our way through the herds.

Pa and the others had set up a temporary camp in the middle of the herds in the middle of the Meadow. We found them sitting on their saddles around a campfire and enjoying a cup of coffee when we arrived.

"Bert Boy," Pa said as our foursome appeared through the sea of pigs and cattle. "Didya find us all a paper?"

"I got two of them," I answered, walking toward them. But before I could add anything else, the snow directly beneath my feet moved suddenly. Scientific studies performed by the Grangerland Alternative Energy, Reclamation, Recycling and Make Your Bed Association proved that the living daylights could, under certain conditions, be used to successfully illuminate a room, and the living daylights which were just scared out of me at that moment would probably have lit a house. I jumped at least six feet straight up.

I landed back on earth as the snow covered head of Tiny Bob popped out in between my legs. "Hey!" he yelled. "I was tryin' to hibernate here."

"Sorry," I said, truly regretting that I had stepped on him when, otherwise, I wouldn't have had to deal with him again until Spring.

As Tiny Bob disappeared back into the snow, Pa said, "Don't

worry 'bout it, Bert Boy. We all thought he was just lookin' fer them sheep."

"Well," he continued, pouring the dregs of his coffee onto the snow. "Should we look at them papers and figure out what we're a gonna do today?"

"What about all of those people?" I asked as my train of thought returned to its track.

"What people?" Vern said, taking a sip of coffee.

"The oneth all around," Nellie said.

Curious, all of the members of the New Old Miss rose from their saddles and gazed out over the herds. Completely surrounded by the cattle and pigs with snow stuck on their backs, it gave you the sense that we were standing in the hole in the middle of a powdered donut. But, sure enough, beyond the outer edge of the donut, past the buffer zone, behind the chain of police officers, a mass of people spread in all directions.

"Well, I'll be damned," E. Lester exclaimed. "Where'd they all come from?"

"I guess we've been so busy enjoying Christmas morning," Vern said. "That we ain't done much more than sit and sip coffee since Nellie and Bert left."

"Well, we made the newspapers," I said, and I began to fill them in on the details of our morning.

I was in the midst of telling them about the reporters when we saw the police line open briefly to allow seven individuals through. And it was obvious that these seven were on their way to see us.

"Who are they?" Little Ben asked, looking at the men stomping through the snow.

"Maybe it's wise men bringin' gifts," Big Bill said hopefully.

"Don't think so, Bill Boy," Pa said. "'Cause I count seven a comin'." This answer seemed to appease Big Bill without diminishing his Christmas spirit. 'Course, I heard seven and, at this distance, wondered if these were the Dwarf Supremists.

"I don't know who they are," Pa continued. "A welcomin' committee, I reckon. But Bert Boy, when they git here, just make sure they don't step on yer brother."

I gladly positioned myself near Tiny Bob, hoping that there was still a chance that he could fall back asleep for a very long winter. In the meantime, the welcoming committee was halfway through the herds and, to my relief, looking more like full sized humans with every step. But, for a welcoming committee, they oddly appeared to be waving their arms frantically as they zigzagged their way through the animals.

"Look at the way thar flappin' thar arms," Big Bill said. "Musta stepped in some dung."

"Could be them new fangled aerobics I've heard 'bout," E. Lester commented as we watched them advancing.

"And I betcha that's the instructor," Vern said, pointing to a bald man who was now in front of the pack. Indeed, this gentleman was waving more frantically than the others and really exaggerating his zigzags. In fact, he'd have to have been a cartoon character to be any more animated.

"Well, I reckon that we'd be appearin' down right discourteous if we didn't go greet our welcomin' committee," Pa said as the seven broke clear of the herd.

"I think yer right," Vern said. "Well, yer probably right. Actually, I ain't sure how it would look, but we'll follow ya anyway." 'Course, by the end of Vern's affirmation, the arm wavers were already upon us.

"Howdy, boys," Pa said extending his hand to the bald headed leader. "Sorry we didn't come over to greet ya'll, but my name's Tex "Eugene" Henry and I think I'm a speakin' fer all of us when I say that we sure did appreciate that aerobic demonstration. Is that the usual welcomin' routine?"

"What are you doing here?" asked the bald man, waving his arms even more frantically than before. "What are you doing here?"

"What do ya mean?" Pa said, taken aback.

"You can't be here," said the bald headed man. "This is Cental Park, a city park. It is owned by the city. You can't be here!" Following his lead, each member of the group was now waving his arms more frantically than before.

"Well, we done staked a claim, Sir," Pa said sternly.

"You can't," said the bald man in a high-pitched whine, before turning to another. "Can he?"

The fellow arm waver shook his head "no". "See, you can't," continued the head of the group, turning back to face Pa. "So I want to know what you're doing here?"

"Well, I don't particularly like yer attitude, so I don't think I'm a gonna tell ya any more than I've done told ya already," Pa said.

Shocked and confused, the bald man stopped waving his arms, cocked his head and looked at Pa. The others followed suit. "But you have to tell me," the leader said puffing his chest. "I'm the Mayor."

I guess our response to that statement showed him that he had just given us even less reason to answer. "No, you can trust me," he continued, his ego deflating quicker than any balloon ever held by Tiny Bobby Pin. "Really."

"Why should we?" Pa asked.

"Because I'm an honest politician," the Mayor said, by now, downright hurt. "Really. Ask anyone from my entourage."

"No, even better," continued the Mayor. "Go ahead, you judge for yourself. Go ahead. Ask me any question."

Someone from the Mayor's entourage tapped him on the shoulder, but the Mayor shushed him. "Go ahead," the Mayor pressed. "Ask me anything. Go ahead."

"Alright," Pa said, probably just to stop the pestering. Then, after thinking briefly, Pa asked, "What do ya do as Mayor?"

"Well," the Mayor said, hestitating for a moment before continuing. "As Mayor, my main job is to run for re-election."

The Mayor then pondered over what he had just said before continuing, "For which you need votes and money. And, until I learn more about you all, you represent potential votes that I might be foolishly tossing away. And, for all I know, you could be very wealthy and might contribute to my present re-election campaign."

The Mayor again stopped briefly to mull things over before concluding. "So, you know," he said. "There's not much point in making false promises and stabbing you in the back yet. Like I said, at least not until I know more." And I have to say that all of us at the New Old Miss took that to be the most honest answer we'd ever gotten from a politician.

"Now, please tell me," the Mayor continued. "What are you doing here?"

"We've done come here and brought all our livestock," Pa said. " 'Cause we all heard that New York City is just a big, old meat market."

Well, the members of the entourage and the Mayor, himself, found this response to be quite amusing.

"That's what we heard back in Texas," Big Bill said, puzzled.

"And in Iowa," Vern added.

The smile vanished and a look of concern quickly crossed the Mayor's face. "So you're from out of town?" the Mayor asked. "I thought maybe you all were from Greenwich Village."

"Nope," said Little Ben.

"That means you aren't registered to vote here," the Mayor surmised.

"No, we ain't," E. Lester said.

"Well, can you at least contribute to my re-election campaign?" the Mayor asked.

"If we had money, we wouldn'ta come here to sell our herds," Pa said and it was true. But, the fact that we were leveling with the Mayor no longer seemed to please him and he once again began frantically gesturing with his arms.

"More homeless," he began shouting. "Can't they leave me alone?"

"We won't be homeless once we build the ranchhouse," Big Bill offered.

"How can I be expected to help people, when they can't help me?" the Mayor screamed. "That's politics!"

"Maybe we'll be able to give ya a little somethin after we sell the cattle," Pa said. And I know that making a political contribution was the last thing in the world Pa wanted to do, but I know he felt that he had to say something to settle the Mayor down before he had himself a stroke.

"I mean we've got some prize winnin' stock here," Pa continued. "Red Branguses and Shorthorns. So, it shouldn't be all that hard to sell these critters. Not if folks know quality and this place is the meat market we've heard it is."

"Meat market!" the Mayor exclaimed, his face changing color like litmus paper dipped in acid. "Do you know what people mean when they call this place a meat market?" And had his entourage not suddenly converged on the Mayor, we would have found out right away. Instead, we had to wait until after the huddle broke.

Now, we couldn't make out what they were all whispering about, but whatever it was caused the Mayor's bright red face to return to its old grey color, which might not have been an improvement. The Mayor also ceased flapping his arms and began nodding his head. And as the huddle approached the ten minute mark, the Mayor resembled one of those bobbily headed figures placed on the dashboard of a pick-up truck which was traveling down an unpaved country road. He even had the same smile on his face.

With that, the entourage parted and the Mayor stepped out, beaming. "Mr. Henry," he said. "When people refer to this place as a meat market, well, they mean exactly what you think they mean. And being the mayor, I'm in a position to make you an offer on all of your animals, pigs included."

"Of course," the Mayor continued. "I will expect that campaign contribution in exchange."

We were stunned. "All?" Pa reiterated. "Ya fellas must have a huge meat market here to be able to transact business so quick-like."

"And we'll pay you the going price in New York City," the Mayor offered. "Which anyone will tell you is grossly overinflated."

Hearing that we were going to be paid much more than we would in Texas certainly piqued our interest. The Mayor sensed this. "Let me explain," the Mayor continued. "We've been inundated by the earliest and worst blizzard of the decade. All arteries into and out of the city have been closed for days and the food supplies are dwindling. Even rich people are getting hungry and I can never let that happen. That's why my advisers suggest buying all your livestock and throwing a big barbeque to feed all of Manhattan."

"Yes, a grand barbeque for anyone who can make it to Central Park," the Mayor said. "What do you say, Mr. Henry? Do we have a deal?"

We all looked to Pa, who was deep in thought. The offer was more than we could ever have hoped for, yet something seemed to be troubling him. "Well, Mr. Mayor," Pa said slowly. "Just one thin. Instead of a political contribution, how 'bout a great recipe fer barbeque sauce?"

The Mayor turned to one of his advisers, who advised him that, contrary to the Mayor's belief that New York had the best of everything, it wasn't particulary known for its barbeque sauce. "Well, okay," the Mayor said disappointedly, as he turned back to Pa. "If it means we have a deal."

Pa turned to Willie. "Willie," Pa said. "I'm a gonna need two of yer beers to git that thar recipe. Any problem?" Willie frowned, but nodded his acquiescence.

Pa turned back to face the Mayor, but before he had a chance to respond, I intercepted him and whispered in his ear. You see, I had anticipated this and had left my spot, deftly positioning myself close to Pa. Now, as I returned to my guard of the Slumbering Bob, Pa pondered what I had said. Finally, he spoke. "Well, Mr. Mayor," he said. "I'm a gonna have to ask one more thin."

The Mayor, who obviously was used to getting his own way, appeared perturbed. 'Course, this was the same look most of the mayors we had encountered had had. Perhaps it was a prerequisite. But Pa continued, undaunted, probably due to the fact that he had had to suffer through the Mayor's pestering and floundering, "I'm a gonna have to ask that that cow over yonder, with the bandana and sunglasses, and that perty little cow next to him, be kept out of any deal."

The Mayor looked over to Nellie and Sir Albert and, obviously not recognizing royalty, simply shrugged his shoulders. "Fine by me," the Mayor said.

"Then, Mr. Mayor," Pa said. "I believe we've got ourselves a deal." The two men concluded with the customary handshake as the rest of us looked on and cheered.

"If this doesn't get me re-elected, I don't know what will," the Mayor said joyfully. He then turned to his people and began pointing. "You and I will go and tell the reporters about what's going on. You, climb up a tree and drop snowballs on the `Day of Outrageous' People. You, figure out how much we owe Mr. Henry and then get him his money. If we don't have enough, raise the subway fares. You, get a pencil and paper and get the recipe for the sauce. You, get these folks a suite in the Plaza until the snow lets up. And you, take their horses and park them, but do it quickly because it's almost ten and the `early bird specials' end soon."

We watched as the Mayor and his advisors scattered. I then looked at the very content faces of Pa, Nellie, Vern, Willie, Clint, Big Bill, Little Ben, E. Lester and Sir Albert and then to the Bob Mound of snow. I took a sweeping look over the recently sold herds, out to the masses of people milling around and then to the few building laying beyond Central Park that were visible through the thick, gray clouds. I felt a warm glow inside of me. We'd soon have money and somewhere there'd be a New Old Miss...because New York, indeed, was nothing but a big meat market!

38

NOW THIS IS GENERALLY the place where you flash ahead and hear what has happened to everyone ten years down the pike. Except I can't do that because I just finished telling you the story as it was happening. I mean, it's still Christmas Day, for gosh sakes. I don't even know what's going to happen tomorrow. But, if you'd like, I can tell you everyone's plans for this afternoon.

Well, Pa read the Post to Big Bill, and now Big Bill has convinced the "Day of Outrageousness" people to join him in his protest against the Christmas Day Sales at the shoe stores on Eighth Avenue. After that, he's thinking about doing New York type things, like standing in a line without knowing why, or joining a crowd watching a disaster, or even sitting in a car and honking at other cars in anticipation of traffic lights turning green.

Little Ben is planning on going out to search for the people who spray painted one of the cows and stole the wagon wheels off of the chuck wagon.

I think Sir Albert and Gerty are going down to a cattle call at the Edison Theatre.

Vern and Pa are going to buy a vacuum cleaner and a lot of extension cords, and, hopefully, get back to the Hudson River before it starts to melt.

Willie wants to learn more about chickens, so he's going to a peep show. 'Course, Clint's going too.

B.B. is still dead, but I might bring him up later with two beers (nothing disgusting intended).

E. Lester saw an ad in the paper for tropical vacation property. So I think he's going to put in a bid on a condominium on an island called Rikker's.

Unfortunately, Tiny Bob couldn't sleep and didn't suffocate and burrowed his way out of the snow. So he is going to go to the Empire State Building and spit from the observatory. (I hope that there's a strong head-wind!)

Me and Nellie, well, we're going to go for a horse and carriage ride around the park. If you thought we were going to do something a little wilder, you have to remember that even though Nellie believes I'm a real cowman, we're still really both just kids.

Harrison Lebowitz

Harrison and his wife, Molly, started Snow Farm Vineyard, Vermont's first commercial vineyard and grape winery in 1996, as a way to keep land open and working in Vermont. This has nothing to do with his writing, but neither did his past career as an Assistant Attorney General for the State of Vermont. He did, however, have his musical "Special Deliveries" produced in New York City. Whether this has anything to do with this, his first novel, is debatable.

Harrison and Molly live with their two children, Tess and Jared, in Vermont.

www.snowfarm.com

1670760

Made in the USA